Charlie gave a little smile. 'It wouldn't work, though, would it? I'd give the game away as soon as I arrived in Montaigne and opened my mouth.'

His smile deepened. 'We would try to limit the amount of time you needed to speak in public. It's all about appearances, really. And when it comes to how you look, you certainly had me and my detectives fooled.'

'But I haven't agreed to this,' Charlie said quickly. 'It's so risky. I mean, there's so much room for things to go wrong. What will happen, for example, if Olivia doesn't turn up before your cut-off date? *I* couldn't possibly marry you.'

She went bright pink as she said this.

Rafe watched the rosy tide with fascination. This girl was such a beguiling mix of innocence and worldliness. But now wasn't the time to be distracted...

THE PRINCE'S CONVENIENT PROPOSAL

BY
BARBARA HANNAY

MILLS & BOON

® and ™ are trademarks owned and used by the trademark owner and/or its licensee. Trademarks marked with ® are registered with the United Kingdom Patent Office and/or the Office for Harmonisation in the Internal Market and in other countries.

First Published in Great Britain 2017
By Mills & Boon, an imprint of HarperCollins*Publishers*
1 London Bridge Street, London, SE1 9GF

© 2016 Barbara Hannay

ISBN: 978-0-263-92265-3

23-0117

Our policy is to use papers that are natural, renewable and recyclable products and made from wood grown in sustainable forests. The logging and manufacturing processes conform to the legal environmental regulations of the country of origin.

Printed and bound in Spain
by CPI, Barcelona

Barbara Hannay has written over forty romance novels and has won a RITA® Award and an *RT Reviewers' Choice* Best Book Award, as well as Australia's Romantic Book of the Year. A city-bred girl, with a yen for country life, Barbara lives with her husband on a misty hillside in beautiful far north Queensland, where they raise pigs and chickens and enjoy an untidy but productive garden.

For Sophie and Milla.

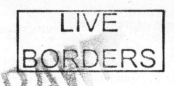

CHAPTER ONE

WEDNESDAY MORNINGS WERE always quiet in the gallery, so any newcomer was bound to catch Charlie's eye as she sat patiently at the reception desk. This morning, her attention was certainly caught by the tall, dark-haired fellow who came striding through the arched doorway as if he owned the place. He was gobsmackingly handsome, but it was his commanding manner that made Charlie almost forget to offer him her customary, sunny and welcoming smile.

A serious mistake. The cut of this fellow's charcoal-grey suit suggested that he actually had the means to purchase one of the gallery's paintings.

And, boy, Charlie needed to sell a painting. Fast. Her father, Michael Morisset, was the artist most represented on these gallery walls and his finances were in dire straits. Again. Always.

Sadly, her charming and talented, but vague and impractical parent was hopeless with money. His finances had always been precarious, but until recently he and Charlie—actually, it had mostly been Charlie who'd struggled with this—had managed to make ends meet. Just. But now, her father had remarried and his new wife had produced a brand-new baby daughter, and his situation was even more desperate.

Charlie was thinking of Isla, her new, too fragile and tiny half-sister, as she flashed the newcomer a bright smile and lifted a catalogue brochure from the pile on the counter.

'Good morning,' she said warmly.

'Morning.' His response was cool, without any hint of an answering smile. His icy grey eyes narrowed as he stopped and stood very still, staring at Charlie.

She squeezed her facial muscles, forcing an even brighter smile as she held out a brochure. 'First time at the gallery, sir?'

Momentary surprise flashed in his eyes, but then he said, 'Of course.'

Charlie thought she caught the hint of an accent, and his gaze grew even chillier, which spoiled the handsome perfection of his cheekbones and jawline and thick, glossy dark hair.

'How are you, Olivia?' he asked.

Huh?

Charlie almost laughed. He looked so serious, but he was seriously deluded. 'I'm sorry. My name's not Olivia.'

The newcomer shook his head. 'Nice try.' He smiled this time, but the smile held no warmth. 'Don't play games. I've come a long way to find you, as you very well know.'

Now it was Charlie's turn to stare, while her mind raced. Was this fellow a loony? Should she call Security?

She glanced quickly around the gallery. A pair of elderly ladies were huddled at the far end of the large space, which had once been a warehouse. Their heads were together as they studied a Daphne Holden, a delicate water colour of a rose garden. The only other visitor, so far this morning, was the fellow in the chair by the window. He seemed to be asleep, most probably a homeless guy enjoying the air-conditioning.

At least no one was paying any attention to this weird conversation.

'I'm sorry,' Charlie said again. 'You're mistaken. My name is not Olivia. It's Charlie.'

His disbelief was instantly evident. In his eyes, in the curl of his lip.

'Charlotte, to be totally accurate,' she amended. 'Charlotte Morisset.' Again, she held out the catalogue. 'Would you like to see the gallery? We have some very fine—'

'No, I'm not interested in your paintings.' The man was clearly losing his patience. 'I haven't come to see the artwork. I don't know why you're doing this, Olivia, but whatever your reasons, the very least you owe me is an explanation.'

Charlie refused to apologise a second time. 'I told you, I'm not—' She stopped in mid-sentence. There was little to be gained by repeating her claim. She was tempted to reach for her handbag, to show this arrogant so and so her driver's licence and to prove she wasn't this Olivia chick. But she had no idea if she could trust this man. For all she knew, this could be some kind of trap. He could be trying to distract her while thieves crept in to steal the paintings.

Or perhaps she'd been watching too much television?

She was rather relieved when a middle-aged couple came into the gallery, all smiles. She always greeted gallery visitors warmly, and Grim Face had no choice but to wait his turn as she bestowed this couple with an extra-sunny smile and handed them each a catalogue.

'We're particularly interested in Michael Morisset,' the man said.

Wonderful! 'We have an excellent collection of his

paintings.' Charlie tried not to sound too pleased and eager. 'The Morrisets are mostly on this nearest wall.' She waved towards the collection of her father's bold, dramatic oils depicting so many facets of Sydney's inner-city landscape. 'You'll find them all listed in the catalogue.'

'And they're all for sale?' asked the woman.

'Except for the few samples of his earliest work from the nineteen-eighties. It's all explained in the catalogue, but if you have any questions, please don't hesitate to ask me. That's why I'm here.'

'Wonderful. Thank you.'

The couple continued to smile broadly and they looked rather excited as they moved away. Behind her back, Charlie crossed her fingers. Her father needed a big sale so badly.

Unfortunately Grim Face was still hanging around, and now he leaned towards her. 'You do an excellent Australian accent, but you can't keep it up. I've found you now, Olivia, and I won't be leaving until we have this sorted.'

'There's nothing to sort.' Charlie felt a stirring of panic. 'You've made a mistake and that's all there is to it. I don't even *know* anyone called Olivia.' She sent a frantic glance to the couple studying her father's paintings.

After she'd given them enough time to have a good look, she would approach them with her gentle sales pitch. Today she had to be extra careful to hit the right note—she mustn't be too cautious, or too pushy—and she really needed this guy out of her hair.

She cut her gaze from his, as if their conversation was ended, and made a show of tidying the brochures before turning to her computer screen.

'When do you get time off for lunch?' he asked.

Charlie stiffened. He was really annoying her. And

worrying her. Was he some kind of stalker? And anyway, she didn't take 'time off for lunch'. She ate a sandwich and made a cup of tea in the tiny office off this reception area, but she wasn't about to share that information with this jerk.

'I'm afraid I'm here all day,' she replied with an imperiousness that almost matched his.

'Then I'll see you at six when the gallery closes.'

Charlie opened her mouth to protest when he cut her off with a raised hand.

'And don't try anything foolish, like trying to slip away again. My men will be watching you.'

His *men*?

What the hell…?

Truly appalled, Charlie pulled her handbag from under the desk, dumped it on the counter, and ferociously yanked the zipper. 'Listen, mate, I'll prove to you that I'm not this Olivia person.' Pulling out her purse, she flipped it open to reveal her driver's licence. 'My name's Charlotte Morisset. Like it or lump it.'

Her pulse was racketing at a giddy pace as he leaned forward to inspect the proffered licence. There was something very not right about this. He had the outward appearance of a highly successful man. Handsome and well groomed, with that shiny dark hair and flashing grey eyes, he might have been a male model or a film star, or even a barrister. A federal politician. Someone used to being in the spotlight.

It made no sense that he would confuse her— ordinary, everyday Charlie Morisset from the wrong end of Bankstown—with anyone from his circle.

Unless he was a high-class criminal. Perhaps he'd heard the recent ripples in the art world. Perhaps he knew that her father was on the brink of finally garnering attention for his work.

My men will be watching you.

Charlie snapped her purse shut, hoping he hadn't had time to read her address and date of birth.

'So you've changed your name, but not your date of birth,' he said with just a hint of menace.

Charlie let out a huff—half sigh, half terror. 'Listen, mister. I want you to leave. Now. If you don't, I'm calling the police.' She reached for the phone.

As she did so Grim Face slipped a hand into the breast pocket of his coat.

White-hot fear strafed through Charlie. He was getting out his gun. Her hands were shaking as she pressed triple zero. But it was probably too late. She was about to die.

Instead of producing a gun, however, he slapped a photograph down on the counter. 'This is the girl I'm looking for.' He eyed Charlie with the steely but watchful gaze of a detective ready to pounce. 'Her name is Olivia Belaire.'

Once again, Charlie gasped.

It was the photo that shocked her this time. It was a head and shoulders photograph of herself.

There could be no doubt. That was her face. Those were her unruly blonde curls, her blue eyes, her too-wide mouth. Even the dimple in the girl's right cheek was the same shape as hers.

Charlie heard a voice speaking from her phone, asking whether she wanted the police, the ambulance or the fire brigade.

'Ah, no,' she said quickly. 'Sorry, I'm OK. It was a false alarm.'

As she disconnected, she stared at the photo. Every detail was exact, including the tilt of the girl's smile. Except no, wait a minute, this dimple was in the girl's left cheek.

Then again, Charlie supposed some cameras might reverse the image.

The girl, who looked exactly like her and was supposed to be Olivia Belaire, was even wearing a plain white T-shirt, just as Charlie was now, tucked into blue jeans. And there was a beach in the background, which could easily have been Sydney's Bondi Beach. Charlie tried to remember what she'd been wearing the last time she'd been to Bondi.

'Where'd you get this photo?'

For the first time, Grim Face almost smiled. 'I took it with my own camera, as you know very well. At Saint-Tropez.'

Charlie rubbed at her forehead, wishing that any part of this made sense. She swallowed, staring hard at the photo. 'Who is this girl? How do you know her?'

His jaw tightened with impatience. 'It's time to stop the games now, Olivia.'

'I'm not—' This was getting tedious. 'What's *your* name?' she asked instead. 'What's this all about?'

Now it was his turn to sigh, to give a weary, resigned shake of his head and to run a frustrated hand through his thick dark hair, ruffling it rather attractively.

Charlie found herself watching with inappropriate interest.

'My name's Rafe.' He sounded bored, as if he was repeating something she already knew. 'Short for Rafael. Rafael St Romain.'

'Sorry, that doesn't ring a bell. It sounds—maybe—French?'

'French is our national language,' the man called Rafe acceded. 'Although most of our citizens also speak English. I live in Montaigne.'

'That cute little country in the Alps?'

He continued to look bored, as if he was sure she was playing with him. 'Exactly.'

Charlie had heard about Montaigne, of course. It was very small and not especially important, as far as she could tell, but it was famous for skiing and—and for something else, something glamorous like jewellery.

She'd seen photos in magazines of celebrities, even royalty, holidaying there. 'Well, that's very interesting, Rafe, but it doesn't—'

Charlie paused. Damn. She couldn't afford to waste time with this distraction. She made a quick check around the gallery. The vagrant was still asleep in the window seat. The old ladies were having a good old chinwag. The other couple were also deep in discussion, still looking at her father's paintings and studying the catalogue.

She needed to speak to them. She had a feeling they were on the verge of making a purchase and she couldn't afford to let them slip away, to 'think things over'.

'I *really* don't have time for this,' she told Rafael St Romain.

Out of the corner of her eye, she was aware of the couple nodding together, as if they'd reached a decision. Ignoring his continuing grim expression, she skirted the counter and stepped out into the gallery, her soft-soled shoes silent on the tiles.

'What did you think of the Morissets?' she asked, directing her question to the couple.

They looked up and she sent them an encouraging smile.

'The paintings are wonderful,' the man said. 'So bold and original.'

'We'd love one for our lounge room,' added the woman.

Her husband nodded. 'We're just trying to make a decision.'

'We need to go home and take another look at our wall space,' the woman said quickly.

Charlie's heart sank. She knew from experience that the chances of this couple returning to make an actual purchase were slim. Most true art lovers knew exactly what they wanted as soon as they saw it.

This couple were more interested in interior décor. Already they were walking away.

The woman's smile was almost apologetic, as she looked back over her shoulder, as if she'd guessed that they'd disappointed Charlie. 'We'll see you soon,' she called.

Charlie smiled and nodded, but as they disappeared through the doorway her shoulders drooped.

She wished this weren't her problem, but, even though she'd moved out of home into a tiny shoebox studio flat when her father remarried, she still looked after her father's finances. It was a task she'd assumed at the age of fourteen, making sure that the rent and the bills were paid while she did her best to discourage her dad from throwing too many overly extravagant parties, or from taking expensive holidays to 'fire up his muse'.

Unfortunately, her new stepmother, Skye, was as unworldly and carefree as her dad, so she'd been happy to leave this task in Charlie's hands. The bills all came to the gallery and Charlie was already trying to figure out how she'd pay the electricity bills for this month, as well as providing the funds for nourishing meals.

Skye would need plenty of nourishment while she cared for Isla, *tiny* little Isla who'd taken a scarily long time to start breathing after she was born. Despite her small size, Charlie's baby sister had looked perfect, though, with the sweetest cap of dark hair, a neat nose and darling little mouth like a rosebud. Perfect tiny fingers and toes.

But the doctors were running some tests on Isla. Charlie wasn't sure what they were looking for, but the thought that something might be wrong with her baby sister was terrifying. Since Isla's birth, her father had more or less lived at the hospital, camping by Skye's bed.

Charlie was dragged from these gloomy thoughts by the phone ringing. She turned back to the counter, annoyed to see that Rafael St Romain in his expensive grey suit hadn't budged an inch. And he was still watching her.

Deliberately not meeting his distrustful grey gaze, she picked up the phone.

'Charlie?'

She knew immediately from the tone of her father's voice that he was worried. A chill shimmied through her. 'Hi.' She turned her back on the exquisitely suited Rafael.

'We've had some bad news about Isla,' her father said. 'There's a problem with her heart.'

Horrified, Charlie sank forward, elbows supporting her on the counter. *Her heart.* 'How—how bad is it?'

'Bad.'

Sickening dizziness swept over Charlie. 'What can they do?'

There was silence on the other end of the phone.

'Dad?'

'The doctors here can't do anything. Her problem is very rare and complicated. You should see her, Charlie. She's in isolation, with tubes everywhere and all these monitors.' Her father's voice was ragged and Charlie knew he was only just holding himself together.

'Surely they can do *something*?'

'It doesn't sound like it, but there's a cardiologist in Boston who's had some success with surgery.'

'Boston!' Charlie bit back a groan. Her mind raced. A surgeon in Boston meant serious money. Mountains of it. Poor little Isla. What could they do?

Charlie knew only too well that her father had little chance of raising a quick loan for this vital operation. He'd never even been able to raise a mortgage. His income flow was so erratic, the banks wouldn't take the risk.

Poor Isla. What on earth could they do? Charlie looked again at the paintings hanging on the walls. She knew they were good. And since her father had married Skye, there'd been a new confidence in his work, a new daring. His latest stuff had shown a touch of genius.

Charlie was sure Michael Morisset was on the very edge of being discovered by the world and becoming famous. But it would be too late for Isla.

'I'm going to ring around,' her father said. 'To see what help I can get. You never know…'

'Yes, that's a good idea,' Charlie told him fervently. 'Good luck. I'll make some calls too and see what I can do. Even if I can get some advice, anything that might help.'

'That would be great, love. Thanks.'

'I'll call again later.'

'OK.'

'Give Skye a hug from me.'

Charlie disconnected, set the phone down, and let her head sink into her hands as she wrestled with the unbearable thought of her newborn baby sister's tiny damaged heart, the poor, precious creature struggling to hold on to her fragile new life.

'Excuse me.'

She jumped as the deep masculine voice intruded into her misery. She'd forgotten all about Rafael St Romain and his stupid photo. Swiping at tears, she turned to him.

'I'm sorry. I don't have time to deal with this Olivia business.'

'Yes, I can see that.'

To her surprise he seemed less formidable. Perhaps he'd overheard her end of the conversation. He almost looked concerned.

'You were speaking with your father,' he said.

Charlie's chin lifted. 'Yes.' Not that it was any of his business.

'Then clearly I am in the wrong. I apologise. The woman I'm searching for has no father.'

'Right. Good.' At least he would leave her in peace now.

'But the likeness is uncanny,' he said.

'It is.' Charlie couldn't deny this. The photo that had supposedly been taken in Saint-Tropez showed a mirror image of herself, and, despite her new worries about Isla, she couldn't help being curious. 'How do you know this Olivia?' she found herself asking. 'Who is she?'

Rafael regarded her steadily and he took a nerve-racking age before he answered. Trapped in his powerful gaze, Charlie flashed hot and cold. The man was ridiculously attractive. Under different circumstances she might have been quite helplessly smitten.

Instead, she merely felt discomfited. And annoyed.

'Olivia Belaire is my fiancée,' he said at last. 'And for the sake of my country's future, I have to find her.'

For the sake of his country's future?

Charlie's jaw was already gaping and couldn't drop any further. This surprise, coming on top of her father's bombshell, was almost too much to take in.

How was it possible that a girl who looked *exactly* the same as herself could live on the other side of the world and somehow be responsible for an entire country's future?

Who was Olivia?

Charlie had heard of doppelgängers, but she'd never really believed they existed in real life.

But what other explanation could there be?

A twin sister?

This thought was barely formed before fine hairs lifted on Charlie's skin. And before she could call a halt to her thoughts, they galloped on at a reckless pace.

This girl, Olivia, had no father, while to all intents and purposes she, Charlie, had no mother.

Charlie's father had always been vague about her mother. Her parents had divorced when Charlie was a baby and her mother had taken off for Europe, never to be heard from or seen again. Over the years, Charlie had sometimes fretted over her mother's absence, but she and her dad had been so close, he'd made up for the loss. Money worries aside, he'd been a wonderful dad.

The two of them had enjoyed many fabulous adventures together, sailing in the South Pacific, hiking in Nepal, living in the middle of rice fields in Bali while her father taught English during the day and painted at night. They'd also had a few very exciting months in New York.

When her father had married Skye, Charlie had been happy to see him so settled at last, and she'd been thrilled when Skye became pregnant. She liked the idea of being part of a bigger family. Now, though, she couldn't help thinking back and wondering why her father had limited his travels to Asia, strictly avoiding Europe. Had he actually been avoiding her mother?

Charlie gulped at the next thought. Had he been afraid that she'd discover her twin sister?

Surely not.

CHAPTER TWO

RAFE WAS REELING as he watched the play of emotions on the girl's face. He was still coming to terms with the frustrating reality that this wasn't Olivia, but her exact double, Charlotte.

Charlie.

The likeness to his missing fiancée was incredible. No wonder his detectives had been fooled. The resemblance went beyond superficial features such as Charlie Morisset's golden curls and blue eyes and her neatly curving figure. It was there in the way she moved, in the tilt of her chin, in the spirited flash in her eyes.

Take away her blue jeans and sneakers and put her in an *haute couture* gown and, apart from her Australian accent, which wasn't too terribly broad, no one in Montaigne would ever tell the difference.

The possibilities presented by this resemblance were so tempting.

Rafe, Crown Prince of Montaigne, needed a fiancée.

He'd been engaged for barely a fortnight before Olivia Belaire took flight. Admittedly, his arrangement with Olivia had been one of hasty convenience rather than romance. They'd struck a business deal in fact, and Rafe understood that Olivia might well have panicked when she'd come to terms with the realities of being married to a prince with enormous responsibilities.

Rafe had come close to panicking, too. One minute he'd been an AWOL playboy prince, travelling the world, enjoying a delightful and endless series of parties…in Los Angeles, London, Dubai, Monaco…with an endless stream of girls to match…redheads, brunettes, blondes… all long-legged and glamorous and willing.

For years, especially in the years since his mother's death, Rafe had been flying high. He and Sheikh Faysal Daood Taariq, his best friend from university, had been A-list invitees at all the most glittering celebrity parties. As was their custom, they'd made quite a hit when they arrived at the wild party in Saint-Tropez.

Just a few short weeks ago.

Such a shock it had been that night, in the midst of the glitz and glamour, for Rafe to receive a phone call from home.

He'd been flirting outrageously with Olivia Belaire, and the girl was dancing barefoot while Rafe drank champagne from one of her shoes, when a white-coated waiter had tugged at his elbow.

'Excuse me, Your Highness, you're needed on the phone.'

'Not now,' Rafe had responded, waving the fellow off with the champagne-filled shoe. 'I'm busy.'

'I'm sorry, sir, but it's a phone call from Montaigne. From the castle. They said it's urgent.'

'No, no, no,' Rafe had insisted rather tipsily. 'Nothing's so important that it can't wait till morning.'

'It's urgent news about your father, Your Highness.'

In an instant Rafe had sobered. In fact, his veins had turned to ice as he'd walked stiff-backed to the phone to receive the news that his father, the robust and popu-

lar ruling Prince of Montaigne, had died suddenly of a
heart attack.

Rafe's memories of the rest of that dreadful night were
a blur. He'd been shocked and grief-stricken and filled
with remorse, and he'd spent half of the night on the
phone, talking to castle staff, to his country's Chancellor, to Montaigne's Chief of Intelligence, to his father's
secretary, his father's publicist—who were now Rafe's
secretary and publicist.

There'd been so much that he'd had to come to terms
with in a matter of hours, including the horrifying, ines-
capable fact that he needed to find a fiancée in a hurry.

An ancient clause in Montaigne's constitution required
a crown prince to be married, or at least betrothed, within
two days of a ruling prince's death. The subsequent marriage must take place within two months of this date.

Such a disaster!

The prospect of a sudden marriage had appalled Rafe.
He'd been free for so long, he'd never considered settling
down with one woman. Or at least, no single woman had
ever sufficiently snagged his attention to the point that
he'd considered a permanent relationship.

Suddenly, however, his country's future was at stake.

Looking back on the past couple of weeks, Rafe was
ashamed to admit that he'd been only dimly aware of the
mining company that threatened Montaigne. But on that
harrowing night he'd been forced to pay attention.

The message was clear. Without a fiancée, Rafe St
Romain would be deposed as Prince of Montaigne, the
Chancellor would take control and the mongrels intent
on his country's ruin would have their way. In a blink
they would tie up the rights to the mineral wealth hidden
deep within Montaigne's Alps.

Among the many briefings Rafe had received that

night, he'd been given an alarming warning from Montaigne's Chief of Intelligence.

'You cannot trust your Chancellor, Claude Pontier. We are certain he's corrupt, but we're still working on ways to prove it. We don't have enough information yet, but Pontier has links to the Leroy Mining Company.'

In other words…if Rafe wasn't married within the required time frame, he would be deposed and the Chancellor could take control, allowing the greedy pack of miners to cause irreparable damage to Montaigne. Given free rein, they would heartlessly tear the mountains apart, wreaking havoc on his country's beautiful landscape and totally destroying the economy based on centuries-old traditions.

With only two days to produce a fiancée, Rafe had turned to the nearest available girl, who had happened to be the extraordinarily pretty, but slightly vacuous, Olivia Belaire. Unfortunately, less than two weeks after their spectacular and very public engagement ball, Olivia had done a runner.

To an extent, Rafe could sympathise with Olivia. The night she'd agreed to step up as his fiancée had been a crazy whirlwind, and she certainly hadn't had time to fully take in the deeper ramifications of marriage to a ruling prince. But Rafe had paid her an exceedingly generous amount, and the terms for their eventual divorce were unstinting, so he found it hard to remain sympathetic now, when his country's problems were so dire.

Despite his wayward playboy history, Rafe loved his country with all his heart and he loved the people of Montaigne, who were almost as famous for the exquisite jewellery they made from locally sourced gemstones as they were for their wonderful alpine cuisine. With the addition of the country's world-class ski slopes, Montaigne offered an exclusive tourist package that had been his country's lifeblood since the eighteenth century.

Montaigne could never survive the invasion of these miners.

Regrettably, his police still hadn't enough evidence to pin Pontier down. They needed more time. And Rafe desperately needed a fiancée.

Damn it, if Charlie Morisset hadn't just received a phone call from her father that had clearly distressed her, Rafe would have proposed that she fly straight home with him. She would be the perfect foil, a lifesaving stand-in until Olivia was unearthed and placated, and reinstated as his fiancée. He would pay Charlie handsomely, of course.

It seemed, however, that Charlie was dealing with some kind of family crisis of her own, so this probably wasn't the choice moment to crassly wave money in her face in the hope that he could whisk her away.

'How on earth did you manage to lose Olivia?'

Rafe frowned at Charlie's sudden, cheekily posed question.

'Did you frighten her off?' she asked, blue eyes blazing. 'You didn't hurt her, did you?'

Rafe was almost too affronted to answer. 'Of course I didn't hurt her.' In truth, he'd barely touched her.

Instantly sobered by the news of his father's death, he had dropped his playboy persona the very moment he and Olivia had left the party in Saint-Tropez. As they'd hurried back to Montaigne, Rafe had reverted to the perfect gentlemanly Prince. Apart from the few tipsy kisses they'd exchanged while they'd danced at the party, he'd barely laid a hand on the girl.

Of course, he'd been grateful to Olivia for agreeing to a hasty marriage of convenience, but since then he'd been busy dealing with formalities and his father's funeral and his own sudden responsibilities.

'I'm sorry to have troubled you,' he told Charlie now with icy politeness.

She gave a distracted nod.

He took a step back, loath to let go of this lifeline, but fearing he had little choice. Charlie Morisset was clearly absorbed by her own worries.

'I think Olivia might be my sister,' she said.

Rafe stilled. 'Is there a chance?'

She nodded. 'I know that my mother lives somewhere in Europe. I—I've never met her. Well, not that I remember—'

Her lower lip trembled ever so slightly, and the tough, don't-mess-with-me edge that Rafe had sensed in Charlie from the outset disappeared. Now she looked suddenly vulnerable, almost childlike.

To his dismay, he felt his heart twist.

'I've met Olivia's mother,' he said. 'Her name is Vivian. Vivian Belaire.'

'Oh.' Charlie looked as suddenly pale and upset as she had when she was speaking to her father on the phone. She seemed to sag in the middle, as if her knees were in danger of giving way. 'That was my mother's name,' she said faintly. 'Vivian.'

Rafe had been on the point of departure, but now, as Charlie sank onto a stool and let out a heavy sigh, he stood his ground.

'I didn't know she had another daugh—' Charlie swallowed. 'What's she like? My mother?'

Rafe was remembering the suntanned, platinum blonde with the hard eyes and the paunchy billionaire husband, who'd had way too many drinks at the engagement ball.

'She has fair hair, like yours,' he said. 'She's—attractive. I'm afraid I don't know her very well.'

'I had no idea I had a sister. I knew nothing about Olivia.'

He wondered if this was an opening. Was there still a chance to state his case?

'I can't believe my father never told me about her.' Charlie closed her eyes and pressed her fingers to her temples as if a headache was starting.

Then she straightened suddenly, opened her eyes and flashed him a guilty grimace. 'I can't deal with this now. I have other problems, way more important.'

Disappointed, Rafe accepted this with a dignified bow. 'Thanks for your time,' he said politely. 'I hope your other problems are quickly sorted.'

'Thank you.' Charlie dropped her gaze to her phone and began to scroll through numbers.

Rafe turned to leave. This dash to the southern hemisphere had been a fruitless exercise, a waste of precious time. His detectives would have to work doubly hard now to find Olivia.

'But maybe I *could* see you this evening.'

Charlie's voice brought him whirling round.

She looked rather forlorn and very *alone* as she stood at the counter, phone in hand. To Rafe's dismay her eyes were glittering with tears.

So different from the tough little terrier who'd barked at him when he first arrived in her gallery.

Maybe I could see you this evening.

He wasn't planning to hang around here till this evening. If Charlie couldn't help him, he would leave Sydney as soon as his private jet was available for take-off.

But the news of her mother and sister had clearly rocked her, and it had come on top of a distressing phone call from her father. With some reluctance, Rafe couldn't deny that he was part-way responsible for Charlie's pain. And he couldn't stifle a small skerrick of hope.

He was running out of time. If this was a dead end, he needed to hurry home, but if there was even a slight chance that she could help...

'I've got the gallery to run and some important family business to sort out,' Charlie said self-importantly. 'But I'd like to know more about Olivia. Maybe we could grab a very quick coffee?'

Was it worth the bother of wasting precious hours for a very quick coffee? The chances of persuading this girl to take off with him were microscopic.

But what other options did he have? Olivia had well and truly gone to ground.

Rafe heard himself saying, 'I could come back here at six.'

Charlie nodded. 'Right, then. Let's do that.'

By the end of the day, Charlie was feeling quite desperate. Her phone calls hadn't produced promising results. Apart from launching a *Save Isla* charity fund, she didn't have too many options. When she called her father she learned that he hadn't fared any better.

After her very quick meeting with Rafe, she and her father planned to meet to discuss strategies, and Charlie knew she would be up all night, setting up a website and a special Facebook page, and responding to the media outlets she'd contacted during the day.

Unfortunately, there would be no time to challenge her father about Olivia. Charlie was deeply hurt that he'd never told her about her twin sister, but right now she had another sister to worry about, and she knew her dad was beside himself with worry. It was totally the wrong time to pester him about Olivia Belaire.

* * *

Promptly at six, Rafe was waiting at the gallery's front door. To Charlie's surprise, he'd changed into a black T-shirt and jeans, and the casual look, complete with a five o'clock shadow and windblown hair, made him look less like a corporate raider and more like—

Gulp.

The man of her dreams.

She quickly knocked that thought on the head. She was already regretting her impulsive request to see him again. There was little she could learn about Olivia over a quick cup of coffee. But Charlie needed to understand why her sister might have agreed to marry such a compellingly attractive guy and then run away from him.

It was bad enough having one sister to worry about. She needed Rafe to set her mind at rest, so she could channel all her attention to Isla's cause.

Suddenly having two sisters, both of them in trouble, was hard to wrap her head around. As for her emotions, she'd have to sort them out later. Right now, she was running on pure adrenaline.

In no time, Charlie and Rafe were seated in a booth in the café around the corner, which was now packed with the after-work crowd. The smell of coffee and Greek pastry filled the small but popular space and they had to lean close to be heard above the noisy chatter.

'We should have gone back to my hotel,' Rafe said, scowling at the crowded booths.

'No,' Charlie responded quite definitely.

'It would have been quieter.'

'But it would have taken time. Time I don't have.'

His eyes narrowed as he watched her, but he'd lost the hawk-eyed detective look. Now he just looked extraordinarily *hot*, and she found herself fighting the tingles and flashes his proximity caused.

Their coffees arrived. A tiny cup of espresso for Rafe and a mug of frothy cappuccino for Charlie, as well as a serving of baklava. Charlie's tummy rumbled at the sight of the flaky filo pastry layered with cinnamon-spiced nut filling. Rafe had declared that he wasn't hungry, but she wasn't prepared to hold back. This would probably be the only meal she'd have time for this evening.

She scooped a creamy dollop of froth from the top of her mug. 'So, the thing I need to know, Rafe, is why my sister ran away from you.'

He smiled. It was only a faint smile, but enough to light up his grey eyes in ways that made Charlie feel slightly breathless. 'I'm afraid I can't answer that,' he said. 'She didn't leave an explanation.'

'But something must have happened. Did you have a row?'

'Not at all. Our relationship was very—' He paused as if he was searching for the right word. 'Very civilised.'

Charlie thought this was a strange word to describe a romantic liaison. Where was the soppiness? The passion? She imagined that getting engaged to a man like Rafe would involve a truckload of passion.

Even so, she found herself believing him when he said he hadn't hurt Olivia. 'So you've heard nothing,' she said. 'You must be terribly worried.'

'I have received a postcard,' said Rafe. 'There were no postage marks. The card was hand delivered, but unfortunately no one realised the significance until it was too late. It simply said that Olivia was fine and she was sorry.'

'Oh.' Charlie offered him an awkward smile of sympathy. No matter what reasons Olivia had for wanting to get out of the engagement, she'd been flaky to just take off, without facing up to Rafe with a proper explanation.

'My mother ran away,' she told him, overlooking the hurt this admission made.

Rafe lifted one dark eyebrow. 'Do you think Olivia might have inherited an escapee gene?'

Charlie was sure he hadn't meant this seriously, but the mere mention of inheritance and genes reminded her of Isla. She had to make this conversation quick, so she could get on with more important matters. 'Look,' she said, frowning, to let him know she was serious. 'I'd really like to know a little more about my sister. Where did you meet her?'

'In Saint-Tropez. At a party.'

'So, she's—well off?'

'Her father—her mother's husband,' Rafe corrected, 'is an extremely wealthy businessman. They have a house in the French Riviera and another in Switzerland, and I think there might also be a holiday house in America.'

'Wow.' *And my father can't even afford to buy one house.* Charlie tried to imagine her sister's life. 'Does she have a job?'

'None that I know of.'

'So, how does she spend her days?'

'Her days?' Rafe's lip curled in a slightly bitter smile. 'Olivia's not exactly a daytime sort of person. She's more of a night owl.'

Charlie blinked at this. She only had the vaguest notions of life on the French Riviera. She supposed Olivia was part of the jet-set who spent their time partying and shopping for clothes. If she emerged in the daylight, it was probably to lie in the sun, working hard on her suntan. Just the same, it bothered her that Rafe wasn't speaking about her sister with any sense of deep fondness. 'And what sort of work do you do?' she asked.

'That's a complicated question.'

She felt a burst of impatience. 'I don't have much time.'

'Then I'll cut to the chase. I'm my country's ruler.'

Charlie stared at him, mouth gaping, as she struggled to take this in. 'A ruler? Like—like a king?'

'Montaigne's only a small principality, but yes.' His voice dropped as if he didn't wish to be overheard. 'I'm the Prince of Montaigne. Prince Rafael the Third, to be exact.'

'Holy—' Just in time, Charlie cut off a swear word. She couldn't believe she'd met a real live prince and was sitting in her local café with him. Couldn't believe that her sister had actually scored a prince as a fiancé. 'You mean I should be calling you Sir, or Your Highness, or something?'

Rafe smiled. 'Please, no. Rafe's fine.'

Almost immediately, another thought struck Charlie. 'Olivia might have been abducted, mightn't she? That postcard might have been a—a hoax.'

Rafe shook his head. 'Security footage in the castle shows her leaving of her own volition. We know she drove her car towards Grenoble. After that—?' He frowned. 'She disappeared.'

'She might have been kidnapped.'

'There's been no request for a ransom.'

'Right.' Charlie gave a helpless shrug. 'And you've had your people searching everywhere? Even down here in Australia?'

'Yes.'

As Charlie sipped her coffee, she tried to put herself in Olivia Belaire's shoes. What would it be like to be engaged to this good-looking Prince? To be marrying into royalty? Would Olivia have been expected to undertake a host of public duties? Would she be required to chair meetings? Run charities? Visit the children's hospital?

At the very thought of a children's hospital, she shivered. *Poor little Isla.*

Fascinating though this conversation was, she'd have to cut it short.

But, as she speared a piece of baklava with her fork, she couldn't help asking, 'Do you think Olivia might have got cold feet? Could she have been worried about the whole royalty thing? All the responsibilities?'

'It's possible.'

'That's hard on you, Rafe. I—I'm sorry.' Lowering the enticing pastry to her plate, Charlie picked up her phone instead. She needed to check the time. She had to meet her father. She really should leave.

As if he sensed this, Rafe said, 'Before you go, I have a proposition.'

'No way,' Charlie said quickly, suddenly nervous. Prince or not, she'd only just met the man and she wasn't about to become embroiled in his troubles. She had enough of her own.

'You could earn a great deal of money,' he said.

Now he had her attention.

CHAPTER THREE

CHARLIE CERTAINLY BRIGHTENED at the mention of money, and Rafe was surprised by his stab of disappointment. After all, her reaction was exactly what he'd expected.

Now, however, caution also showed in Charlie's expressive face, and that was also to be expected.

'Why would you offer me money?' she asked.

'To entice you to stand in as your sister.'

She stared at him as if he'd grown an extra head. 'You've got to be joking.'

'I'm perfectly serious.'

Leaning back, she continued to watch him with obvious distrust. 'You want me to pretend to be your fiancée?'

'Yes.'

'Oh, for heaven's sake, that's ridiculous. Why?'

At least, she listened without interrupting while he explained. She leaned forward again, elbows on the table, chin resting in one hand, blue eyes intent, listening as if transfixed. Rafe told her about the inconvenient clause in Montaigne's constitution, about the country's mineral wealth and the very real threat of a takeover, and the possibility of ruin for the people who meant so much to him.

Charlie didn't speak when he finished. She sat for a minute or two, staring first at him and then into space with a small furrow between her neatly arched brows. Then she picked up her phone.

'Excuse me,' she said without looking up from the small screen. 'I'm just researching you.'

Rafe smiled. 'Of course.' He drained his coffee and sat back, waiting with barely restrained patience. But despite his tension, he thought how pleasant it was to be in a country where almost nobody knew him. Of course, his bodyguards were positioned just outside the café, but in every other way he was just an ordinary customer in a small Sydney coffee shop, chatting with a very pretty girl. The anonymity was a luxury he rarely enjoyed.

'Wow,' Charlie said, looking up from her phone. 'You're the real deal.'

Rafe's moment of fantasy was over. 'So,' he said. 'Would you consider my proposal?'

She grimaced. 'I hate to sound mercenary, but how much money are we talking about?'

'Two hundred and fifty thousand dollars US.'

Charlie's eyes almost popped out of her head. Her first instinct was to say no, she couldn't possibly consider accepting such a sum. But then she remembered Isla.

Fanning her face with her hand, she took several deep breaths before she answered. 'Crikey, Rafe, you sure know how to tempt a girl.'

Wow—not only would she be able to help Isla, she would be a step closer to finding out about Olivia as well. How could she pass up such an opportunity to meet her long-lost sister and maybe get some answers?

But even as she played with these beguiling possibilities Charlie gave Rafe a rueful smile. 'It wouldn't work, though, would it? I'd give the game away as soon as I arrived in Montaigne and opened my mouth.'

Yes, her Aussie accent *was* a problem. 'Do you speak French?'

'*Oui.*'

'You learnt French here in Australia?' Rafe asked in French.

'I went to school in New Caledonia,' Charlie replied with quite a passable French accent. 'I lived there for a few years with my father. Our teacher was a proper Frenchwoman. Mademoiselle Picard.'

Rafe smiled with relief. Charlie's French might be limited, but she could probably get by. 'I think you would manage well enough. Olivia isn't a native French speaker.'

'As long as I dropped the crikeys?'

His smile deepened. 'That would certainly help, but we would try to limit the amount of time you needed to speak in public. It's all about appearances, really. And when it comes to how you look, you certainly had me and my detectives fooled.'

'But I haven't agreed to this,' Charlie said quickly. 'It's so risky. I mean, there's so much room for things to go wrong. What will happen, for example, if Olivia doesn't turn up before your cut-off date? *I* couldn't possibly marry you.'

She went bright pink as she said this.

Rafe watched the rosy tide with fascination. This girl was such a beguiling mix of innocence and worldliness. But now wasn't the time to be distracted.

'I'm confident we'll find Olivia,' he assured her. 'But whatever happens, you have my word. If you come to Montaigne with me, you'll be free to leave at the end of the month, if not sooner.'

'Hmm... What about—?' Charlie looked embarrassed. 'You—you wouldn't expect me to actually behave like a fiancée, would you? In private, I mean?'

This time Rafe manfully held back his urge to smile. 'Are you worried that I'd expect to ravish you on a nightly basis?'

'No, of course not.' She dropped her gaze to the half-eaten baklava on her plate. 'Well, yes...perhaps. I guess...'

'There's no need to worry,' he said more gently. 'Again, you have my word, Charlie. If you agreed to this, I would proudly escort you to public appearances as my fiancée, but in both public and in private I'd be a total gentleman. You'd have your own suite of rooms in the castle.'

Just the same, the thought of taking Charlie to bed was tempting. Extremely so. Despite her innocent, cautious façade, Rafe sensed an exciting wildness in her, an essential spark he'd found lacking in her sister.

But, sadly, his years as a playboy prince were behind him. Now responsibility for his country weighed heavily. If Charlie agreed to return with him to Montaigne, the engagement would be a purely political, diplomatic exercise, just as it had been with Olivia.

Charlie was very quiet now, as if she was giving his proposal serious thought.

'So what do you think?' he couldn't help prompting, while trying desperately to keep the impatience from his voice.

Charlie looked up at him, all big blue eyes and dark lashes, and he could see her internal battle as she weighed up the pros and cons.

Rafe wished he understood those cons. Was she worried about leaving her job at short notice? Were there family commitments? Did this involve the phone call from her father? A jealous lover?

He frowned at this last possibility. But surely, if there

was a serious boyfriend on the scene, Charlie would have mentioned him by now.

'I can't pretend I'm not interested, Rafe,' she said suddenly. 'But I need to talk to—to someone.'

So...perhaps there was a boyfriend, after all. Rafe tried not to frown.

'When do you need a decision?' she asked.

'As soon as possible. I hoped to fly out tonight.'

'Tonight? Can you book a flight that quickly?'

'I don't need to book. I have a private jet.'

'Of course you do,' Charlie said softly and she rolled her eyes to the ceiling. 'You're a prince.' She gave a slow, disbelieving shake of her head, but then her gaze was direct as she met his. 'What time do you want to leave, then?' she asked.

Now. 'Ten o'clock? Eleven at the latest.' He pulled a chequebook from his pocket and filled in the necessary details, including his scrawled signature. 'Take this with you,' he said as he tore off the cheque.

Charlie took it gingerly, almost as if it were a time bomb. She swallowed as she stared at it. 'You'd hand over that amount of money? Just like that? You trust me?'

Rafe didn't like to point out that his men would be tailing her, so he simply nodded.

She folded the cheque and slipped it into her handbag and she looked pale as she rose from her seat. 'I'll be as quick as I can,' she said. 'Give me your phone number and I'll text you.'

CHAPTER FOUR

MICHAEL MORISSET, WHO had the same curls and clear blue eyes that Charlie had inherited, looked as if he'd aged ten years when she met him at the hospital.

It was frightening to see her normally upbeat and care-free father looking so haggard and worn.

Skye looked even worse. Only a few short days ago, the happy mother had been glowing as she proudly showed off her sweet newborn daughter. Now Skye looked pale and gaunt, with huge dark circles under her eyes. Her shoulders were stooped and even her normally glossy auburn hair hung in limp strands to her shoulders.

Charlie's eyes stung as she hugged her stepmother. She couldn't imagine how terrified Skye must be to know that her sweet little daughter had only the most tenuous hold on life.

'Would you like to see Isla?' Skye asked.

Charlie nodded, but her throat closed over as her father and Skye took her down the hospital corridor, and she had to breathe in deeply through her nose in an attempt to stay calm.

The baby was in a Humidicrib in a special isolation ward and they could only look at her through a glass window.

Isla was naked except for a disposable nappy, and she

was lying on her side with her wrinkled hands folded together and tucked under her little chin. A tube had been inserted into her nose and was taped across her cheek to hold it in place. Monitor wires were taped to her tummy and her feet. Such a sad and scary sight.

'Oh, poor darling.' The cry burst from Charlie. She couldn't help it. Her heart was breaking.

She tried to imagine a doctor operating on such a tiny wee thing. Thank heavens she had found the money for the very best surgeon possible. She suppressed a nervous shiver. This was hardly the time to dwell on the details of what earning that money entailed. Her baby sister was her focus.

As she watched, Isla gave a little stretch. One hand opened, tiny fingers fluttering, bumping herself on the chin so that she frowned, making deep furrows across her forehead. Now she looked like a little old lady.

'Oh,' Charlie cried again. 'She's so sweet. She's gorgeous.'

She turned to her father and Skye, who were holding hands and gazing almost fearfully at their daughter.

'I've found a way to raise the money,' Charlie told them quickly.

Skye gasped. 'Not enough to take her to Boston, surely?'

'Yes.'

Skye gave a dazed shake of her head. 'With a special nurse to accompany her?'

'Yes, there's money to cover all those costs.'

'Oh, my God.'

Skye went white and clutched at her husband's arm, looking as if she might faint.

'Are you sure about this, Charlie?' her father demanded tensely. 'I don't want Skye to get her hopes up and then be disappointed.'

Charlie nodded. 'I have the cheque in my handbag.' Nervously, she drew out the slim, astonishing slip of paper. 'It might take a few days before the money's deposited into your bank account, but it's a proper bank cheque. It's all above board.'

'Good heavens.' Her father stared at the cheque and then stared at his daughter in disbelief. 'How on earth did you manage this? What's this House of St Romain? Some kind of church group? Who could be so generous?'

This was the awkward bit. Charlie had no intention of telling her dad and Skye about Rafe and the fact that she'd agreed to be a stand-in as a European prince's pretend fiancée. For starters, they wouldn't believe her—they would think she'd taken drugs, or had been hit on the head and was hallucinating.

But also, telling them about Rafe would involve telling them about Olivia, and this wasn't the right moment to bring up that particular can of worms. Charlie was angry about her father's silence over such an important matter as her sister. On the way to the hospital she'd allowed herself a little weep about her absent mother and unknown twin sister, but she'd consoled herself that by accepting the role of fake fiancée she was actually taking a step closer to finding the truth.

For now, though, they had to stay focused on Isla.

'Dad, you have my word this money is from a legitimate source and there's nothing to worry about. But it's complicated, I'll admit that. You'll have to trust me for now. You've got enough to worry about with Isla. Let me take care of the money side of things.'

'I hope you haven't gone into debt, Charlie. You know I won't be able to pay this back.'

'You don't have to worry about that either. The only issue will be finding someone to run the gallery while I'm—' Charlie quickly changed tack. 'I'll be—busy organising everything. Do you think Amy Thornton might be available?'

'I'm pretty sure Amy's free. But for heaven's sake, Charlie—' For a long moment her father stared at her. 'If you don't want to tell me, I'm not going to press you,' he said finally. 'I do trust you, darling. I know you won't be breaking any laws.'

'Of course not. I've managed to find a generous—' Charlie swallowed. 'A generous benefactor, who wishes to remain anonymous.'

'How amazing. That's—that's wonderful.'

Charlie forced a bright smile. 'So now your job is to get busy with talking to doctors and airlines and everything that's involved with getting Isla well.'

'I don't know what to say.' Tears glistened in her father's eyes. 'Thank you, Charlie.' His voice was ragged and rough with emotion. 'Not every girl would be so caring about a half-sister.'

The three of them hugged, and Skye was weeping, but to Charlie's relief her father quickly broke away to find a nursing sister. In no time he and the nurse were making the necessary arrangements. Her dad was stepping up to the mark and adopting full responsibility.

She was free to go.

She'd never realised how scary that could be.

A frenetic hour later Charlie had rung Amy Thornton and secured her services at the gallery for the next month. She'd showered, changed into jeans and a sweater for the long flight, and had taken her cat, Dolly, next door to be minded by Edna, a kind and very accommodating elderly neighbour.

As she frantically packed, she couldn't believe she was actually doing this. She didn't dare to stop and think too hard about her sudden whirlwind decision—she knew she'd have second, third and fourth thoughts about the craziness of it all. The only safe way to keep her swirling emotions under control was to keep busy.

Finally, she was packed and ready with her passport, which was, fortunately, up to date.

Rafe arrived just as Charlie was sitting on her suitcase trying to get it closed. He shot a curious and approving glance around her tiny flat with its bright red walls and black and white furnishings, which she was quietly rather proud of, and which normally included her rather beautiful black and white cat.

Then he eyed her bulging luggage and frowned.

'I know it's winter in Montaigne,' Charlie offered as her excuse. 'So I threw in every warm thing I have. But I'm not sure that any of my stuff is really suitable for snowy weather.'

Or for an aspiring princess, she added silently.

Rafe passed this off with a shrug. 'You can always buy new warm clothes when you get there.'

Yes, she could do that if she hadn't already reallocated his generous payment. She felt a tad guilty as she snapped the locks on her suitcase shut.

Rafe picked it up. 'I have a taxi waiting.'

'Right.' Charlie stifled a nervous ripple. This was going to work out. And it wasn't a completely foolish thing to do. It was worthwhile. Really, it was. She would provide a front for Rafe while he got things sorted with Olivia and saved his country from some kind of economic ruin. And little Isla was getting a very important chance to have a healthy life.

Straightening her shoulders, she pinned on a brave smile. 'Let's get this show on the road,' she told Rafe.

To her surprise, he didn't immediately turn to head for the door. He took a step forward, leaned in and kissed her on both cheeks. She caught a whiff of expensive after-shave, felt the warm brush of his lips on her skin.

'Thank you for doing this, Charlie.' His eyes blazed with surprising emotion and warmth. 'It means a lot to me.'

Charlie wasn't sure what to say. When people did un-expectedly nice things she had a bad habit of crying. But she couldn't allow herself to cry now, so she nod-ded brusquely. Then she followed him out, shut the door, and slipped the key under the mat outside Edna's door, as they'd arranged.

As she did so, Edna's door opened to reveal the old lady with Dolly in her arms.

'We thought we'd wave you off,' Edna said, beaming a jolly smile as she lifted one of Dolly's white paws and waggled it. But then Edna saw Rafe and she forgot to wave or to smile. Instead she stood there, like a statue, eyes agog.

Great.

Charlie suppressed a groan. When she'd told her neigh-bour about her hastily arranged flight, she hadn't men-tioned a male companion. Now *everyone* in their block of flats would know that Charlie Morisset had taken off on reckless impulse with a tall, dark and extremely hand-some stranger.

Conversation was limited as the taxi whizzed across Syd-ney, although Rafe did comment on the beauty of the harbour and the magnificent Opera House. In no time, they arrived at a private airport terminal that Charlie hadn't even known existed.

There was no queue, no waiting, no taking her shoes off for Security, not even tickets to be checked. Her passport was carefully examined though, by a round little Customs man with a moustache, who did a lot of bowing and scraping and calling Rafe 'Your Highness'. Then their luggage was trundled away and there was no more to do.

Rafe's plane was ready and waiting.

Oh, boy. Charlie had been expecting a smallish aircraft that would probably need to make many stops between Australia and Europe. This plane was enormous.

'Do you own this?' she couldn't help asking Rafe.

He chuckled. 'I don't need to *own* a jet. They're very easy to charter, and I have a priority listing.'

'I'm sure you do,' she muttered under her breath.

At that point, she might have felt very nervous about flying off into the unknown with a man she'd only just met, but Rafe took her arm as they crossed the tarmac, tucking it companionably under his, and somehow everything felt a little better and safer. And he kept a firm steadying hand at her elbow as they mounted the steps and entered the plane.

Then Charlie forgot to be nervous. She was too busy being impressed. And overawed.

The interior of Rafe's chartered jet was like no other plane she'd ever seen or imagined. It was more like a hotel suite—with padded armchairs and sofas, and a beautiful dining table.

Everything was exquisite, glamorous and tasteful, decorated in restful blues and golds. As they went deeper into the plane, there were wonderful double beds—two of them, Charlie was relieved to see—complete with banks of pillows, soft wall lamps, and beautiful gold quilts.

The only things to remind her that this was a jet were the narrowness of the space and the lines of porthole windows down each side.

'OK,' she said, sending Rafe a bright grin. 'I'm impressed.'

'I hope you have a comfortable flight.'

'There'd have to be something wrong with me if I didn't.'

He looked amused as he smiled. 'Come and take a seat ready for take-off.'

Rafe's bodyguards had boarded the plane as well, but they disappeared into a section behind closed doors, leaving Rafe and Charlie in total privacy as they strapped themselves into stupendously luxurious white leather chairs. An excessively polite, young female flight attendant appeared, dressed demurely in powder blue and carrying a tray with glasses of champagne, complete with strawberries and a platter with cheese and grapes and nuts.

Oh, my. Until now, Charlie had been too busy and preoccupied to give much thought to what being a prince's fiancée involved, but it seemed this gig might be a ton of fun. Despite her worries about Isla and about all the unknowns that lay ahead of her, she should try to relax and enjoy it.

The flight was a breeze. First there was a scrumptious meal of roasted leek soup, followed by slow-cooked lamb and a tiny mousse made from white chocolate and cherries, and to drink there was wonderful French champagne.

Charlie gave Rafe a blissful smile as she patted her

lips with the napkin. 'This is so delicious,' she said, for perhaps the third or fourth time.

He looked slightly bemused and she wondered if she'd gone a bit too far with her praise.

Of course, she'd been out with guys who'd fed her beautiful meals before this, but it was still an experience she could never get tired of. At home, she'd done most of the cooking before her father's marriage, and she now cooked for herself in the flat, but she'd never seemed to have time to learn more than the basics. Fancy gourmet food was a treat.

After dinner, Rafe said he had business to attend to and was soon busy frowning at his laptop. Charlie, yawning and replete, changed into pyjamas and climbed into an incredibly comfortable bed.

She expected to lie awake for ages mulling over the amazing and slightly scary turn her life had taken in one short day, but with a full tummy, an awesomely comfy bed, and the pleasant, deep, throbbing drone of the plane's engines, she fell asleep quickly.

Rafe suppressed a sigh as he watched Charlie fall asleep with almost childlike speed. Was that the sleep of innocence? He hadn't slept well for weeks—since the night of his father's death. There always seemed to be too much to worry about. First his guilt and despair that he'd been so caught up in his good-time life that he'd missed any chance to bid his father farewell. And then the weighty realities of assuming his sudden new responsibilities.

Now he scanned the emails he'd downloaded before boarding the plane, but there was still no good news about Olivia, or about the intelligence surveillance on Claude Pontier.

Rafe was confident that it wouldn't be long now, before they caught Pontier out. Montaigne's Head of Police, Chief Dameron, was a wise, grey-haired fellow, approaching retirement, so he had a wealth of experience. He'd come up through the ranks, earning his promotions through hard work and diligence, but he'd also been trained by the FBI.

Consequently, his combination of old-school police procedures with the latest technical surveillance savvy was invaluable. Rafe had every faith in him.

Now Rafe looked again towards the bed where Charlie slept, curled on her side with golden curls tumbling on the pillow, and he was surprised by the tenderness he felt towards this girl who'd so readily stepped into her sister's shoes. He wondered if their similarities were more than skin deep.

He suspected that the two girls' personalities were quite different, found himself hoping for this, in fact. And that made no sense at all.

When Charlie woke, the flight attendant was offering her a tray with orange juice and a pot of coffee.

'We'll be landing in Dubai in less than an hour,' she was told.

Really?

A glance through the doorway showed Rafe, already up and dressed and sitting on one of the lounges, working on his computer again. Or perhaps he'd been working all night? Charlie downed her orange juice and hurried to her private bathroom to change out of her pyjamas and wash her face.

She took her tray with the coffee through to the lounge.

'Good morning.' Once again, Rafe's smile held a hint of amusement. 'You slept well?'

'Unbelievably well,' Charlie agreed.

She settled into a lounge and took a sip of coffee. 'I didn't realise we'd be landing in Dubai. I guess we need to refuel?'

'It's not a long stop,' he said. 'But yes, we need to re-fuel and my good friend, Sheikh Faysal Daood Taariq, wants to give us breakfast.'

'Did you say a—a sheikh?'

'That's right.'

Charlie stared at Rafe in dismay. The thought of break-fast with a sheikh was even more confronting than step-ping onto a private jet with a prince. She took a deeper sip of her coffee, as if it might somehow clear her head. 'Are you sure I should come to this breakfast?'

'Well, yes, of course,' said Rafe. 'You're my fiancée.'

'Oh, yes.' This demanded more coffee. 'Yes, of course.' Charlie's hand shook ever so slightly as she refilled her cup from the silver pot. The deeper ramifications of be-coming her sister Olivia were only just sinking in.

This, now, was her reality check. When she stepped off this plane, she would no longer be Charlie Morisset.

'You'll like Faysal,' Rafe told her with a reassuring smile. 'I've known him for years. We met when we were both at Oxford.'

'I—I see. And he's a proper sheikh, but you just call him Faysal?'

'Yes, and you can call him Faysal, too. He's very re-laxed and used to westerners.'

'But will I need to wear a headscarf, or curtsy or any-thing?'

Rafe grinned. 'Not today. Not in his home.'

'What about shaking hands? Is that OK?'

'Offering your hand would be perfectly acceptable. You'll find Faysal is a charming gentleman.'

'Right.' Charlie looked down at her hands and realised

she should probably have painted her nails. She looked at her simple T-shirt and trousers. 'I should probably change into something a bit dressier.'

'Not at all. You'll be fine, Charlie. Relax.' Rafe closed his laptop and slipped it into an overhead locker. 'It's time to strap ourselves back into the seat belts for landing.'

The flight attendant collected their coffee trays, and, once they were belted, she disappeared as the plane began its descent.

In her seat beside Rafe, Charlie couldn't resist asking more questions. 'So, this Faysal—how many wives does he have?'

This brought another chuckle. 'None at all so far. He's still enjoying the life of a bachelor.'

'Right. So he's a playboy?'

'Of course,' Rafe said with a knowing smile.

And I suppose you were a playboy, too, before your father died.

This sudden realisation bothered Charlie more than it should have. Why should she care about Rafe's sex life? It was none of her business—although it did make her wonder again about why Olivia had run away from him.

'And for your information, Faysal's father only has *four* wives,' Rafe said.

'Oh?' she replied airily. 'Only four?'

Rafe shrugged. 'It's a sign of the times. His grandfather had forty.'

Good grief.

After only a very short time in Dubai, Charlie realised how truly ignorant she was about this part of the world. Of course, she'd expected to see regal and haughty, dark-bearded men in flowing white robes, and she knew these men were extraordinarily wealthy and heavily into horse-racing and speed-cars and living the high life. But she hadn't been prepared for the over-the-top opulence.

On the short journey from the airport to Sheikh Faysal Daood Taariq's home, she saw a car painted in gold—and yes, Rafe assured her, it was *real* gold—and another studded with diamonds. And good grief, there was even, in one bright red sports car, a leopard!

A proper live, wild creature. Massive, with a glorious coat of spots and a silver lead around its neck. The leopard was sitting in a front passenger seat beside a handsome young man in white robes and dark sunglasses.

Gobsmacked, Charlie turned to Rafe. 'That wasn't really a leopard, was it?'

He grinned. 'It was indeed.'

'But it couldn't be. How can they?'

Rafe shrugged. 'Welcome to Dubai. Extravagance abounds here and dreadfully expensive exotic pets are all the rage.'

'But surely—' Charlie wanted to protest about the dangers. About animal rights, but she stopped herself just in time.

'Listen, Charlie.' They were in the back seat of a huge limousine and Rafe leaned a little closer, speaking quietly. 'Try not to be too surprised by anything you see here.' He waved his hand to the view beyond the car's window, as they passed a grand palace at the end of an avenue lined on both sides with fountains and palm trees.

'I can't help being amazed,' she said somewhat meekly. But she knew she had to try harder. 'I guess Olivia's used to all this,' she said. 'Her jaw wouldn't be dropping every five minutes.'

Rafe nodded. 'Exactly.'

In that moment, Charlie realised something else.

'You've brought me here to your friend's house as a test, haven't you? It's a kind of trial run for me?'

Rafe's only answer was a smile, but Charlie knew she was right. Visiting his good friend, Faysal, was a kind of fast-track apprenticeship for her in her new role as Rafe's fiancée. If she made any gross mistakes here, the errors would remain 'in house' so to speak.

But she wasn't going to make mistakes. She could do this. In Sheikh Faysal's home, she would ensure that she had perfect posture and perfect manners. She would remember to stand straight, sit with her knees together, and never cross her legs, always be polite and eat neatly, and—

And it would be exhausting to be a full-time princess.

But Charlie was determined to pass any test Rafe St Romain presented. Of course, she could hold her tongue and play the role she'd been assigned. After all, he was paying her *very* handsomely.

Now, with her thoughts sorted, she realised that their car was turning. Huge iron gates were rolling open to allow them entry to a gravelled drive and a tall, white, three-storeyed house decorated with arches.

The car stopped at a heavily embossed front door, which opened immediately to reveal a dark-haired, olive-skinned man almost as handsome as Rafe.

'Rafe and Olivia!' he cried, throwing wide his arms. 'How lovely to see you both again. Welcome!'

Breakfast at Faysal's was wonderful, as always, and to Rafe's relief Charlie behaved admirably.

They dined on the terrace beside the swimming pool, where they were served Arabic coffee made from coffee beans ground with cardamom and saffron, as well as spicy chick peas and *balabet*, a dish of sweetened vermicelli mixed with eggs and spices. There were also delicious pancakes flavoured with cardamom and coloured with saffron and served with date syrup.

Charlie was on her best behaviour, and Rafe knew she was trying hard not to be too overly impressed by everything she saw and tasted. But he could also tell that she was enjoying the meal immensely, possibly even more than she'd enjoyed last evening's meal on the plane.

Just the same, she managed not to gush over the food, and she only jumped once when Faysal called her Olivia.

She couldn't quite hide her fascination with her surroundings, though. Her bright blue eyes widened with obvious delight at the fountains and the terraced gardens and the arcade decorated with exquisite blue and gold tiled mosaics. And Rafe thought she was just a little too impressed by Faysal, who was, as always, handsome and ultra-charming.

Nevertheless, the meeting went rather well, and Rafe was feeling relaxed when Charlie retired to the powder room.

As soon as she'd left, however, Faysal, who had dressed today in European trousers and a white polo shirt instead of his customary white robes, looked across the table to Rafe with a narrowed and sceptical dark gaze.

'So,' he said, his lips tilting with amusement. 'Who the hell is that girl, Rafe?'

Inwardly groaning, Rafe feigned ignorance. 'You know who she is. She's my fiancée, Olivia. What game are you playing?'

'That's the very same question I want to ask you. You're trying to pull a swift one over me, old boy.' Faysal nodded to the corridor where Charlie had disappeared. 'That girl is Olivia's double, I'll grant you that, but, unless she's had a complete personality transplant, she is not the girl I met in Saint-Tropez and again at your engagement ball.'

Rafe sighed heavily as he remembered the extravagant ball he'd hosted. At the time he'd needed to make a big stir about his engagement and to show Chancellor Pontier how serious he was. He hoped there hadn't been too many guests as astute as Faysal. 'Is it really that obvious?'

Faysal's smile was sympathetic as he nodded. 'I'll admit I observe women with a deeper interest than most.'

This was true, but still Rafe was afraid he had a problem.

'Her name's Charlie,' he said. 'Or rather, Charlotte. She's Olivia's twin sister. I tracked her down in Australia.'

'Australia? So that was the accent.'

Rafe grimaced. 'Is that what gave her away? Her accent?'

'Not really.' Faysal eyed Rafe with a level and serious gaze.

'What, then?' Rafe demanded impatiently.

'Her sincerity.'

Hell.

Rafe knew exactly what Faysal meant. There was a genuineness about Charlie that had been totally absent in her sister. He gave a helpless shrug. 'I can't do much about that.'

'No,' Faysal observed quietly. Then he frowned. 'So what happened to Olivia? She hasn't been abducted, has she?'

'No, I wouldn't be sitting here passing the time of day with you if that was the case.' Rafe shrugged. 'She ran away.'

Faysal looked only mildly surprised. 'She panicked, in other words.'

'Yes, I think she must have.'

His friend gave a slow, thoughtful nod. 'Getting engaged to that girl wasn't your smartest move, my friend.'

'I know.' Rafe sighed again. 'As you know, it was all about convenience. It was such a shock when my father died. So unexpected.'

'The pressures of being an only child,' Faysal mused. 'If your mother had still been alive…'

Faysal didn't finish the sentence, but Rafe knew exactly what he was implying. His mother had died three years ago, but if she'd still been alive she would have seen through Olivia Belaire in a heartbeat. And in no time at all, his mother would have produced a list of a dozen or more highly suitable young women for him to choose from.

These girls would have been from good schools and families. They would probably have all had university degrees and perfect deportment and grooming and impeccable manners and be interested in good works. The list of his mother's requirements for a princess were numerous. She had never approved of the girls Rafe had dated.

His criteria for selecting a female companion had been quite different from his mother's. But those carefree days were over.

'If you can see through Charlie,' he said, somewhat dispiritedly, 'I've got a problem on my hands, haven't I?'

His friend shook his head and smiled. 'No, not a problem, Rafe. If you play your cards correctly, I'd say your Charlie could be quite an asset.'

No, Rafe thought, *Faysal's reading this wrong.* His friend might have approved of Charlie's prettiness and sincerity, but he hadn't seen her horror at the thought of actually having to marry him.

'She's a temporary stopgap,' he said firmly. 'That's all.'

CHAPTER FIVE

'So, ARE YOU going to give me a performance appraisal?'

Charlie and Rafe were back in the plane and taking off for Europe when she posed this question.

She'd tried her hardest to be cool and sophisticated in Faysal's home and she needed to know if her efforts had been satisfactory. After all, there wasn't much time to lift her act before they arrived in Montaigne.

She was watching Rafe intently, waiting for his answer, and she didn't miss his frown, although he very quickly hid it behind a smooth smile.

'You were perfect,' he said.

'Are you sure?' She'd tried really hard to lose her accent, but she suspected that he wasn't being totally honest. 'I need to hear the truth, Rafe. I don't want to let you down.'

Which was a noble way of saying that she didn't want to face the embarrassment of being caught out.

'You were fine,' he said with a hint of impatience.

Charlie wasn't sure that 'fine' was good enough, but she didn't want to pester him and become annoying. She consoled herself that Rafe would have told her if she'd made a major blunder.

'So there's nothing you need to warn me about before I arrive in your country?' she tried one more time.

Rafe smiled. 'No, just be yourself, Charlie. It would be different if you really were my fiancée, but for now, I think you'll do well just as you are.'

'Right.' Charlie wished the mention of Rafe's 'real' fiancée didn't bother her so much.

'Just try to look as if you're enjoying yourself,' he said.

She couldn't help smiling. 'That shouldn't be too hard.'

It was true. Everything about this trip so far had been wonderfully exciting. If Charlie hadn't been so worried about poor little Isla, she would have looked on this as the adventure of a lifetime.

As soon as they reached their cruising height, Rafe opened his laptop again. Apparently, he was studying everything he could about mining, so that he could outwit the Leroy Mining Company who wanted to wreck his Alps.

For most of the flight Charlie watched movies. Her head still buzzed with a host of questions—questions about Rafe, about his family and his country, and what he expected of her—but he was clearly preoccupied. And, as he'd made it quite clear, she didn't have the responsibility of a 'real' job.

That belonged to Olivia.

Her sister.

Charlie felt a deep pang at the thought of the girl who was her mirror image. *Her sister.* They shared the same mother. Had shared the same *womb*. The same DNA.

How could her father have kept this secret from her? Learning about it now, Charlie felt hurt. Deeply hurt, as if she'd been denied something precious. The other half of herself.

She wondered how on earth the decision had been

made. Obviously her parents had decided to split and take a child each. But how had they made that choice?

Tossed a coin? Drawn straws?

Charlie wouldn't dwell on the fact that her mother had rejected her and chosen Olivia. It could warp her mind if she let that sink in too deeply. The important thing to remember was that she loved her father very much. She'd had a wonderful childhood and they'd shared many adventures, and they had a great relationship. She couldn't imagine her life without her sweet, dreamy dad.

But she also couldn't deny that her feelings about Olivia were incredibly complicated. On one level she longed to meet her sister and get to know her, but on another level she was stupidly jealous that Olivia was going to marry this deadly handsome Prince.

When Rafe found her.

They arrived in Grenoble mid-afternoon, descending through thick clouds into a world of whiteness. Snow blanketed every rooftop and field and Charlie was so excited she could hardly drag herself from the window when the flight attendant delivered her coat and scarf.

'Do you have boots?' Rafe asked, eyeing Charlie's flimsy shoes. 'You might need them.'

'They're packed away in my suitcase.'

'Hmm.' He came closer and fingered the fabric of her coat.

Charlie could tell by his frown that the coat was inadequate.

'This should be OK to get you from here to my car,' he said. 'But you'll have to get something thicker and warmer for Montaigne.'

'Yes, I dare say.' The new coat would probably need to be a good deal more glamorous, too, Charlie thought, as she noted the elegant cut of Rafe's thick overcoat. In other words, she would have to spend a big chunk of her meagre savings on a coat that she'd only need for a couple of weeks. But she couldn't bring herself to ask Rafe for more money.

Despite Rafe's warning, Charlie wasn't prepared for the blast of frigid air that hit her as she stepped out of the plane. The cold seemed to bite straight through her coat and penetrate to her very bones.

'Are you OK?' Rafe asked, slipping an arm around her shoulders. 'Charlie, you're shivering. Here, take my coat.'

'No, it's all right. We're almost there.'

Welcome warmth enveloped them as they left the tarmac and the airport's doors slid open for them. But now there was something else to worry about.

'Are there likely to be paparazzi here?' she asked.

Rafe slanted her a smile. 'There shouldn't be. I've tried to keep my movements undercover.'

Just the same, Charlie turned up the collar on her coat and tried to look relaxed when heads turned their way. She kept a fixed little smile in place as she walked with Rafe to the chauffeur waiting with a sleek black, unmarked car. All was well. So far.

Grenoble lay at the very foot of the Alps, so it wasn't long before the car was climbing the mountainous slopes. Snowflakes drifted all around them, and Charlie watched through the car windows in delight.

'It doesn't snow in Sydney,' she told Rafe. 'I've seen snow in the Blue Mountains and on the tops of the peaks in Nepal, but we were there in summer. I've never seen it like this. With snow simply *everywhere*.'

It was only then that she caught Rafe's warning frown

and his quick glance to the chauffeur sitting just in front of him.

Oh, help.

Charlie flinched. What an idiot she was. Of course, this chauffeur would talk to the rest of Rafe's staff about the strange change in their master's fiancée. Damn. She'd only just arrived and already she'd made a huge blunder.

Her face was burning as she pressed her lips tightly together. She was such a fool. Turning away sharply, she held her eyes wide open to try to hold back any hint of tears.

Until now, she hadn't doubted that she could do this, but with this first silly gaffe the enormity of her task almost overwhelmed her. There would be so many chances to make mistakes—with servants, with government officials, with Rafe's friends, shopkeepers…

Rafe reached for her hand and she jumped, but his touch was gentle.

'Don't worry,' he murmured, giving her hand an encouraging squeeze.

'But—' Charlie nodded meaningfully towards the back of the chauffeur's head.

'It's OK,' Rafe said quietly, still holding her hand. 'I'll speak to him.' After a bit, he added, 'You'll probably prefer not to have a personal maid.'

Heavens no. Charlie supposed Olivia might have had a maid, but she was bound to make way too many slip-ups under that level of vigilant attention. 'I don't think a maid will be necessary,' she said carefully.

Rafe nodded.

Deeply grateful, Charlie managed a weak smile. 'I'll get the hang of this,' she promised.

'Of course you will.'

His hand was warm on hers.

Already, she was beginning to like Rafe. Too much.

The early twilight was growing darker by the minute.
Below them, the lights of Grenoble twinkled prettily, and
as the road wound ever upwards, night pressed in. They
passed clusters of steep-roofed chalets that glowed with
welcoming warmth, but for most of the journey the Alps
loomed dark and slightly ominous, the car's headlights
catching huge rocky outcrops topped with snow.

Charlie wondered how long it would take to reach
Montaigne, but she refrained from asking Rafe and once
again exposing her ignorance. It wasn't easy for a natural chatterbox to remain silent, but discretion was her
new watchword.

From time to time, Rafe talked to her about matters
that he needed to attend to over the next few days. Meetings, luncheons, more meetings, dinners.

'You'll be busy,' Charlie said, and she wondered what
she would do while Rafe was buzzing around attending
to his princely duties.

'You'll probably need to attend some of these func-
tions,' he said. 'Especially the dinners, but I'll try to keep
your duties light. You'll have plenty of time for shopping.'

Shopping. *Oh, dear.*

It was about an hour and a half later that they reached
Montaigne perched high in an Alpine valley. The capital
city was incredibly pretty, bathed in the clear moonlight,
with lights shining from a thousand windows. The valley
looked like a bowl of sparkling, golden flakes.

'Home,' said Rafe simply.

'It's very beautiful,' Charlie told him.

He nodded and smiled. 'You must be so tired. It's been
a long journey.'

They were pulling up at the front steps of a fairy-tale castle. Charlie forgot her tiredness. She was far too excited.

'*Bonsoir,* Your Highness. *Bonsoir, mademoiselle.*'

A dignified fellow in a top hat and a braided great-coat opened the car door for them. Another man collected their luggage.

Rafe ushered Charlie up a short flight of snow-spotted steps and through the huge open front doors. A woman aged around fifty and dressed in a neat navy-blue skirt and jacket greeted them with a smile.

'Good evening, Chloe.' Rafe addressed her quickly in French, as she greeted them and took their coats. 'Made-moiselle Olivia is very tired, so we'll retire early this evening, but we'd like some coffee and perhaps a little soup?'

'Yes, I'll have it sent up straight away, Your Highness.'

'That would be very good, thank you.'

Charlie managed with difficulty to refrain from staring about her like an awestruck Aussie tourist, but Rafe's castle was amazingly beautiful. There were white marble floors and enormous flower arrangements, huge gold-framed mirrors, chandeliers, and a grand marble stair-case carpeted in deep royal blue.

Despite her nervousness, she planned to drink in every moment that she spent here, and one day she would tell her grandchildren about it. But she wasn't sure she could ever get used to hearing Rafe addressed as 'Your High-ness'. Thank heavens she was only *mademoiselle*.

'I'll show you to your room,' Rafe told her.

To her surprise, they didn't proceed up the staircase. A lift had been fitted into the castle.

'My grandfather had this lift installed for my grandmother,' Rafe told her. 'Grandmère had a problem with her knees as she got older.'

'It must make life a lot easier for everyone else, too,' said Charlie.

'Yes. Here we are on the second floor. Your room is on the right.'

Charlie's room was, in fact, an entire suite, with a huge bedroom, bathroom and sitting room. And although the castle seemed to be heated, there was even a fireplace, where flames burned a bright welcome, and off the bedroom a small study, complete with a desk, a telephone and an assortment of stationery ready for her use.

The whole area was carpeted in a pretty rose pink with cream and silver accessories, and there were at least three bowls of pink roses. Charlie's suitcase had already been placed at the foot of the bed and it looked rather shabby and out of place.

'This is rather old-fashioned compared with your flat in Sydney,' Rafe said.

'But it's gorgeous,' protested Charlie, who couldn't believe he would even *try* to make a comparison. 'Oh, and look at the view!' She hurried over to the high, arched window set deep in the stone wall with a sill wide enough for sitting and dreaming.

Below, the lights of Montaigne glowed warm and bright in the snowy setting.

'I can't believe this.' She was grinning as she turned back to Rafe. 'It's so incredibly picture perfect.'

'There's a remote control here beside the bed.' Rafe picked it up and demonstrated. 'It makes the glass opaque for when you want to sleep.'

'How amazing.' Charlie watched in awe as the glass grew dark and then, at another flick of the switch, became clear again. 'It's magic. Like being in a fairy tale. Aren't you lucky to actually live here?'

His smile was careful. 'Even fairy tales have their dark and dangerous moments.'

'Well, yes, I guess.' Charlie wasn't sure if he was joking or serious. 'I suppose there are always wicked witches and wolves and evil spells.' And in Rafe's case, a wicked Chancellor and evil miners who wanted to wreck his country. 'But at least fairy tales give you a happy ending.'

'Unless you're the wolf,' suggested Rafe.

Charlie frowned at him. 'You're very pessimistic all of a sudden.'

'I am. You're right. I apologise.' But Rafe still looked sad as he stood there watching her.

Charlie wondered if he was thinking about his father who had died so recently. Or perhaps he was thinking about Olivia, wishing his real fiancée were here in his castle, preparing for their marriage. Instead he was left with an improvised substitute who would soon leave again.

Or were there other things worrying him? He'd mentioned the mining threat, but he probably had a great many other issues to deal with. Affairs of state.

She was pondering this when he smiled suddenly. 'I must say I'm not surprised that you believe in happy endings, Charlie.'

She thought instantly of Isla. 'It's terribly important to think positively. Why not believe? It's better than giving up.'

He dismissed this with a shrug. 'But it's a bit like asking me if I believe in fairies. Happy endings are all very well in theory, but I find that real life is mostly about compromise.'

Compromise?

Charlie stared at him in dismay. She'd never liked the idea of compromise. It seemed like such a cop-out. She never wanted to give up on important hopes and dreams and to settle for second best.

She wanted to protest, to set Rafe straight, but there was something very earnest in his expression that silenced her.

She thought about his current situation. He'd been forced to arrange a hasty, convenient marriage to save his country, instead of waiting till he found the woman he loved. That was certainly a huge compromise for both Rafe and for Olivia.

When Rafe looked ahead to the future, he could probably foresee many times when he would be required to set aside his own needs and desires and to put duty to his country first.

It was a chastening thought. Charlie supposed she'd been pretty foolish to come sailing in here, all starry-eyed, and immediately suggest that living in a castle was an automatic ticket to a fairy-tale life. She was about to apologise when there was a knock at the door.

A young man had arrived with their supper.

'Thanks, Guillaume,' Rafe said as the fellow set a tray on the low table in front of the fire. To Charlie, he said, 'I thought we'd be more comfortable eating in here tonight.' When Guillaume had left, he added, 'You don't mind if I join you?'

'No, of course not.' After all, it was what the servants would expect of an engaged couple.

They sat on sofas facing each other. The coffee smelled wonderful, as did the chicken soup, and the setting was incredibly cosy. Charlie looked at the flickering flames, the bowls of steaming soup and the crusty bread rolls.

The scene was almost homely, hardly like being in

a royal castle at all, and for Charlie there was an extra sprinkle of enchantment, no doubt provided by the hunky man who, having shed his overcoat, looked relaxed again now in his jeans and dark green sweater.

Rafe's comments about compromise were sobering though, and no doubt they were the check she needed. Royals might not be dogged by the money worries that had plagued her for most of her life, but their money came with serious responsibilities.

Was that why Olivia ran away?

When they finished their soup, Rafe called for a nightcap, which was promptly delivered, and as he and Charlie sipped the rich, smooth cognac he watched the play of firelight on Charlie's curly hair, on her soft cheeks and lips. It was only with great difficulty that he managed to restrain himself from joining her on her sofa.

But man, he was tempted. There was a sweetness about Charlie that—

No, he wasn't going to make comparisons with her sister. He couldn't waste time or energy berating himself for the error of judgement that had landed him with Olivia Belaire. Regret served no useful purpose.

'Tomorrow, when you're ready, my secretary, Mathilde, will bring you a list of your engagements,' he said, steering his thoughts strictly towards business. 'Including your shopping and hair appointments.'

Charlie looked worried. 'But I won't have *appointments* for *shopping*, will I?'

'Yes. The stores find it helpful to plan ahead. They can make sure that the right staff is available to give you the very best assistance.'

'I see.' Charlie still looked worried. 'Will your secretary also give me a list of the sorts of clothes I need?'

'No, Monique at Belle Robe will look after that. If you show Monique your list of engagements, she'll be able to advise you on dresses, shoes, handbags or whatever.'

'I—I see.'

Was it his imagination, or had Charlie grown pale?

Why? Surely all women loved shopping? Her sister had enthusiastically embraced the shopping expeditions he'd paid for. Unfortunately, Olivia had also taken all those clothes with her when she left. They would have fitted Charlie perfectly.

'You'll have to try to enjoy the experience,' he said.

'Yes, of course. I'll try to behave like Olivia. I suppose she loved shopping.'

'Yes, she had quite a talent for it.'

Charlie lifted a thumbnail to her mouth as if she wanted to chew it. Then she must have realised her mistake and quickly dropped her hand to her lap with her fist tightly curled. 'So I need to be enthusiastic,' she said. 'I can do that.'

'And don't worry about the expense.'

To his dismay, Charlie looked more worried than ever. 'What's the matter, Charlie?'

She flashed him a quick, rather brave little smile. 'No problem, really. It's just that I'm so used to living on a budget and it's hard to throw off the habits of a lifetime.'

Rafe couldn't remember ever dating a girl who was cautious with money. This was a novel experience. 'These clothes won't have price tags,' he reassured her. 'So you needn't know the cost. And remember they're just costumes. They're your uniform, if you like, an important part of the job.'

'Of course.'

'And you don't have to worry about jewellery either,'

he said next. 'There's a huge collection here in the castle vault. All my mother's and grandmother's things.'

'How—how lovely.'

'I imagine that sapphires and diamonds will suit you best.'

Charlie fingered one of her simple, pearl stud earrings, and Rafe suppressed yet another urge to join her on the couch, to trace the sweet pink curve of her earlobe, preferably with his lips. Then he would kiss her smooth neck—

He sat up straighter, cleared his throat. 'And you'll have a driver to take you everywhere.'

'Thank you.'

'Are you sure you wouldn't like a maid as well? A female companion?'

Charlie shook her head. 'If I had another girl hanging out with me, I'd be sure to chatter and give myself away.'

He smiled, knowing that this was true. Charlie was so honest and open, but he wished she weren't still looking so worried. He felt much better when she was smiling. He'd been growing rather used to her smiles.

He hoped his next suggestion wouldn't make her even more worried. 'I was hoping you might be able to visit a children's hospital,' he said carefully. 'It would be very helpful for your image.'

The change in Charlie was instantaneous. Her shoulders visibly relaxed and she uncrossed her legs and, yes, she actually smiled. 'Sure,' she said. 'I'd love that. I love kids. That's a great idea.'

The sudden reversal was puzzling until Rafe remembered that his men had reported Charlie visiting a hospital in Sydney just before she'd made her final decision to accompany him to Montaigne.

What was her interest in hospitals? He hadn't asked his men to follow up on this, but now he recalled the upsetting phone call from her father and wondered if that was the connection. He would have liked to question Charlie about it. But if she'd wanted to tell him, she would have done so by now, and there were limits to how far he could reasonably expect to pry into her private affairs.

After all, their relationship was strictly business.

Charlie yawned then, widely and noisily, and Rafe was instantly on his feet. 'It's time I left you. You need to sleep.'

'I *am* pretty stuffed,' she admitted with a wan smile.

They both stood. Beside them, the fire glowed and danced.

'Goodnight, Charlie.'

'Goodnight, Rafe.'

Her eyes were incredibly blue, their expression curious, and he supposed she was wondering if he planned to kiss her.

He certainly wanted to kiss her. Wanted to rather desperately. He wanted to taste the sweetness of her soft lips. Wanted to kiss her slowly and comprehensively, right there, on the sofa, by the warmth of the fire. Wanted to feel the softness of her skin, feel the eagerness of her response. Rafe imagined that Charlie's uninhibited response would be rather splendid.

'I'll see you in the morning,' she said, eyeing him cautiously.

Rafe came to his senses. 'Yes.' He spoke brusquely, annoyed by his lapse. 'I usually have breakfast at seven-thirty, but you will be tired from the jet lag, so sleep as long as you wish. There's a phone by your bed, so just call for a maid when you wake. Have coffee, breakfast, whatever you want, brought here to your room. Take your time.'

'Thank you.'

Stepping forward, he kissed her politely on both cheeks. *'Bonne nuit,'* he said softly, and then turned and left her without looking back.

Don't do it, Rafe told himself as he walked away. *Don't mess with this girl. You know you'll only end up hurting her.*

Problem was, the habits Rafe had developed during his years of freedom were strong. He'd grown used to having almost any girl he fancied, usually without any strings attached.

Now he was surrounded by restrictions and almost every breath he took had a string attached. The press was watching him. Chancellor Pontier was watching him. For all he knew, the whole country was watching him. His enemies were waiting for him to stuff up, while his people were waiting for him to step up to the mark.

At times the weight of expectation and responsibility pressed so heavily Rafe could barely breathe. Even Charlie, despite her willingness to help him, was just another responsibility.

For her sake, he had to remember that.

Charlie checked her phone before she went to bed, but there was no message from her father. She pressed the remote to darken the window and climbed into bed. The sheets were smooth and silky, they smelled of lavender and were trimmed with exquisite lace and embroidery. The pillow was soft but firm.

Nevertheless, she lay awake for ages, worrying about Isla. Did no news mean good news? Or was her father too busy to bother with texting? Were he and Skye and Isla already in the air on their way to Boston?

How was Isla?

She remembered the lecture she'd given Rafe about positive thinking. She should follow her own advice. She had to believe that all would be well. Isla's tiny heart would survive the long plane flight and the highly skilled doctors in Boston would make her well. The money Rafe had so generously handed over would be put to good use and this whole crazy venture would be worthwhile.

The money...

This was another thing for Charlie to worry about. How on earth could she afford the clothes she needed to carry off the role of Prince Rafael's fiancée? Why on earth hadn't she foreseen this problem?

Anxiously she tossed and turned, playing with the notion of coming clean, of telling Rafe about Isla and explaining what she'd done with his money. But there were problems with this revelation.

First, there was a chance that Rafe might not believe her and they could end up having a row about it. It was an unlikely outcome, Charlie admitted. Rafe appeared to be quite generous and reasonable.

But Charlie certainly didn't want to take advantage of his good nature. The thing was, she'd struck a deal with him and now she had to keep up her end of the bargain. To ask for more money on top of his ample payment would feel totally shabby.

Besides, if she tried to tell Rafe about her baby sister's condition and the impending surgery, she would almost certainly offload all her fears and then blubber all over him.

This was the last thing Prince Rafael of Montaigne needed. He hadn't brought her here to listen to her problems.

He had enough problems of his own.

Once she'd thought things through to this point, Charlie felt calmer. Lying in the darkness, she watched the flickering firelight and she thought about the lovely evening she and Rafe had spent together. She remembered the moment before he'd left when he stood there in the firelight, looking at her. So tall and dark and sexy, with an expression in his eyes that had set her heart thumping.

So intense he'd looked. For a giddy moment, she'd thought he was going to kiss her. Properly. Passionately. Her heart had carried on like a crazy thing, thrashing about like a landed fish.

Such a ridiculous reaction. Perhaps she could blame the jet lag. Tomorrow she'd feel much more like her old self.

CHAPTER SIX

WHEN CHARLIE WOKE the next morning, she took a moment to get her bearings. She couldn't remember another time she'd ever woken to such sumptuous surroundings.

She reached for the remote and pressed the button, and—hey, presto! Bright sunlight streamed into her room.

She wondered how late she'd slept and snatched up her phone to check the time. It was nine o'clock, and there were four new messages on her phone.

Three messages were from her father. One told her that he and Skye and Isla were leaving for Boston. Another gave her their flight's departure and arrival times. A third message asked where she was.

Charlie didn't answer this specifically.

Have a safe flight, she wrote. Sending my love to you and to Skye and Isla. All's well here. C xxx.

She'd crossed so many time zones, she didn't even try to calculate where they might be by now. It was just good to know Isla was on her way and, at this point, all was well. Charlie sent up a prayer.

Keep Isla safe. Hang in there, sweetheart.

The last text message was from Rafe.

Good morning. I hope you've slept well. My secretary, Mathilde, would like to meet with you at eleven. Is this suitable?

Quickly she typed back that this would be fine.

Great, wrote Rafe. Any problems, give me a call.

Charlie wondered where he was. Then her tummy rumbled. She needed breakfast. Rather nervously, she lifted the phone beside the bed.

Immediately a woman's voice at the other end said, '*Bonjour*, Mademoiselle Olivia.'

'Oh,' said Charlie. '*Bonjour.*' In her best French she asked, 'Could I please have some coffee in my room?'

'Certainly, *mademoiselle*. Would you also like breakfast? An omelette perhaps?'

'An omelette would be lovely. *Merci.*'

'It will be with you very soon, Mademoiselle Olivia.'

'Thank you.'

This done, Charlie heaved a huge sigh of relief. Her first hurdle might have been a rather low bar in the scheme of things, but at least she'd cleared it without mishap.

A much higher hurdle came later, after the secretary Mathilde had given Charlie her engagement itinerary. She was expected to start clothes shopping this very day.

Not only did Charlie need a warmer overcoat, a new outfit was required for dinner this evening, another to wear for a daytime engagement the next day and a special gown for a gala event to be held in the castle in two evenings' time.

Charlie almost whimpered when she saw the list. She knew Rafe never dreamed that she would be paying for these clothes out of her own money, but she felt she had no other option. The problem was, her bank account wouldn't stretch to *four* expensive items of clothing, all fit for a princess. She would be lucky if she could afford one of these outfits, which meant she had no alternative but to get a cash advance on her credit card.

Ouch.

Shivering inside her inadequate coat, Charlie stepped out of the castle to find that fresh snow had fallen during the night. Now, in the early afternoon, it was clear and sunny, but the air was freezing. A chauffeur was waiting for her at the foot of the steps.

He was understandably surprised when Charlie asked him to take her to a bank before delivering her to Belle Robe, but he discreetly refrained from making any comment. Fortunately, the bank teller didn't seem to recognise her as the Prince's intended bride. Her cards were accepted without a hitch and she was able to withdraw a sickening amount of money.

Belle Robe was around the next corner.

Gulp.

Charlie had seen expensive clothing boutiques in Sydney, so she was used to store windows decorated with elegant mannequins dressed in glamorous gowns, but she'd never been inside one of these places before. Now she tried hard not to be overawed by the top-hatted doorman, the wide expanses of cream carpet, the gilt-framed floor-to-ceiling mirrors.

Madame Monique, who'd been assigned to attend to Charlie's needs, was pencil thin with cut-glass cheekbones and she was dressed in a severely straight black dress of fine wool. She also wore glasses with trendy black and white frames and her iron-grey hair was pulled tightly back into a low ponytail.

Another woman might have looked plain in such restrained attire but Monique managed to look incredibly elegant. No doubt her bright scarlet lipstick and nail polish helped.

Charlie supposed she should have painted her nails, too. She wondered if Olivia had always worn nail polish. It was another detail she should have checked with Rafe.

Monique was very organised and had a page set aside for Charlie in a thick gold-edged notebook. 'Welcome back again, Mademoiselle Olivia,' she said with a careful smile.

'Thank you,' said Charlie. 'How are you, Monique?'

Surprise flashed briefly in the woman's eyes, as if she hadn't expected this question. 'I'm very well, thank you, *mademoiselle*.' Her smile brightened. 'And now, His Highness has ordered quite a few more items for you, I believe.'

'Yes, I'm afraid so.'

Monique looked a little puzzled at this and Charlie winced. *Afraid so?* Had she really said that? What an idiot she was. She would have to behave far more confidently if she wanted to convince the people of Montaigne that she was Olivia Belaire. She was supposed to *adore* shopping.

She laughed quickly to try to cover her gaffe. 'So,' she said, brightly. 'I'm sure you have some wonderful suggestions.'

'Of course,' said Monique. 'I have a very good idea what suits you now, so I've made a few selections to get us started.'

'Lovely,' Charlie enthused. 'I can't wait to try them on.'

They started with the coats and it was so hard to choose between a beautiful long red coat with a leather belt and another in black and white houndstooth. Eventually, with a little prompting from Monique, Charlie settled on the red.

For this evening's dinner, she chose a timelessly styled blue dress made from exquisitely fine wool. It was rather figure-hugging and designed to catch the eye, but Charlie supposed it was the sort of thing Rafe wanted her to wear. She tried not to blush when she saw her reflection in the mirror, but, heavens, she'd had no idea she could look so glamorous.

'Do you know what the daytime event for tomorrow will be?' asked Madame Monique, watching Charlie closely.

Charlie was relieved that she could answer this. 'I believe I'll be visiting the children's hospital.'

The woman's eyebrows rose, but she made no comment as she showed Charlie a rather demure dress in grey with a box neckline and a wide band around the waist.

'Hmm,' said Charlie. 'That's lovely, but do you have anything that's a bit more—fun?'

'Fun, Mademoiselle Olivia?' Madame Monique was clearly surprised.

Charlie wondered if she'd used the wrong French word. 'Something more appealing to the children, something a little more—relaxed?'

'Oh, I see, of course.' Monique went back to her racks, frowning.

Charlie followed her. The clothes were extremely elegant, but there were rather a lot of beiges and greys and blacks. She was wondering if she would be better off just wearing a pair of jeans and one of her own sweaters when something caught her eye.

'What about this?' she said, lifting out a hanger to inspect the dress more closely. It was a feminine shift dress with elbow-length sleeves and a delicate all-over print of little red sail boats with white sails on a navy-blue background. 'This would be perfect. Do you have it in my size?'

Now Monique looked worried. 'But, *mademoiselle*, don't you remember? You already have this dress. You bought it two weeks ago.'

'Oh.' Charlie wished she could sink through the floor. 'Yes, of course,' she said shakily. 'How silly of me. I—I took it home to Saint-Tropez, you see, when I—when I visited my mother—and I—'

It was awful to lie so blatantly and just saying the word 'mother' felt terribly wrong. She couldn't quite finish the sentence, but if Monique was baffled, and Charlie was sure that she had to be, she discreetly covered the reaction.

'What about this?' Monique lifted out a white dress with black polka dots and a short black jacket. 'I think this would suit you beautifully. And it certainly looks… *détendu*.'

This outfit did indeed suit Charlie very well and it had the right playful vibe she'd been hoping for. It was added to the stash, along with an *oh-my-God* evening gown of pale sea-green satin that was the most elegant and glamorous thing Charlie had ever clapped eyes on, let alone worn.

She felt a little faint as she wondered what the price tag might be.

'And now for your shoes,' said Monique.

The fainting sensation grew stronger for Charlie. *Oh, dear.* She had to sit down.

Monique fussed. 'Mademoiselle Olivia, are you all right? What can I get you? A glass of water perhaps? Coffee?'

'Perhaps some water,' said Charlie. 'Thank you.'

Monique tut-tutted when she returned with the water. 'Perhaps you are not well, *mademoiselle*.'

'No, I'm fine,' Charlie insisted, after taking several reviving sips. 'It's probably—' She was about to use jet lag as an excuse when she remembered that her sister, Olivia, hadn't been flying halfway across the world in a jet. 'I'm just a bit tired,' she said instead. 'And I was wondering—before we start on the shoes, would you mind telling me how much I have spent so far?'

This time, Madame Monique didn't try to cover her surprise. Her eyebrows shot high above her black and white spectacle frames. 'But you know there's no need to concern yourself, my dear. This goes on the St Romain account, does it not?'

Charlie had no idea what arrangement Rafe had made with Olivia. All she knew was that he'd paid her, Charlie, an extremely generous sum and she wouldn't dream of asking him for anything more.

'I'm paying for today's purchases,' she said, but as the words left her mouth she saw Monique's expression of jaw-dropping shock and knew that she'd made yet another mistake.

The dinner that evening was an official affair with some of Montaigne's most important businessmen and their wives. Charlie wore the blue wool dress and a new pair of skin-toned high heels that she hoped would go with almost everything, although Madame Monique had persuaded her that she needed black boots to go with her overcoat.

'You look beautiful,' Prince Rafael told her when he saw her.

'Thanks.' It was the first time that day that Charlie had seen him and, to her dismay, just watching him walk into the drawing room in a dark suit and tie caused a jolt to her senses. To make matters worse, he reached for her hand.

Ridiculous tingles shot over her skin.

'Did your shopping expedition go well?'

'Yes, thanks. Monique—was very helpful.' Although Charlie was miserably aware that tongues would be wagging at Belle Robe.

'Something very strange has happened to Olivia Belaire, the Prince's fiancée. I think she must be unwell. She looked very pale.'

'Can you believe she wanted to pay for the clothes with cash? And then she didn't have enough.'

At some stage this evening she would have to confess to Rafe that she'd needed to use his money as well, but she was sure she should leave it until after the dinner.

Rafe must have noticed her distress. He gave her hand an encouraging squeeze. 'I think you need jewellery to set that dress off. Sapphires perhaps?'

Charlie gulped, touched a hand to her bare throat. Before she could answer, Rafe was summoning Jacques, his right-hand man—or perhaps his valet, Charlie wasn't sure—telling him to bring the single-strand Ceylon sapphires.

'Don't look so worried,' Rafe told her as the man hurried away. His smile was a little puzzled. 'I've never met a woman who didn't like shopping or jewellery.'

Charlie shrugged. 'If you transplant an ordinary Aussie girl into a fairy-tale European kingdom, you've got to expect a few surprises.'

Rafe's eyes gleamed as he smiled. This time he lifted her hand to his lips. 'Touché,' he murmured.

To Charlie's dismay, he left a scorch mark where his lips touched her hand.

* * *

The sapphires were promptly delivered and they were perfect to complement the simple lines of her sky-blue dress—a single strand of deep blue oval stones surrounded by delicate clusters of tiny white diamonds and set in white gold.

'Allow me,' Rafe said, lifting the necklace and securing it around Charlie's neck.

The skin around his eyes crinkled this time when he smiled. 'Perfect,' he said softly. 'Oh, and there are matching earrings. You might like to wear them as well. Take a look in the mirror.'

Charlie was a little stunned by her reflection. Who was this elegant creature?

But her cheeks were flushed pink and her fingers fumbled as she tried to fit the earrings to her lobes. Crikey, she had to calm down or she'd drop a royal sapphire and have the Prince of Montaigne down on his knees, searching for it in the thick carpet.

At last the earrings were secure.

'You look like a princess,' Rafe told her.

Yes, it was amazing what expensive clothes and jewellery could do for a girl. Charlie drew a deep breath. Tonight she would have to pretend that she was a princess-to-be. Princess Charlie or, rather, Charlotte.

What a laugh.

Any urge to laugh soon died when Rafe took her hand again. She was super-aware of his warm, *naked* palm pressed against hers, of his long fingers interlaced with hers, as he led her down the formal staircase to greet their guests.

She kept her smile carefully in place and concentrated hard on remembering everyone's names as she was introduced, but the task would have been a jolly sight easier if her pretend fiancé hadn't kept touching her. For Rafe, it meant nothing to place a hand at her elbow, on her shoulder, at the small of her back. For Charlie, it was intensely, breath-robbingly distracting.

The castle's dining room was a long rectangular space decorated with rich red wallpaper as a background for impressive paintings and gold-framed mirrors. An enormous picture window with a spectacular view of the valley took up most of the far wall. The table was exquisitely set with candles and flowers, gleaming silver and shining glassware, and everything was arranged so perfectly that Charlie could imagine a ruler had been used to align the place settings.

Throughout the delicious four-course meal, Rafe conversed diplomatically with his important guests, but his eyes constantly sought Charlie out. Many times he sent her a smouldering smile across the table.

She knew his smiles weren't genuinely flirtatious. He was playing the role of an affectionate fiancé for the sake of their guests. So, of course, she tried to remain cool and collected, to pay studious attention to the conversations all around her. Actually, she had no choice but to pay *very* careful attention, because everyone spoke rather rapidly in French and she could only just keep up with them. And she tried hard to not let Rafe's sexy smiles affect her too deeply.

Unfortunately, her body had a mind of its own, firing off heat flashes whenever her gaze met Rafe's across the table. It didn't help that she was terribly worried about the conversation she must have with him as soon as his guests had departed.

* * *

It was late when everyone finally left. Much to Charlie's amazement, the men had withdrawn to linger over coffee and cognac—she thought that kind of antiquated custom had gone out with the ark.

'This is when the men settle their important business,' one of the wives told her as their coffee was served. 'They're all so worried about this Leroy Mining Company.'

'While we just want to gossip,' said another woman, an attractive brunette.

Seeing their expectant smiles, Charlie was suddenly nervous again. Were these businessmen's wives expecting her to supply them with gossip? What would Olivia have done in her shoes? She hadn't a clue.

She didn't even know if these women had known Olivia.

'I'm all ears,' Charlie said, managing an extra-bright smile, despite the roiling tension in her stomach.

For a moment the women looked baffled. Clearly, this wasn't the response they'd expected. They were hoping for news from her, but just when things were about to get very awkward one of the women laughed, as if Charlie had actually cracked a wonderful joke, and then the others joined in.

After that, knowing it was her duty as hostess to lead the conversation, Charlie asked them if they were coming to the ball on the night after next and it seemed that all of them were. From then on, she was fielding questions about which band would be playing on the night of the ball and whether Princess Maria or Countess von Belden had been invited.

'I'm sorry,' Charlie said. 'I've been visiting my mother In Saint-Tropez and I've left all those arrangements to Rafael.'

* * *

Somehow, she got through the interrogation without too many sticky moments. She wondered if Rafe had ensured that the guests were first-timers who hadn't met her sister. Even so, the night was an ordeal. She was battling jet lag and she was almost dropping with exhaustion. This 'princess' gig was so much harder than it looked from the outside.

She was sure Rafe must be tired, too, but after the guests left he still came to her room, as he'd warned her he must, for his expected 'nightly visit'.

'Thank heavens that's over,' he said, taking off his coat and carelessly draping it on the end of a sofa, then flopping into the deep cushions and loosening his tie and the buttons at his throat.

Charlie hadn't meant to stare as he performed this small act, but everything about the man was so utterly eye-catching. She found herself mesmerised by the jutting of his jaw as he loosened his collar, by the sudden exposure of his tanned throat, and even the way he sat with his elbows hooked over the back of the sofa, his long legs sprawled casually.

Everything about this Prince was super-attractive and manly.

Rafe caught her watching him. She looked away quickly, cheeks flaming, and then tried to make herself comfortable as she sat on the opposite sofa. But it was hard to feel comfortable with a huge weight on her mind.

There was only one thing for it, really—she had to get her worries off her chest quickly, before Rafe launched into another cosy fireside chat.

Charlie sat forward with her back straight, her hands tightly clasped in her lap. 'Rafe, I have a confession to make.'

Unfortunately, he merely looked amused, which wasn't at all helpful. 'I thought something must be troubling you.'

'Did it show tonight? I'm sorry. Do you think your guests noticed?'

'No, Charlie, relax.' He gave a smiling, somewhat indulgent shake of his head. 'It's just that I've learned to read the signs. There's a certain way you hold your mouth when you're distracted or worried, but as far as anyone else is concerned you were perfect tonight. You look very lovely, by the way.'

'Yes, you told me.' She refused to take his flattery seriously. 'It's the dress, of course.'

This brought another slow, knowing smile tilting the corners of his sexy mouth. 'Of course. We'll blame the dress. Now, what's your problem?'

Charlie's problem was the same problem that had dogged her all her life. 'Money.'

'Money?' Rafe looked understandably puzzled. 'So what's the problem exactly? You have too little or too much money?'

She couldn't imagine ever being worried about having too much money. 'Too little, of course. I'm sorry, I—'

A crease furrowed between Rafe's dark brows. 'Dare I ask about the two hundred and fifty thousand dollars I gave you? I know it's not really any of my business, but you haven't spent that already, have you?'

'Well, yes—I have—actually.' Charlie almost added an apology as she made this confession, but stopped herself just in time. She would only make matters worse if she behaved as if she were guilty. 'I'm only telling you this, because I went shopping today, and I tried to buy the clothes out of my own savings. But I didn't have quite enough, not for the shoes and boots, as well as the coat and the dresses.'

'But *you* weren't expected to pay for the clothes out of your own purse. Surely Monique explained?'

'I think she may have tried to. She said something about a St Romain account, but I wanted to pay for them, Rafe. You've already given me so much money.'

'Which you've managed to spend in forty-eight hours. That's no mean feat, Charlie.'

She had no answer for this. At least Rafe didn't ask her what she'd spent the money on. She still felt too tense about Isla to try to talk about that situation.

No doubt he assumed she'd bought a yacht or an apartment, or even that she'd used his money to pay off old debts.

A deafening silence followed her admission. In the midst of the awkwardness, she heard a *ping* from her phone, which she'd left on her bedside table.

'Do you mind if I get that?' she asked.

'By all means.' Rafe gave a stiff nod of his head and he spoke with excessive, almost chilling politeness.

Charlie knew she'd disappointed him and she might have felt guilty if she hadn't been so very anxious about her family. They must be in Boston by now. Her stomach was churning as she dashed to the phone.

CHAPTER SEVEN

RAFE KNEW IT was foolish to feel disappointed in Charlie simply because she'd dispensed with his money so easily. She was perfectly entitled to do what she liked with the cheque he'd given her.

She was fulfilling her obligations—she'd accompanied him to Montaigne and was acting as a stand-in for her sister, and that was all he'd asked of her. How she spent the money was none of his business.

Besides, he was using Charlie to his own ends, so he was in no position to make moral judgements about the girl.

To Rafe's annoyance, these rationalisations didn't help. He *was* disappointed. Unreasonably, illogically, stupidly disappointed.

Unfortunately, in the same short couple of days that it had taken Charlie to spend his payment, he'd allowed her—an unknown girl from the bottom of the planet—to steal under his defences.

Thinking back over the past forty-eight hours, Rafe couldn't believe that he'd allowed Charlie to cast a spell over him. But, surely, that must be what had happened. Somehow, despite the lectures he'd given himself, he'd allowed himself to become intrigued by the possibility that he'd discovered a rare creature—a lovely, sexy girl with genuine *heart*, who wasn't a grasping opportunist.

Foolishly, he'd decided that Charlie was different from her sister Olivia and from the other frustratingly shrewd and calculating young women in his social circles.

Rafe had been beguiled by Charlie's air of apparent naivety, and, even though he'd known that she wouldn't remain in his life beyond a few short weeks, he'd wanted to thoroughly enjoy the novelty of her company while he could.

She'd been a refreshing experience.

Or so he'd thought.

He consoled himself that he wasn't the only one who'd been hoodwinked. Even his good friend, Sheikh Faysal, had been taken by Charlie and had made remarks about her sincerity.

What had Faysal said? *'If you play your cards correctly, I'd say your Charlie could be quite an asset.'*

Ha! They'd both been conned.

Charlie was nervous as she picked up the phone. As she'd hoped, it was a message from her father.

Arrived safely. Dr Yu has assessed Isla and it's all systems go. Surgery scheduled for nine a.m. tomorrow EDT. Thank you, darling!! Love you loads, Dad & Skye xx

It was such a relief to hear from him. Almost immediately, Charlie could feel her shoulders relax and her breathing ease. Isla was in the best possible place, under the care of the brilliant doctors in Boston.

But her relief brought a welling of tears and she had to close her eyes to stop them from spilling. She drew in a deep breath, and then another.

She wasn't ready to share this news with Rafe. It was too private, too desperately scary to talk about. And it wasn't over yet. Poor little Isla still faced surgery and that was probably the most dangerous time of all.

Opening her eyes again, she caught a glimpse of Rafe's cautious, frowning expression. She supposed he'd been watching her, but as she returned to the sofa he paid studious attention to his own phone, which he slipped back into his pocket as she sat down.

For a tense moment, neither of them spoke. And then they both spoke together.

'That was a message from my father,' Charlie said.

'I was just checking the weather forecast,' said Rafe.

They stopped, eyed each other awkwardly.

'All's well with my family,' offered Charlie.

'There's more snow predicted,' said Rafe.

Charlie managed a tiny smile. 'At least I have a warm coat now.'

'Yes.'

She swallowed, wondering what on earth they could talk about when the mood was so strained. Rafe's smiles had vanished. There was no chance of regaining the warmth of last evening's conversation.

She touched the sapphires, lying cool and solid against her throat. 'Do these need to be returned to a vault, or something?'

Rafe nodded. 'I'll see to it.'

He sat, watching her with a hard-to-read, brooding gaze as she removed the necklace and the earrings and placed them back in their velvet-covered box. This time, he made no attempt to help her. Without the jewellery, she felt strangely naked.

'So, tomorrow you go to the children's hospital,' Rafe said.

Charlie nodded. 'Yes.'

'I hope that's not too much of an imposition.'

'No, I think I'll enjoy it.' She would feel closer to her family. The connection was important.

Another awkward silence fell and Rafe stared at her thoughtfully. 'I don't have any pressing appointments in the morning. I'll accompany you.'

This was a surprise—and not a pleasant one either. Under normal circumstances, Charlie wouldn't have minded. She enjoyed Rafe's company very much, probably *too* much. But now she was sure he was only going to the hospital to keep an eye on her, which meant he didn't trust her, and that possibility disturbed her.

'I'll look forward to your company,' she said quietly, knowing she had little choice.

Rafe nodded, then stood. 'The breakfast room is on the ground floor, in the south wing. I'll see you there at eight tomorrow?'

'Yes—sir.' Charlie couldn't help adding the cheeky 'sir'. Rafe was being so stodgy and formal.

He didn't smile, but one dark eyebrow lifted and a flicker of something that might have been amusement showed briefly in his eyes. He left quickly, though, with a curt *'bonne nuit'*. No kisses on the cheek tonight.

Visiting a children's hospital with a prince in tow was a very different experience from any previous hospital visit that Charlie had made.

After a polite and rather formal exchange at breakfast, she and Rafe left the castle in a sleek black, chauffeur-driven car that sported the blue and gold flags of Montaigne fluttering from its bonnet. And as they passed through the snowy streets, people turned to stare, to point and to wave excitedly. Finally, when the car pulled up outside the hospital, there was a group of reporters hovering on the footpath.

From the moment the chauffeur opened the door for Charlie, cameras were flashing and popping and she felt so flustered she almost stumbled and landed in the newly snow-ploughed gutter. The possibility of such an ignominious christening for her long red coat and knee high boots ensured that she navigated the footpath super carefully. Rafe's hand at her elbow helped.

A team of doctors, nurses and administrators from the hospital greeted them on the front steps. Charlie remembered to smile while Rafe introduced her as his fiancée, Olivia Belaire, and she did her level best to remember names as she shook everyone's hand.

Then the hospital team, plus Rafe and Charlie and the reporters, all processed inside.

Charlie leaned in to speak in a whisper to Rafe. 'Surely, all these flashing cameras will frighten the sick children?'

'They won't all be allowed into the wards,' Rafe assured her.

Indeed, as Charlie's and Rafe's coats were taken and they continued to the wards, only one television cameraman and one newspaper journalist were allowed to continue, along with the entourage of hospital staff. Charlie decided to ignore the other adults as best she could. The children were her focus and they were delightful.

Over the next hour or so, she and Rafe met such a touching array of children. Some were very sick and confined to bed, while others were more mobile and were busy with various craft activities. They talked to a little boy in a wheelchair who was playing a game on a tablet and another boy presented Rafe with a colourful portrait of himself and Olivia, both wearing golden crowns.

A little girl wearing a white crocheted cap to cover her bald head performed a beautiful curtsy for them.

'Oh, how clever you are!' Charlie told her, clapping madly. Prince Rafael, however, went one better. Responding with a deep bow, he took the little girl's hand and gallantly kissed her fingers.

The smile on the child's face was almost as huge as the lump in Charlie's throat and she knew this was a moment she would remember forever.

Of course, the cameras were flashing and whirring throughout these exchanges, but by now Charlie, glad of her jaunty polka-dot dress, had learned to ignore them. They moved on to a room that looked like a kindergarten where children were sitting at tables and busy with crêpe paper and scissors and wire.

'So what are you doing?' Charlie asked, kneeling down to the children's level.

'We're making roses,' she was told by a little girl with a bandage over one eye. 'And we made one for you!'

'Oh!'

Charlie's gratitude and praise for the pink and purple concoction were heartfelt and, although she felt quite emotional at times, she managed to keep her smile in place. Until they reached the sick babies.

Suddenly, her stomach was churning. At least there were no babies awaiting heart surgery in this ward, but she was given a warm, blanketed bundle to hold, and from the moment the little one was placed in her arms she was battling tears.

Of course, she was thinking of Isla, and of course, the cameramen zoomed in close, capturing every emotion. She didn't dare to catch Rafe's eye.

* * *

They were driving back to the castle, after morning tea with a selection of hospital staff, before Rafe commented on the experience. 'That seemed to go well,' he said, although he didn't look particularly happy.

'It was amazing,' Charlie declared firmly. 'The children were so excited to see you, Rafe. That little girl with the curtsy was gorgeous. I hope she gets better. Her doctor said he was optimistic.'

'That's good,' Rafe said warmly. 'Everyone loved you—especially the children, but you were a hit with the staff as well.'

Charlie couldn't help feeling chuffed. 'I guess I was channelling my inner princess.'

Rafe's response was an incomprehensible smile, and he looked more worried than pleased.

What was wrong? Charlie wondered with a sigh. She felt a spurt of impatience. She'd done her level best this morning. He'd said she'd done well. What more did he want?

'Why do you look so worried, Rafe? I thought you just told me that the visit went well. I thought you were happy.'

'Of course the visit went well. You were perfect.' He gave a slow shake of his head. 'That's the problem.'

This made no sense at all. 'Excuse me?'

'You've set rather a high standard for Olivia to follow.'

'Oh.' Charlie hadn't considered this possibility. 'Are you suggesting that visiting a children's hospital might not be her cup of tea?'

'Exactly,' Rafe said grimly.

Charlie had no answer for this. She'd done what she'd been asked to do. She could do no more. 'Do you think there'll be a photo in the newspaper tomorrow?'

Rafe nodded. 'Almost certainly.'

'I wonder if Olivia will see it. Gosh, imagine how shocked she'll be.'

This brought another frown from Rafe. 'At least, she might make contact then.'

'And that's a good thing, surely?'

But his expression was still serious and thoughtful as he looked away out through the car's window. A woman and a little girl out on the street saw him and waved excitedly, but he seemed too preoccupied to notice. He didn't wave back.

Charlie, feeling sorry for them, waved instead.

The car returned to the castle and Charlie expected that Rafe would leave her now. She had no other commitments for the day, but he would almost certainly be busy. She wasn't looking forward to the next few hours of anxiously pacing the floor, trying to fill in time until she heard news from her father.

In the castle's enormous, white-marbled entrance, she hesitated, expecting Rafe to dismiss her.

Instead, he stood, tall and wide shouldered, in his large, heavy wool overcoat, with his black leather gloves clasped in one hand, watching Charlie with unexpected vigilance, almost as if she were a puzzling, troublesome child.

She was getting rather tired of trying to understand what this Prince really wanted of her. She was about to demand what his problem was when he spoke.

'Charlie, can I ask a personal question?' His manner was perfectly polite, but there was an intensity in his grey gaze that made her suddenly nervous.

In an attempt to cover this, she shrugged, rather like a teenager put on the spot by an inquisitive parent. 'I guess. What do you want to know?'

'Would you be prepared to explain why I've seen you on the verge of tears on at least three separate occasions now?'

Her cheeks flamed hotly. 'Three times?'

'Yes,' said Rafe. 'You've been upset twice on the phone when you were speaking to your father and then today at the hospital with that tiny baby in your arms.'

'You're—you're very observant.'

'Look, I don't want to pry, Charlie,' Rafe said more gently. 'I'm fully aware that I dragged you away from your life in Sydney without really asking if it was convenient, but if something is causing you distress, perhaps I should know.'

She would burst into tears if she tried to talk about Isla, especially now with the scheduled surgery only hours away. 'I'm just a bit tense,' she hedged.

Rafe's grey eyes narrowed. 'And this tension relates to your father?'

'Sort of...yes.' It was the best she could manage. She crossed her arms tightly over her chest and hoped this was the end of Rafe's interrogation.

'Is there any way I can help?'

This was so unexpected.

Charlie had never had a drop-dead handsome man offer to help her. For a moment she was tempted to pretend that Rafe really was her fiancé, to tell him everything that was bothering her as she threw herself into his arms and sobbed on his strong, capable shoulder.

Just in time, she dragged her thoughts back to reality. 'It's kind of you to offer to help, Rafe. But, actually, I haven't talked to you about—my concerns—because I knew you might want to help. And you can't really, and if you did try, then there'd probably be all kinds of publicity and—'

'I can avoid publicity when I need to,' Rafe cut in. 'My press secretary is very good at managing these things.'

Charlie supposed this was true. There would be many times when a royal needed to avoid the press, and other times when he would welcome the attention. She supposed Rafe had been well aware that his presence at the hospital today would be a draw-card for journalists. Perhaps, Charlie realised now, he'd been using the hospital visit as some kind of bait to lure Olivia out of hiding.

This thought drew Charlie up sharply. But she didn't want to think too deeply about Rafe's relationship with Olivia. She especially didn't like to contemplate the regrettable reality that Rafe planned to go ahead with his marriage to her sister, even though he didn't love her and she clearly didn't love him.

On the other hand, when Charlie considered what she'd been prepared to do to save Isla, she supposed Rafe might go to any length to save his country. It was all rather depressing, really.

And Rafe was still waiting for her answer.

She pulled her phone from her pocket to check the time. It was only midday, and by her calculations Isla's surgery was scheduled for three pm Montaigne time. She still had to wait hours and hours before she knew the outcome.

'I appreciate your concern,' she told him. 'But now is not a good time to talk about it.'

'When will be a good time?' Rafe persisted.

'By the end of the day.' She had no idea how she would fill in the rest of the day. 'I just wish this day would go faster,' she said, thinking aloud.

'So, why don't you allow me to divert you for an hour or so with lunch in one of our finest restaurants?'

Charlie was momentarily dumbstruck. 'Aren't you too busy?'

'Not today. I've kept my schedule clear.' A smile shimmered in his eyes as he waited for her answer.

'Will there be lots of people staring at us?'

'Not at this place. Most of Cosme's clientèle are famous in their own right. Come on, Charlie. I'll drive you there myself. Let me show you a little more of my country and one of my favourite places.'

The smile he gave her now would have done Prince Charming proud, and Charlie had to admit that the thought of a pleasant lunch in a lovely restaurant was way more appealing than pacing alone in her room and uselessly worrying.

Really, when the man invited her so nicely, she'd be churlish to refuse, wouldn't she?

Rafe drove to Cosme's in a flashy silver sports car, with the hood up against the biting cold. As far as Charlie could tell, most of the city's roads seemed to be narrow and winding, which must have made life difficult for the guys with the snowploughs. Many streets were ancient and cobbled and crowded in by tall buildings made from centuries-old stone. She was sure she would have been nervous if she'd been behind the wheel, but Rafe drove his car skilfully and with obvious enjoyment.

She wondered how often he got to taste this kind of freedom, although she supposed he wasn't ever completely free. His minders were still following at a discreet distance.

The restaurant, simply called Cosme's, was in an old building that might have once been a castle. Two pine trees stood like sentries in huge pots on either side of a bright red door, making a bright splash of welcome colour.

Inside, Charlie and Rafe, with their coats and scarves taken care of, were led up a winding stone staircase to a spacious dining area made completely of stone and warmed by a blazing, crackling fire, a proper open fire with logs. The other diners scarcely paid them any attention as they were shown to their table set in an alcove.

It was all wonderfully simple, but perfect—a starched white tablecloth, gleaming, heavy silver, a small candle in a pottery holder and another spectacular view.

Charlie was rapt as she looked out through their alcove's arched window to the pale winter sky and a steep, snow-covered mountainside. 'This is absolutely gorgeous, Rafe. Thank you for bringing me here.'

He grinned. 'The pleasure's all mine. But wait till you try the food.'

The menu was large and of course everything was in French.

'You know the menu well,' Charlie said. 'I think I'd like you to choose. What do you suggest I should try?'

'Well, you can't beat the traditional French favourites,' Rafe suggested. 'Cosme has perfected them. I'm sure you'd enjoy his *soupe à l'oignon.*'

'Oh, yes.' A proper French onion soup on a cold winter's day sounded perfect.

'But perhaps, first, you would like to try an entrée? How about something local, like goat's cheese baked with Alpine honey?'

Charlie grinned. 'Yes, please. It sounds amazing.'

And, of course, it was totally delicious. For Charlie, who was used to cramming in a hasty sandwich at her desk in the gallery, this leisurely, gourmet lunch was the ultimate luxury.

As she tasted her first sip of a divine vintage Chablis, she couldn't help asking, 'Has Olivia been here?'

Amusement flickered in Rafe's eyes and at the corners of his mouth. 'Actually, no, she hasn't.'

She knew it was small-minded of her to be pleased about this. Surely it was shameful to have feelings of sibling rivalry for a sister you'd never even met.

Charlie's soup arrived, along with a veal dish for Rafe. The soup was wonderfully rich and savoury with a to-die-for golden, cheesy bread crust. It was so good she couldn't talk at first, apart from raving, but after a bit she encouraged Rafe to tell her more about Montaigne.

She was keen to learn more about its history and its traditions, about the mining threat and his plans for his country's future. So he told her succinctly and entertainingly about the country's history and the jewellery-making craftspeople and the famous Alpine skiers. As he talked she could feel how genuinely he loved this small principality and its people.

Charlie decided there was something very attractive about a man whose vision extended beyond his own personal ambitions. Not that she should dwell on Prince Rafael of Montaigne's attractions.

She was halfway through the soup, when she asked, in a burst of curiosity, 'What's it like to be you, Rafe? To be a prince? Does it do your head in sometimes?'

He frowned. 'My head in?'

'Does it ever feel unreal?'

He seemed to find this rather amusing. 'Mostly, it feels all too real.'

'But you must have met a lot of famous people. I guess you must have an awesome Christmas card list.'

This time Rafe laughed out loud, a burst of genuine mirth. 'Yes, I suppose it is an awesome list,' he said eventually.

'Will you add me?' Charlie couldn't resist asking. 'After all this is over?'

Any amusement in his face died. 'Yes,' he said quietly. 'If you'd like a Christmas card, I'd be happy to add you to my list, Charlie.'

The thought of being back in Australia and finding Prince Rafael's card in the mail wasn't as cheering as it should have been.

Charlie promptly changed the subject. 'Do you ever wish you could just be plain old Rafe St Romain?'

He wasn't smiling now. 'Many, many times. But hardly anyone can have exactly what they want, can they?'

'I—I guess not.'

'That's why life's a compromise.'

'Yeah,' said Charlie softly. But today she really needed a fairy tale for Isla. 'I suppose your parents drummed that into you?'

He gave this a little thought before he answered. 'It was my granny, actually. She was a crusty old thing, prone to giving lectures. Her favourite lesson was about the need to put duty before personal happiness. I must admit, I ignored her advice for as long as I could.'

'How long was that? Until your father died?'

His eyes widened. 'You're very perceptive, aren't you?'

Charlie dropped her gaze. 'Sorry, I have a bad habit of asking nosy questions.'

But Rafe shook this aside. 'You're quite right,' he said. 'I spent far too long living the high life. It's my deepest regret that my father died not knowing if I'd give up the nonsense and step up to the mark as his heir.'

His jaw was stiff as he said this, his mouth tight, as if he was only just holding himself together. An unexpected welling of emotion prompted Charlie to reach out, to give his hand a comforting squeeze.

Rafe responded with a sad little smile that brought tears to her eyes.

'Anyway,' he said quickly. 'I don't think Granny was ever very happy herself, and she was forever warning me that I couldn't expect to be as carefree and contented as my parents were.'

'Well, at least you must be reassured to know that your parents were happy.'

'Yes.' This time Rafe's smile wasn't quite as sad. 'My mother was from Russia. She was the daughter of a count. Her name was Tanya and she was very beautiful. My father worshipped her.'

'Wow.'

Charlie thought how sad it was that Rafe, by contrast, was arranging to marry for convenience, to save his country, tying himself into a contract with a girl he didn't seem to particularly admire.

If her sister ever came out of hiding.

To Charlie this seemed like a compromise of the very worst kind.

'By the way,' he said suddenly, changing their mood with a sudden warm smile, 'you should finish this meal with one of Cosme's chocolate eclairs. That's a happy ending you can always rely on.'

'Oh,' Charlie moaned. 'I don't think I have room.'

'We can ask for a tiny bite-size one. I promise, they're worth it.'

Charlie checked her phone again as they were getting back into the car. Rafe had noticed her checking it twice, very quickly, during the meal.

'When do you expect to hear something?' he asked.

She looked at him, her blue eyes wide, almost fearful.

'You're obviously waiting for a phone call,' he said.

She nodded sadly. 'But it won't come for ages yet. It's only just starting.'

Rafe had turned on the ignition and was about to drive off, but now he waited. Charlie had been relaxed and animated during lunch, but now she was tense and pale. 'What has just started, Charlie?'

She opened her mouth, as if she was going to tell him, and then, annoyingly, shut it again.

Rafe sat very still, but with poorly contained patience. 'What?' he asked again, but she didn't reply.

He watched her trembling chin, knew she was struggling not to cry, and couldn't believe how the sight of her distress bothered him as much as it frustrated him. He almost demanded there and then that she tell him about it.

He certainly would have done so, if they weren't in a car on a narrow street with curious pedestrians on either side. Instead, with grim resignation, he put his foot down on the accelerator and the car roared off.

When Rafe pulled up at the castle steps a valet was waiting to open Charlie's door and to park the car. Charlie wondered if ancient dungeons had been turned into underground car parks and she might have asked Rafe about this, but the question died when he linked his arm with hers and kept a firm hold on her as they went up the steps and inside the huge front doors.

'We'll have coffee in Olivia's room,' he told the waiting Chloe.

Charlie had expected to be alone now. She wanted to focus on Isla, to send positive thoughts while she waited for news. Just in time, she remembered not to show that she minded Rafe's company. No matter how tense she was, she couldn't let him down in front of the watchful eyes of his staff. She was supposed to be his loving fiancée, after all.

She waited until they were in the lift. 'You don't need to come to my room, Rafe.'

His eyes were cool grey stones. 'But I choose to.'

He said this with such compellingly regal authority Charlie knew it was pointless to argue. She supposed she should be grateful for his company. Try as she might to send positive thoughts, she would probably end up sitting alone, unhelpfully imagining all kinds of gruesomeness as a surgeon's scalpel sliced through poor Isla's tiny chest.

Upstairs once again, she and Rafe sat opposite each other on the sofas. It was a scene that was beginning to feel very familiar, with the fire flickering, the huge window offering them its snowy view of the city and a coffee pot and their mugs sitting on the low table between them.

'Shall I pour?' Charlie asked.

Rafe nodded gravely. 'Thank you.'

The coffee was hot and strong. Charlie took two sips then set her mug down.

'How long do you have to wait for this news?' Rafe asked.

'I don't know. I guess it depends—' It was ridiculous to avoid telling him now. 'I have no idea how long it takes to operate on a not quite two weeks old baby's heart.'

She watched the shock flare in his eyes.

'This is your little half-sister?' he said, eventually.

Charlie swallowed. 'You knew?'

'I knew you had a baby sister, your stepmother's child. You visited her in Sydney before you left.'

She supposed his 'men' had told him this. 'Her name's Isla,' she said. 'She was born with a congenital heart defect.'

'Oh, Charlie.'

She held up a hand to stop him. 'Don't be nice to me, or I'll cry.'

Rafe stared at her, his expression gravely thoughtful. 'Where is this surgery taking place?'

'In America. In Boston. The surgeon is supposed to be brilliant. The best.'

'I'm sure you can rely on that brilliance,' Rafe said, and this time his voice was surprisingly gentle.

Charlie nodded. Already, after getting this sad truth out in the open, she was breathing a little more easily.

Rafe was looking at his phone. 'I guess the Internet should be able to tell us how long these sorts of operations might take.'

'I guess.' Charlie hugged her coffee mug to her chest as she watched him scroll through various sites.

'Hmm…looks like it could take anything from two and a half hours to over four hours.'

'Oh, God.'

Poor Isla.

Rafe looked up from his phone, his gaze direct, challenging. 'This is what you wanted the money for, isn't it?'

The tears she'd warned him about welled in her eyes. Fighting them, Charlie pressed her lips together. She nodded, swallowed deeply before she could speak. 'Do you mind?'

'Mind? No, of course I don't mind. How could I mind about my money being spent on something so—so decent and honourable?' His mouth twisted in a lopsided, sad smile.

'Oh, Charlie,' he said again and his voice was as gentle as she'd feared it would be.

Oh, Charlie.

With just those two words, Rafe unravelled the last shreds of her resolve.

The tension of the past few days gave way. She could feel her face crumpling, her mouth losing its shape. Then suddenly Rafe was on the sofa beside her and he was drawing her into his arms, bringing her head onto his shoulder.

For a brief moment, Charlie savoured the luxury of his muscled strength, the reassuring firmness of his considerable chest through the soft wool of his sweater, but then the building force of her pent-up emotions broke through and she wept.

CHAPTER EIGHT

RAFE KNEW THIS was wrong. A weeping Charlie in his arms was not, in any way, shape or form, a part of his plans. But he was still trying to digest her news and its implications.

Surely he shouldn't be so deeply moved by the fact that Charlie had used his money for such a worthy cause?

It had been much easier to assume that she'd wasted it.

Now, disarmed by the truth, Rafe knew he had to get a grip, had to throw a rope around the crazy roller coaster of emotions that had slugged him from the moment Charlie hurled herself into his embrace.

These emotions were all wrong. So wrong. He'd struck a business deal with this girl, and a short term one at that. She was a conveniently purchased stopgap. Nothing more. He wasn't supposed to feel aching tenderness, or a desperate need to help her, to take away her worries.

The problem was—this girl had already become so much more than a lookalike body double that he could parade before Montaigne like a puppet. Charlie Morisset was brave and unselfish and warm-hearted and, when these qualities were combined with the natural physical attributes she shared with her beautiful sister, she became quite dangerous. An irresistible package.

But somehow Rafe had to resist her appeal. He'd made

his commitment. He'd chosen Olivia as his fiancée. They'd signed a contract, and even though she'd disappeared he was almost certain she was playing some kind of game with him and would turn up when it suited her.

Meanwhile, Charlie was being predictably sensible. Already, she was pulling out of his arms and gallantly drying her eyes, and making an admirable effort to regain her composure.

She gave him a wan smile and they drank their cooling coffee. Outside, the afternoon was turning to early twilight.

Rafe stood and went to the window, looking out. 'It's not snowing. Perhaps we should go for a walk. All the lights are coming on, so it should be quite pleasant, and you still have a long time to wait.'

He was sure a long walk in fresh air and a chill wind were what they both needed. Anything was safer than staying here on the sofa with Charlie. The temptations were huge, overwhelming, but only a jerk would take advantage of her when she was so distraught.

'Won't you be mobbed if you try to walk out on the streets?' Charlie asked.

'It's not too bad at this time of the year. With an overcoat and a woolly cap and scarves, I can more or less stay incognito.' He smiled at her. She should have looked pathetic, so wan and puffy-eyed from crying, but she brought out the most alarming protectiveness in him. He held out his hand to haul her to her feet. 'Come on.'

Charlie had the good sense to recognise that Rafe's suggestion of a walk was the right thing to do under the circumstances. Sitting here, feeling sick and scared, was not going to help anyone in Boston. She could change into jeans and a sweater, and she'd bought a warm hat, as well as a scarf and gloves, so she would be well protected against the cold.

Besides, it was incredibly considerate of Rafe to put up with her weeping and to devote this entire day to her. The least she could do was accept his kind suggestion.

Outside, the sky and the air were navy blue, on the very edge of night. Lamplight glowed golden, as did the lights from shops and houses, from the headlights of cars. Pulling their hats low and winding their scarves tighter, they set off together, with Charlie's arm linked in the crook of Rafe's elbow.

Ahead stretched the long main street that led from the castle. On either side were pastel-coloured buildings from different eras, mostly now converted into shops, hotels and restaurants.

'This section of the city is called Old Town,' Rafe told her. 'New Town starts on the far hillside, beyond that tall clock tower.'

He seemed to enjoy playing tour guide, pointing out the significance of the clock tower and the statue of his great-great-grandfather in full military regalia, complete with medals. When they rounded the next corner and came across a small cobblestoned plaza with a charming statue of a young boy with a flock of goats, Rafe told her the story of the goatherd who was Montaigne's national hero.

'His name was Guido Durant,' Rafe said. 'He acted as a kind of unpaid sentry up in the high Alps. When the Austral-Hungarians were making their way through a narrow pass in winter, planning to invade our country, Guido dug at rocks and stones and managed to get a snow slide going. It turned into a full-blown avalanche and blocked their way. Then he ran through the night all the way to the castle to warn my great-great-grandfather.'

'So he's Montaigne's version of William Tell?' Charlie suggested.

Rafe shot her a surprised smile. 'You know about William Tell?'

'Of course. My father used to love telling me that story. He used to play the opera, too, turning the music up really loud. It's very dramatic.'

'Yes, it is,' Rafe agreed. 'It was one of my father's favourite operas, actually.'

'My father's, too.' Charlie laughed. 'Crikey, Rafe, we do have something in common after all.'

'So we do,' he said quietly and his grey eyes gleamed as their gazes connected, making Charlie feel flushed and breathless. For a crazy moment, she thought he was going to do something reckless like haul her into his arms and her skin flashed with heat, as if she'd been scorched by a fireball.

Then the moment was over.

They walked on and the smell of cooking reached them from the many cafés, but they weren't very hungry after their substantial lunch.

Montaigne's capital city was packed with charm. Charlie loved the cobblestoned alleys, the arched doorways with fringes of snow, the shop windows with beautifully crafted wares, including jewellery that Rafe told her was locally made from gemstones found right here in the Alps. She especially loved the glimpses into cosy cafés where laughing people gathered.

'Can you ever go into places like that?' she asked him, as they passed a group at a bar who were guffawing loudly, obviously sharing a huge joke.

He shrugged. 'I have a few favourite cafés where I like to meet with friends.'

'Thank heavens for that.'

'Are you worried about me, Charlie? You think I'm not happy?'

'Well, no, of course not,' she said, which wasn't true. She wasn't sure that anyone who believed life was a compromise could really be happy.

His smile was complicated as he tucked her arm more snugly in his.

They went on, past a tenth-century cathedral, which, according to Rafe, had beautiful frescoes in its cloisters, past a museum of culture and local history, a monastery where a choir was practising, sending beautiful music spilling into the night.

Once again, Charlie imagined herself at some point in the distant future, when she was middle-aged and married to some respectable, ordinary Aussie man, telling others, perhaps her children, about this magical mountain kingdom that she'd once visited with a handsome prince.

She didn't suppose anyone would believe her.

Rafe's phone rang twice during their walk, but the calls seemed to be business matters that he was able to deal with quite quickly. Just once, Charlie checked her phone. There wasn't any news about Isla. She had known there wouldn't be, but she'd had to check anyway.

Always, throughout the walk, her fear about her baby sister sat like a heavy rock in her chest.

They were almost back at the castle, passing a market stall that sold arts and crafts and local honey, when Charlie heard the ping of a text message.

Her heart took off like an arrow fired from a bow. She came to a dead stop in a pool of yellow lamplight, felt sick, burning, and was almost too scared to look at her phone.

Rafe stood watching her, his eyes brimming with gentle sympathy. He smiled, a small encouragement.

Terrified, Charlie drew the phone out from the depths of her overcoat pocket. She was so scared she could hardly focus on the words.

Isla out of surgery and Dr Yu is happy. She'll be in Intensive Care for about four days, but so far all good. Love, Dad xxx

'Oh!' She wanted to laugh and cry at once.

Unable to speak, she held up her phone for Rafe to read the message, but she was shaking so badly, he had to clasp her hand tightly to steady it before he had any chance of reading it.

'She made it!' His cry was as joyous as Charlie's and he looked so relieved for her that she couldn't help herself. Launching towards him, she threw her arms around his neck, and hugged him hard, and then, impulsively, she kissed him. On the mouth.

No doubt it was an unwise move for an Australian commoner to kiss a European crown prince in such a public place. Fortunately the Crown Prince didn't seem to mind. In fact he gathered the commoner into his arms, almost crushing her as he held her tightly against him, and he returned her kiss with breath-robbing, fiery passion.

It seemed fitting to go into a café to celebrate the good news. Rafe took Charlie's hand and showed her a place tucked away in a back street that seemed to be carved out of stone like a cave. As they went inside, another welcoming fire burned in a grate, rows of bottles and glasses reflected back the cheerful light, and although there were one or two excited glances and elbow nudges from curious customers, they didn't hassle the newcomers as they perched on tall wooden stools at the bar.

Charlie's head was spinning.

Calm down, girl, it was just a kiss.

But it wasn't just *any* old kiss. She knew she'd never been kissed with such intensity, such excitement, had never experienced such a soul-searing thrill.

But he's a prince, a jet-setter, a playboy. He's had masses of practice. A kiss like that means nothing to him.

Could she be sure? It had felt very genuine.

Yes, that's the problem.

She had to stop thinking about it. Had to concentrate on Isla.

None of this would have happened if Isla had been well.

Rafe ordered *vin chaud*, which proved to be a delicious mulled wine laced with cinnamon, cloves and juniper berries.

'Here's to Isla,' he said, clinking his glass against Charlie's.

'Yes. To Isla.' Charlie lifted her glass. 'Hang in there for another four days, kiddo.' She took a sip. 'Wow, this is amazing.'

'It's a favourite drink with the skiers,' Rafe told her.

'I can certainly understand why.' Charlie drank a little more. 'I've never been skiing.'

He pretended to be shocked. 'That's something we'll have to remedy.'

The thought of skiing with Rafe was thrilling, but Charlie doubted they would have time. Apart from the hospital visit this morning, today had been unusually free of engagements. The private time alone with Rafe had been an unexpected bonus, but she knew he had commitments that were bound to keep him very busy. And tomorrow evening, there was to be the grand ball.

Charlie had never been to a ball and the very thought of it made her nervous. She would have to wear that beautiful, and incredibly expensive, pale green gown, and her schedule tomorrow included appointments with a hairdresser and a beautician.

It was best not to think about that tonight while they lingered over their *vin chaud*.

Eventually, they continued on their way, stopping to buy hot roasted chestnuts from a stall on a street corner and eating them from a paper cone. When they reached the castle, Rafe ordered a light supper to be brought to Mademoiselle Olivia's room.

In the lift, Charlie gave herself a stern lecture.

Forget about that kiss. You started it, remember?

Yes, and Rafe was just being kind.

Kind? Really?

That's probably how a playboy expresses kindness.

It won't happen again.

Delicious mini-pizzas arrived, topped with caramelised onions, black olives and Gruyère cheese. And there were cherries for dessert along with a pot of the most divine hot chocolate.

As they enjoyed their supper, Rafe filled Charlie in about the important dignitaries who would attend the ball tomorrow evening.

'You won't be expected to know everyone,' he assured her. 'But I'll ask Mathilde to give you a list with photos, so you can at least learn some of the names.'

'That would be helpful, thank you.' Charlie remembered something else that was bothering her. 'What about the dancing?'

'Ah, yes.' Rafe frowned. 'I should have thought about that earlier. Can you waltz?'

'No, not really. I mean—we learnt a little ballroom dancing at school and I've watched people waltzing on TV. I know it's basically one-two-three, one-two-three, but—' Charlie grimaced awkwardly. 'I don't suppose there'll be any disco dancing?'

Rafe smiled. 'There'll be some, I should imagine. But you'll be expected to know how to waltz.'

'Could Olivia waltz?'

'Yes. She's quite a good dancer, I must admit.'

Damn. 'Any chance we could have a bit of practice before tomorrow night?'

'Of course,' Rafe said without hesitation.

It was silly to feel so self-conscious, almost blushing at the thought of dancing in his arms, their bodies lightly brushing.

'You don't want to start worrying about that now, though,' he said. 'I'll see you tomorrow evening, say an hour early, before the ball, and we can have a little practice. Your room's carpeted, so it won't be the same as dancing on a proper dance floor, but at least we can run through the basics. I'm sure you'll pick it up very quickly.'

'OK. Thank you.'

The charming meal was a lovely end to a perfect day. All too quickly, it seemed to Charlie, it was time for Rafe to leave. He rose from the sofa, taking both her hands in his and drawing her to her feet.

Her heart began a silly kind of drumming.

Stop it.

'Thanks for giving up so much time to be with me today,' she said. 'It's been—' She was about to tell him it had been wonderful, a stand-out, red-letter day that she would never forget. But perhaps over-the-top enthusiasm wasn't wise at this point. It was time to remind herself that this was only a role that she was being paid to fulfil.

Instead of gushing, she said carefully, 'I appreciated your company. It was—very nice.'

'Very nice?' Rafe repeated in a tone that implied she had somehow insulted him.

'Well...yes.'

Leave it at that, Charlie. Too bad if he's disappointed. It's important to keep your head.

Perhaps Rafe understood. He responded with a courteous nod. 'I enjoyed the day, too. You're great company, Charlie, and I was very pleased to share the good news about your little sister.'

It felt strained to be so formal after the closeness they'd shared today, but Charlie told herself that this new, careful politeness was desirable. This was how matters must be between herself and the Prince. Even though Rafe was still holding her hands, it was time to retreat from being overly familiar.

It was time to remember the reality of their situation. She was only a temporary fill-in until Olivia was found—or until Olivia returned of her own accord.

Charlie was pleased to have her thoughts sorted on this matter, but then Rafe spoiled everything by clasping her hands more tightly and holding them against his chest.

Big mistake. She could feel his heart beating beneath her palm.

In response, her own heart was hammering. She tried to ignore it.

'You're a very special girl,' he said with a wry smile. 'Note I said *special*, not just very *nice*.'

'Special is open to interpretation,' Charlie said more curtly than she meant to.

'So it is.' Rafe lifted her hands to his lips. 'Perhaps

you'd prefer nice?' Keeping his grey gaze locked with hers, he kissed her hand, and his lips traced a seductive path over her knuckles.

Of course, Charlie's skin burned and tingled wherever his lips touched, and she knew what would come next. At any moment, Rafe would take her into his arms again and he would kiss her. Already, she could imagine the exquisite devastation of his lips meeting hers.

She had never wanted a kiss more, but she had to remember why this shouldn't happen.

'D-don't play with me, Rafe.'

He frowned as he stared at her, trying to read her.

Time seemed to stand still.

And poor Charlie was already regretting her plea, as the wicked vamp inside her longed for Rafe to go on kissing her hands, kissing her mouth, kissing any part of her that took his fancy.

But he was letting her hands go. 'Forgive me, Charlie. I did not intend to take liberties.'

It was ridiculous to feel so disappointed. Charlie knew she should be relieved that her message had got through to the playboy Prince.

'I'll see you at breakfast in the morning,' he said politely. 'Sleep well.'

With another formal bow, he backed out of the room, but the blazing signal in his eyes was anything but formal, and there was no way Charlie could miss its message. She only had to say the word and Rafe would drop the formalities. In a heartbeat, she would be in his arms, in his bed, discovering what it was like to make love to a prince. All night long.

Somehow, she stood super still until the door closed behind him.

Oh, help. Now she would have the devil's own job getting to sleep.

CHAPTER NINE

NEXT MORNING, WHEN Charlie went down to the breakfast room, she half expected to find that Rafe had left already, but he was still at the table, polishing off a croissant stuffed with smoked salmon and scrambled eggs. After a restless night, she felt a little uncertain about his mood, but he greeted her with a smile.

'*Bonjour*, Olivia.'

'*Bonjour,*' she responded carefully, knowing there were servants within hearing range.

Rafe immediately shot a pointed glance towards the newspaper on the table beside him.

The headline jumped out at Charlie.

OLIVIA LOOKS FORWARD TO MOTHERHOOD!

She gasped, caught Rafe's eye. He gave a helpless shrug.

The headline was accompanied by a photo of Charlie standing in the hospital's nursery in her new black and white polka-dot dress, holding the snugly wrapped baby and gazing at it wistfully, while Rafe watched with a smile that might easily be interpreted as fond.

The accompanying story began: *Olivia Belaire's motherly instincts were on clear display yesterday when she and Prince Rafael visited Montaigne's Royal Children's Hospital...*

Charlie skipped the rest of the story to check out another smaller headline.

ROYAL-IN-WAITING BRINGS CURTSIES AND SMILES.

The photograph beneath this caption showed Charlie and Rafe in the children's ward, standing close together, grinning with delight and applauding as the little girl in the crocheted cap performed her curtsy.

Charlie wondered what Olivia would make of these stories, if she saw them.

'Are you happy with this?' she asked Rafe, holding up the paper.

'My press officer's happy, so that's the main thing.' Over his coffee cup, he smiled at her again. 'You did well. I told you that yesterday. Everyone loved you.'

Charlie supposed she should be pleased, but she didn't really know how to feel about this. It was all too weird, and now that she wasn't quite so stressed about Isla she found herself wondering about her other sister. Olivia.

What was the real reason for Olivia's decision to take off? Would these photos of her double bring her out of hiding? If so, when would she show up? How would that scene play out?

Charlie couldn't help wondering if Rafe had thought this charade through properly, considering all possible consequences.

Then again, Charlie knew that for herself there was only one possible outcome. As soon as Olivia returned, Charlie's role at Montaigne would be over, which meant she could be gone from here within a matter of days.

Hours?

In no time she would find herself back in Sydney, back in her little flat that she'd decorated so carefully. She would be reunited with Dolly, her cat, and she'd see all her friends again and resume her role at the gallery. Once again she would be living in hope that she might sell her father's paintings for an enormous sum.

Taking her seat at the breakfast table, Charlie wished she felt happier about the prospect of going home. It didn't make sense to feel miserable about going back to her own world and her old life, the life that had been perfectly satisfactory until she'd been so suddenly plucked from it.

Her low mood was annoying. Puzzling, too. She knew she couldn't have fallen in love with Rafe in such a short space of time. And anyway, even if she had, foolishly, lost her head, it couldn't be an emotion of the lasting kind.

She was simply dazzled…starstruck. This man and his castle and his beautiful principality were all part of a fairy tale, after all. This world wasn't real—not for an everyday average Aussie girl.

'Is everything all right?' Rafe asked her in French.

Charlie blinked and it took her a moment to compute his simple question. 'Of course,' she said at last. 'I was just wondering when a certain person might be found.'

'Oh, yes, I know.' He frowned. 'It's very frustrating.'

Charlie suspected that Rafe might have said more, but a young man with carefully slicked-back hair, dressed in a pristine white shirt and black trousers, appeared to pour her coffee and to politely offer her warmed platters of food awaiting her selection. She copied Rafe and took a croissant with scrambled eggs and a little smoked salmon.

'I'm going to be busy for most of today,' Rafe told her as the young man hovered to pour his second cup of coffee and to make sure Charlie had everything she needed.

'But I've arranged for Mathilde to give you that VIP guest list with the photos.'

'Thank you.'

'And I won't forget our arrangement to meet prior to the ball. I think seven o'clock should give us enough time.'

'Yes, I'll make sure I'm ready.' Charlie was rather looking forward to their dancing lesson.

Rafe nodded. 'There's nothing else you need today?' And then almost immediately, he answered his own question. 'Of course, you'll need jewellery for tonight.'

'Well, yes, I suppose I shall.'

'What colour is your gown?'

Charlie thought about the beautiful gown hanging in her wardrobe. She remembered the slinky sensation of the fully lined satin and the way it had clung and rippled about her body as she moved. Now that the ball was drawing close, she was a bit self-conscious about wearing it in public.

'It's a sort of pale green.' she said. 'Not an apple green, a pale—I don't know, a smoky green, perhaps?' The colour was hard enough to describe in English, but trying to do so in French was almost impossible. Charlie knew she was making a hash of it. 'I think Monique may have called it sea foam, or something like that.'

'Sea-foam green?' Rafe's grey eyes widened. He didn't look impressed.

Charlie lifted her hands in a helpless gesture. 'Don't worry, Rafe, it works. That colour shouldn't suit me with my blue eyes, but it seems to.'

'I'm sure it's very beautiful, Char—Olivia.' It was the first time Rafe had ever slipped up with her name. Was it a sign that he was nervous about her performance tonight? This would be her first real test in front of all the most important people in Montaigne. She was beginning to wish that she'd chosen a nice safe white or blue dress.

But then, to her surprise, Rafe said, 'I can't wait to see you wearing it.' And he sent her a smile so smouldering it should have been illegal. Charlie was too busy catching her breath to reply.

'I imagine,' he said next, 'that pearls and diamonds might be best suited to your sea foam.'

'Yes,' Charlie agreed, very deliberately calming down, despite the exciting prospect of wearing royal pearls and diamonds. 'I think they'd be perfect.'

'Good. I'll arrange to have them sent to your room before seven.'

'Thank you.'

It was yet another day of new experiences. Charlie had been to hair salons before, of course, and had once indulged in a spray tan at a beauty salon in Sydney. But she'd never been to a suite of salons as grand and luxurious as the place Rafe's chauffeur delivered her to for today's appointments.

She'd certainly never been so pampered. By the end of the day she'd been given a warm oil body massage and a winter hydrating facial, as well as a manicure, pedicure and eyebrow wax—and of course, there had been a beautiful healthy lunch that included a ghastly looking green smoothie that was surprisingly delicious.

Charlie's hair had been given a special conditioning treatment, too, and her scalp had been massaged, her curls trimmed.

'Oh, my God, Olivia! Your hair has grown so much since your last cut!'

Charlie merely nodded at this. 'It grows fast,' she agreed, crossing her fingers under her cape.

After a short but intense discussion among the hairdressers about the Prince's expectations for the ball, Charlie's hair was styled into a glamorous updo. And then her make-up was applied. She'd been rather nervous about this. She was worried that the make-up would be too heavy, that it would involve false eyelashes and she'd end up looking like a drag queen. She wanted to be able to recognise herself when she saw her reflection.

There was no problem with recognition, however. In fact, the results were amazing. The girl in the mirror was the same old Charlie, but her skin now had a special glow, a feat she had never managed before without making her nose shiny. Her eyes seemed to have acquired an extra sparkle and glamour. Her hair was glossy, her curls artistically tamed. The result was faultless.

Charlie was a little overawed by this newly refined and sophisticated version of herself. She *almost* felt like a princess. She quickly stomped on that thought before it took root.

By seven o'clock the names and faces on the supplied list had all been memorised—Charlie had tested herself several times—and she was dressed and ready. The seafoam dress still looked good, she was relieved to see.

It was sleeveless with a scooped neckline and an elegant, low cowl back, but it was the slinky way the dress flowed, responding to every subtle movement of her body, that made it so special.

She had never gone out of her way to draw attention to herself, but she knew this was the sort of dress that would let everyone, male and female, know she was in the room. The addition of Rafe's heirloom pearls and diamonds—delivered by his valet, Jacques—completed her transformation. She had expected a necklace and earrings, but there was a tiara as well, which Jacques kindly helped her to secure.

When the valet left she was rather stunned when she saw herself in the mirror. The dress was a dream, the make-up dewy-perfect. The elegant up-sweep of her hair and the gleaming pearls and sparkling diamonds of the tiara had combined to create the perfect image of a princess.

Charlie Morisset was in for a *big* night.

For Rafe's sake, she only hoped she could get through it without making too many blunders.

Rafe was due at any moment and, rather than waiting for him to knock, Charlie opened her door, ready for his arrival. As she did so she heard strange noises—blasts and ripples of music floating up the staircase from the grand ballroom on the lower floor. Trumpets, clarinets, saxophones and flutes. The band was warming up.

Excitement and anticipation pinged inside her and she drew a quick, steadying breath. Not that it did her any good, for a moment later Rafe stepped out from a doorway across the hall and she completely forgot how to breathe.

He was dressed in a formal black military uniform with gold braid on his shoulders, a colourful row of medals and a diagonal red and gold sash across his broad chest. His dark hair, as black as a raven's wing, gleamed in the light of overhead chandeliers and he looked so handsome and so splendidly royal that Charlie's knees began to tremble.

Drop-dead gorgeous had just been redefined.

It didn't help that Rafe had come to a complete standstill when he saw her, or that his smile was replaced by a look of total surprise.

The trembling in Charlie's knees spread to the rest of her body and she might have stumbled if she hadn't kept a death grip on the door handle. She wished that Rafe would say something—*anything*—but he simply stood there, staring at her with a bewildered smile.

After an ice age or two, she managed to speak. 'Are you coming in?'

Rafe nodded and she stepped back to allow him to enter her room. 'That's an amazing uniform,' she said, hoping to ease the obvious tension. 'You look very—regal.'

'And you look, *literally*, breathtaking, Charlie.' He turned to her and gave a shaky smile as he let his burning gaze ride over her from head to toe and back again. 'You're going to steal the show tonight.'

She managed to smile. 'You had your doubts about the sea foam.'

Rafe shook his head. 'I knew you would choose well.'

'I'm glad it's OK, then.'

'OK? *C'est superbe. Magnifique!*'

As Charlie closed the door Rafe stepped towards her, reaching for her hands. His grey eyes were shining so brightly they'd turned to silver. A knot in his throat moved as he swallowed. 'My dear Charlie,' he whispered, taking her hands in his and drawing her nearer. 'I think I've made the most terrible mistake in bringing you here.'

Charlie's throat was suddenly so painfully tight she could barely squeeze out a response.

'Why is that?' she managed at last.

Rafe's mouth twisted, as if he was trying for a smile, but couldn't quite manage it. 'I don't know how I'll ever be able to let you go.'

Oh, Rafe.

She wanted to weep, to melt in his arms, to acknowledge the unmistakable emotions that eddied between them, to give in to the sizzling chemistry. But a warning voice in her head reminded her that she had to be sensible.

In less than an hour they were expected to host a royal ball that would be attended by all the local VIPs, including Rafe's enemies. Being seen at such an occasion was the very reason she'd been brought to Montaigne. Decorum was required. Dignity, not passion.

She shook her head at him. 'Don't pay me compliments, sir. Not now. You'll make me cry, and that will spoil my make-up, and I'm sure it cost you a small fortune.'

A rueful chuckle broke from him. 'I've never met a girl so worried about money. But, OK, no more compliments.'

'Good.' Although Charlie feared that a dancing lesson with Rafe would be even more dangerous than his compliments.

'I'll have to kiss you instead,' Rafe said next. 'Perhaps there is no make-up here?'

Before she quite realised what was happening Rafe touched his fingers to her bare shoulder and, before she could gather her wits to stop him, he pressed his warm, sexy lips to the same patch of skin.

Charlie gasped as his lips brushed her in the gentlest of caresses. Her skin tingled and flamed. The blood in her veins rushed and zapped.

'Or perhaps here?' Rafe murmured as he pressed another kiss to Charlie's neck and caused a starburst of heat, just above the pearls and diamonds.

'What about here?' he whispered, and Charlie had no choice but to cling to him, grabbing at the stiff cloth of his jacket, closing her eyes, as he kissed the sensitive skin just beneath her ear. And then gently nibbled at her earlobe.

She tried to tell herself that he was just being a playboy, and she might have believed this, if she hadn't already seen that shimmer of a deeper emotion in his eyes.

And now she was only too painfully aware of the truth about her own feelings. She was in love with this man. Totally. Utterly. Deeply.

It didn't make sense, she knew it was wrong, but she couldn't help it. From the moment she'd left Australia, this Prince had charmed every cell in her body. Right now, she was powerless.

'You do crazy things to me, Charlie.' Rafe's arms tightened around her and his voice was hoarse and breathless as he whispered close to her ear. 'You make me want to forget everything, throw off my responsibilities. You make me want to believe in your fairy tales.'

Oh, Rafe. Charlie's throat ached with welling tears. *What have we done?*

And now, his grey eyes were fierce, burning with an intensity that was almost scary, as he ever so gently touched the backs of his fingers to her cheek. 'I've never really believed in love till now. But my problem was that I'd never met the right girl. And now I have. Now I want to believe.'

Emotion and longing rioted through Charlie. She thought she might burst.

Rafe's sad smile was breaking her heart. 'Is it safe to kiss your lips?' he whispered.

She knew she should step back, tell him no. If he kissed her mouth, heaven knew what else might happen.

But it was so hard to be sensible. To her dismay, she heard herself say, 'I have a new lipstick for touch ups.'

Idiot.

It was all the invitation the Prince needed. Slipping his arms around Charlie's waist, he gathered her closer, and now she could smell the expensive cloth of his jacket, the light cologne on his skin.

His lips found hers and her heart seemed to burst into flames. She tipped her head to access the dizzying pleasure, and worried, fleetingly, that her tiara might slip, but this worry and all others were shoved aside as Rafe's lips worked their magic. His kiss was all-seeking and possessive, commanding every shred of her attention.

Happiness and hunger in equal parts rose through Charlie like a bubbling geyser. She no longer cared that she'd fallen under this Prince's spell. She would happily hand him her heart on a platter.

With unforgivable ease, he had won her completely and, as his kiss deepened deliciously, a soft moan of deepest pleasure escaped her.

But the moan was cut short as the door burst open.

A woman's voice yelled, 'What the hell's going on?'

CHAPTER TEN

OLIVIA.

The woman bursting through the door couldn't be anyone else. An exact replica of Charlie, she was dressed in a magnificent white fur coat and elegant, knee-high white boots. She looked stunning. Stunning and very angry.

Ignoring Rafe, the newcomer directed her glaring gaze straight to Charlie. 'What the hell are you doing here?'

'Olivia.' Rafe had gone pale, but he managed to sound calm. 'What impeccable timing you have.'

Slamming the door behind her, Olivia flounced past them into the room and flung her expensive copper-toned handbag onto the nearest sofa. 'Don't talk to me about timing, Rafe. I deserve an explanation. What's going on? What's *she* doing here?'

Hearing herself called 'she', Charlie felt weirdly dislocated from this scene, as if a real-life version of herself had taken centre stage, and she was an invisible spectre watching on.

'I'll explain in due course,' Rafe told her coolly. 'Just as soon as you've apologised for your disappearance. You knew full well that you'd cause me enormous problems by taking off like that, without warning or explanation. You knew my country was left in grave danger.'

Olivia pouted. 'I always planned to come back.'

Rafe looked unimpressed. 'It would have been helpful if you'd informed me of your plans.'

This brought a shrugging eye roll from his fiancée. Olivia reminded Charlie of a petulant teenager.

Rafe was standing with his shoulders braced, his eyes wary but determined. 'Where have you been, Olivia?'

'In Monaco.' She gave another offhand shrug, as if her answer was obvious. 'I needed to—see someone.'

Charlie could sense the fury mounting in Rafe as he glared at her sister.

Olivia pouted back at him. 'You haven't explained what she's doing here.'

'Isn't it obvious? You know very well that I needed a fiancée. A *visible, available* fiancée.' Rafe turned to Charlie and his grey eyes now betrayed a mix of sadness and resignation. With a courteous nod to her, he said, 'Charlie, allow me to introduce you to your sister, Olivia Belaire. Olivia, this is Charlotte Morisset, from Australia.'

If Charlie had dreamed of being greeted by Olivia with a sisterly hug, she was promptly disappointed. Olivia didn't so much as offer a handshake, let alone a kiss on the cheek. Instead she lowered herself onto the arm of the nearest sofa, letting her fur coat fall open to reveal a tight, tiny, copper silk dress.

Then she crossed her legs, which looked rather long and sexy in the knee-high white boots. 'Yes,' she said airily. 'I know who she is. I rang my mother and got the whole story from her.'

'So you never knew about me either?' Charlie couldn't help asking. 'Not till today?'

'No.' As she said this, Olivia finally lost some of her belligerence. 'It was a terrible shock to see those photos of you at the hospital.'

Charlie could well believe this. She remembered her own shock and disbelief back in Sydney when Rafe had first shown her the photo of the girl on the beach in Saint-Tropez. It was astonishing to think that she and this girl had shared their mother's womb, had been babies together until their parents' divorce.

She wondered what had caused the bust up. Had the birth of twins been the final blow for an already shaky relationship between a woman who loved the high life and a dreamy, impoverished artist? She saw her puzzlement reflected in Olivia's blue eyes. No doubt her sister was asking herself similar questions.

'How on earth did you find her?' Olivia asked Rafe.

'My men were searching high and low for you, Olivia, but you were very good at keeping under the radar. And then we were sure we'd found you in Sydney.'

'But that's ridiculous. Why on earth would I go to Australia?' Olivia said this as if Australia were still a penal colony.

'We have beaches, too,' Charlie couldn't help snapping. 'Beaches and snowfields and casinos. Sydney's not Mars, you know?'

Rafe sighed, shifted his cuff to check the gold watch on his wrist. 'Anyway, we don't have much time to thrash this out now. There's a grand ball due to start in less than thirty minutes.'

'Yes, so I gathered from all the fuss downstairs. Obviously, that's why you two are all dressed up.' Olivia's eyes narrowed as she studied Charlie in her finery. Then she smiled archly and gave another shrug. 'Well, I'm back now.'

'For how long?' asked Rafe.

'For as long as you need me, Rafey. I've sorted everything out with my boyfriend.'

This brought a further stiffening of Rafe's shoulders, a deeper frown. 'You never mentioned a boyfriend.'

Olivia gave yet another nonchalant shrug. 'I know. Andre and I had a fight just before I met you. Well, a bit of a tiff. I'd gone home to Saint-Tropez in a huff.'

Rafe glared at her now and Charlie could imagine what he was thinking—that Olivia had agreed to the fiancée role in a fit of spite to get back at her boyfriend. How awful.

'But surely this fellow's not prepared to let you marry me?' Rafe said.

Olivia's jaw jutted stubbornly. 'He is, actually. He's prepared for me to complete the terms of our contract.'

So there was a contract. It was all signed and sealed. Charlie felt ice water pool in her stomach. For her, then, this was it. Her exit line. She was no longer needed.

As if to confirm this, Olivia shot another glance Charlie's way. 'It was good of you to fill in for me, Charlotte.'

'It was *indeed* very good of Charlie,' Rafe cut in coldly. 'She dropped everything to help me out.'

'Yes, but I'm sure you paid her very well.'

This brought another glare from Rafe as Olivia sat there in her fur coat and boots, with one crossed leg swinging, while she smiled at him shrewdly. He looked as if he would have liked to shake her, but instead he clasped his hands behind his back and stood with the stiff, unhappy dignity of a prince who had been schooled by his granny to put duty before personal desires.

Rafe should have known this would happen. It was no doubt typical of Olivia to turn up at the very worst possible moment, but he couldn't believe he'd made such a serious error of judgement and recklessly chosen her in a moment of panic. He was a fool, the very worst version of a thoughtless idiot.

And now, what about Charlie? What the hell had he been thinking when he'd started kissing her? Damn it, he hadn't merely kissed her, he'd been seducing the poor girl, when he'd known all too well that he had absolutely no right to toy with her emotions.

There was no point in trying to excuse himself now, by trying to pretend that Charlie was simply irresistible. Sure, he'd found himself daydreaming about her constantly and, yes, he was desperate to make love to her. Even though they'd only shared a kiss or two, he'd sensed an exciting wildness in Charlie that had only fired his own desire to greater heights. Their few, sweet kisses had been just enough to tease him, to give birth to a deep and painful longing, the whisper of a promise, a burning question without any answers.

It had been such a delightful surprise to discover that a girl who looked so much like Olivia could be so very different beneath the surface. Beyond the beauty, there'd been so much to *love* about Charlie—her openness, her sudden surprise questions, her selfless concern for her baby half-sister. But all these differences should have warned him to protect Charlie, not to expose her.

Olivia might have been out of sight, but, although Rafe had only known her for a painfully brief time, he'd been almost certain that she would turn up again, when she was good and ready. And he'd also been fully aware that he'd signed a contract with her, a contract which he now had no choice but to honour.

The terms of their contract were clear. Rafe was paying Olivia a sum of money that was enormous, even by his standards, to take on the role of his wife. At a future date, when Pontier and the Leroy Mining Company threats were satisfactorily resolved, Olivia would then be free to divorce him. No doubt, she would go back to this boyfriend, who would enjoy sharing her profits. By then, Rafe should supposedly have found a more suitable bride.

These plans had all been so clear and watertight.

Before he'd walked into a certain art gallery in Sydney.

And now… Rafe couldn't bear to see the hurt and shock and disappointment in Charlie's eyes. He knew full well that he'd caused her this pain. He'd played with her feelings unforgivably.

He'd gambled recklessly with his own feelings as well. In a moment of weakness he'd allowed himself to imagine—or to hope, at any rate—that life wasn't the compromise he'd always believed it to be, and that Charlie's happy endings were indeed possible.

Fool.

Now there was no way to resurrect this situation without making things worse for Charlie.

'So.' Olivia was smiling smugly as she finally rose from her perch on the arm of the sofa. 'It's obvious from the little scene I've so recently interrupted that you two have grown quite pally.' The smile she sent Rafe and then Charlie was condescending in the extreme.

Charlie had no choice but to ignore the piercing pain in her heart. She tried to hide her distress with a defiant tilt of her chin. But she didn't dare to catch Rafe's eye.

'But like it or not, it's time for me to relieve you of your duties, Charlotte,' Olivia said next. 'I'm sure you'll agree that *I* should attend tonight's ball with Prince Rafael.'

Nó-o-o! Just in time, Charlie jammed her lips tightly together to hold back her cry of protest.

It didn't really help that Rafe looked angry, as if this new possibility hadn't occurred to him.

'That's not very practical,' he told Olivia. 'As you can see, Charlie's all ready to—'

But Olivia, having thrown Charlie a quick look that was probably meant to be pitying, stopped him with a raised hand. 'If I'm to be your wife, Rafe, I'm the one who needs to meet all these important people tonight.'

Rafe's eyes narrowed. 'In theory, that's true. But the ball's about to begin,' he said. 'And Charlie has gone to a great deal of trouble.'

'I'm sure she has, and, yes, she looks beautiful,' Olivia admitted grudgingly. 'And I suppose I should apologise if my arrival has been a trifle inconvenient, but *I* want to go to the ball. I believe I should go. It doesn't make sense for her to carry on as my double now that I'm here.'

Olivia didn't quite stamp her foot, but she might as well have. The insistence in her voice was equally compelling.

Rafe, however, could match her stubbornness. 'Olivia, be reasonable. It's too late.'

'Oh, for heaven's sake, Rafe, don't tell me you're taking her side.'

'It's not a matter of taking sides.'

Charlie couldn't stand this debate. 'It's not too late,' she shouted.

The other two turned and stared at her, both obviously surprised that she'd spoken up.

'It's not too late,' Charlie said again, hoping desperately that her voice wasn't shaking. 'It won't take me long to get changed.' She knew there was no other choice, really.

Olivia was right. Rafe had made a legal and binding commitment, and, as his future wife, Olivia should be at the ball tonight, mixing with Montaigne's VIPs.

Charlie knew that Rafe was aware of this. He'd only protested because he felt sorry for her.

And that was rubbish.

There was no point in feeling sorry for her. She'd completed her commitment and now she was free. Free to leave Montaigne. Why prolong the torture by attending a silly ball and dancing with a ridiculously handsome prince, spending an entire night at his side, pretending to be his chosen bride?

All those touches and smiles from the Prince would be sure to completely break her already shattered heart. She'd been stupid to allow herself to get so hung up on him. Now, there really was no valid reason for her to stay another moment in these clothes, living the lie.

'I can be undressed in a jiffy,' she told them. 'At least we know Olivia and I are the same size.'

Rafe looked grim.

Olivia looked satisfied and ever so slightly triumphant.

Charlie lifted her head even higher. 'If you'll excuse me—'

With that, she retired to her adjoining bedroom, walking very deliberately with her shoulders back and her head bravely high, closing the door quietly but firmly behind her.

'Would you like a hand?' Olivia called after her.

'No, thanks!'

Don't cry, Charlie warned herself as she sank back against the closed door. *Don't you dare waste a moment on crying. You'll only look ridiculous with make-up streaking down your cheeks and you'll slow down this whole horrible, inevitable process.*

Best to get it over with.

Drawing a deep, shuddering breath, she stepped away

from the door and turned her back on the full-length mirror with its taunting reflection. Methodically, she began to undress.

First she unpinned the tiara and set it on the quilted bedspread. The pearl and diamond earrings and necklace came off next and Charlie placed them carefully back in their box, which she set on the bed beside the tiara. She kicked off her silver shoes, set them neatly on the floor at the end of the bed.

With the removal of each item, she could feel herself stepping further and further away from Rafe. She tried not to think about the exciting ballroom downstairs, the musicians on their special dais, the white-coated waiters with their silver trays of drinks, the enormous flower arrangements, the brilliant chandeliers, the enormous ballroom floor polished to a high sheen. Not to mention the long staircase where she and Rafe had planned to descend, her arm linked with his, as they went to receive his official guests.

Unlike Cinderella, she wouldn't have to leave before midnight—she wouldn't make it to the ball at all.

She knew she was foolish to feel so disappointed. She'd only ever been a stopgap, a fill-in. It was time to get out of the dress.

The zipper for the ball gown was discreetly hidden within a side seam beneath her left arm. Charlie carefully slid the zipper down, then gently, somewhat awkwardly, eased out of the gown.

The silk-lined satin whispered and rustled about her as she dragged it over her head, taking care not to smudge the shiny fabric with her make-up. She really could have done with help for this manoeuvre, but eventually she got the dress off without a lipstick smear, or a split seam.

She arranged the gown on a hanger on the wardrobe

door. The pale sea-foam satin shimmered, making her think, rather foolishly, of mermaids. Hadn't there been a poem she'd learned long ago about a forsaken merman?

One last look at the white-wall'd town...

For heaven's sake! Her mind was spinning crazily, throwing up nonsense. *Stop it!*

She let out the breath she'd been holding, collected the white towelling bathrobe from a chair where she'd left it, pulled it on and tied the sash at her waist. She took the carefully chosen lipstick from her evening bag and set it on the bed, where Olivia could find it, beside the jewellery.

There. It was done. She was no longer a princess, not even a pretend one. She was Charlie Morisset once more.

Unfortunately, this thought brought no sweet rush of relief.

Resolutely, she returned to the bedroom door and opened it.

Rafe and Olivia were still there, more or less where she'd left them. They were standing rather stiffly and neither of them looked happy and Charlie wondered what they'd been saying to each other.

'Over to you, Olivia,' she said quietly.

'Thank you, Charlotte.'

'Would you like me to help you?'

'I—' Olivia hesitated. 'I'm not sure. I'll call out if I need you.'

'OK.'

As the door closed on her sister, Charlie rounded on Rafe, needing to speak her piece before he could try to apologise, as she was sure he would.

'It's OK,' she told him quickly. 'I'm fine about this,

Rafe. Honestly. If I'd gone to the ball, I probably would have made a hash of things, getting people's names wrong, making mistakes with my French, standing on your toes when we were trying to waltz.'

His sad smile was almost her undoing. 'You've been very gallant, Charlie, but I do owe you an apology.'

Why? For kissing me?

She would break down if he tried to apologise for that.

'Save it for later,' she said as toughly as she could. 'I'll be fine here in my room, if someone could send me a little supper.'

'Of course.'

'I'm assuming I can keep this room for tonight?'

'Most definitely. I wouldn't dream of asking you to leave. There are other rooms that Olivia can use. And I'll arrange for a special meal to be sent up for you.'

'Your staff will be gobsmacked to realise there are two of us.'

'Perhaps, but they're trained to be very discreet. Just the same, I'll have a word with them to smooth the waters.'

Charlie nodded. 'Thank you.' She looked down at her bare feet beneath the white bathrobe. After the pedicure, her toes were looking especially neat and smooth with pretty, silvery green nail polish. She supposed it had been a whimsical choice to wear nail polish to match the seafoam dress when her toes wouldn't even be seen. Anyone would think she'd been planning to wear glass slippers.

Hastily, she lifted her gaze from her feet, only to realise that Rafe was staring at them, too. Feeling self-conscious, she rubbed one bare foot against the other as she tried to banish stupid thoughts about what might have happened tonight, after the ball, if she and Rafe had opted to pick up where their kiss had left off.

Before she could stop her reckless thoughts, they rushed away, and she was picturing the two of them in bed—her bed, his bed—it didn't matter whose bed—and it wasn't just her feet that were bare.

Stop it!

'Have you had news about Isla this afternoon?' Rafe asked.

Desperately grateful for the change of subject, Charlie smiled. 'I was able to speak to my dad,' she told him. 'Isla's still doing well.' Dad said the doctors were very happy with her progress and he sounded so relieved. It was lovely to hear the happiness in his voice.'

Rafe nodded. 'That's very good news.'

'It is.'

She was wondering what they might talk about next, when a voice called from inside.

'Charlotte, can you give me a hand with this tiara?'

'Coming,' Charlie called back, and she hurried to her sister's assistance, without another glance in Rafe's direction.

She'd thought she was prepared for the sight of Olivia in the ball gown, in *her* ball gown, but the reality was even more startling than anything she'd imagined.

Olivia was stop-and-stare gorgeous. The softly shimmering gown clung to her body in all the right places, the deep cowl back was divine, and the pale fabric rippled sensuously as she moved.

'Wow!' Charlie said. 'I hope you like the gown.'

Olivia grinned. 'It's adorable, isn't it?'

'Yeah,' Charlie said flatly.

'A good choice. Is it from Belle Robe?'

Charlie nodded.

'Monique's brilliant.' Olivia grinned. 'I'm looking forward to another shopping spree. But right now I need a couple of pins to anchor the ends of this tiara.'

'Yes, I can do that.' Charlie obliged, marvelling as she did so at the incredible similarity between her hair and her sister's. It was amazing now, up close, to see that Olivia's tresses were the exact same colour of wheat, had the same amount of curl, were the same texture. She was suddenly overwhelmed by the enormity of their connection.

They'd come from the same egg. For nine months they'd nestled together in the same womb. She wondered who had been born first. Had her father been present for their birth?

Olivia, however, was busily applying another layer of Charlie's lipstick. 'Well,' she said. 'I think I'm ready.'

'You look lovely,' Charlie told her. 'Like a proper princess.'

'That's the general idea.' Olivia picked up the beaded silver evening bag, popped the lipstick inside.

Charlie blinked, desperate to hide any hint of tears as her lookalike headed for the door.

Just before she reached it, Charlie had to ask, 'Why did you do it, Olivia? When you already had a boyfriend, why did you agree to marry Rafe?'

Her sister smiled archly. 'For the same reason as you, my dear Charlotte. For the money, of course.'

CHAPTER ELEVEN

CHARLIE DIDN'T WATCH Olivia and the Prince as they left for the ball. Excusing herself quickly, she retired to her room. Tears threatened, but she gave herself a mental shake. She'd known from the start of this mad adventure with Rafe that it would all end with her sister's return, so it made absolutely no sense to feel sorry for herself.

But she wasn't going to beat herself up either. Sure, she'd been reckless. Any way you looked at it, agreeing to pretend to be a foreign prince's fiancée was pretty damn crazy. Many would call it foolish in the extreme.

But Charlie consoled herself that at least her original motives hadn't been merely mercenary, and Isla was out of the woods, so that was a huge positive. Her mistake had been getting sidetracked by all the trimmings—a handsome and charming prince and his beautiful castle and his gorgeously romantic Alpine principality.

And at least she'd learned one or two things from this wildly unreal experience. She no longer believed any of that nonsense about fairy tales and happy endings. Sadly, Rafe's depressingly realistic theory was correct. Life *was* a compromise.

For Charlie Morisset, it was time to remember who she really was. An everyday, average girl from Down Under. And a poor one at that.

Right, come on, girl. Get a grip on reality. Deep breath.

* * *

When the first strains of waltz music drifted up from the ballroom, she turned on the television. She'd hardly watched any TV since she'd arrived in Montaigne, but tonight she curled up on the sofa in front of the fire and scrolled through channels till she found a romantic movie, so old it was in black and white. It was also in French, without subtitles, but Charlie could just keep up.

She refused to think about the laughter and the music and glamour downstairs and she refused to give a moment's thought to Olivia dancing in Rafe's arms. The film was very good, and she managed to remain deeply engrossed until a knock at the door signalled the arrival of her dinner.

'Please, come in,' she called.

Guillaume appeared, bearing a heavily laden tray and looking deeply distressed. 'His Highness ordered a special dinner for you, *mademoiselle*.'

Charlie smiled bravely. 'How kind of him.'

Guillaume set the tray on the coffee table, then gave a deep bow. He looked as if he might have been going to say something of great importance, but after standing with his mouth open for a rather long and awkward moment, he swallowed, making his Adam's apple jerk nervously, then said simply, *'Bon appetit, mademoiselle.'*

'Merci, Guillaume.' For his sake, Charlie replied with as much dignity as she could muster, while seated in her bathrobe, and she waited until he'd gone before she examined her meal.

As the door closed behind him, she lifted the lid on a small casserole dish and was greeted by the tantalising aroma of beef in red wine with herbs and mushrooms. On checking out the other covered dishes, she found *foie gras* and toast fingers, and wedges of several different cheeses. Yet another little dish housed crème caramel.

Oh, and there was a selection of Belgian chocolates! And as if these luxuries weren't enough, there was a bottle of Shiraz *and* an ice bucket with champagne, plus the appropriate glasses.

I could get well and truly plastered.

It was a tempting thought. Charlie could have used a little cheering up, although the last thing she wanted was to leave the castle with a hangover. Even so, it was very thoughtful of Rafe to make sure she had such a wonderful selection.

And it didn't help at that moment, to remember the Prince's many kindnesses.

Rafe wasn't just the hunkiest guy she'd ever met. He really was, despite his princely status and his many regal responsibilities, the most thoughtful man she'd ever known. She was used to her dad's vagaries, and none of her boyfriends had been especially considerate or caring. Rafe, however, had gone out of his way to make sure she'd thoroughly enjoyed her short stay in his country.

And then, of course, there were his kisses…

Would she ever forget the way he'd kissed her tonight, taking such exquisite care not to mess her make-up? All those delicious sexy kisses to her neck, to her throat and ears…

Until their caution gave way to passion.

Oh, such blissful passion!

No wonder she needed to cry.

It was hours later when Charlie's phone rang. She had fallen asleep on the sofa at some unearthly hour, having found a second movie to watch while drinking yet another big glass of the deliciously hearty red wine. It took her a moment to find her phone among the scattered dishes on the coffee table. Her fingers finally closed around it just as it was due to ring out.

'Hello,' she said sleepily.

'Charlie, I'm sorry if I've woken you. It's Dad.'

A chill skittered through her. Suddenly terrified for Isla, Charlie sat up quickly, heart thumping. 'Yes, Dad? How's Isla?'

'Isla's OK,' her father said quickly. 'Actually, she's better than OK. She's coming out of ICU tomorrow.'

'Oh, that's wonderful.'

'Yes, it is. I'm not ringing with bad news, Charlie. It's good news, rather amazing news, actually. It's about my paintings.'

'Really?' Charlie was waking up fast. 'Don't tell me you've sold one?'

'Not just one painting, Charlie. I've sold five!'

'Oh, wow! How?' She was wide awake now. 'Tell me all about it.'

And, of course, her dad was more than happy to recount his amazing story. 'I happened to meet this fellow here in Boston called Charles Peabody. He works here at the hospital, some kind of world-famous surgeon, actually, absolutely loaded. Anyway, Dr Yu introduced us, just out of politeness, but it turns out Peabody's wife was born in Sydney, so he has a bit of a soft spot for the place. *And* he's apparently something of an art collector.'

'That was very handy.'

'Wasn't it? It's as if my stars were all aligned. Anyway, we were yarning and I happened to mention my paintings.'

'As you do.'

Her father laughed. 'Of course. Anyway, Peabody was really interested. Afterwards, he got in touch with his

New York dealer, who was able to show him my paintings online. And he fell in love with the painting of the alley. You know the one—you've always liked it, too—*View from Cook's Alley*?'

'Yes, of course,' said Charlie. 'That's always been my favourite.'

It was a remarkable painting, she'd always believed. It showed a view down a steep, narrow alley that had grimy, old buildings on either side that served as a frame for a sparkling view of Sydney Harbour. The slice of the bright blue sky and sunlit water with pretty sailing boats and the curve of the Harbour Bridge made a startling contrast to the narrow dark alley with dank gutters, a stray cat and newspapers wrapped around the bottom of a lamp post.

'That's so fantastic, Dad. I always knew someone would realise you're a genius. I'm so happy for you. I hope this Peabody fellow is paying you top dollar?'

'Top dollar? You wouldn't believe the sum the dealer managed to sell it for. I still can't bring myself to say it out loud, in case it breaks a spell or something.'

Charlie chuckled. No wonder she was superstitious. She got it from her dad.

'But the amazing thing is,' her father went on, 'the dealer's already sold four more paintings to American collectors—in New York, in Seattle, San Francisco and New Orleans. After all these years, it seems I've become an overnight international success.'

Charlie's laugh was a little shaky. She was feeling teary again. 'That's so fantastic. Totally deserved, of course.'

'Thanks, darling.' Her dad's voice sounded a bit choked now. 'And I mean that. I owe you heartfelt thanks, Charlie. I'm pretty sure I would have fallen by the wayside without you there to prop me up more than once.'

Charlie had to swallow the lump in her throat before she could speak. 'And these sales might never have happened if it wasn't for Isla,' she said.

'Correction. They wouldn't have happened if it wasn't for you, Charlie. I don't know how you found that money, or who the kind benefactor was, but we're so, so grateful.'

Now she gripped the phone harder, fighting more tears.

'You know what this means, don't you, love?' her father said next.

'Your money worries are over.' At last. Finally. 'Dad, you so totally deserve this.'

'But it also means I can pay you back for Isla's operation, and you can pay whoever you borrowed the money from.'

'Yeah.' Charlie knew it made no sense to be sobered by this prospect. The timing was perfect. Now she wasn't only free to leave Montaigne, she would also be able to hand the money back to Rafe, even though he didn't expect it, and her ties with him would be severed. Neatly. Cleanly. Permanently.

If only she could find a way to feel happy about that.

As dawn broke over the castle, Rafael St Romain paced the carpeted floor in his private suite. He was bone weary, but he was also bursting with impatience. Except for the night of his father's death, this night of the Grand Ball had turned out to be the most unexpectedly significant and pivotal night of his life. As a result, he hadn't slept a wink.

It had all begun quite early in the evening. The business of greeting the long line of guests was just coming to an end, when the head of police, Chief Dameron, stepped up to Rafe, leaning close to his ear.

'We've got him,' he whispered excitedly.

Rafe immediately knew who the man was referring to. It had to be Montaigne's Chancellor, Claude Pontier.

The news was exhilarating, but Rafe hid his surprise behind a frown. 'You've made an arrest?'

'Better than an arrest, Your Highness. Would it be possible to have a private audience?'

The last of the guests had been presented, so Rafe excused himself, murmuring his apologies to Olivia, before retiring with his police chief to a small salon. There he was given details of the good news. The police had intercepted several important phone calls from Claude Pontier and now they had irrefutable evidence of his corrupt dealings with the Leroy miners who threatened Montaigne with so much damage.

Chief Dameron handed Rafe a document. 'And here is Pontier's signed resignation.'

This time Rafe's jaw dropped. 'He's resigned as Chancellor? Already?'

'Yes, Your Highness.' Chief Dameron allowed himself a small smile. 'Given the man's options, resignation seemed to be his wisest choice.'

Rafe was elated, of course, but he didn't like to think too deeply about the techniques his police might have used to persuade the Chancellor to roll over so quickly. Dameron was a gracious and gentlemanly old fellow, but Rafe could almost imagine him threatening Pontier with some ancient punishment for treason, possibly involving menacing machinery and dark, unpleasant dungeons.

'Well,' he said, shaking off these thoughts as the good news sank in. 'We'll need to appoint a new Chancellor.' Which also meant he had the chance to appoint a citizen who was unquestionably sympathetic to his country's best interests.

The police chief nodded. 'If you'll pardon my forwardness, Your Highness, might I make a suggestion?'

'By all means.'

'I'd like to highly recommend the Chief Justice, Marie Valcourt, as someone very suitable to be the next Chancellor.'

'Ah, yes.' Rafe smiled. Marie Valcourt was indeed an excellent choice. Apart from her inestimable legal skills, she was fiercely loyal to Montaigne. Her family's history in this region went back almost as far as his own. Besides, he rather liked the idea of a woman as Chancellor. His father would possibly roll in his grave, but it was time his country moved with the times.

'I'm sure we can trust Marie to act with Montaigne's best interests at heart,' he said.

'I'm certain of it.' Chief Dameron's smile broadened. 'If this were medieval times, Justice Valcourt would be donning blue-grey armour and standing at the city gates, sword in hand.'

Rafe laughed. 'She's a wonderful champion of our cause, that's for sure. A first-class suggestion, Chief.'

After that, it was almost bizarre how quickly everything had turned around. By midnight, while the Grand Ball continued with music and waltzing and an endless flow of champagne, Rafe had consulted in private chambers with his minsters and, with their consent, he'd spoken at some length to Justice Marie Valcourt. Within a matter of hours, he had appointed her as Montaigne's new Chancellor.

It had been well after midnight when the final guests eventually left. Of course, Olivia had known that something was in the wind, but fortunately she'd been happy enough to spend the evening dancing with just about every available male.

Olivia had done this with very little complaint, for which Rafe was excessively grateful, and afterwards, as he explained the new situation to her, he couldn't blame her for being instantly wary.

'So what does this mean for me, Rafe?'

'Chancellor Valcourt agrees that the constitutional requirements regarding my marriage are totally out of date and unnecessary,' Rafe told her. 'There's to be a special meeting of Cabinet tomorrow to repeal the old law. I'm assured it will be passed, without contest, which means—'

'I'm no longer needed here,' Olivia supplied.

He nodded. 'If that's what you wish, yes, you are free.'

'I can tear up our contract?'

'Yes, you can.'

'But I can keep the money?'

He suppressed a weary smile. 'Of course.'

Olivia brightened instantly. 'That—that's very kind, Rafe.'

'No, it's you who has been kind,' he assured her. 'I'm very grateful to you for stepping up to the plate. My country would have been in deep trouble without your help.'

'And Charlotte's help, too,' Olivia said with unexpected generosity. Then her eyes narrowed as she shot Rafe a cagey glance. 'I suppose my sister will go home now as well?'

'I suppose—'

Rafe paused in his pacing and stood at the window, looking out over the familiar view of snowy rooftops, which were only just visible in the pre-dawn light. It was almost eight. A reasonable hour, surely? He didn't think he could wait much longer before he went to Charlie's room.

Of course, he wanted to ask her to stay.

All night, during the ball, throughout the political manoeuvres and the diplomatic tensions, Rafe had been battling with thoughts of Charlie and their interrupted kiss. He couldn't get the honeyed taste of her kisses out of his mind. He kept remembering the exquisite pleasure of holding her in his arms, her breasts pressed against his chest, her stomach crushing against his hard arousal.

He kept hearing the soft needy sighs she'd made as she wound her arms more tightly around him, driving him insane with the knowledge that she was as ready as he was.

Now that he'd had hours to pace impatiently, his memories of her were at fever point. Rafe desperately needed more of Charlie. He needed her spontaneity and responsiveness. He'd been waiting all night.

He was dizzy with wanting. He wanted her. Now.

At eight-fifteen Rafe left his room, his pulses drumming crazily as he crossed the carpeted hallway to Charlie's door. He knocked quietly, and held his breath as he waited for her response.

There was no sound from within.

Perhaps she was still asleep? He waited a little longer, listening intently for the smallest sounds, but Charlie's suite was fully carpeted, so her footsteps would almost certainly be silent.

After what felt like an age, but was probably no more than thirty seconds, Rafe knocked again, more loudly this time.

There was still no response. He remembered the two bottles of wine he'd sent to her room last night. Perhaps she'd been a little too indulgent and was sleeping it off?

He called, 'Charlie? Charlie, are you awake? It's Rafe.'

When there was still no response from within he began to worry. Swift on the heels of his worry came action.

Pushing the door open, Rafe marched into the sitting room, where Charlie had dined last night. It was all very tidy now. No sign of her meal. Even the cushions on the sofas were plumped and in place.

The door to Charlie's bedroom was closed, however. Rafe crossed to it and knocked again. 'Charlie?'

Again, there was no answer and he felt a fresh stirring of alarm.

'Charlie!' he cried more loudly, pushing open the door as he did so.

The bed was empty.

In fact it was neatly made up. And there was no sign of her belongings. Thoroughly alarmed, Rafe flung the wardrobe doors open. The long red coat, the blue dinner dress and the black and white polka-dot outfit from Belle Robe were still hanging there—but not the ball gown, which was now in Olivia's possession. All Charlie's other clothes and her suitcase were gone.

He knocked on the door to the en-suite bathroom, then opened it. Again, it was empty and cleared of Charlie's things.

Dismayed, Rafe went back to the bedroom. And that was when he saw the small folded sheet of white paper on the snowy pillow. With a cry, he snatched it up.

He hardly dared to read its contents. By now, he had no doubt that the news wouldn't be good.

His fears were quickly confirmed.

Dear Rafe,
  Goodbye and thanks so much for everything. Your country is beautiful and you've been a wonderful host. It's been an amazing experience.
  My bank will be in touch to repay you the money in full. I wish you and Olivia every happiness.

Oh, and I've borrowed your chauffeur.
Apologies for the inconvenience,
Charlie xx

If Rafe had thought he'd cared about Charlie before this, now the true weight of his feelings crashed down on him. The thought of losing her was as painful as cutting his own heart out with a penknife.

He couldn't possibly let her go without making sure she understood how he felt.

He wasted no time on a second reading of her note. Grabbing his phone, he speed-dialled his chauffeur.

'Tobias, where are you?'

'Good morning, Your Highness. I have just driven Mademoiselle Morisset to Grenoble.'

'You're there already?'

'Yes, Your Highness.'

Rafe cursed. It was rather telling that Tobias had referred to Charlie by her correct name—*Morisset*. 'I gave you no such instructions,' he barked.

'Forgive me, Your Highness, but you told me to make myself available to the *mademoiselle* at all times.'

This was damn true, Rafe remembered now, through gritted teeth. And perhaps he shouldn't be surprised that Charlie had won over his staff. 'So you're already at the airport?'

'I am, sir.'

'And Mademoiselle Morisset has already booked her flights.'

'I believe so, Your Highness.' After a small silence. 'Yes, she has.'

Damn.

As Rafe disconnected he was already racing through the castle. He had no choice but to drive his own car down the mountain as quickly as possible. No matter what risks were involved, he couldn't let Charlie simply fly away.

It was freezing when Charlie stepped out of the car at Grenoble airport. She almost wished she'd brought her lovely new overcoat with her, but she was determined to leave behind everything that meant she was in any way indebted to the Prince.

Now, she knew that Tobias had been speaking to Rafe on the phone. In other words, Rafe knew where she was, so on the off chance that he might, for some crazy reason, try to follow her, she shouldn't linger over farewells.

She needed to get away, to get safely home to Sydney and to put this whole heartbreaking experience behind her.

'Thank you, Tobias,' she said as he set her suitcase on the footpath. 'I really appreciate everything you've done for me, especially your skilful driving down those steep snowy roads.'

'Thank you, *mademoiselle*. It's been my pleasure.'

'I hope Prince Rafael won't be too angry with you for bringing me here this morning,' she said.

Tobias shrugged. 'Don't give it another thought. Would you like me to help you with your suitcase?'

'No, thank you. It has wheels. It's as easy as pie.' She pinned on a smile as she held out her hand. 'Goodbye, then, Tobias.'

'*Adieu, mademoiselle.* I wish you a safe journey.' To Charlie's surprise, a look of genuine warmth shone in the chauffeur's eyes as he smiled. 'I and the rest of the castle staff will miss you, *mademoiselle*.'

Miss me? This was so unexpected, Charlie felt a painful lump in her throat. Her vision grew blurry. Why, oh, why was she so susceptible to people saying nice things about her?

She managed a shaky, crooked smile. 'I'll miss you, too. I've had a wonderful stay in your country.'

Then quickly, before she made a total fool of herself, she grabbed the handle of her suitcase, yanked it into its extended position, gave a hasty wave, and hurried away, dragging the wobbling suitcase behind her as she went through the airport's huge sliding glass doors.

Rafe drove as quickly as he dared down the steep, winding mountain road. Of course, there were princely responsibilities that he should have been attending to this morning, but right now finding Charlie before she boarded a plane was far more important than anything else.

He couldn't bear to think that Charlie might slip away before they had a proper conversation. Charlie knew nothing about the way his entire situation had changed overnight. He had to tell her that he was free from the pressure to marry her sister. More importantly, he had to tell her the truth that lay in his heart.

Unfortunately, it was going to be a damned difficult conversation to get right. Rafe needed Charlie to understand the true strength and depth of his feelings for her.

Some might say this was an unreasonable expectation, given that Rafe hadn't really understood these feelings himself until this morning. It was only when he'd read Charlie's note and realised that he was going to lose her that he'd faced a moment of terrifying truth. Everything had been suddenly, frighteningly clear.

Charlie Morisset was desperately important to his future happiness.

Rafe had known many women—all glamorous, beautiful or charming in their own way—but he'd never known a woman like Charlie. Charlie was not only beautiful and sexy, but she was honest and genuine and caring and funny and kind.

In just a few short days, she had become so much more than a girlfriend Rafe wanted to bed. She'd become a rare and real friend. She'd answered a deep need in himself that he hadn't even realised existed. Until now.

Unhappily, he knew it would be asking a great deal to expect Charlie to believe in the truth of his rapid transformation. It would be especially difficult when time was so pressing. Charlie had every right to tell him to take a flying leap.

Rafe cursed aloud, but it wasn't the particularly sharp bend in the roadway that bothered him. It was the harrowing possibility that he might let Charlie go.

And yet…if he was honest, he had to admit that he had used the girl to his own ends, with very little regard for her finer feelings. Now he wanted to make amends, but there was only the briefest window of opportunity to set things right.

As the Prince of Montaigne spun the steering wheel back and forth, negotiating yet another set of hairpin bends at the fastest possible speed, he tried to practise what he must say to his no-nonsense, straight-shooting Australian.

If only it could be as easy as it was in the movies when a guy chasing a girl could win her with a simple *I love you.*

CHAPTER TWELVE

CHARLIE FELT CALMER once she'd emerged from the long queue in Customs and was safely in the departure lounge. In less than an hour now she would be on a flight home to Sydney via Paris, this time without a diversion to Dubai and a handsome sheikh's residence.

She bought herself a cappuccino, a croissant and a paperback novel. She chose a murder mystery, rather than a romance. It would probably be years before she could bear to read another romance. She now knew better than to believe in happy ever after.

Settling at a table in the corner of the café, she took a sip of her coffee and opened the paperback with a great sense of purpose.

Focus, girl, focus.

The story was set in the American Midwest, thousands of kilometres from anywhere Charlie had ever been. It was midsummer, apparently, and the hero cop had a doozy of a hangover. There was a body lying in the middle of a cornfield. Flies were buzzing around it.

Charlie sighed and closed the book. She wasn't normally squeamish, but this morning she wasn't in the mood for blood and gore. Problem was, she wasn't in the mood for any form of entertainment, really.

Her mind, her whole body, felt numb. She broke off a

corner of her croissant. She hadn't had any breakfast and she should have been hungry, but even the sweet pastry filled with strawberry jam seemed tasteless.

It was as if her senses had been dulled. She had left Montaigne and sent herself into self-imposed exile, and nothing would ever be the same again.

No Rafe.

Forget him.

But how could she forget him? How could she forget the whole prince-Alpine-castle fairy tale? The gorgeous lunch at Cosme's. The walk with Rafe through the snowy streets, holding hands. The look in his eyes when he saw her in the ball gown. His kiss.

Oh, help, that kiss.

How was a girl supposed to get over something as life-changing as that?

Heading to the opposite hemisphere is supposed to help. Aren't distance and time supposed to cure all wounds?

Yes, once she was back in Sydney, surrounded by everything that was familiar and dear, she'd feel so much better. All she wanted was for this flight to be over.

She needed to be home.

Rafe's car skidded to a halt in the airport car park. As he leapt from the driver's seat an attendant glared at him. Rafe pressed several large notes into the man's beefy hand. 'Be a good fellow and park this for me.'

'But—'

'This is an emergency.'

Without waiting to see the attendant's reaction, Rafe took off on foot, racing into the airport terminal, heedless of the surprised stares of staff and travellers. He was a man on a mission, a desperate mission as far as he was concerned. He *had* to see Charlie. He couldn't let her go back to Australia without speaking to her, without making sure she understood that everything about his situation had changed.

Mathilde had tracked down Charlie's flight and had texted him the details. Now, in the middle of the busy airport, he scanned the list of flights that were preparing for departure.

Already, Charlie's flight was boarding. A chill swept through him. He still had to wrangle with Security and Customs, had to persuade them to let him get through to her.

But he would do this. He was the Prince of Montaigne. With luck, someone at the Customs gates would recognise him, but if that didn't happen he would wave his royal passport in their faces and make them understand.

He would do whatever was necessary to stop that plane.

Flying home was going to be a very different matter from the flight in Rafe's luxurious chartered jet. Charlie was crammed into economy class beside a little Japanese man who seemed to go to sleep as soon as he sat down and a very large American businessman who only just managed to get his seat belt done up.

Wedged between them, Charlie tried to look on the bright side. She could watch back-to-back movies if necessary and, if she didn't sleep, at least she would be home inside twenty-four hours and then she could sleep for a week.

She had hoped to keep Rafe out of her thoughts, but she found herself wondering if he was awake yet. No doubt he'd slept in quite late after the Grand Ball, but he might be up by now.

Had he seen her note? Would he be upset that she'd left without saying a proper goodbye? Or would he simply move Olivia back into her room and get on with his life?

This possibility was so depressing, Charlie picked up her novel and tried again to read, forcing herself to concentrate on the words on the page and to ignore the questions in her head, the heavy weight in her chest.

'Miss Morisset?'

Charlie had actually made it to page three—after having read the second page several times—when she heard her name. She looked up to see a pretty, auburn-haired flight attendant fixing her with a wide-eyed, fearful stare, almost as if she suspected Charlie of being a terrorist or something equally horrifying.

Charlie tried not to panic. 'Yes?' she said.

'Could you please come with me?' the attendant asked.

A shaft of white-hot panic shot through Charlie. What could possibly have gone wrong now? Was there a mistake with her ticket? She'd never bought a plane ticket using her phone before. But surely a problem would have been picked up at the airport desk. Not now, at the last moment.

Despite her profuse apologies, the large American wasn't happy about getting out of his seat to make room to let Charlie past. She tried to ignore all the curious stares of the other passengers, but her cheeks were flaming as she followed the flight attendant back down the long narrow aisle, through business class and first class, where people were already sipping champagne, to the very front of the plane.

'What's the matter?' she asked, when the attendant finally stopped at the plane's front door. 'Is there a problem with my ticket?'

'There's someone here who needs to speak to you,' the girl said, nodding towards the air bridge. Her eyes were bigger than ever, and a couple of other attendants were also staring at Charlie.

Crikey, anyone would think she was a celebrity or something. Or had something terrible happened? Was it a message from her father? Were the police trying to contact her?

Stiff with fear, Charlie forced her feet to move forward, through the doorway. Then she saw the tall, dark-haired, masculine figure in a long charcoal overcoat and her knees almost caved.

It didn't make sense. What was he doing here? Was she dreaming?

'Charlie!' A huge smile lit up Rafe's handsome face as he stepped forward, reaching for her hands.

'Wh-what are you d-doing here?'

'I had to see you. I couldn't let you go.'

'Why? Is something wrong?'

'No, not at all. Everything's fine, in fact. Very fine indeed. That's why I had to see you, to let you know.'

And suddenly, standing in the air bridge, holding her hands tightly in his, Rafe told her a crazy story about his Chancellor and some Chief Justice and an overnight change in Montaigne's laws. He said that he and Olivia weren't going to marry after all, and now he wanted Charlie to know how he really felt about her.

Her head was spinning.

'I haven't slept all night for thinking of you,' Rafe said.

Charlie hadn't slept for thinking about him, but she wasn't about to admit that now when her mind was made up. She'd put too much hard thinking into reaching this point.

Now she didn't know whether to laugh or to cry. This

was like something out of a dream—or a nightmare; she wasn't sure which.

'I want you to stay.' Rafe's gaze was intense. 'I need you to come back with me, Charlie, so I can explain everything to you properly. I want us to have another chance. A proper chance.'

Another chance.

Charlie's whole body swayed dizzily. It was just as well Rafe was holding her hands or she might have fallen.

He stepped closer, and she smelled the faintest trace of his cologne as he leaned in to speak softly in her ear. 'I know this is the wrong place and the wrong time, but I've fallen in love with you, Charlie.'

In love. In love. In love.

The words circled in her head, but they felt unreal, like part of a magic spell.

Rafe clasped her hands more tightly. 'Please come back to Montaigne with me.'

Oh-h-h.

She couldn't believe this was happening now.

It was everything she wanted. It was too much to take in. Her poor heart was soaring and swooping like a bird caught in a whirlwind. She longed to lean into Rafe, to be wrapped in his strong arms, to just let him sweep her away.

But she had to be sensible. She had to remember how she'd sat in her room in the early hours of this morning, alone in Rafe's castle, thinking carefully and rationally about everything that had happened between them. She had reminded herself then how very, very easy it was to be blinded by this handsome Prince, by his charm, by his wealth and power.

She knew she had to be super careful now, or she could make a very serious mistake.

* * *

Rafe saw the fear in Charlie's pale face and his heart sank. Had he done this to her? Surely he hadn't made her feel so scared? It was the last thing he wanted. 'Charlie, I only want to talk to you, to try to explain.'

She was shaking her head. 'I'm sorry, Rafe. It's too much. Too much pressure.'

'But I wouldn't try to force you into anything.'

'You already have,' she said.

'No, Charlie, I—'

He was silenced by the stubborn light in her eyes. It reminded him of the tough little terrier he'd met in the Sydney art gallery. Right now Charlie looked both tough *and* scared.

'You're trying to get me off this plane, Rafe. What's that if it's not bullying?' Charlie's lovely mouth twisted as if she was trying very hard not to cry.

Again, she shook her head. 'Believe me, I've thought this through properly. We come from totally different worlds. We connected for a couple of days and it was fun. But you were right all along. Happy endings are for dreamers. Real life is all about compromise and common sense.'

Despair ripped through Rafe. He couldn't bear to lose her, to let things end this way.

'Thanks for everything, but I'm going home,' Charlie told him quietly, and then, before he could find the all-important words that might stop her, she turned. Her shoulders were ramrod-straight as she walked back into the plane.

The flight attendants quickly turned from their whispering huddle when Charlie appeared, but not before she heard snatches of their conversation.

'Rafael...'

'Prince of Montaigne...'

'Playboy...'

She didn't bother to speak to them. With her head high, her eyes stinging but dry, she made the hideously long journey back down the aisle to her seat.

Her large neighbour wasn't happy about having to get out again to let her past. She thanked him and, as soon as she was buckled in her seat, she found the eye mask for sleeping and slipped it on.

Eventually, the huge plane rolled forward on the tarmac, gathering speed, and she told herself over and over that she'd done the right thing, the only sensible thing. She could only hope that if she kept saying this until she reached Sydney, she might at last believe it.

CHAPTER THIRTEEN

Six weeks later

AFTER YET ANOTHER unsuccessful job interview, Charlie climbed the stairs to her flat, lugging grocery bags with food for her cat, as well as the ingredients for her own dinner.

She was now at the end of her second full week of job hunting and she'd lost count of the number of interviews she'd endured. If she'd known it would be this difficult to get another job, she might not have accepted the gallery's redundancy so readily. Not that she'd had much option.

From the moment her father had been heralded as the art world's latest sensation, the directors of the gallery where Charlie had worked for five years had promptly decided to employ experts with 'proper' qualifications. Charlie hadn't been to university, so her intimate knowledge of the work of local artists hadn't counted.

The dismissal had upset her for a day or two. Her father had protested and wanted to fight for her to stay, but she'd begged him not to cause a fuss. In her heart of hearts, she'd already accepted that it was time to move on. After all, the gallery was a constant reminder of a certain tall, commanding figure who'd come striding through the doors to turn her world upside-down.

Now it was late on a Friday. Charlie reached the landing at the top of the steps and set down her shopping while she fished in her jeans pocket for her keys. It was a warm afternoon at the end of summer. Edna from next door had left her door open to catch a breeze and the smell of her baking wafted down the hallway.

The tempting aroma of freshly baked chocolate cake was accompanied by the sound of voices—Edna's voice and a masculine baritone. Judging by the happy chatter, the two of them were having a jolly old time. Disturbingly, the man's voice reminded Charlie of Rafe's.

So annoying to have yet another reminder of the man she was trying so hard to forget. Pushing the key roughly into the lock, Charlie shoved at the door, holding it open with her knee, while she gathered up the shopping bags.

Meow!

Her darling cat, Dolly, pattered down the hall, eager to greet her. 'Hello, beautiful girl, you're going to love me when you see what I've bought for your dinner.'

Dolly answered with another meow and rubbed her silky black and white body against Charlie's shins. Then she began to sniff at the shopping bags.

Charlie was closing the door when Edna's voice called from the next flat, 'Yoo-hoo! Is that you, Charlie?'

'Yes, Edna, just home.' Charlie tried to inject a little enthusiasm into her response, but she knew from experience that Edna liked to drag her in for a cuppa and to meet her friends. She wasn't in a sociable mood this evening.

If she was honest, she hadn't been in a sociable mood for weeks. A broken heart could do that to a girl, and losing her job hadn't helped. Charlie's dad and her neighbour had both commented on her low moods, but so far they'd been tolerant, sensing that something 'deep' was the cause. However, she knew their tolerance would turn to annoyance before too long.

'Ah,' said Edna's voice.

Charlie turned to see her neighbour beaming from her doorway.

'I told him you should be home soon,' said Edna.

Told *him*?

Charlie's heart began a fretful kind of pounding. 'Told who?' she asked shakily.

Edna's beaming grin broadened. 'Your lovely friend.'

'My—'

Rafe appeared in the hallway behind Edna, and Charlie froze. He was dressed in casual blue jeans and a white T-shirt. His black hair was a little longer and shaggier than she remembered, and his jaw was shadowed by the hint of a beard. He seemed a little leaner and more strained, and yet Charlie thought he'd never looked more gorgeous.

Why was he here?

She had relived the details of their farewell a thousand times, torturing herself with questions about what might have happened if she'd gone with Rafe instead of walking away.

Regrets? Yes, she'd had more than a few, but for the sake of her sanity she'd chosen to believe that she'd done the right thing, the only sensible thing.

Now, amazingly, after six long weeks, here Rafe was. Truly. In the flesh. Charlie was so blindsided she couldn't speak, couldn't think how to react. Could only stand there stupefied.

'Hello, Charlie,' he said.

She might have nodded. She couldn't be sure.

'Rafe told me you weren't expecting him,' Edna explained self-importantly, almost hugging herself with excitement. 'Isn't this a lovely surprise for you?'

'I—guess,' Charlie muttered faintly.

Her neighbour turned to Rafe. 'Well, I really enjoyed meeting you again, Rafe, and thank you so much for our lovely chat.'

'Thank you for the tea and chocolate cake,' he responded with his customary courtesy.

'I'll leave you two to have a really nice catch-up now.' Edna winked rather obviously at him.

Crikey, thought Charlie. *The poor woman would probably have a heart attack if she knew she was winking so brazenly at a European prince.*

With a final smiling wave, Edna closed her door.

Charlie swallowed as she looked at Rafe. Her impulse was to rush into her flat and slam the door in his face, but that would be childish, not to mention rude. And it would leave her with too many unanswered questions.

Her second thought was to hold Rafe at bay, here on the landing, while she demanded that he explain exactly why he had come all this way. She was still thinking this through when Rafe spoke.

'How's your baby sister?' he asked.

It was the last thing Charlie had expected him to say and, in an instant, she could feel her resistance crumbling.

'Isla's doing really well,' she said. 'She's home again and she's getting fatter. She even gave her first smile last week.'

'That's wonderful.'

'Yes, it is.' He looked so gorgeous and, with so much emotion shimmering in his eyes, Charlie wanted to hurl herself into his arms. 'I guess you'd better come inside,' she said instead.

'Thank you, Charlie. I'd like that.'

In the hallway, she bent to pick up her shopping.

'Here, let me.' Rafe bent down too and their hands bumped together as they both tried to grab the bags at the same moment.

Lightning flashes engulfed Charlie. She stepped away, her hands clenched to her sides as she thanked him weakly. 'Can you bring the bags through to the kitchen?'

She couldn't believe she was conversing about ordinary everyday things like her shopping bags with Rafe St Romain. Shouldn't she be *demanding* to know exactly why he was here? Why he'd crossed hemispheres to be here?

But those questions felt too huge. Charlie had spent six long weeks trying to get over this man. Unfortunately, she now knew for sure that her efforts had been in vain. The mere sight of him stirred up every last vestige of the old longing and pain.

Oh, help!

Dolly rubbed at her ankles again, meowing more insistently. 'She can smell her dinner,' Charlie said, glad of the distraction. 'I'd better feed her, or she'll drive us mad.'

'By all means.'

She nodded to a red kitchen stool. 'Pull up a pew. Or if you'd prefer, you can sit in the lounge. I won't be long.'

'Here in the kitchen is fine, thanks.'

'Would you like another cup of tea?'

Rafe smiled, rubbed a hand over his flat stomach. 'No, thanks, I'm swimming in tea.'

'Wine?'

He shook his head, and smiled again. 'Take care of your cat.'

Charlie felt as if she'd woken in the middle of a weird dream as she unwrapped the fish she'd bought for Dolly and set it on a chopping board to dice. 'When did you arrive in Sydney, Rafe?'

'A couple of hours ago.'

'You must be feeling jet-lagged.'

'It's not too bad.'

She transferred the fish to Dolly's stainless-steel feeding bowl, set it on the floor, where Dolly greeted it with ecstatic, purring delight.

Rafe laughed. 'That's one happy cat.'

'It's a special treat. Fresh fish is like *foie gras* and champagne for her.' Charlie washed her hands at the sink, dried them on a hand towel hanging on a hook, then turned back to Rafe without quite meeting his gaze. Under normal circumstances she would start cooking her own meal now.

These were anything but normal circumstances.

'I was hoping that you might be free,' Rafe said. 'So I could take you out to dinner tonight.'

'Oh, I—um—' Charlie's head spun dizzily as she imagined dining somewhere glamorous with this man. He would be sure to choose a restaurant with sensational gourmet food, first-class wines, candlelight and ambience by the truckload. She saw herself falling under his spell. Again.

Be careful, girl.

'Actually, I—I was about to cook my dinner,' she told him. 'Why don't you join me here?' She couldn't quite believe she'd said that, but she could hardly send him packing, and surely it was far safer to eat in her kitchen than to go to a restaurant? At least she would be able to keep busy here. She could distract herself with any number of small kitchen tasks.

'There's enough for two,' she said. 'That's if you don't mind a Thai prawn stir-fry?'

Rafe's grey eyes gleamed with an intensity that made her heart stumble. 'Thank you, Charlie. I'd like that very much.'

She swallowed. Now she felt stupidly nervous about cooking a meal in front of this Prince, even though she'd made the dish so many times she could practically do it in her sleep.

'What can I do to help?' Rafe asked.

She blinked at him. 'Do you know how to cook? Have you ever been in a kitchen?'

He smiled. 'Not since I was a small boy, but I used to love sneaking downstairs to help the cooks to peel apples, or to cut out gingerbread men.'

It was an endearing thought, and, despite her qualms, Charlie set two chopping boards and two knives on the counter. 'You can help with chopping the veggies, then. I'll do the onions—I'd hate to see a grown man cry. You can do the carrots. Or would you prefer—?'

'Carrots are fine.'

It was surreal. Six weeks ago, they had parted at the door of an international jet amidst a huge amount of embarrassment and tension and now there were still huge questions hanging in the air. But Rafe seemed perfectly happy to help with preparing their dinner as if they were an old couple who'd lived harmoniously together for ages.

Charlie showed him how to cut carrots on the diagonal for stir-frying, rather than in strips or rounds.

'Stir-frying needs to be very quick and this way there's more of the carrot's surface area coming in contact with the heat.'

He nodded. 'That makes sense.'

As they chopped capsicum, shallots and fresh ginger Charlie asked about Tobias and Mathilde, Guillaume and Chloe. Rafe told her they were all well.

He looked up from his task, sending her a glance that hinted at amusement. 'They all asked to be remembered to you.'

'Oh.' This was a surprise. Her face flamed as she nipped the ends off snow peas, and she refrained from asking any more questions as she set jasmine rice cooking on a back burner.

Charlie found the fish sauce she needed and combined it with soy sauce, sesame oil and honey in a small bowl. Luckily the prawns were already peeled, so she could avoid that messy task.

As she set the wok on the gas flame she wondered what Rafe was *really* thinking. She felt tense as a bowstring. Questions kept popping into her head, but they were so very personal and important that to ask them felt as reckless as running through a field of unexploded landmines.

She forced herself to concentrate on her task, working calmly and methodically, cooking the prawns in the hot oil with garlic and chilli.

'When do the vegetables go in?' Rafe asked as he came to stand beside her.

'Soon. They only take a few minutes.'

'It smells sensational.'

Her skin was flaming—not from the cooking heat, but from his proximity. 'Would you—ah—mind setting the table? The plates and bowls are in the cupboard up there.' She pointed. 'And the cutlery's in that drawer.'

Rafe set the table with black place mats and white china and Charlie's red-handled cutlery, while Charlie transferred the stir-fry and the rice into two black and white ceramic bowls.

'Wine!' she announced. She suddenly, most definitely, needed wine. 'There's a nice cold white chilling in the fridge. I'll get the glasses.'

But she'd run out of delaying tactics. In a matter of moments, everything was ready. Rafe was sitting opposite her at her dining table, and he was smiling—looking unaccountably happy, actually—and drop-dead sexy in his casual jeans and T-shirt. And Charlie knew her efforts to keep herself busy and diverted had been no help whatsoever.

Even without the glamour of a fancy restaurant and mood lighting, even here in her ordinary little flat with a simple home-cooked meal, Prince Rafael of Montaigne was as attractive and charming as ever. And she was still totally, hopelessly under his spell.

Worse, she knew they could no longer avoid the important conversations they'd been dancing around, although Rafe seemed in no hurry to broach them.

'This is delicious,' he said. 'The flavours are fantastic.'

'I'm glad you like it.' The meal wasn't exactly flash.

'I love it, Charlie. This is exactly what I hoped for.'

'Prawn stir-fry?'

He chuckled. 'To see you in your natural environment.'

'You make me sound like some kind of rare animal.'

'Sorry.' He gave a dismayed shake of his head. 'Am I making a hash of this?'

Was he? Charlie thought he was being rather lovely, just as he'd been in Montaigne, although she was still uncertain and confused about the purpose of his surprise visit.

'You were right,' Rafe said suddenly, after he'd helped himself to another spoonful of veggies. 'I should never have tried to drag you off that plane. I was an egotistical bully. I realised that, as soon as you turned and walked away from me. I couldn't believe I'd been so crass.'

He looked so repentant, the final wedge of resistance in Charlie's heart melted.

'I shouldn't have run away,' she admitted. 'I should have at least stayed at the castle until I'd thanked you for your wonderful hospitality. I should have said goodbye properly.'

Rafe shrugged. 'I couldn't really blame you for rushing off. You'd been through the wringer. I'd dragged you across the world and you had the stress of trying to pretend to be someone else. Not to mention all the worry about your little sister.'

'And I also had a certain playboy prince kissing me senseless when he wasn't supposed to.'

The smoulder in Rafe's eyes sent Charlie's skin flaming again. 'I'm not going to apologise for kissing you.'

The air seemed to crackle with the chemistry sparking between them. Charlie dropped her gaze. 'It was pretty awkward to have Olivia turning up just at that moment—'

'It was,' Rafe agreed. 'Her timing was uncanny.'

He set down his fork. To Charlie's surprise, he smiled and leaned back in his chair, looking totally relaxed.

'So how is Montaigne's political situation now?' she asked, having deliberately avoided searching the Internet for news of his country. It had seemed sensible to try to put the whole experience behind her, but now, with Rafe here in her flat, dining at her table, she needed to get her facts straight before her brain went into total meltdown. 'Is everything settled?'

Rafe nodded. 'Our new Chancellor is brilliant. Leroy Mining have pulled in their horns. Everything's back to the way it should be as far as I'm concerned.'

'That must be a relief. And where's Olivia these days?'

'On her honeymoon, I imagine.'

Charlie's eyes widened. 'She's married already? To her fellow in Monaco?'

'Yes. His name's Frederick Hugo.' Rafe took a lazy

sip of his wine. 'And she has also spilled her story to the press.'

'About you—and—'

'And about you,' Rafe supplied smoothly. 'Olivia's big reveal. It was a double-page spread in a really popular glossy. Everything out in the open about how she only became engaged to me to help Montaigne, and the real love of her life was Frederick.'

'Gosh.'

Rafe didn't look the slightest bit put out. 'No doubt the magazine paid her a fortune. That's fine.' He smiled. 'She's saved me from having to explain how there came to be two of you.'

Charlie swallowed. 'So that's in the magazines, too? About Olivia and me being identical twins?'

'Yes, including photos of you at the hospital. Olivia declared she was ever so grateful that her sister stepped in when she had her little crisis.'

'So now your whole country knows who I really am?'

'Well, those who read gossip magazines, at any rate. But it means,' Rafe added carefully, 'that if you ever wanted to come back to Montaigne, we wouldn't have to worry about awkward explanations.'

'I—I see.'

'Of course,' he added, 'I'm being plagued with questions about you, especially about why I let you go.'

Charlie found this hard to believe. 'Who would ask about me?'

Rafe smiled again. 'Absolutely everyone. My staff. My good friend Faysal. Monique at Belle Robe. The people at the hospital. Just about anyone who's met you, Charlie.'

She had no idea what to say to this. She was astonished that these people even remembered her, let alone cared about her. Totally flustered, she stood abruptly and wondered if it was too soon to start clearing the table.

Rafe stood too and he moved towards her, reached for her hand before she could try to pick up a plate.

'Charlie,' he said softly.

'What?' She could barely hear her nervous response above the thumping of her heart.

'You were right to be cautious. We do hardly know each other.' His hand closed around hers. 'But I meant what I said at the airport. I want us to have a second chance.'

A second chance...

Charlie was as enchanted by Rafe's touch, by the pressure of his fingers wrapped around hers, as she was by his words. But there were things she needed to sort out. This man was supposed to be finding himself a wife to help him to rule Montaigne. He had access to the wealthiest and most beautiful women in Europe and he now had time to court one of these women properly. So what was he doing in a suburban flat in Sydney?

'What sort of second chance are we talking about, Rafe? Last time you wanted me to pretend to be your fiancée.'

'I know, I know.' He gave a soft groan. 'Looking back it was crazy, but it was the best crazy thing I've ever done.'

Now he reached for her other hand and held them both together, cradled against his chest.

Charlie could feel the heat of him through his thin white T-shirt, feel the thud of his heartbeats. She blinked back tears and tried to breathe. *Don't cry. Not now.*

'Charlie, I've missed you so much I thought I was going out of my mind.'

She couldn't speak. All the air had been sucked out of her lungs.

'But I owe it to you to do better,' Rafe said. 'I want us to go about dating the way any other couple might. No pressure, no huge expectations. Just the two of us getting to know each other, seeing how things work out.'

'Where—where might this happen?'

'Here. In Sydney.'

'You mean, you'd stay here in Sydney?'

'For a while, a couple of weeks at least. I'd love to explore this place with you. Bondi Beach, the harbour, maybe the Blue Mountains.'

It was Charlie's idea of bliss and she could no longer think of reasonable objections. 'Well, I don't happen to have a job any more, so I'm actually free.'

'That's handy.' Laughter shone in Rafe's eyes.

Charlie tried to smile back at him, but she couldn't see him now for tears.

It didn't matter. Rafe's arms were around her. Strong and reassuring and safe. She closed her eyes, let her head rest against his chest. It felt like coming home.

He didn't kiss her immediately. For long lovely moments he just held her close as if she was the most precious thing in the world. And when his lips finally found hers, his kiss was lazy and lingering, and the magic was there from the first contact.

Charlie felt the heat and the power of him flowing through her, touching flashpoints, igniting the yearning that had never really gone away.

Rafe in jeans and a T-shirt, here in Australia, was every bit as sexy and dangerous as he'd been in his castle in full princely regalia. Desire curled through Charlie like smoke. Like smoke and flames and she wanted to press close to him, to wriggle against him, to tear off her clothes.

Between increasingly frantic kisses, she asked, 'Have you booked into a hotel?'

'Yes. Somewhere near the harbour.'

'But you said you wanted to see me in my natural environment.'

Rafe smiled. 'That's true, I do.'

'Then you should cancel your booking,' she suggested recklessly. 'Stay here.'

She heard the sharp rasp of his breath. 'That would be perfect.'

Then in a burst of unbelievable confidence, she said, 'But, of course, you'd need to check my bedroom first. Make sure the mattress is up to scratch.'

Now he laughed. 'Have I ever told you I love the way you think, Charlie girl?'

In one easy motion he swept her high, holding her with an arm beneath her knees and another around her shoulders. 'Which way is the bedroom?'

Charlie pointed.

Of course, she knew she should be nervous about directing a royal prince to her boudoir. She had no idea what happened when a girl let a fairy tale and real life collide. But she was too entranced to analyse the problem, too impressed by Rafe's strength, by the easy way he carried her as if she were a featherweight.

'It's like a glamorous cave in here,' he said as he set her down on the snowy white bed in her black-walled bedroom with just a single lamp glowing in the corner.

'I got carried away with the black and white theme.'

'It's great. I love it.' He sat on the bed beside her, and her body hummed with anticipation as he leaned over her, supporting himself with a hand on the mattress on either side of her.

Please, she whispered silently. She'd never felt so ready, so wanting.

Bending closer, he kissed her throat, her chin, her brow and, in that moment, as her eyes drifted closed, he pressed gentle kisses to her eyelids, and Charlie forgot the whole prince thing. This was Rafe and that was all that mattered. Rafe, the hunkiest *and* the nicest guy she'd ever met, who'd come all this way to get to know her.

'I've missed you so much I thought I was going out of my mind,' he'd said.

He kissed her mouth, teasing her lips apart with his tongue, and any last efforts to think dissolved as sensation claimed her, washing over her in heated, hungry waves. She wound her arms around his neck, and her hips bucked, needing him closer still.

It should have been gentle and lingering, this first time, but they'd been waiting too long. Need built fast and furiously, breaking through any final barriers of politeness. Everything went a little wild and slightly desperate as they helped each other out of their clothes and then scrambled to be close again. Skin to skin.

At the centre of the wildness there was happiness, too. For Charlie, a fierce, bubbling, over-the-top joy. She and the man who'd stolen her heart were together at last, and everything was OK. It was perfect.

It was ten days later when Charlie got the phone call. For Rafe they had been ten glorious days, spent exclusively with Charlie, exploring Sydney, dining out, cooking at home, talking, talking, making love. A kind of honeymoon without the wedding. A perfection they both knew couldn't last.

On this particular day they had been to the Blue Mountains, hiking, checking out the gift shops and dining in a hotel with an amazing view of craggy cliffs and a deep, tree-studded valley. Rafe was driving his hire car back into Charlie's garage when her phone rang. She had to fish the phone out of her bag.

'I've no idea who this can be,' she said as she checked the caller ID. She climbed out of the car to answer the call.

Rafe collected their sweaters from the back seat, locked the car, and indicated to Charlie that he would go ahead to open the flat.

Still intent on the phone conversation, she nodded.

He was in the kitchen, giving Dolly a welcome scratch behind her ears, when Charlie came in. Charlie's eyes were wide, as if she'd had a shock, but there was also a tightness in her expressive face that suggested she might not want to share her news.

'That was unexpected,' she said, setting her phone on the kitchen counter.

'Is everything OK?' Rafe asked cautiously.

'Well, I guess. I've been offered a job.'

An unwelcome chill spread over his skin. Charlie had already told him about her father's sudden rise to fame and the changes at the art gallery where she used to work. But they hadn't talked about her future plans. They'd been busy making the most of their time together, and Rafe had promised Charlie there would be no pressure or expectation, so he'd been careful to hold any discussion about the future at bay. Charlie hadn't mentioned any job prospects.

'It's weird,' she said now. 'I've applied for all kinds of positions and been knocked back and now I'm offered a job I never even applied for.'

Rafe's throat tightened. 'What kind of offer?'

'To run another art gallery at the Gold Coast. In

Queensland.' Her eyes widened and it was clear she was impressed. 'There's a big tourist market up there,' she said. 'A huge turnover.'

'A big responsibility, then.' Rafe spoke quietly, despite the chilling lump of dread that had settled in his gut.

Now he regretted his reticence to talk about their future. He hadn't wanted to rush Charlie, to overwhelm her with the truth about his deep feelings for her. But the past days had only served to prove to him how important she was to him.

In every way, Charlie was the most desirable woman he'd ever known, but his feelings went way beyond their incredible chemistry. With her own special brand of wisdom, Charlie brought the perfect balance to his world.

As he juggled the privileges of royalty with its responsibilities, he needed this sunny, open-hearted and genuine girl in his life. By his side.

Hell. Had he left it too late?

Charlie stood very still with her arms folded tightly over her chest, trying hard not to mind that Rafe had taken her news so calmly, as if he wasn't in any way a part of her future.

A big responsibility, then.

Was that all he could say?

After ten of the best days of her life? After ten ecstatically beautiful days filled with fun and laughter and their deepening friendship, not to mention sublimely satisfying sex?

Foolishly, she'd spent these ten days falling more deeply and helplessly in love with the man, despite the fact that there'd been no talk at all about where any of this was leading.

Now Charlie hugged herself tighter and tried not to

panic. But Rafe was taking her news so calmly. Too calmly. Had she been a total fool? Had she totally misunderstood where their relationship was heading?

Was the new job opportunity a turning point? Was Rafe about to gently let her go?

It was really nice knowing you, Charlie, but I'm royalty after all, and I'm afraid you're not quite up to scratch.

'I didn't realise you were still job-hunting,' Rafe said.

Charlie shrugged miserably and kept her gaze on the black and white floor tiles. 'I wasn't really hunting for this job.'

'If I'd known you were looking for work, I might have spoken earlier,' he said. 'I'd like to offer you a job.'

She stiffened. A job offer from Rafe was like a slap in the face. What did he have in mind? To employ her as some kind of secretary-cum-mistress?

How dared he?

'No, thanks,' she snapped, jamming her lips tightly together to bite back the sob that threatened.

'Because being my wife is a kind of job, I'm afraid.'

At first, Charlie thought she'd misheard him.

'As you know,' Rafe went on with uncharacteristic earnestness, 'there are certain expectations and responsibilities. But I think—no, I don't just think, I *know* you'd be brilliant at that particular job, Charlie. So I was hoping you'd do me the honour—'

He stopped talking and looked at her with a smile that was both shy and hopeful.

Charlie stopped hugging herself. Instead she gripped the counter before her knees gave way. 'I'm sorry,' she said shakily. 'I think I might have missed something. What exactly are you asking me?'

And that was when it happened. Tall, impossibly handsome Rafael St Romain, Prince of Montaigne, got down on one knee on her kitchen floor and placed a hand over his heart.

'I love you, Charlie. I suspect I've been in love with you from the day I first met you, but now I know it for certain and it's a relief to be able to tell you at last.'

Oh.

'I'm desperate to spend the rest of my life with you.'

'Oh-h-h-h.'

'And I'm shamelessly begging you to marry me.'

'Oh, Rafe.' Charlie dashed at tears with one hand while she held her other hand out to him. 'I've been the same.' Her voice was very wobbly as she linked her fingers with his. 'I didn't know it was possible to love someone so deeply. I had no idea till I met you.'

The intensity in his face was heart-stopping. 'So you'll marry me?'

Charlie was grinning now, with tears streaming down her face. 'Only if you get up off that floor and kiss me.'

Leaping to his feet, Rafe was more than happy to oblige. 'I promise I'll make you happy,' he said as he gathered Charlie close.

'And if marrying you is a job, my first job will be to keep you happy, too,' she told him.

A pleading meow sounded at their feet. Charlie felt a silken pressure against her ankles and looked down to a swishing black and white tail. 'Oh, dear. If we get married, what will happen to Dolly?'

Rafe smiled. 'No worries, as you Aussies say. She'll fit in just fine in the castle.'

And then he kissed her and, despite the thousand wonderful kisses they'd shared, this was the very best kiss of all.

EPILOGUE

THE BELLS RANG LOUDLY, pealing from churches all over Montaigne, echoing from the mountainsides and rolling down the valleys. Loudest of all were the bells from the cathedral where Prince Rafael and his bride, Princess Charlotte, were to be married.

The joyful sounds surrounded Charlie and her dad as they drove through the streets, lined with crowds of cheering well-wishers who were waving flags or home-made signs.

We love you, Charlie!
Bonne chance!
Félicitations!

Charlie couldn't help being overwhelmed by all the excitement and goodwill. She felt quite nervous by the time she and her father arrived at the cathedral and the bells were replaced by thundering organ music, lifting to the magnificent soaring ceilings.

Is this real? Is this really happening to me?

As she stood in the enormous cathedral doorway, Charlie trembled as she saw the splendour of it all— the stained-glass windows, the candles, the bishop in his robes, the pews filled with grand-looking strangers. She was almost too scared to look properly at Rafe, who stood at the far end of the very long aisle, incredibly splendid in a red jacket with gold braid and black trousers. She was so overcome she feared she might weep.

In that moment, however, her eye was caught by a bobbing flash of deep purple right at the front of the congregation. Someone had turned to grin and to wave excitedly. Charlie realised it was Edna.

Her neighbour had been over the moon to be invited to the royal wedding and today she looked magnificent in a purple lace suit, with a lavender fascinator, complete with feathers, perched rather precariously on her head.

The sight of her old neighbour's familiar beaming grin was enough to calm Charlie.

She looked again at Rafe. And he smiled.

His smile was for her. Only for her. She could feel his love reaching her down the full length of the red-carpeted aisle, and she knew that, despite the over-the-top pomp and ceremony, Rafe was just a normal guy who needed her. He had told her this over and over during the past few days.

They loved each other. They might be a royal couple, but they were also good mates. Everything was OK.

With a happy, calming, deep breath, Charlie turned her attention to Arielle, her flower girl, who had just arrived in the car that followed close behind.

Arielle was one of the first people Charlie had visited on her return to Montaigne. The little girl's hair had grown back since the day they'd first met in the hospital, when she'd worn a crocheted cap and had won Rafe and Charlie's hearts with her curtsy. On Charlie's second visit, she had met Arielle's parents as well. Since then her friendship with the family and with many other patients had deepened.

Today the excited little girl looked beautiful with her

mop of short dark curls adorned by a circlet of roses that matched her floor-length dress of palest pink. Olivia looked beautiful too in a gown in the same shade. She'd been thrilled and touched when Charlie had invited her to be her matron of honour.

And Suze, Charlie's best friend since kindergarten, was also a bridesmaid, looking perfectly lovely, but slightly overawed by the fact that her groomsman partner was a handsome sheikh.

Now, with everyone assembled, Charlie sent them all a final smile and then linked arms with her dad. Michael Morisset had taken a while to get used to the idea of his daughter marrying a prince. At first he'd thought Charlie was pulling his leg. It was too preposterous to believe.

Fortunately, once he'd got to know Rafe, he'd calmed down. Eventually, he'd declared his prospective son-in-law to be a regular 'good bloke'.

'I was worried Rafe wouldn't understand how lucky he was,' Charlie's father had confided. 'But he seems to truly appreciate how wonderful you are, my duckling, so I'm happy to give you my blessing.'

Now her dad smiled at her. His eyes were a tad too shiny, but he still looked happy. 'I'm so proud of you, kiddo,' he said fondly, a beat before the organist struck the opening chords of the processional hymn.

The congregation rose, the music swelled and flowed, and Charlie kept her smile just for Rafe as she made her way down the long, long aisle. Throughout the procession, her Prince didn't take his eyes from her and his message was clear and shining.

This day wasn't just a happy ending, it was the very happiest of new beginnings.

* * * * *

*If you loved this story and want to enjoy
another wedding romance look out for
SLOW DANCE WITH THE BEST MAN
by Sophie Pembroke.*

*If you love nothing more than a Cinderella story
you won't want to miss
Therese Beharrie's fabulous debut book
THE TYCOON'S RELUCTANT CINDERELLA!*

"Allow me?" he asked, reaching for the bow on her faux fur stole.

Ophelia gave him a quiet nod as he tugged on the end of the satin ribbon. He loosened the bow and opened the stole a bit. Just enough to offer a glimpse of the spectacular diamonds around her neck.

"There," he said. "That's better."

Ophelia swallowed, unable to move, unable to even breathe while he touched her. She'd dropped her guard. Only for a moment. And now…

Now he was no more than a breath away, and she could see her reflection in the cool gray of his irises. He had eyes like a tempest, and there she was, right at the center of his storm. Looking beautiful and happy. Full of life and hope. So much like her old self, the old Ophelia—the girl who'd danced through life, unfettered and unafraid—that she forgot all the reasons why she shouldn't kiss this man. This man who had such a way of reminding her who she used to be.

"I'm sorry." She removed her hand from Artem's face and slid across the leather seat, out of his reach "I shouldn't have… I'm sorry."

"Ophelia," he said with more patience in his tone than she'd ever heard. "It's okay."

But it wasn't okay. *She* wasn't okay.

"Showtime," he muttered.

Showtime.

* * *

Drake Diamonds:
Looking for love that shines as bright
as the gems in their window!

HIS BALLERINA BRIDE

BY
TERI WILSON

First Published in Great Britain 2017
By Mills & Boon, an imprint of HarperCollins*Publishers*
1 London Bridge Street, London, SE1 9GF

© 2016 Teri Wilson

ISBN: 978-0-263-92265-3

23-0117

Our policy is to use papers that are natural, renewable and recyclable products and made from wood grown in sustainable forests. The logging and manufacturing processes conform to the legal environmental regulations of the country of origin.

Printed and bound in Spain
by CPI, Barcelona

Teri Wilson is a novelist for Mills & Boon. She is the author of *Unleashing Mr. Darcy*, now a Hallmark Channel Original Movie. Teri is also a contributing writer at HelloGiggles.com, a lifestyle and entertainment website founded by Zooey Deschanel that is now part of the *People* magazine, *TIME* magazine and *Entertainment Weekly* family. Teri loves books, travel, animals and dancing every day. Visit Teri at www.teriwilson.net or on Twitter, @TeriWilsonauthr.

For the classic-movie lovers out there
who dream of little black dresses, diamonds
and breakfast on Fifth Avenue.

"People will stare. Make it worth their while."

—Harry Winston

Chapter One

They say diamonds are a girl's best friend. Ophelia Rose had a tendency to disagree. Strongly.

Not that Ophelia had anything against diamonds per se. On the contrary, she adored them. Just two months ago, she'd earned an entire college degree in diamonds. Gemology, technically. Every piece of jewelry she'd designed for her final independent study project featured a diamond as its centerpiece. They were something of a pet jewel of hers. So naturally, working at Drake Diamonds was her dream job. It was her dream job *now*, anyway. Now that all vestiges of her former life had pretty much vanished.

Now that she'd been forced to start over.

She still loved diamonds. In truth, only *certain* diamonds had been getting on her nerves of late. Diamonds of the engagement variety. The level of stress that those particular gems were causing her was enough to make her seriously question their best-friend status. Unfortunately, engagement diamonds were something of an occupational hazard for someone who worked on the tenth floor of Drake Diamonds.

Ophelia pasted on a smile and focused on the glittering jewels in the display case before her and the way they dazzled beneath the radiant store lights. *Breathe. Just breathe.*

"This is the one. Princess cut. It's perfect for you..." The man sitting across from Ophelia slipped a 2.3-carat solitaire onto the ring finger of the woman sitting beside him and cooed, "...princess."

"Oh, stop. You're going to make me cry again," his fiancée said, gazing at the diamond on her hand. Sure enough, a lone tear slipped down her cheek.

Ophelia slid a box of rose-scented tissues toward the princess.

In the course of a typical workday, Ophelia went through at least two boxes of tissues. Twice that many on the weekend, along with countless flutes of the finest French champagne and dozens of delicate petits fours crafted to look like the distinctive Drake Diamonds blue gift box crowned with its signature white ribbon. Because shopping for an engagement ring at Drake Diamonds was an experience steeped in luxury, as it had been since 1830.

Her current customers couldn't have cared less about the trappings, particularly the edible ones. Their champagne flutes were nearly full and the petits fours completely untouched. Ophelia was fairly certain the only things they wanted to consume were each other.

It made her heart absolutely ache.

Six months had passed since Ophelia's diagnosis. She'd had half a year to accept her fate, half a year to come to terms with her new reality. She'd never be the girl with the diamond on her finger. She'd never be the bride-to-be. Multiple sclerosis was a serious, chronic illness, one that had altered every aspect of her existence. It had been difficult enough to let this uninvited guest turn her life upside down. She wouldn't let it do the same to someone else. That much she could control.

She couldn't dictate a lot of things about her new life. But her single status was one of them. And she was perfectly fine with it. She had enough on her plate with work, volunteering at the animal shelter and staying as healthy as possible. Not to mention coping with everything she'd left behind.

Still.

Being reminded on a daily basis of what she would never have was getting old.

"Look at that. It's a perfect fit." She smiled at the happy couple, and her throat grew tight. "Shall I wrap it for you?"

"Yes, please." The besotted man's gaze never left his betrothed. "In one of those fancy blue boxes?"

Ophelia nodded. "Of course. It's my pleasure."

She gathered the ring and the petits fours—which the bride declared were in flagrant violation of her wedding diet—and padded across the plush blue carpet of the sales floor toward the gift-wrap room. After dropping off the diamond ring, where it would be boxed, wrapped and tied with a bridal-white bow, she made her way to the kitchen to dispose of the tiny cakes.

She stopped and stared at the counter and the endless rows of pristine silver plates and champagne flutes. Once her current customers left, she'd be passing out another pair of fancy desserts. Another duo of champagne glasses. To yet another couple madly in love.

I can't keep doing this.

This wasn't the plan. The plan was to work in jewelry design, to sketch and create the pieces in those glittering display cases. Catering to the lovesick was definitely *not* the plan.

She knew she should be grateful. She had to start somewhere. As far as the sales team went, working on the tenth floor in Engagements was the most coveted position in the building. She simply needed to bide her time until she could somehow show upper management what she could do, and get transferred to the design department.

One day at a time. I can do this.

She could totally do it. But maybe all those happily engaged couples would be easier to stomach with a little cake.

Why not? No one was looking. Everyone was on the sales floor.

Ophelia had never been much of a rule breaker. She'd never broken *any* rules, come to think of it. Funny how being the good girl all her life hadn't stopped her world from falling apart. Life wasn't fair. She should have known that by now.

She closed her eyes and bit into one of the petits fours. As it melted in her mouth, she contemplated the healing powers of sugar and frosting. Cake might not be the best thing for the body, but at the moment, it was doing wonders for her battered soul.

Finally, she'd uncovered the one good thing about no longer being a professional ballet dancer. Cake. She couldn't remember the last time she'd had a bite of the sweet dessert. Not even on her birthday.

"My God, where have you been all my life?" she whispered.

"Excuse my tardiness," a sultry male voice said in return.

Oh, God.

Ophelia's eyes flew open.

Much to her dismay, the bemused retort hadn't come from the petit four. It had come from her boss. Artem Drake, in the flesh. His tuxedo-clad, playboy flesh.

"Mr. Drake." Her throat grew tight.

What was he even doing here? No one at Drake Diamonds had laid eyes on him since he'd inherited the company from his father. Unless the photos of him on *Page Six* counted.

And good grief. He was a thousand times hotter in person than he was on the internet. How was that even possible?

Ophelia took in his square chin, his dark, knowing gaze and the hint of a dimple in his left cheek, and went a little bit weak in the knees. The fit of his tuxedo was impeccable. As was the shine of his patent leather shoes. But it was the look on his face that nearly did her in. Like the cat who got the cream.

The man was decadence personified.

She swallowed. With great difficulty. "This isn't what it looks like."

She couldn't be seen eating one of the Drake petits fours. They were for customers, not employees. Not to mention the mortification of being caught moaning suggestively at a baked good. She dropped it like a hot potato. It landed between them on the kitchen floor with a splat. A crumb bounced onto the mirror surface of one of Artem's shoes.

What on *earth* was she doing?

He glanced down and lifted a provocative brow. Ophelia's insides went all fluttery. Perfect. She'd already made an idiot of herself and now she was borderline swooning over an eyebrow. Her *boss's* eyebrow.

"Oh, good," he said, his deep voice heavily laced with amusement. "Thanks for clearing that up. For a minute, I thought I'd stumbled upon one of my employees eating the custom-made, fifteen-dollars-per-square-inch snacks that we serve our customers."

Those petits fours were fifteen dollars apiece? That seemed insane, even for Drake Diamonds. They were good, but they weren't that good.

Ophelia glanced at the tiny cake at her feet, and her stomach growled. Okay, maybe they were that good. "Um…"

"So what's the story, then? Are you a runaway fiancée hiding in my kitchen?" His gaze flitted to the floor again. "Are those pretty feet of yours getting cold?"

"A fiancée? Me? No. Definitely not." Once upon a time, yes. But that, like so many other things, had changed. "I mean, no. Just…no."

Stop talking. She was making things so much worse, but she couldn't seem to think straight.

Those pretty feet of yours…

"So you do work for me, then?" He crossed his arms and leaned against the kitchen counter, the perfect picture of elegant nonchalance.

What was he doing, wearing a tux at ten in the morning, anyway? On a weekday, no less. Was this some kind of billionaire walk of shame?

Probably. She thought about the countless photos she'd seen of him with young, beautiful women on his arm. Sometimes two or three at a time. *Walk of shame. Definitely.*

"I do," she said. I do. *I do.* Wedding words. Her neck went instantly, unbearably hot. She cleared her throat. "I work in Engagements."

The corner of his lips twitched. So he thought that was funny, did he? "And your name is?"

"Ophelia." She paused. "Ophelia Rose." At least she had her wits about her enough to identify herself by her actual, real last name and not the stage name she'd been using for the last eight years. Out of everything in her life that had changed, no longer calling herself Ophelia Baronova had been the most difficult to accept. As if that person really, truly no longer existed.

She doesn't.

Ophelia bit her lower lip to keep it from trembling.

Artem Drake crossed his arms. "I suppose that makes me your boss."

This was getting weird.

"Come now, Ophelia Rose. Don't look so sad. I'm not going to fire you for biting into temptation." One corner of Mr. Drake's perfect mouth lifted into a half grin. "Literally."

Clearly, he knew a thing or two about temptation. How was it possible for a man to so fully embody sex?

"Good." She forced a smile. Being fired hadn't actually crossed her mind, although she supposed it should have. It was just kind of difficult to take Artem seriously, since he hadn't darkened the door of Drake Diamonds in the entire time she'd worked there. But if he thought the sadness behind her eyes was because she was afraid of him, so be it. That was fine. Better, actually. She wasn't about to bare her messed-up soul to her employer.

Her employer...

When would she have another opportunity to talk to Artem Drake one-on-one? Never, probably. Because she sure wasn't planning on sneaking off to the kitchen anymore. And who knew when he'd show up again? She had to make the most of this moment. If she didn't, she'd regret it. Just as soon as she went back out on the sales floor among all those engaged couples.

It was now or never.

But maybe she should scrape the cake off the floor first.

Artem Drake was having difficulty wrapping his mind around the fact that the goddess of a woman who'd just dropped to her knees in front of him worked for him. But to be fair, the concept of anyone in this Fifth Avenue institution answering to him was somewhat laughable.

Granted, his last name was on the front of the building. And the gift bags. And those legendary blue boxes. But he'd never had much to do with running the place. That had been his father's job. And now that his father was gone, the responsibility should fall on the shoulders of his older brother, Dalton. Dalton lived and breathed Drake Diamonds. Dalton spent so much time here that he had a foldout sofa in his office. Hell, Artem didn't even *have* an office.

Nor did he have any idea how much those silly little cakes cost. He'd pulled a number out of thin air. And now he'd nearly made the goddess cry. Maybe he was cut out to run the place, after all. His dad had loved making people cry.

Besides, *goddess* wasn't quite the right word. There was something ethereal about her. Delicate. Unspeakably graceful. She had a neck made for diamonds.

Which sounded exactly like something his father would say.

"Stand up," Artem said, far more harshly than he'd intended. But if she didn't get up off her knees, he wouldn't have any hope of maintaining an ounce of professional behavior.

She finished dabbing at the mess with a napkin and stood, her motions so effortlessly fluid that the air around her seemed to dance. "Yes, sir."

He rather liked the *sir* business. But he needed to do

what he'd come here to do and get the hell out of this place. He pushed away from the counter and straightened his cuff link. Singular. One of them had managed to go missing since the symphony gala the night before. Maybe he'd pick up a new pair on his way out. *After* he'd waved the proverbial white flag in his brother's face.

He cleared his throat. "While this has been interesting, to say the least, I have some business to attend to. And I'm sure you have work to do, as well."

Could he sound more ridiculous? *I have some business to attend to. And I'm sure you have work to do, as well*. He'd never spoken like that in his life. Dalton, yes. All the time. That's probably how he spoke to his girlfriends.

"Wait," Ophelia blurted, just as he took a step toward the door. "Please, Mr. Drake. Sir."

He turned. "Yes, Miss Rose?"

"I'd like to schedule a meeting with you. At your convenience, of course." She lifted her chin, and her neck seemed to lengthen.

God, that neck. Artem let his gaze travel down the length of it to the delicate dip between her collarbones. A diamond would look exquisite nestled right there, set off by her perfect porcelain skin. Artem had never seen such a beautiful complexion on a woman. She almost looked as though she'd never set foot outdoors. Like she was crafted of the purest, palest marble. Like she belonged in a museum rather than here. What in God's name was she doing working behind a jewelry counter, anyway?

He lifted his gaze back to her face, and her cheeks went rosebud pink. "A meeting? With me?"

He'd heard worse ideas.

"Yes. A business meeting," she said crisply. "I have some design ideas I'd like to present. I know I work in sales at the moment, but I'm actually a trained gemologist."

Artem wasn't sure why he found this news so surprising, but he did. Few people surprised him. He wished more of them did. Ophelia Rose was becoming more intriguing by the minute.

She was also his *employee*, at least for the next ten minutes or so. He shouldn't be thinking about her neck. Or the soft swell of her breasts beneath the bodice of the vintage sea-foam dress she wore. Or what her delicate bottom would feel like in the palms of his hands. He shouldn't be thinking about any of the images that were currently running through his mind.

"A gemologist? Really?" he said, somehow keeping his gaze fixed on her face. God, he deserved a medal for such restraint.

She nodded. "I've have a degree from the New York School of Design. I graduated with honors."

"Then congratulations are in order. Perhaps even a celebration." He just couldn't help himself. "With cake."

Her blush deepened a shade closer to crimson. "Honestly, I'd rather have that meeting. Just half an hour of your time to show you my designs. That's all I need."

She was determined. He'd give her that. Determined and oh-so-earnest.

And rather bold, now that he thought about it. He

had, after all, just walked in on her shoving cake in her mouth. Cake meant for lovebirds prepared to drop thousands of dollars for a Drake diamond. She had a ballsy streak. Sexy, he mused.

Artem wondered how much he was paying her. He hadn't a clue. "I'm sorry, but I can't."

She took a step closer to him, and he caught a whiff of something warm and sweet. Vanilla maybe. She smelled like a dessert, which Artem supposed made perfect sense. "Can't or won't?"

He shrugged. "I guess you could say both."

She opened her lovely mouth to protest, and Artem held up a hand to stop her. "Miss Rose, before you waste any more of your precious time, there's something you should know. I'm resigning."

She went quiet for a beat. A beat during which Artem wondered what had prompted him to tell this total stranger his plans before he'd even discussed them with his own flesh and blood. He blamed it on his hangover. Or possibly the sad, haunted look in Ophelia's blue eyes. Eyes the color of Kashmir sapphires.

It didn't seem right to let her think he could help her when he'd never even see her again.

"Resigning?" She frowned. "But you can't resign. This is Drake Diamonds, and you're a Drake."

Not the right Drake. "I'm quitting my family business, not my family." Although the thought wasn't without its merits, considering he'd never truly been one of them. Not the way Dalton and their sister, Diana, had.

"But your father left you in charge." Her voice had gone as soft as feathers. *Feathers.* A bird. That's what she reminded him of—a swan. A stunning, sylphlike swan. "That matters."

He shook his head. She had no clue what she was talking about, and he wasn't about to elaborate. He'd already said too much. And frankly, it was none of her business. "I assure you, this is for the best. I might add that it's also confidential."

"Oh, I won't tell anyone."

"I know you won't." He pointed at the petit four that she'd scraped up off the floor, still resting in her palm. "You'll keep my secret, and I'll keep yours. Does that sound fair, princess?"

His news wouldn't be a secret for long, anyway. Dalton's office was right down the hall. If Artem hadn't heard Ophelia's sensual ode to cake and made this spontaneous detour, the deed would already be done.

He'd enjoyed toying with her, but now their encounter had taken a rather vexing turn. As much as he liked the thought of half an hour behind closed doors with those lithe limbs and willowy grace, the meeting she so desperately wanted simply wasn't going to happen. Not with him, anyway.

Maybe Dalton would meet with her. Maybe Artem would suggest it. *I quit. Oh, and by the way, one of the sales associates wants to design our next collection...*

Maybe not.

"Okay, then. It was nice meeting you, Mr. Drake." She offered him her free hand, and he took it. "I'm so very sorry for your loss."

That last part came out as little more than a whisper, just breathy enough for Artem to know that Ophelia

Rose with the sad sapphire eyes knew a little something about loss herself.

"Thank you." Her hand felt small in his. Small and impossibly soft.

Then she withdrew her hand and squared her shoulders, and the fleeting glimpse of vulnerability he'd witnessed was replaced with the cool confidence of a woman who'd practically thrown cake at him and then asked for a meeting to discuss a promotion. There was that ballsy streak again. "One last thing, Mr. Drake."

He suppressed a grin. "Yes?"

"Don't call me princess."

Chapter Two

"Really, Artem?" Dalton aimed a scandalized glance at Artem's unbuttoned collar and loosened bow tie. "That penthouse where you live is less than three blocks away. You couldn't be bothered to go home and change before coming to work?"

Artem shrugged and sank into one of the ebony wing chairs opposite Dalton's desk. "Don't push it. I'm here, aren't I?"

Present and accounted for. Physically, at least. His thoughts, along with his libido, still lingered back in the kitchen with the intriguing Miss Rose.

"At long last. It's been two months since Dad died. To what do we owe the honor of your presence?" Dalton twirled his pen, a Montblanc. Just like the one their father had always used. It could have been the same one, for all Artem knew. That would have been an appropriate bequest.

Far more appropriate than leaving Artem in charge of this place when he'd done nothing more than pass out checks and attend charity galas since he'd been on the payroll.

The only Drake who spent less time in the building than he did was their sister, Diana. She was busy training for the Olympic equestrian team with her horse, which was appropriately named Diamond.

Artem narrowed his gaze at his brother. "I've been busy."

"Busy," Dalton said flatly. "Right. I think I remember reading something about that in *Page Six*."

"And here I thought you only read the financial pages. Don't tell me you've lowered yourself to reading *Page Six*, brother."

"I have to, don't I? How else would I keep apprised of your whereabouts?" The smile on Dalton's face grew tight.

A dull ache throbbed to life in Artem's temples, and he remembered why he'd put off this meeting for as long as he had. It wasn't as if he and Dalton had ever been close, but at least they'd managed to be cordial to one another while their father was alive. Now it appeared the gloves were off.

The thing was, he sympathized with Dalton. Surely his older brother had expected to be next in line to run the company. Hell, everyone had expected that to be the case.

He didn't feel too sorry for Dalton, though. He was

about to get exactly what he wanted. Besides, Artem would *not* let Dalton ruin his mood. He'd had a pleasant enough evening at the symphony gala, which had led to a rather sexually satisfying morning.

Oddly enough, though, it had been the unexpected encounter with Ophelia Rose that had put the spring in his step.

He found her interesting. And quite lovely. She would have made it almost tolerable to come to work every day, if he had any intention of doing such a thing. Which he didn't.

"Has it occurred to you that having the Drake name in the papers is good PR?" Artem said blithely.

"PR. Is that what they're calling it nowadays?" Dalton rolled his eyes.

It took every ounce of Artem's self-restraint not to point out how badly his brother needed to get laid. "I didn't come here to discuss my social life, Dalton. As difficult as you might find it to believe, I'm ready to discuss business."

Dalton nodded. Slowly. "I'm glad to hear that, brother. Very glad."

He'd be even happier once Artem made his announcement. So would Artem. He had no desire to engage in this sort of exchange on a daily basis. He was a grown man. He didn't need his brother's input on his lifestyle. And he sure as hell didn't want to sit behind a desk all day at a place where he'd never been welcomed when his father had been alive.

According to the attorneys, his father had changed the provisions of his will less than a week before he'd died. One might suppose senility to be behind the change, if not for the fact that his dad had been too stubborn to lose his mind. Shrewd. Cold. And sharp as a tack until the day he passed.

"Listen," Artem said. "I don't know why Dad left me in charge. It's as much of a mystery to me as it is to you."

"Don't." Dalton shook his head. "It doesn't matter. What's done is done. You're here. That's a start. I've had Dad's office cleaned out. It's yours now."

Artem went still. "What?"

Dalton shrugged one shoulder. "Where else are you going to work?"

Artem didn't have an answer for that.

Dalton continued, "Listen, it's going to take a few days to get you up to speed. We have one pressing matter, though, that just can't wait. If you hadn't rolled in here by the end of the week, I was going to beat down your door at the Plaza and insist you talk to me."

Whatever the pressing matter was, Artem had a feeling that he didn't want to hear about it. He didn't need to. It wasn't his problem. This idea that he would actually run the company was a joke.

"Before the heart attack…" Dalton's voice lost a bit of its edge.

The change in his composure was barely perceptible, but Artem noticed. He'd actually expected his brother to be more of a mess. Dalton, after all, had been the jewel in their father's crown. He'd been a son, whereas Artem had been a stranger to the Drakes for the first five years of his life.

"…Dad invested in a new mine in Australia. I didn't even know about it until last week." Dalton raised his brows, as if Artem had something to say.

Artem let out a laugh. "Surely you're not suggesting that he told *me* about it."

His brother sighed. "I suppose not, although I wish he had. I wish someone had stopped him. It doesn't matter, anyway. What's done is done. The mine was a bust. It's worthless, and now it's put the business in a rather precarious position."

"Precarious? Exactly how much did he spend on this mine?"

Dalton took too long to answer. He exhaled a slow, measured breath and finally said, "Three billion."

"Three billion dollars." Artem blinked. That was a lot of money. An astronomical amount, even to a man who lived on the eighteenth floor of the Plaza and flew his own Boeing business jet, which, ironically enough, Artem used for pleasure far more than he did for business. "The company has billions in assets, though. If not trillions."

"Yes, but not all those assets are liquid. With the loss from the mine, we're sitting at a twenty-five million dollar deficit. We need to figure something out."

We. Since when did any of the Drakes consider Artem part of a *we*?

He should just get up and walk right out of Dalton's office. He didn't owe the Drakes a thing.

Somehow, though, his backside remained rooted to the spot. "What about the diamond?"

"*The* diamond? The *Drake* diamond?" Dalton shook

his head. "I'm going to pretend I didn't hear that. I know you're not one for sentimentality, brother, but even you wouldn't suggest that we sell the Drake diamond."

Actually, he would. "It's a rock, Dalton. A pretty rock, but a rock nonetheless."

Dalton shook his head so hard that Artem thought it might snap clear off his neck. "It's a piece of history. Our family name was built on that rock."

Our family name. Right.

Artem cleared his throat. "How much is it worth?"

"It doesn't matter, because we're not selling it."

"How much, Dalton? As your superior, I demand that you tell me." It was a low blow. Artem would have liked to think that a small part of him didn't get a perverse sort of pleasure from throwing his position in Dalton's face, but it did. So be it.

"Fifty million dollars," Dalton said. "But I repeat, it's not for sale, and it never will be."

Never.

If Artem had learned one thing since becoming acquainted with his father—since being "welcomed" into the Drake fold—it was that *never* was an awfully strong word. "That's not your call, though, is it, brother?"

Ophelia hadn't planned on stopping by the animal shelter on the way home from work. She had, after all, already volunteered three times this week. Possibly four. She'd lost count.

She couldn't go home yet, though. Not after the day she'd had. Dealing with all the happily engaged couples was bad enough, but she was growing accustomed to it. She didn't have much of a choice, did she? But the unexpected encounter with Artem Drake had somehow thrown her completely off-kilter.

It wasn't only the embarrassment of getting caught inhaling one of the fifteen dollar petits fours that had gotten her so rattled. It was him. Artem.

Mr. Drake. Not Artem. *He's your boss, not your friend. Or anything else.*

He wasn't even her boss anymore, she supposed. Which was for the best. Obviously. She hadn't exactly made a glowing first impression. Now she could start over with whoever took his place. So really, there was no logical reason for the acute tug of disappointment she'd felt when he'd told her about his plans to resign. None whatsoever.

There was also no logical reason that she'd kept looking around all afternoon for a glimpse of him as he exited the building. Nor for the way she'd gone all fluttery when she'd caught a flash of tuxedoed pant leg beyond the closing elevator doors after her shift had ended. It hadn't been Artem, anyway. Just another, less dashing man dressed to the nines.

What was her problem, anyway? She was acting as though she'd never met a handsome man before. Artem Drake wasn't merely handsome, though. He was charming.

Too charming. Dangerously so.

Ophelia had felt uncharacteristically vulnerable in the presence of all that charm. Raw. Empty. And acutely aware of all that she'd lost, all that she'd never have.

She couldn't go home to the apartment she'd inherited from her grandmother. She couldn't spend another evening sifting through her grandmother's things—the grainy black-and-white photographs, her tattered pointe shoes. Her grandmother had been the only family that Ophelia had known since the tender age of two, when a car accident claimed the lives of her parents. Natalia Baronova had been more than a grandparent. She'd been Ophelia's world. Her mother figure, her best friend and her ballet teacher.

She'd died a week before Ophelia's diagnosis. As much as Ophelia had needed someone to lean on in those first dark days, she'd been grateful that the great Natalia Baronova, star ballerina of Ballet Russe de Monte Carlo in the 1940s and '50s, died without the knowledge that her beloved granddaughter would never dance again.

"Ophelia?" Beth, the shelter manager, shook her head and planted her hands on her hips as Ophelia slipped off her coat and hung it on one of the pegs by the door. "Again? I didn't see your name on the volunteer schedule for this evening."

"It's not. But I thought you could use an extra pair of hands." Ophelia flipped through the notebook that contained the animals' daily feeding schedule.

"You know better than anybody we always need help around here, but surely you have somewhere else to be on a Friday night."

Nowhere, actually. "You know how much I enjoy spending time with the animals." Plus, the shelter was now caring for a litter of eight three-week-old kittens that had to be bottle-fed every three hours. The skimpy volunteer staff could barely keep up, especially now that the city was blanketed with snow. People liked to stay home when it snowed. And that meant at any given moment, one of the kittens was hungry.

Beth nodded. "I know, love. Just be careful. I'd hate for you to ruin that pretty dress you're wearing."

The dress had belonged to Ophelia's grandmother. In addition to mountains of dance memorabilia, she'd left behind a gorgeous collection of vintage clothing. Like the apartment, it had been a godsend. When she'd been dancing, Ophelia had lived in a leotard and tights. Most days, she'd even worn her dance clothes to school, since she'd typically had to go straight from rehearsal to class at the New York School of Design. She couldn't very well show up to work at Drake Diamonds dressed in a wraparound sweater, pink tights and leg warmers.

Neither could she simply go out and buy a whole new work wardrobe. Between her student loan bills and the exorbitant cost of the biweekly injections to manage her MS, she barely made ends meet. Plus there were the medical bills from that first, awful attack, before she'd even known why the vision out of her left eye sometimes went blurry or why her fingers occasionally felt numb. Sometimes she left rehearsal with such crippling fatigue she felt as if she were walking through Jell-O. She'd blamed it on the stress of dealing with her grandmother's recent illness. She'd blamed it on the rigorous physical demands of her solo role in the company production of *Giselle*. Mostly, though, she'd simply ignored her symptoms because she couldn't quite face the prospect that something was seriously wrong.

Then one night she'd fallen out of a pirouette. Onstage, midperformance. The fact that she'd been unable to peel herself off the floor had only made matters worse.

And now she'd never perform again.

Sometimes, in her most unguarded moments, Ophelia found herself pointing her toes and moving her foot in the familiar, sweeping motion of a rond de jambe. Then she'd close her eyes and remember the sickening thud as she'd come down on the wooden stage floor. She'd remember the pitying expressions on the faces of her fellow dancers and the way the crimson stage curtains had drawn closed on the spectacle with a solemn hush. Her career, her life, everything she'd worked for, had ended with that whisper of red velvet.

She had every reason to be grateful, though. She had a nice apartment in Manhattan. She had clothes on her back and a job. She'd even had the forethought to enroll in school while she'd been dancing, because she'd known that the day would come when she'd be unable to dance for a living. She just hadn't realized that day would come so soon. She'd thought she'd had time. So much time. Time to dance, time to love, time to dream.

She'd never planned on spending her Friday nights feeding kittens at an animal shelter, but it wasn't such a bad place to be. She actually enjoyed it quite a bit.

"I'll be careful, Beth. I promise." Ophelia draped a towel over the front of her dress and reached into the cabinet above a row of cat enclosures for a bottle and a fresh can of kitten formula.

As she cracked the can open and positioned it over the tiny bottle, her gaze flitted to the cage in the corner. Her hand paused midpour when she realized the wire pen was empty.

"Where's the little white kitten?" she asked, fighting against the rapidly forming lump in her throat.

"She hasn't been adopted, if that's what you're wondering." Beth cast her a knowing glance. "She's getting her picture taken for some charity thing."

"Oh." Ophelia hated herself for the swell of relief that washed over her. The shelter's mission was to find homes for all their animals, after all. Everyone deserved a home. And love. And affection.

The lump in her throat grew tenfold. "That's too bad."

"Is it?" Beth lifted a sardonic brow.

Ophelia busied herself with securing the top on the bottle and lifting one of the squirming kittens out of the pen lined with a heating pad that served as a makeshift incubator. "Of course it is."

She steadfastly refused to meet Beth's gaze, lest she give away her true feelings on the matter, inappropriate as they were.

But there was no fooling Beth. "For the life of me, I don't know why you won't just adopt her. Don't get me wrong—I appreciate your help around here. But I have a sneaky suspicion that the reason you came by tonight has more to do with visiting your fluffy friend than with feeding our hungry little monsters. You're besotted with that cat."

"And you're exaggerating." The orange kitten in Ophelia's hand mewed at a volume that belied its tiny size. Ophelia nestled the poor thing against her chest, and it began suckling on the bottle at once. "Besides, I told you. I can't have a pet. My apartment doesn't allow them."

It was a shameless lie. But how else was she supposed to explain her reluctance to adopt an animal she so clearly adored?

The truth was that she'd love to adopt the white Persian mix. She'd love coming home to the sound of its dainty feet pattering across the floor of her empty apartment. If the cat could come live with her, Ophelia would let it sleep at the foot of her bed, and feed it gourmet food from a can. If…

But she couldn't do it. She was in no condition to let anyone depend on her for their survival. Not even an animal. She was a ticking time bomb with an unknown deadline for detonation.

Ophelia braced herself for an ardent sales pitch. Beth obviously wasn't buying the excuses she'd manufactured. Fortunately, before Beth went into full-on lecture mode, they were interrupted by none other than the adorable white cat they'd been discussing. The snow-white feline entered the room in the arms of a statuesque woman dressed in a glittering, sequined floor-length dress.

Ophelia was so momentarily confused to see a woman wearing an evening gown at the animal shelter that at first she didn't seem to notice that the sequin-clad Barbie was also on the arm of a companion. And that companion was none other than Artem Drake.

Him.

Again? Seriously?

She could hardly believe her eyes. What on earth was he doing here?

For some ridiculous reason, Ophelia's first instinct was to hide. She didn't want to see him again. Especially here. Now. When he had a glamorous supermodel draped all over him and Ophelia was sitting in a plastic chair, chest covered in stained terry cloth while she bottle-fed a yelping orange tabby. And, oh, God, he was dressed in another perfect tuxedo. Had the man come strutting out of the womb in black tie?

She wondered what he'd look like in something more casual, a pair of soft faded jeans, maybe. Shirtless. Heck, as long as she was fantasizing, bottomless. Then she wondered why, exactly, she was wondering about such things.

"My, my, who do we have here?" Artem tilted his head.

Ophelia had been so busy dreaming of what he had going on beneath all that sleek Armani wool that she'd neglected to make herself invisible. Super.

"Um…" She struggled for something to say as his gaze dropped to her chest. Her nipples went tingly under his inspection, until she realized he was looking at the kitten, not her. Of course.

Why, oh, why hadn't she gone straight home after work?

He lifted his gaze so that he was once again looking her directly in the eyes. "Miss Rose, we meet again."

"You two know each other?" Beth asked, head swiveling back and forth between Ophelia and Artem.

Ophelia shook her head and centered all her concentration on not being attracted to him, while the orange kitten squirmed against her chest. "No, not really," she said.

"Why, yes. Yes, we do," Artem said at that exact instant.

The grin on his face was nothing short of suggestive. Or maybe that was just his default expression. Resting playboy face.

Heat pooled in her center, much to her mortification and surprise. She couldn't remember the last time she'd experienced anything remotely resembling desire. Unless this morning in the kitchen of Drake Diamonds counted. Which, if she was being honest, it most definitely did.

Beth frowned. Artem's date lifted an agitated brow.

Ophelia clarified the matter before Ms. Supermodel got the wrong idea and thought she was one of his sexual conquests, which no doubt were plentiful. "We've met. But we don't actually know one another." *Not at all*.

Artem directed his attention toward Beth and, by way of explanation, said, "Miss Rose works for me."

Worked, past tense, since he'd resigned from his family's business. Who did that, anyway?

"Drake Diamonds." Beth nodded. "Of course. Ophelia's told me all about it. I'm sure I don't need to tell you what a treasure you've found in her. She's one of our best volunteers. Such a hard worker."

"A hard worker," Artem echoed, with only a subtle hint of sarcasm in his smoky voice. Then, presumably to ensure that Ophelia knew he hadn't forgotten about her indiscretion in the kitchen, he flashed a wink in her direction. "Quite."

The wink floated through her in a riot of awareness. *He's not flirting with you. He's goading you.* There was a difference. Right?

Beth continued gushing, oblivious to Artem's sarcastic undertones. "I don't know what we'd do without her. She's such a cat lover, here almost every night of the week. Weekends, too."

So now she sounded like a lonely cat lady. Perfect. "Beth, I'm sure Mr. Drake isn't here to hear about my volunteer work." Again, why exactly *was* he here?

"Oh, sorry. Of course he isn't. Mr. Drake, thank you so much for the generous donation on behalf of your family, as well as for being photographed with one of our charges. Having your picture in the newspaper with one of the animals will definitely bring attention to our cause." Beth beamed at Artem.

So he'd given a donation to the shelter. A *generous* donation...and right when Ophelia had been wishing for something that would make him seem less appealing. Thank goodness she'd no longer be running into him at work. He was too...too *much.*

"My pleasure," Artem said smoothly, and ran a manly hand over the white kitty still nestled in his date's arms.

Ophelia's kitty.

Not hers, technically. Not hers at all. But that didn't stop the sting of possessiveness she felt as she watched the cat being cuddled by someone else. And not just *any*one else. Someone who was clearly on a date with Artem Drake.

It shouldn't have mattered, but it did. Very much.

"That's actually Ophelia's favorite cat you have there." Beth smiled.

"She's awfully sweet," Artem's date cooed.

Ophelia felt sick all of a sudden. What if Artem's companion adopted it? *Her* cat? She took a deep breath and fought against the image that sprang to her mind of the woman and Artem in the back of a stretch limo with the white kitten nestled between them. Did everything in life have to be so unfair?

"Is it now?" Artem slid his gaze toward Ophelia. "Your favorite?"

She nodded. There was no sense denying it, especially since she had that odd transparent feeling again. Like he could see straight into her heart.

"I keep insisting Ophelia should adopt her." An awkward smile creased Beth's face. Artem's date still had a firm grip on the kitten. Clearly, Beth was hinting that Ophelia needed to speak now or forever hold her peace.

She needed to get out of here before she did something monumentally stupid like snatch the kitten out of the woman's arms.

"I should be going." Ophelia stood and returned the tiny orange kitten to the incubator. "It was lovely seeing you again, Mr. Drake. Beth."

She nodded at Artem's date, whose name she still didn't know, and kept her gaze glued to the floor so she wouldn't have to see the kitten purring away in the woman's arms.

Artem ignored Ophelia's farewell altogether and looked right past her, toward Beth. "How much is the kitten? I'd like to purchase it for Miss Rose."

What?

"That would be delightful, Mr. Drake. The adoption fee is fifty dollars, but of course we'll waive it for one of our generous donors." Beth beamed.

Artem plucked the kitten out of his date's arms. Ophelia had to give the woman credit; she didn't hesitate to hand over the cat, but kept a firm grip on Artem's bicep. Ophelia felt like reassuring her. *He's all yours.* She wasn't going home with her former boss.

Nor was she going home with the kitten. "Mr. Drake, I need to have a word with you. *Alone.*"

Beth weaved her arm around Artem's date's elbow and peeled her away. "Come with me, dear. I'll give you a tour of our facility."

Beth gave Ophelia a parting wink as she ushered the woman out the door toward the large kennels. Surely she wasn't trying to play matchmaker. That would have been absurd. Then again, everything about this situation was absurd.

Ophelia crossed her arms and glared at Artem. "What do you think you're doing?"

He shrugged. "Buying you a cat. Consider it an early Christmas bonus. You're welcome, by the way."

"No." She shook her head.

Was he insane? And did he have to stand there, looking so unbelievably hot in that tuxedo, while he stroked the kitten like he was Mr. December in a billionaires-with-baby-animals wall calendar?

"No?" His blue eyes went steely. Clearly, he'd never heard such a sentiment come out of a woman's mouth before.

"No. Thank you. It's a generous gesture, but..." She glanced at the kitten. Big mistake. Her delicate little nose quivered. She looked impossibly helpless and tiny snuggled against Artem's impressive chest. How was Ophelia supposed to say no to that face? How was she supposed to say no to *him*? She cleared her throat. "...but no."

He looked distinctly displeased.

Let him be angry. Ophelia would never even see him again. *That's what you thought this morning, too.* She lifted her chin. "I really should be going. And you should get back to your date."

"My date?" He smiled one of those suggestive smiles again, and Ophelia's insides went instantly molten. Damn him. "Is that what this is about? You're not jealous, are you, Miss Rose?"

Yes. To her complete and utter mortification, she was. She'd been jealous since he'd waltzed through the door with another woman on his arm. What had gotten into her?

She rolled her eyes. "Hardly."

"I'm not quite sure I believe you."

Ophelia sighed. "Why are you doing this?"

"What exactly is it that I'm doing?"

"Being nice." She swallowed. She felt like crying all of a sudden, and she couldn't. If she did, she might not ever stop. "Trying to buy me a cat."

He shrugged. "The cat needs a home, and you like her. Why shouldn't you have her?"

There were so many reasons that even if Ophelia wanted to list them all, she wouldn't have known where to start. "I told you. I can't."

Artem angled his head. "Can't or won't?"

He'd thrown back at her her own words from their encounter at Drake Diamonds, which made Ophelia bite back a smile. The man was too charming for his own good. "Mr. Drake, as much as I'd love to, I cannot adopt that cat."

He took a step closer to her, so close that Ophelia suddenly had trouble taking a breath, much less forming a valid argument for not taking the kitten she so desperately wanted. Then he reached for her hand, took it in his and placed it on the supple curve of the cat's spine.

The kitty mewed in recognition, and Artem moved their linked hands through her silky soft fur in long, measured strokes. Ophelia had to bite her lip to keep from crying. Why was he doing this? Why did he care?

"She likes you," he said. And as if he could read her mind, he added, "Something tells me you two need each other. You come here nearly every day. You want this kitten. You need her, but you won't let yourself have her. Why not?"

Because what would happen if Ophelia had another attack?

No, not *if.* When. Her illness was officially called relapsing-remitting MS, characterized by episodic, clearly defined attacks, each one more neurologically devastating than the last. Ophelia never knew when the next one would come. A year from now? A month? A day? What would she do with the cat then, when she was too sick to care for it?

The kitten purred, and the sensation vibrated warmth through Ophelia's hand, still covered with Artem's. God, this was tortuous. She jerked her hand away. "Mr. Drake, I—"

Before she could say another word of protest, he cut her off. "I'll adopt the cat. You take care of her for me, and I'll give you your meeting," he said.

His voice had lost any hint of empathy. He sounded angry again, as if she'd forced him into making such a suggestion.

"My meeting?" She swallowed. It would have been an offer too good to be true, if it were possible. Thank God it wasn't. "And how are you going to arrange such a meeting, now that you no longer work at Drake Diamonds?"

"I'm a Drake, remember?" As if she could forget. "And there's been a change of plans. I do, in fact, still work there."

"Oh," she said, stunned. "I don't understand."

He offered no explanation, just handed her the kitten.

She held out her arms without thinking. What was happening? She hadn't agreed to his ludicrous proposition, had she? "Wait. If you didn't resign, what does that mean, exactly?"

"It means I'm still your boss." He turned on his heel and brushed past her toward the kennels. He was leaving, just like that? He paused with his hand on the door.

"Take that cat home with you, Miss Rose. I trust I'll see you tomorrow in my office?"

She couldn't let him manipulate her like this. At best, it was unprofessional. At worst…well, she didn't even want to contemplate the worst-case scenario. She could not take the kitten, no matter how much she wanted to. Even temporarily. She couldn't be Artem Drake's cat sitter. She absolutely couldn't.

He stood there staring at her with his penetrating gaze, as if they were engaged in some sort of sexy staring contest.

One that Ophelia had no chance of winning.

"Fine."

Chapter Three

Artem arrived at Drake Diamonds the next morning before the store even opened, which had to be some kind of personal record. He couldn't remember the last time he'd been there during off-hours. If he ever had.

Dalton, on the other hand, had been making a regular practice of it for most of his life. In recent years, for work. Naturally. But back when they'd been teenagers, when Dalton had been more human and less workaholic robot, Artem's brother had gotten caught with a girlfriend in the middle of the night, in the middle of the first-floor showroom, in flagrante delicto.

It remained Artem's favorite story about his brother, even if it marked the moment when he'd discovered that Dalton had been the only Drake heir who'd been entrusted with a key to the family business while still in prep school.

He wished it hadn't mattered. But it had. In truth, it still did, even though those feelings had nothing to do with the business itself.

He'd never had any interest in hanging around the shop on Fifth Avenue. To the other Drakes, it was a shrine. To the world, it was a historic institution. Drake Diamonds had been part of the Manhattan landscape since its crowded, busy streets teemed with horse-drawn carriages. To young Artem, it had always simply been his father's workplace.

And now it was his. Same building, same office, same godforsaken desk.

What was he doing? Dalton didn't need him. Not really. Wasn't his brother in a better position to save the company? Dalton was the one familiar with the ins and outs of the business. His bedroom in Lenox Hill was probably wallpapered with balance sheets.

All Dalton's life, he'd worn his position as a Drake like a mantle, whereas to Artem it had begun to feel like a straitjacket. Now that his father was gone, there was no reason why he couldn't simply shrug it off and move on with his life. In addition to his recent promotion, he'd been left a sizable inheritance. Sizable enough that he could walk away from his PR position with the company and never again have his photo taken at another dull social event if he so chose. There was no reason in the world he should willingly get out of bed at an ungodly predawn hour so he could walk to the store and sit behind his father's desk.

Yet here he was, climbing out of the back of his black town car on the corner of Fifth Avenue and Fifty-seventh Street.

He told himself that his decision to stay on as CEO, at least temporarily, had nothing to do with Ophelia. Because that would be preposterous.

Yes, she was lovely. Beyond lovely, with her fathomless eyes, hair like spun gold and her willowy, fluid grace. And yes, he'd lost more sleep than he cared to admit thinking about what it would feel like to have those impossibly graceful legs wrapped around his waist as he buried himself inside her.

Her simplest gestures utterly beguiled him. Innocent movements, like the turn of her wrist, made him want to do wholly inappropriate things. He wanted to wrap his fingers around her wrists like a diamond cuff bracelet, pin her arms over her head and trace the exquisite length of her neck with his tongue. He wanted that more than he'd wanted anything in a long, long time.

Artem was no stranger to passion. He'd experienced desire before, but not like this. Nothing like this.

He found it frustrating. And quite baffling, particularly when he found himself doing things like sitting behind a desk, adopting animals and dismissing a perfectly good date, choosing instead to go home and get in bed before midnight. Alone.

His temples throbbed as he stepped out of the car and caught a glimpse of himself in the reflection of the storefront window. He'd dressed the part of CEO in a charcoal Tom Ford suit, paired with a smooth silk tie in that dreadful Drake Diamond blue. *Who are you?*

"Good morning, Mr. Drake." The store's doorman greeted him with a tip of his top hat and a polite smile.

Standing on the sidewalk in the swirling snow, clad in a Dickensian overcoat and Drake-blue scarf, the doorman almost looked like a throwback to the Victorian era. Probably because the uniforms had changed very little since the store first opened its doors. Tradition ruled at Drake Diamonds, even down to how the doormen dressed.

"Good morning." Artem nodded and strode through the door.

He made his way toward the elevator on the opposite side of the darkened showroom, his footsteps echoing on the gleaming tile floor. Then his gaze snagged on the glass showcase illuminated by a radiant spotlight to his right—home to the revered Drake Diamond.

He paused. Against its black velvet backdrop, the diamond almost appeared to be floating. The most brilliant star, shining in the darkest of nights.

He walked slowly up to the showcase, inspecting the glittering yellow stone mounted at the center of a garland necklace of white diamonds. Upon its discovery in a South African mine in the late 1800s, it had been the third largest yellow diamond in the world. Artem's great-great-great-great-great-grandfather bought it on credit before it had even been properly cut. Then he'd had it shaped and set in Paris—in a tiara of all things—before bringing it to New York and putting it on display in his new Fifth Avenue jewelry store. People had come from all over the country to see the breathtaking diamond. That single stone had put old man Drake's little jewelry business on the map.

Would it really be so bad to let it go? Drake Diamonds was world famous now. Sure, tourists still flocked to the store and pressed their faces to the glass to get a glimpse of the legendary diamond. But would things really change if it were no longer here?

He glanced at the plaque beneath the display case. It gave the history of the diamond, its various settings and the handful of times it had actually been worn. The last sentence of the stone's biography proclaimed it the shining star in the Drake family crown.

Artem swallowed, then looked back up at the diamond.

Ophelia's face materialized before him. Waves of gilded hair, sparkling sapphire eyes and that lithe, swan-like neck…with the diamond positioned right at the place where her pulse throbbed with life.

He blinked, convinced he was seeing things. A mirage. A trick of the mind, like a cool pool of glistening water before a man who hasn't had a drink in years.

It was no mirage. It was her.

Standing right behind him, only inches away, with her exquisite face reflected back at him in the pristine pane of glass. And damned if that diamond didn't look as though it had been made just for her. Placed deep in the earth billions of years ago, waiting for someone to find it and slip it around her enchanting neck.

"Beautiful, isn't it?" Her blue eyes glittered beneath the radiant showroom lights, lighting designed to make gemstones shimmer and shine. Somehow she sparkled brighter than all of them.

Beautiful, indeed.

"Quite," Artem said.

She moved to stand beside him, and her reflection slipped languidly away from the necklace. "Sometimes I like to come here and look at it, especially at times like this, when the store is quiet. Before all the crowds descend. I think about what it must have been like to wear something like this, back in the days when it was actually worn. It seems almost a shame that it's become something of a museum piece, don't you think?"

"I do, actually." At the moment, it seemed criminal the diamond wasn't draped around her porcelain neck. He could see her wearing it. The necklace and nothing else. He could imagine that priceless jewel glittering between her beautiful breasts, an image as real as the snow falling outside.

He shoved his hands in his pockets before he used them to press her against the glass and take her right there against the display case until the gemstone inside fell off its pedestal and shattered into diamond dust. The very idea of it made him go instantly hard.

And that's when Artem knew.

Ophelia did, in fact, have something to do with his decision to stay on as head of Drake Diamonds. She may have had *every*thing to do with it.

He ground his teeth and glared at her. He didn't enjoy feeling out of control. About anything, but most especially about his libido. Artem was a better man than his father had been. He had to believe that.

Ophelia blinked up at him with those melancholy eyes that made his chest ache, seemingly oblivious to the self-control it required for Artem to have a simple conversation with her. "Is it true that it's only been worn by three women? Or is that just an urban myth?"

"Yes, it's true." He nodded. A Hollywood star, a ballerina back in the forties and Diana Kincaid Drake. Only three. That fact was so much a part of Drake mythology that Artem wouldn't have been able to forget it even if he'd tried.

"I see," she whispered, her eyes fixed dreamily on the diamond. She almost looked as though she were trying to see inside it, to the heart of the stone. Its history.

Then she blinked, turned her back on the necklace and focused fully on Artem, her trance broken. "About our meeting..."

"Ah, yes. Our meeting." Out of the corner of his eye, he spotted Dalton making his entrance through the store's revolving door. Artem lowered his voice, although he wasn't quite sure why. He had nothing to hide. "Shall I assume my kitten is tucked snug inside your home, Miss Rose?"

"Yes." Her cheeks went pink, and her bow lips curved into a reluctant smile.

So he'd been right. She'd wanted that kitten all along. Needed it, even though she'd acted as though he'd been forcing it on her.

He'd done the right thing. For once in his life.

"So." She cleared her throat. "Shall I make an appointment with your assistant so I can show you my designs?"

"What did you name her?" he asked.

Ophelia blinked. "I'm sorry?"

"The kitten." Somewhere in the periphery, Artem saw the curious expression on his brother's face and ignored it altogether. "Have you given her a name yet?"

"Oh." Her flush deepened a shade, as pink as primroses. "I named her Jewel."

For some reason, this information took the edge off Artem's frustration. Which made no sense whatsoever. "Then I suppose you and I have business to discuss, Miss Rose. I'll have my assistant get you the details." He gave her a parting nod and headed to the elevator, where Dalton stood waiting. Watching.

Somehow it felt as if their father was watching, too.

Ophelia stood poised on the black-and-white marble terrace while snowflakes whipped in the frosty wind. Despite the chill in the air, she hesitated.

"Welcome to the Plaza, miss." A doorman dressed in a regal uniform, complete with gold epaulettes on his shoulders, bowed slightly and pulled the door open for her with gloved hands.

A hotel. Artem Drake had summoned her to a *hotel*. Granted, the Plaza was the most exclusive hotel in Manhattan, if not the world, but still.

A hotel.

Did he think she was going to sleep with him? Surely not. She was worried over nothing. He was probably waiting for her in the tearoom or something. Although, as refined as he might be, Ophelia couldn't quite picture him taking afternoon tea.

"Thank you." She nodded politely at the doorman. After all, this wholly awkward scenario wasn't his fault. She wondered if she was supposed to tip him for opening the door for her. She had no clue.

Crossing the threshold into the grand lobby of the Plaza was like entering another world. Another decade. She felt like she'd walked into an F. Scott Fitzgerald novel. The decor was opulent, gilded with an art deco flavor reminiscent of Jay Gatsby.

Ophelia found it breathtakingly beautiful. If she'd known such a place existed less than a mile from her workplace, she would have been coming here every afternoon with her sketchbook and jotting down ideas. Drawings of geometric pieces with zigzag rows of gemstones that mirrored the glittering Baccarat chandeliers and the gold inlaid design on the gleaming tile floor.

Maybe she'd do those designs. If this meeting went as well as she hoped, maybe she'd end up with a job in the design department and she could come here and sketch to her heart's content. And maybe she'd actually see some of her designs come to fruition instead of just taking up space in her portfolio.

She tightened her grip on her slim, leather portfolio. It was Louis Vuitton. Vintage. Another treasure she'd found in her grandmother's belongings. It had been filled to bursting with old photographs from Natalia Baronova's time at the Ballet Russe de Monte Carlo. Ophelia had spent days studying those photos when she'd come home from her time in the hospital.

In the empty hours when she once would have been at company rehearsal dancing until her toes bled, she'd relived her grandmother's legendary career instead. Those news clippings, and the faded photographs with her grandmother's penciled notations on the back, had kept Ophelia going. She'd lost her health, her family, her job. Her life. All she'd had left was school and her grandmother's memories.

Ophelia had clung to those memories, studied those images until she made them her own by incorporating what she saw into her jewelry designs. The result was an inspired collection that she knew would be a success…if only someone would give her a chance and look at them.

She took a deep breath. If there was any fairness at all in the world, this would be her moment. And that *someone* would be Artem Drake.

"May I help you, miss?" A man in a pristine white dinner jacket and tuxedo pants smiled at her from behind the concierge desk.

"Yes, actually. I'm meeting someone here. Artem Drake?" She glanced toward the dazzling atrium in the center of the lobby, where tables of patrons sipped glasses of champagne and cups of tea beneath the shade of elegant palm fronds. Artem was nowhere to be seen.

She fought the sinking feeling in her stomach. *It doesn't mean anything. He could simply be running late.*

"Mr. Drake is in penthouse number nine. This key will give you elevator access to the eighteenth floor." The concierge slid a discreet black card key across the desk.

Ophelia stared at it. She'd never been so bitterly disappointed. Finally, *finally*, she'd thought she'd actually spotted a light at the end of the very dark tunnel that had become her life. But no. There was no light. Just more darkness. And a man who thought she'd meet him at a hotel on her lunch hour just to get ahead.

The irony was that's exactly what everyone in the company had thought when she'd begun dating Jeremy, the director. The other dancers had rolled their eyes whenever she'd been cast in a lead role. As if she hadn't earned it. As if she hadn't been dancing every day until her toes bled through the pink satin of her pointe shoes.

It hadn't been like that, though. She'd cared for Jeremy. And he'd cared for her, too. Or so she'd thought.

"Miss?" The concierge furrowed his brow. "Is there something else you need?"

Yes, there is. Just a glimmer of hope, if you wouldn't mind...

"No." She shook her head woodenly, and reached for the card key. "Thank you for your help."

She marched toward the elevator, her kitten heels echoing off the gold-trimmed walls of the palatial lobby. She didn't know why she was so upset. Or even remotely surprised. She'd seen all those photos of Artem in the newspaper, out every night with a different woman on his arm. Of course he'd assumed she'd want to sleep with him. She was probably the only woman in Manhattan who *didn't*.

Except she sort of did.

If she was honest with herself—painfully honest—she had to admit that the thought of sex with Artem Drake wasn't exactly repulsive. On the contrary.

She would never go through with it, of course. Not now. *Especially* not now. Not *ever*. It was just difficult to think about Artem without thinking about sex, especially since she went weak in the knees whenever he looked at her with those penetrating eyes of his. Eyes that gave her the sense that he could see straight into her aching, yearning center. Eyes that stirred chaos inside her. *Bedroom eyes.* And now she was on her way to meet him. In an actual bedroom.

Bed or no bed, she would *not* be sleeping with him.

The elevator stopped on the uppermost floor. She squared her shoulders and stepped out, prepared to search for the door to penthouse number nine.

She didn't have to look very hard. It was the only door on the entire floor.

He'd rented a hotel room that encompassed the entire floor? She rolled her eyes and wondered if all his dates got such royal treatment. Then she reminded herself that this was a business meeting, not a date.

If she had any sense at all, she'd turn around and walk directly back to Drake Diamonds. But before she could talk herself into leaving, the door swung open and she was face-to-face with Mr. Bedroom Eyes himself.

"Mr. Drake." She smiled in a way that she hoped conveyed professionalism and not the fact that she'd somehow gone quite breathless.

"My apologies, Miss Rose. I'm on the phone." He opened the door wider and beckoned her inside. "Do come in."

Ophelia had never seen such a large hotel room. She could have fit three of her apartments inside it, and it was absolutely stunning, decorated in cool grays and blues, with sleek, modern furnishings. But the most spectacular feature was its view of Central Park. Horse drawn carriages lined the curb alongside the snow-covered landscape. In the distance, ice skaters moved in a graceful circle over the pond.

Ophelia walked right up to the closest window and looked down on the busy Manhattan streets below. Everything seemed so faraway. The yellow taxicabs looked like tiny toy cars, and she could barely make out the people bundled in dark coats darting along the crowded sidewalks with their scarves trailing behind them like ribbons. Snow danced against the glass in a dizzying waltz of white, drifting downward, blanketing the city below. The effect was rather like standing inside a snow globe. Absolutely breathtaking.

"Um-hmm. I see," muttered Artem, standing a few feet behind her with his cell phone pressed against his ear.

Ophelia turned and found him watching her.

He didn't so much talk *to* whoever was on the other end as much he talked *at* them. He sounded rather displeased, but even so, he never broke eye contact with her throughout the call. "Despite the fact that this seems a rather…questionable…time to make such a donation, we must honor our commitment. I know you don't like to involve yourself with the press, brother, but think about the headlines if we backed out. Not pretty. And might I add, it would be my face they'd print a photo of alongside the negative chatter. So that's my final decision."

The person on the receiving end of his tirade was clearly Dalton. Ophelia felt guilty about overhearing such a conversation, so she averted her gaze. No sooner had she looked away than she caught sight of an enormous bed looming behind Artem.

My God, it's a behemoth.

She'd never seen such a large bed. It could have fit a dozen people.

Her face went hot, and she looked away. But as Artem wrapped up his call, her gaze kept returning to the bed and its sumptuous, creamy-white linens.

"Again, my apologies." Artem tossed his phone on the nearby sectional sofa and walked toward her. "Please, let me take your coat. Do make yourself comfortable."

She took a step out of his reach. "Mr. Drake, I'm afraid you've got the wrong impression."

"Do I?" He stopped less than an arm's length away, just close enough to send a wave of awareness crashing over her, while at the same time not quite crossing the boundary of respectability. "And what impression is that?"

"This." She waved a shaky hand around the luxurious room, trying—and failing—to avoid looking at the bed.

Artem followed her gaze. When he turned back toward her, an angry knot throbbed in his jaw. He lifted an impetuous brow. "I'm afraid I don't know what you mean, Miss Rose. Do you care to elaborate?"

"This room. And that bed." Why, oh, why, had she actually mentioned the bed? "When I said I wanted to show you my designs, that was precisely what I meant. I've no idea why you arranged to rent this ridiculous suite. The hourly rate for this room must be higher than my yearly salary. It's absurd, and thoroughly inappropriate. I have no interest in sleeping with you. None. Zero."

She really wished she hadn't stammered on the last few words. She would have preferred to sound at least halfway believable.

Artem's eyes flashed. "Are you quite finished?"

"Yes." She ordered her feet to walk straight to the door and get out of there. Immediately. They willfully disobeyed.

"I live here, Miss Rose. This is my home. I did not, as you so boldly implied, procure a rent-by-the-hour room in which to ravage you on your lunch break." He paused, glaring at her for full effect.

He lived here? In a penthouse at the Plaza?

Of course he did.

Ophelia had never been so mortified in her life. She wanted to die.

Artem took another step closer. She could see the ring of black around the dreamy blue center of his irises, a hidden hint of darkness. "For starters, if my intention was to ravage you, I would have set aside far more than an hour in which to do so. Furthermore, I'm your employer. You are my employee. Despite whatever you may have heard about my father, sleeping with the staff is not the way I intend to do business. Occasionally, the apple does, in fact, fall farther from the tree than you might imagine."

Ophelia had no idea what he was talking about, but apparently she'd touched a nerve. For the first time since setting eyes on Artem Drake—her *boss*, as he took such pleasure in pointing out time and time again—he looked less than composed. He raked an angry hand through his hair, mussing it. He almost looked like he'd just gotten out of bed.

Stop. God, what was wrong with her? She should *not* be thinking about Artem in bed. Absolutely, definitely not. Yet somehow, that was the one and only thought in her head. Artem, dark and passionate, tossing her onto the mammoth-sized bed behind him. The weight of him pressing down on her as he kissed her, entered her...

Her throat grew tight. "Good, because I have no interest whatsoever in sleeping with my boss."

Been there, done that. Got the T-shirt. Never again.

Artem narrowed his gaze at her. "So you mentioned."

Ophelia nodded. She wasn't sure she could manage to say anything without her voice betraying her. Because the more she tried to convince him that she didn't want to sleep with him, the more she actually wanted to. Assuming it was possible to want two very contradictory things at the same time.

But apparently he did *not* want to sleep with her, which was fine. No, not merely fine. It was good. She should be relieved.

Then why did she feel so utterly bereft?

"Now that we've established how ardently opposed we both are to having sex with one another—" His gaze flitted ever so briefly to her breasts, or maybe she only imagined it, since her nipples felt sensitive to the point of pain every time he looked at her "—perhaps you should show me your designs."

Her designs. The very reason she'd come here in

the first place. She swallowed around the lump in her throat. "Yes, of course."

He motioned toward the sleek, dark table in the center of the room. Ophelia opened her portfolio and carefully arranged her sketches, aware of his eyes on her the entire time. She felt every glance down to her core.

He picked up the first of her four large pages of bristol paper. "What do we have here?"

She took a deep breath. *This is it. Try not to blow it any more than you already have.* "Those are a collection of rings. I call them ballerina diamonds."

The subtlest of smiles came to his lips. "Ballerina diamonds? Why is that?"

"Each ring has a large center stone. See? That stone represents the dancer. The baguettes surrounding the center diamond are designed to give the appearance of a ballerina's tutu." She gestured around her waist, as if she were wearing one of the stiff classical tutus that she once wore onstage.

"I see." He nodded.

She allowed herself to exhale while he studied her drawings. She hadn't realized how exposed she would feel watching him go over her designs. These pieces of jewelry were personal to her. Deeply personal. They allowed her to keep a connection to her old self, her former life, in the only way she could.

She wanted him to love them just as much as she did, especially since no one in the design department at Drake Diamonds would even agree to meet with her.

"These are lovely, Miss Rose," he said. "Quite lovely."

"Thank you."

"What do we have here? A tiara? It almost looks familiar." He picked up the final page, the one she was the most nervous for him to see.

"That's intentional. It's a modernized version of the tiara that once held the Drake Diamond."

He grew very still at the mention of the infamous jewel.

Ophelia continued, "As you know, the original tiara was worn by Natalia Baronova. My collection calls for the stone to be reset in a new tiara that would honor the original one. I think it would draw a great number of people to the store. Don't you?"

He returned the sketch to the stack of papers and nodded, but Ophelia couldn't help but notice that his smile had faded.

"Mr. Drake…"

"Call me Artem," he said. "After all, we did nearly sleep together."

He winked, and once again Ophelia wished the floor of his lavish penthouse would open up and swallow her whole.

She cleared her throat. "I want to apologize. You've been nothing but kind to me, and I jumped to conclusions. It's just that I was involved with someone at work once before, and it was a mistake. A big mistake. But I shouldn't have assumed…"

Stop talking.

She was making things worse. But she wanted to be given a chance so badly that she was willing to lay everything on the line.

"Ophelia," he said, and she loved the way her name

sounded rolling off his tongue. Like music. "Stop apologizing. Please."

She nodded, but she wasn't quite finished explaining. She wanted him to understand. She *needed* him to, although she wasn't sure why. "It's just that I don't do that."

He angled his head. "What, exactly?"

"Relationships." Heat crawled up her neck and settled in the vicinity of her cheeks. "Sex."

Artem lifted a brow. "Never?"

"Never," she said firmly. "I'm not a virgin, if that's what you're thinking. It's just not something I do." *Since my diagnosis...*

Maybe she should tell him. Maybe she should just spill the beans and let him know she was sick, and that's why she'd been so adamant about not adopting the kitten. It was why she would never allow herself to sleep with him. Or anyone else. Not that she'd really wanted to...until now. Today. In this room. With him.

She should tell him. Didn't she have an obligation to be honest with her employer? To tell the truth?

Except then he'd know. He'd know everything, and he wouldn't look at her anymore the way he was looking at her now. Not like she was something to be fixed. Not like she was someone who was broken. But like she was beautiful.

She needed a man to look at her like that again. Not just any man, she realized with a pang. *This* man. Artem.

He gazed at her for a long, silent moment, as if weighing her words. When he finally spoke, his tone was measured. Serious. "A woman needs to be adored, Ophelia. She needs to be cherished, worshipped." His gaze dropped to her mouth, and she forgot how to breathe. "Touched."

And, oh, God, he was right. She'd never in her life needed so badly to be touched. Her body arched toward him, like a hothouse orchid bending toward the light of the sun. She wrapped her arms around herself, in desperate need of some kind of barrier.

"Especially a woman like you," he whispered, his eyes going dark again.

She swallowed. "A woman like me?"

Sick? Lonely?

"Beautiful," he whispered, and reached to cup her cheek with his hand.

It was the most innocent of touches, but at that first brush of Artem Drake's skin against hers, Ophelia knew she was in trouble.

So very much trouble.

Chapter Four

It took Dalton less than a minute to confirm what Artem already knew.

"These designs are exceptional." Dalton bent over the round conference table in the corner of their father's office—now Artem's office—to get a closer look at Ophelia's sketches. "Whose work did you say this was?"

Artem shifted in his chair. "Ophelia Rose."

Even the simple act of saying her name awakened his senses. He was restless, uncomfortably aroused, while doing nothing but sitting across the table from his brother looking at Ophelia's sketches. He experienced this nonsensical reaction every time she crossed his mind. It was becoming a problem. A big one.

He'd tried to avoid this scenario. Or any scenario that would put the two of them in a room together again. He really had. After their electrically charged meeting in his suite at the Plaza ten days ago, he'd kept to himself as much as possible. He'd barely stuck his head out of his office, despite the fact that every minute he spent between those wood-paneled walls, it seemed as though his father's ghost was breathing down his neck. It was less than pleasant, to say the least. It had also been the precise reason he'd chosen to meet Ophelia in his suite to begin with.

He'd needed to get out. Away from the store, away from the portrait of his father that hung behind his desk.

Away from the prying eyes of his brother and the rest of the staff, most notably his secretary, who'd been his dad's assistant for more than a decade before Artem had "inherited" her.

Not that he'd done anything wrong. Ophelia was an employee. There was no reason whatsoever why he shouldn't meet with her behind closed doors. Doing so didn't mean there was anything between them other than a professional relationship. Pure business. He hadn't crossed any imaginary boundary line.

Yet.

He'd wanted to. God, how he'd wanted to. But he hadn't, and he wouldn't. Even if keeping that promise to himself meant that he was chained to his desk from now on. He needed to be able to look at himself in the mirror and know that he hadn't become the thing he most despised.

His dad.

Of course, there was the matter of the cat. Artem supposed animal adoption wasn't part of the ordinary course of business. But he could justify that to himself easily enough. Like he'd said, the kitten had been an early Christmas bonus. A little unconventional, perhaps, but not *entirely* inappropriate.

If he'd tried to deny that he wanted her, he'd have been struck down by a bolt of lightning. Wanting Ophelia didn't even begin to cover it. He craved her. He *needed* her. His interest in her went beyond the physical. Beneath her strong exterior, there was a sadness about her that he couldn't help but identify with. Her melancholy intrigued him, touched a part of him he seldom allowed himself to acknowledge.

Any and all doubt about how badly he needed to touch her had evaporated the moment she'd told him that she didn't allow herself the pleasure of sexual companionship. Why would she share something so intimate with him? Even more important, why couldn't he stop thinking about it?

Since their conversation, he'd thought of little else.

Something was holding her back. She'd been hurt somehow, and now she thought she was broken beyond repair. She wasn't. She was magic. Hope lived in her skin. She just didn't know it yet. But Artem did. He saw it in the porcelain promise of her graceful limbs. He'd felt it in the way she'd shivered at his touch.

If he'd indeed crossed a forbidden line, it had been the moment he'd reached out and cupped her face. Something electric had passed between them then. There'd been no denying it, which was undoubtedly why she'd promptly gathered her coat and fled.

Artem had made a mistake, but it could have been worse. Far worse. The list of things he'd wanted to do to her in that hotel room while the snow beat against the windows had been endless. He'd exercised more restraint than he'd known he'd possessed. The very idea of a woman like Ophelia remaining untouched was criminal.

Regardless, it wouldn't happen again. It couldn't. And since he could no longer trust himself to have a simple conversation with Ophelia without burying his hands in her wayward hair and kissing her pink peony mouth until she came apart in his hands, he would just avoid her altogether. It was the best way. The only way.

There was just one flaw with that plan. Ophelia's jewelry designs were good. Too good to ignore. Drake Diamonds needed her, possibly as much as Artem did.

"Ophelia Rose?" Dalton frowned. "Why does that name sound familiar?"

"Because she works here," Artem said. "In Engagements."

Dalton waved a hand at the sketches of what she'd called her ballerina diamonds. "She can do *this*, and we've got her working in sales?"

"*You* have her working in sales." After all, Artem hadn't had a thing to do with hiring her. "I'd like to move her to the design team, effective immediately. I've been going over the numbers. If we can fast-track the production of a new collection, we might be able to reverse some of the financial damage that Dad did when he bought the mine."

Some. Not all.

If only they had more time…

"Provided it's a success, of course," Dalton said. "It's a risk."

"That it is." But what choice did they have? He'd already investigated auctioning off the Drake Diamond. Even if he went through with it, they needed another course of action. A proactive one that would show the world Drake Diamonds wasn't in any kind of trouble, especially not the sort of trouble they were actually in.

Over the course of the past ten days, while Artem had been actively trying to forget Ophelia, he'd been doing his level best to come up with a way to overcome the mine disaster. It had been an effective distraction. Almost.

Time and again, he'd found himself coming back to Ophelia's designs, running his hands along those creamy-white pages of cold-press drawing paper. Obviously, given the attraction he felt toward Ophelia, promoting her was the last thing he should do. Right now, he could move about the store and still manage to keep a chaste distance between them. Working closely with her was hardly an ideal option.

Unfortunately, it happened to be the *only* option.

"Let's do it," Dalton said.

In the shadow of his father's portrait, Artem nodded his agreement.

Ten days had passed since Ophelia had shown Artem her jewelry designs. Ten excruciating days, during which she'd seen him coming and going, passing her in the hall, scarcely acknowledging her presence. He'd barely even deigned to look at her. On the rare occasion when he did, he'd seemed to see right through her. And morning after morning, he kept showing up on *Page Six*. A different day, a different woman on his arm. It was a never-ending cycle. The man went through women like water.

Which made it all the more frustrating that every time Ophelia closed her eyes, she heard his voice. And all those bewitching things he'd said to her.

A woman needs to be adored, Ophelia. She needs to be cherished, worshipped.

Touched.

Ophelia had even begun to wonder if maybe he was right. Maybe she did need those things. Maybe the ache she felt every time she found herself in the company of Artem Drake was real. It certainly felt real. Every electrifying spark of arousal had shimmered as real as a blazing blue diamond.

Then she'd remembered the look on Jeremy's face when she'd told him about her diagnosis—the small, sad shake of his head, the way he couldn't quite meet her gaze. There'd been no need for him to tell her their affair was over. He'd done so, anyway.

Ophelia had sat quietly on the opposite side of his desk, barely hearing him murmur things like, *too much*, *burden* and *not ready for this*. The gravity of his words hadn't even registered until later, when she'd left his office.

Because for the duration of Jeremy's breakup speech, all Ophelia's concentration had been focused on not looking at the framed poster on the wall behind him—the company's promotional poster for the *Giselle* production, featuring Ophelia herself standing en pointe, draped in ethereal white tulle, clutching a lily. She wasn't sure if it was poetic or cruel that her final role had been the ghost of a woman who'd died of a broken heart.

That was exactly how she'd felt for the past six months. Like a ghost of a woman. Invisible. Untouchable.

But when Artem had said those things to her, when he'd reached out and cupped her face, everything had changed. His touch had somehow summoned her from the grave.

She'd embodied Giselle's resurrected spirit dancing in the pale light of the moon, without so much as slipping her foot into a ballet shoe. Her body felt more alive than it ever had before. Liquid warmth pooled in her center. Delicious heat danced through every nerve ending in her body, from the top of her head to the tips of her pointed toes. She'd been inflamed. Utterly enchanted. If she'd dared open her mouth to respond, her heart would have leaped up her throat and fallen right at Artem's debonair feet.

So she'd done the only thing she could do. The smart thing, the right thing. She'd run.

She'd simply turned around and bolted right out the door of his posh Plaza penthouse. She hadn't even bothered to collect her designs, those intricate colored pencil sketches she'd labored over for months.

She needed to get them back. She *would* get them

back. Just as soon as she could bring herself to face Artem again. As soon as she could forget him. Clearly, he'd forgotten about her.

That's what you wanted. Remember?

"Miss Rose?"

Ophelia looked up from the glass case where she'd been carefully aligning rows of platinum engagement rings against a swath of Drake-blue satin. Artem's secretary, the one who'd given her the instructions to meet him at the Plaza a week and a half ago, stood on the other side, hands crossed primly in front of her.

Ophelia swallowed and absolutely forbade herself to fantasize that she was being summoned to the hotel again. "Yes?"

"Mr. Drake has requested a word with you."

A rebellious flutter skittered up Ophelia's thighs. She cleared her throat. "Now?"

The secretary nodded. "Yes, now. In his office."

Not the hotel, his office. Right. That was good. Proper.

It required superhuman effort to keep the smile on her face from fading. "I see."

"Follow me, please."

Ophelia followed Artem's secretary across the showroom floor, around the corner and down the hall toward the corporate offices. They passed the kitchen with its bevy of petits fours atop gleaming silver plates, and Ophelia couldn't help but feel a little wistful.

She took a deep breath and averted her gaze. At least all this was about to end, and she could go back to the way things were before he'd ever walked in on her scarfing down cake. She assumed the reason for this forced march into his office was to retrieve her portfolio.

Although wouldn't it have been easier to simply have someone return it to her on his behalf? Then they wouldn't have been forced to interact with one another at all. He'd never cross Ophelia's mind again, except when Jewel purred and rubbed up against her ankles. Or when she saw him looking devastatingly hot in the society pages of the newspaper every morning. Or the other million times a day she found herself thinking of him.

"Here you go." Artem's secretary pushed open the door to his office and held it for her.

Ophelia stepped inside. For a moment she was so awestruck by the full force of Artem's gaze directed squarely at her for the first time since the Plaza that the fact they weren't alone didn't even register.

"Miss Rose," he said. For a millisecond, his focus drifted to her mouth, then darted back to her eyes.

Ophelia's limbs went languid. There was no legitimate reason to feel even the slightest bit aroused, but she did. Uncomfortably so.

She pressed her thighs together. "Mr. Drake."

He stood and waved a hand at the man sitting opposite him, whom Ophelia had finally noticed. "I'd like to introduce you to my brother, Dalton Drake."

Dalton rose from his chair and shook her hand. Ophelia had never thought Dalton and Artem looked much alike, but up close she could see a faint family resemblance. They had the same straight nose, same chiseled features. But whereas Dalton's good looks seemed wrapped in dark intensity, Artem's devil-may-care expression got under her skin. Every time.

It was maddening.

"It's a pleasure to meet you, Miss Rose," he said, in a voice oddly reminiscent of his brother's, minus the timbre of raw sexuality.

Ophelia nodded, unsure what to say.

What was going on? Why was Dalton here, and why were her sketches spread out on the conference table?

"Please, have a seat." Dalton gestured toward the chair between him and Artem.

Ophelia obediently sat down, flanked on either side by Drakes. She took a deep breath and steadfastly avoided looking at Artem.

"We've been discussing your work." Dalton waved a hand at her sketches. "You have a brilliant artistic eye. It's lovely work, Miss Rose. So it's our pleasure to welcome you to the Drake Diamonds design team."

Ophelia blinked, unable to comprehend what she was hearing.

Artem hadn't forgotten about her, after all. He'd shown her designs to Dalton, and now they were giving her a job. A real design job, one that she'd been preparing and studying for for two years. She would no longer be working in Engagements.

Something good was happening. Finally.

"Thank you. Thank you so much," she breathed, dropping her guard and fixing her gaze on Artem.

He smiled, ever so briefly, and Ophelia had to stop

herself from kissing him right on his perfect, provocative mouth.

Dalton drummed his fingers on the table, drawing her attention back to the sketches. "We'd like to introduce the new designs as the Drake Diamonds Dance collection, and we plan on doing so as soon as possible."

Ophelia nodded. It sounded too good to be true.

Dalton continued, "The ballerina rings will be the focus of the collection, as my brother and I both feel those are the strongest pieces. We'd like to use all four of your engagement designs, plus we'd like you to come up with a few ideas for companion pieces—cocktail rings and the like. For those, we'd like to use colored gemstones—emeralds or rubies—surrounded by baguettes in your tutu pattern."

This was perfect. Ophelia had once danced the Balanchine choreography for *Jewels*, a ballet divided into three parts, *Emeralds*, *Rubies* and *Diamonds*. She'd performed one of the corps roles in *Rubies*.

"Can you come up with some new sketches by tomorrow?" Artem slid his gaze in her direction, lifting a brow as her toes automatically began moving beneath the table in the prancing pattern from *Rubies'* dramatic finale.

Ophelia stilled her feet. She didn't think he'd noticed, but she felt hot under his gaze all the same. "Tomorrow?"

"Too soon?" Dalton asked.

"No." She shook her head and did her best to ignore the smirk on Artem's face, which probably meant he was sitting there imagining her typical evening plans of hanging out with kittens. "Tomorrow is fine. I do have one question, though."

"Yes, Miss Rose?" Artem leaned closer.

Too close. Ophelia's breath froze in her lungs for a moment. *Get yourself together. This is business.* "My inspiration for the collection was the tiara design. I'd hoped that would be the centerpiece, rather than the ballerina rings."

He shook his head. "We won't be going forward with the tiara redesign."

Dalton interrupted, "Not yet."

"Not ever." Artem pinned his brother with a glare. "The Drake Diamond isn't available for resetting, since soon it will no longer be part of the company's inventory."

Ophelia blinked. She couldn't possibly have heard that right.

"That hasn't been decided, Artem," Dalton said quietly, his gaze flitting to the portrait of the older man hanging over the desk.

Artem didn't bat an eye at the painting. "You know as well as I do that it's for the best, brother."

"Wait. Are you selling the Drake Diamond?" Ophelia asked. It just wasn't possible. That diamond had too much historical significance to be sold. It was a part of the company's history.

It was part of *her* history. Her grandmother had been one of only three women to ever wear the priceless stone.

"It's being considered," Artem said.

Dalton stared silently down at his hands.

"But you can't." Ophelia shook her head, vaguely aware of Artem's chiseled features settling into a stern expression of reprimand. She was overstepping and she knew it. But they couldn't sell the Drake Diamond. She had plans for that jewel, grand plans.

She shuffled through the sketches on the table until she found the page with her tiara drawing. "Look. If we reset the diamond, people will come from all over to see it. The store will be packed. It will be great for business."

Ophelia couldn't imagine that Drake Diamonds was hurting for sales. She herself had sold nearly one hundred thousand dollars in diamond engagement rings just the day before. But there had to be a reason why they were considering letting it go. Correction: Artem was considering selling the diamond. By all appearances, Dalton was less than thrilled about the idea.

Of course, none of this was any of her business at all. Still. She couldn't just stand by and let it happen. Of the hundreds of press clippings and photographs that had survived Natalia Baronova's legendary career, Ophelia's grandmother had framed only one of them—the picture that had appeared on the front page of the arts section of the *New York Times* the day after she'd debuted in *Swan Lake*. The night she'd worn the Drake Diamond.

She'd been only sixteen years old, far younger than any other ballerina who'd taken on the challenging dual role of Odette and Odile, the innocent White Swan and the Black Swan seductress. No one believed she could pull it off. The other ballerinas in the company had been furious, convinced that the company director had cast Natalia as nothing more than a public relations ploy. And he had. They knew it. She knew it. Everyone knew it.

Natalia had been ostracized by her peers on the most important night of her career. Even her pas de deux partner, Mikhail Dolin, barely spoke to her. Then on opening night, the company director had placed that diamond tiara, with its priceless yellow diamond, on Natalia's head. And a glimmer of hope had taken root deep in her grandmother's soul.

Natalia danced that night like she'd never danced before. During the curtain call, the audience rose to its feet, clapping wildly as Mikhail Dolin bent and kissed Natalia's hand. To Ophelia's grandmother, that kiss had been a benediction. One dance, one kiss, one diamond tiara had changed her life.

Ophelia still kept the photo on the mantel in her grandmother's apartment, where it had sat for as long as she could remember. Since she'd been a little girl practicing her wobbly plié, Ophelia had looked at that photograph of her grandmother wearing the glittering diamond crown and white-ribboned ballet shoes, with a handsome man kissing her hand. Her grandmother had told her the story of that night time and time again. The story, the diamond, the kiss…they'd made Ophelia believe. Just as they had Natalia.

If the Drakes sold that diamond, it would be like losing what little hope she had left.

"Is that agreeable to you, Miss Rose?" Dalton frowned. "Miss Rose?"

Ophelia blinked. What had she missed while she'd been lost in the past? "Yes. Yes, of course."

"Very well, then. It's a date." Dalton rose from his chair.

Wait. What? A date?

Her gaze instinctively flew to Artem. "Excuse me? A date?"

The set of his jaw visibly hardened. "Don't look so horrified, Ophelia. It's just a turn of phrase."

"I'm sorry." She shook her head. Maybe if she shook it hard enough, she could somehow undo whatever she'd unwittingly agreed to. "I think I missed something."

"We'll announce the new collection via a press release on Friday afternoon. You and Artem will attend the ballet together that evening and by Saturday morning, the Drake Diamond Dance collection will be all over newspapers nationwide." Dalton smiled, clearly pleased with himself. And why not? It was a perfect PR plan.

Perfectly horrid.

Ophelia couldn't go out with Artem, even if it was nothing but a marketing ploy. She definitely couldn't accompany him to the ballet, of all places. She hadn't seen a live ballet performance since she'd been one of the dancers floating across the stage.

She couldn't do it. It would be too much. Too overwhelming. Too heartbreaking. *No. Just no.* She'd simply tell them she wouldn't go. She was thankful for the opportunity, and she'd work as hard as she possibly could on the collection, but attending the ballet was impossible. It was nonnegotiable.

"That will be all, Miss Rose," Artem said, with an edge to his voice that sent a shiver up Ophelia's spine. "Until Friday."

Then he turned back to the papers on his desk. He'd finished with her. Again.

Chapter Five

Ophelia looked down at the ring clamp that held her favorite ballerina engagement design. Not a sketch. An actual ring that she'd designed and crafted herself.

It was really happening. She was a jewelry designer at Drake Diamonds, with her own office overlooking Fifth Avenue, her own drafting table and her own computer loaded with state-of-the-art 3-D jewelry design software. She hadn't used such fancy equipment since her school days, but after spending the morning getting reacquainted with the technology, it was all coming back to her. Which was a good thing, since she clearly wasn't going to get any help from the other members of the design team.

She recognized the dubious expressions on the faces of the other designers. They looked at her the same way the ballet company members had when Jeremy had chosen her as the lead in *Giselle*. Once again, everyone assumed her relationship with the boss was the reason she'd been promoted. Except this time, she had no connection with her boss whatsoever.

At least that's what she kept telling herself.

She did her best to forget about office politics. She had a job to do, after all.

In fact, she'd been so busy adapting to her new reality that she'd almost managed to forget that she was scheduled to attend the ballet with Artem on Friday night. *Almost*. The fact that she wasn't experiencing daily panic attacks in anticipation of stepping into the grand lobby of Lincoln Center was due to good old-fashioned denial. She could almost pretend their "date" wasn't actually going to happen, since Artem had gone back to keeping his distance.

She'd seen him a grand total of one time since their meeting with Dalton. Just once—late at night after the store had closed. Ophelia had stopped to look at the Drake Diamond before she'd headed home to feed Jewel. She hadn't planned on it, but as she'd crossed the darkened showroom, her gaze had been drawn toward the stone, locked away in its lonely glass case. Protected. Untouched.

She'd begun to cry, for some silly reason, as she'd gazed at the gem, then she'd looked up and spotted Artem watching from the shadows. She'd thought she had, anyway. Once she'd swept the tears from her eyes, she'd realized there had been no one else there. Just her. Alone.

Her day-to-day communication at the office was mostly with Dalton. On the occasions when Artem needed something from her, he sent his secretary, Mrs. Burns, in his stead. So when Mrs. Burns walked into Ophelia's office on Friday morning, she wasn't altogether surprised.

Until the secretary, hands clasped primly at her waist, stated the reason for her visit. "Mr. Drake would like to know what you're wearing."

The ring clamp in Ophelia's hand slipped out of her grasp and landed on the drafting table with a clatter. "Excuse me?"

Four days of nothing. No contact whatsoever, and now he was trying to figure out what she was wearing? Did he expect her to take a selfie and send it to him over the Drake Diamonds company email?

Mrs. Burns cleared her throat. "This evening, Miss Rose. He'd like to know what you're planning to wear to the ballet. I believe you're scheduled to accompany him tonight to Lincoln Center."

Oh. That.

"Yes. Yes, of course." Ophelia nodded and tried to look as though she hadn't just jumped to an altogether ridiculous assumption. *Again.*

Maybe the fact that she kept misinterpreting Artem's intentions said more about her than it did about him. It *did*, she realized, much to her mortification. It most definitely did. And what it said about her, specifically, was that she was hot for her boss. Her kitten-buying, penthouse-dwelling, tuxedo-wearing playboy of a boss.

Ugh.

She supposed she shouldn't have been surprised. After all, every woman on the island of Manhattan—and undoubtedly a good number of the men—would have willingly leaped into Artem Drake's bed. There was a big difference between the infatuated masses and Ophelia, though. They could sleep with whomever they wanted.

Ophelia could not. Not with Artem. Not with anyone. The fact that doing so would likely put her fancy new job in jeopardy was only the tip of the iceberg.

"Miss Rose?" Mrs. Burns eyed her expectantly over the top of her glasses.

Ophelia sighed. "Honestly, why does he even care what I wear?"

"Mr. Drake didn't share his reasoning with me, but I assume his logic has something to do with the fact that you're a representative of Drake Diamonds now. All eyes will be on you this evening."

All eyes will be on you.

Oh, God. Ophelia hadn't even considered the fact that she'd be photographed on Artem's arm. At the ballet, of all places. What if someone recognized her? What if they printed her stage name in the newspaper?

Then everyone would know. *Artem* would know.

She swallowed. "Mrs. Burns, do you suppose it's really necessary for me to be there?"

The older woman looked at Ophelia like she'd just sprouted an extra head. "The appearance is part of the publicity plan for the new collection. The collection that you designed."

Right. Of course it was necessary for her to go. She should *want* to be there.

The frightening thing was that part of her did want to be there. She wanted to hear the whisper of pointe shoes on the stage floor again. She wanted to smell the red velvet curtain and feel the cool kiss of air-conditioning in the wings. She wanted to wear stage makeup—dramatic black eyeliner and bright crimson lips. One last time.

She just wasn't sure her heart could take it. Not to mention the fact that she'd be revisiting her past alongside Artem. She didn't want to feel vulnerable in front of him. Nothing good could come from that.

But she didn't exactly have a choice in the matter, did she?

She did, however, have the power to deny his ridiculous request. "Tell Mr. Drake he'll know what I'm wearing when he sees me tonight. Not to worry. I'm fully capable of dressing myself in an appropriate manner for the ballet."

Artem's secretary seemed to stifle a grin. "I'll certainly pass that message along."

Of course, an hour later, Mrs. Burns was back in Ophelia's office with a second request regarding her fashion plans for the evening. Again Ophelia offered no information. She was sure she'd find something appropriate in Natalia's old things, but she couldn't think about it right now. Because thinking about it would mean it was really happening.

Then after lunch, Mrs. Burns was back a third time, with instructions for Ophelia to arrive promptly at

Artem's suite at the Plaza at seven o'clock. Drake Diamonds would send a car to pick her up a half hour prior.

Ophelia wanted to ask why on earth it was necessary to convene at his penthouse beforehand. Honestly, couldn't they just meet at Lincoln Center? But all this back and forth with Mrs. Burns was starting to get ridiculous.

Maybe one day, in addition to her office, her drafting table and her computer, Ophelia would eventually have her own secretary. Then there would be no need to communicate with Artem at all. They could simply talk to one another through their assistants. No lingering glances. No aching need in the pit of her stomach every time he looked at her. No butterflies.

Better yet, no temptation.

Artem glanced at the vintage Drake Diamonds tank watch strapped round his wrist. It read 7:05. Ophelia was late.

Brilliant.

He'd been on edge for days, and her tardiness was doing nothing to help his mood.

For once in his life, he'd exercised a modicum of self-control. He'd done the right thing. He'd kept his distance from Ophelia Rose. Other than one evening when he'd spied her looking at the Drake Diamond after hours, he hadn't allowed himself to even glance in her direction.

And he'd never been so bloody miserable.

She'd seemed so pensive standing in the dark, staring at the diamond, her face awash in a kaleidoscope of cool blues and moody violets reflected off the stone's surface. What was it about that diamond? If the prospect didn't sound so ridiculous, Artem would have believed it had cast some sort of spell over her. She'd looked so beautiful, so sad, that he'd been unable to look away as the prisms of color moved over her porcelain skin.

And when amethyst teardrops had slid down her lovely face, he'd been overcome by a primal urge to right whatever wrong had caused her sorrow. Then she'd seen him, and her expression had closed like a book. Thinking about it as he paced the expanse of his suite, he could almost hear the ruffle of pages. Poetic verse hiding itself away. Sonnets forever unread.

And now?

Now she was late. It occurred to him she might not even show. Artem Drake, stood up by his evening companion. That would be a first. It was laughable, really.

He had never felt less like laughing.

As he poured himself a drink, a knock sounded on the door. Finally.

"You're late," he said, swinging the door open.

"Am I fired?" With a slow sweep of her eyelashes, Ophelia lifted her gaze to meet his, and Artem's breath caught in this throat.

She'd gathered her blond tresses into a ballerina bun—fitting, he supposed—exposing her graceful neck and delicate shoulders, wrapped in a white fur stole tied closed between her breasts with a pearly satin bow. Her dress was blush pink, the color of ballet slippers, and flowed into a wide tulle skirt that whispered and swished as she walked toward him.

Never in his life had he gazed upon a woman who looked so timelessly beautiful.

Seeing her—here, now, in her glorious flesh—took the edge off his irritation. He felt instantly calmer somehow. This was both a good thing and a very bad one.

He shot a glance at the security guard from Drake Diamonds standing quietly in the corner of the room, and thanked whatever twist of fate had provided a chaperone for this moment. His self-control had already worn quite thin. And as stunning as he found her dress, it would have looked even better as a puff of pink on the floor of his bedroom.

"Fired? No. I'll let it slide this time." He cleared his throat. "You look lovely, Miss Rose."

"Thank you, Mr. Drake." Her voice went breathy. As soft as the delicate tulle fabric of her dress.

She'd been in the room for less than a minute, and Artem was as hard as granite. It was going to be an undoubtedly long night.

"Come," he said, beckoning her to the long dining table by the window.

Since they were already behind schedule, he didn't waste time on pleasantries. And chaperone or no chaperone, he needed to get her out of this hotel room before he did something idiotic.

"Artem?" Ophelia's eyes grew wide as she took in the assortment of jewelry carefully arranged on black velvet atop the table. A Burmese ruby choker with eight crimson, cushion-cut stones and a shimmering band of baguettes and fancy-cut diamonds. A bow-shaped broach of rose-cut and old European-cut diamonds with carved rock crystal in millegrain and collet settings. A necklace of single-cut diamonds alternating with baroque-shaped emerald cabochon drops. And so on. Every square inch of the table glittered.

Ophelia shook her head. "I don't understand. I've never seen any of these pieces before."

"They're from the company vault," Artem explained. "Hence the security detail." He nodded toward the armed guard standing silently in the corner of the room.

Ophelia followed his gaze, took in the security officer and looked back up at Artem. "But you're the CEO."

"I am indeed." *CEO.* Artem was beginning to get accustomed to the title, which in itself was cause for alarm. This was supposed to be temporary. "Insurance regulations require an armed guard when assets in excess of one million dollars leave the premises. Think of him as a bodyguard for the diamonds."

The security guard gave a subtle nod of his head.

Ophelia raised a single, quizzical brow. "A million dollars?"

"Of course, if I'd known what you'd planned on wearing tonight, I could have selected just one appropriate item instead of transforming my suite into the equivalent of Elizabeth Taylor's jewelry box."

"Oh." She flushed a little.

Had she been any other woman, Artem would have suspected her coyness to be an act. A calculated, flirtatious maneuver. But Ophelia wasn't just any other woman.

He'd seen her at the office. At work, she was bright, confident and earnest. Far more talented than she realized. And always so serious. Serious, with that ever-present hint of melancholy.

But whenever they were alone together, her composure seemed to slip. And by God, was it a turn-on.

Artem liked knowing he affected her in such a way. He liked knowing he was the one who'd put the pretty pink glow in her cheeks. He liked seeing her blossom like a flower. A lush peony in full bloom.

Hell, he loved it all.

"Wait." Ophelia blinked. "These aren't for me."

"Yes, Ophelia, they are. For tonight, anyway. Just a little loan from the store." He shrugged one shoulder, as if he did this sort of thing every night, for every woman he stepped out with. Which he most definitely did not. "Choose whichever one you like. More than one if you prefer."

Ophelia's hand fluttered to her neck with the grace of a thousand butterflies. "Really?"

"You're representing Drake Diamonds," he said, by way of explanation.

"I suppose I am." She gave a little tilt of her head, then there it was—the smile he'd been waiting for. More dazzling than the treasure trove of jewels at her disposal. "I think a necklace would be lovely."

She pulled at the white satin bow of her little fur jacket. At last. Artem's fingers had been itching to do that since she'd crossed the threshold. He hadn't. Obviously. The diamonds he could explain. Undressing her in any fashion would have stepped over that boundary line that he was still determined not to cross.

He wondered if his father had been at all cognizant

of that line. Had he thought, even once, about the ramifications of his actions? Or had he taken what he wanted without regard to what would happen to his family, his business, his legacy?

Artem's jaw clenched. He didn't want to think about his father. Not now. He didn't want to think about how he himself represented everything that was wrong with the great Geoffrey Drake. Artem Drake was nothing but a living, breathing mistake of the highest order.

And his father was always there, wasn't he? A larger than life presence. A ghost haunting those he'd left behind.

Artem was tired of being haunted. It was exhausting. Tonight he wanted to live.

He gave Ophelia a quiet smile. "A necklace it is, then."

Ophelia had never felt so much like Cinderella. Not even two years ago when she'd danced the lead role in the company's production of the fairy tale.

As for jewels, from the outrageously opulent selection at Artem's penthouse, she'd chosen a necklace of diamond baguettes set in platinum that wrapped all the way around her neck in a single, glittering strand. It fit almost like a choker, except in front it split into three strands, each punctuated with large, brilliant cut diamonds. The overall effect was somehow dazzling, yet delicate.

It wasn't until Artem had fastened it around her neck that he'd told her the necklace had once belonged to Princess Grace of Monaco. Ophelia had been concentrating so hard on not reacting to the warm graze of his fingertips against her skin that she'd barely registered what he'd said. Now, as she sat beside him in the sleek black limousine en route to Lincoln Center, her hand kept fluttering to her throat.

She was wearing Princess Grace's necklace. How was that even possible?

She wished her grandmother were alive to see her right now. Ordinarily, she never let herself indulge in such wishes. Natalia Baronova's heart would break if she knew about the illness that had ended her granddaughter's dance career. But wouldn't she get a kick out of seeing Ophelia dressed in one of her grandmother's vintage gowns, wearing Grace Kelly's jewelry?

She smiled and her gaze slid toward Artem, who was watching her with great intensity.

"Allow me?" he asked, reaching for the bow on her faux fur stole.

Ophelia gave him a quiet nod as he tugged on the end of the satin ribbon. He loosened the bow and opened the stole a bit. Just enough to offer a glimpse of the spectacular diamonds around her neck.

"There," he said. "That's better."

Ophelia swallowed, unable to move, unable to even breathe while he touched her. She'd dropped her guard. Only for a moment. And now...

Now he was no more than a breath away, and she could see her reflection in the cool blue of his irises. He had eyes like a tempest, and there she was, right at the center of his storm. Looking beautiful and happy. Full of life and hope. So much like her old self—the girl who'd danced through life, unfettered and unafraid—that she forgot all the reasons why she shouldn't kiss this man. This man who had such a way of reminding her of who she used to be.

Her heart pounded hard in her chest, so hard she was certain he could hear it. She parted her lips and murmured Artem's name as she reached to cup his chiseled jaw. His eyes locked with hers and a surge of heat shot straight to her lower body. She licked her lips, and there was no more denying it. She wanted him to kiss her. She wanted Artem's kiss and more. So much more.

His fingertips slid from her stole to her neck, down her throat to her collarbone. There was a reverence in his touch, like a blessing. And those words that had haunted her so came flooding back.

A woman needs to be adored, Ophelia. She needs to be cherished, worshipped.

"Mr. Drake, sir, we've arrived." The limo's intercom buzzed, and the driver's voice startled some sense back into Ophelia.

What was she *doing*?

She was letting a silly diamond necklace confuse her and make her think something had changed when, in fact, *nothing* had. She was still sick. And she always would be.

"I'm sorry." She removed her hand from Artem's face and slid across the leather seat, out of his reach. "I shouldn't have… I'm sorry."

"Ophelia," he said, with more patience in his tone than she'd ever heard. "It's okay."

But it wasn't okay. *She* wasn't okay.

As if she needed a reminder, Lincoln Center loomed in her periphery. Inside that building, dancers with whom she'd trained less than a year ago were getting ready to perform, winding pink ribbons around their ankles in dressing rooms filled with bouquets of red roses. Jeremy, the man who'd once asked her to marry him, was inside that building, too. Only he was no longer watching her go through her last-minute series of pliés and port de bras. He was watching someone else do those things. He was kissing someone else's cheek in the final moments before the curtain went up. Another dancer. An able-bodied girl. One who wouldn't have to be carried off the stage when she fell down because she'd lost her balance. One who could do more than three pirouettes before her vision went blurry. One who wouldn't have to give herself injections twice a week and be careful not to miss her daily 8000 IU of vitamin D.

A girl who wasn't broken.

Not that she missed Jeremy. She didn't. She'd confused her feelings for him with her love of dance. If she'd ever had a proper lover, that lover was ballet. Ballet had fed her soul. And now? Now she was starving. Her body needed to move. As did her heart. Her soul.

Artem reached for her hand, but she shook her head and fixed her gaze out the car window, where a group of paparazzi were gathered with cameras poised at the ready.

She couldn't let him touch her again. If she did, there was no telling what she'd do. She was too raw, too tender, too hungry. And Artem Drake was too...

...too *much*.

She'd just have to pretend, wouldn't she? She'd have to act as though the way he looked at her and the things he said didn't make her want to slip out of her fancy dress and slide naked into his lap right there in the back of the Drake Diamonds limousine.

Artem looked at her. Long and hard, until her hands began to shake from the effort it took to keep pretending she was fine. The driver cleared his throat, and Artem finally directed his gaze past her, toward the photographers waiting on the other side of the glass.

"Showtime," he muttered.

Yeah. Ophelia swallowed around the lump in her throat. *Showtime.*

Chapter Six

Artem smiled for the cameras. He made polite small talk. He answered questions about the press release that Dalton had issued earlier in the day announcing the new Drake Diamonds Dance collection. He did everything he always did in his capacity as public relations front man for the company.

It was business as usual. With one very big exception—this time, Ophelia stood beside him.

He'd been attending events like this one for the better part of his adult life, and rarely had he done so alone. Having a pretty woman on his arm went with the territory. Logically, Ophelia's presence shouldn't have made a bit of difference. Logic, however, had little to do with the torturous ache he felt when he placed his hand on the small of her back or cupped her elbow as they walked up the broad steps to the entrance of Lincoln Center. Logic certainly wasn't behind the surge of arousal he'd felt when he'd placed the diamonds around her graceful neck. Logic hadn't swirled between them in the backseat of the car. That had been something else entirely. Some forbidden form of alchemy.

The fulfillment of what had nearly happened in the limousine tormented him. The kiss that wasn't even a kiss. The look in her eyes, though. That look had been as intimate as if she'd touched her lips to his. Perhaps even more so.

He could still feel the riotous beat of her pulse as he'd traced the curve of her elegant neck with his fingertips. Most of all, he could still see the glimmer in her sapphire eyes as she'd reached out to touch his face. Eyes filled with insatiable need. Sweet, forbidden hunger that rivaled the ravenous craving he'd been struggling against since the moment he'd caught her eating that silly cake.

God, what was wrong with him? He was a grown man. A man of experience. He shouldn't be feeling this wound up over a woman he barely knew, particularly one whom he had no business sleeping with.

On some level he loathed to acknowledge, he wondered if what he was experiencing was in any way similar to what his father had felt any of the myriad times he'd strayed. But Artem knew that wasn't the case. His father had been a selfish bastard, with little or no respect for his wedding vows. End of story. Artem wasn't even married, for God's sake. With good reason. He didn't have any intention of repeating the past.

Besides, this attraction he felt for Ophelia was different in every possible way. *She* was different.

Maybe it was her vulnerability that he found so intriguing. Or perhaps it was her unexpected ballsy streak. Either way, this strange pull they felt toward one another was without precedent. That much had become clear in the back of the limousine. With a single touch of her hand on his face, he'd known that she felt it, too. Whatever this was.

And now here they were, in the grand lobby of Lincoln Center, surrounded by people and cameras and blinding flashbulbs. Yet for all the distractions, Artem's senses were aware of one thing and one thing only— the whisper-thin fabric of her lovely dress beneath his hand as he guided her through the crowd. Just a fine layer of tulle between his flesh and hers.

It was enough to drive a man mad.

He somehow managed to answer a few more questions from lingering reporters before handing the usher their tickets and moving beyond the press of the crowd into the inner lobby.

"Welcome, Mr. Drake." The usher smiled, then nodded at Ophelia. "Good evening, miss."

"Thank you," she said, glancing at the ticket stubs as he passed them back to Artem.

Artem kept his hand planted on the small of her back as he led her to the lobby bar. It took every ounce of self-control he possessed not to keep that hand from sliding down, over the dainty, delectable curve of her behind, in plain view of everyone.

Get ahold of yourself.

His hand had no business on her bottom. Not here, nor anyplace else. Things were so much simpler when he could stick to the confines of his office.

Just as Artem realized he'd begun to think of the corner office as his rather than his father's, Ophelia turned to face him. Tulle billowed beneath his fingertips. He really needed to take his hands off her altogether. He would. Soon.

"I haven't even asked what we're seeing this evening. What's the repertoire?" She frowned slightly, as if trying to remember something. Like she had a catalog of ballets somewhere in her pretty head.

Artem hadn't the vaguest idea. Mrs. Burns had handed him an envelope containing the tickets as he'd walked out the door at five o'clock. He examined the ticket stubs and his jaw clenched involuntarily.

You've got to be kidding me.

"Artem?" Ophelia blinked up at him.

"Petite Mort," he said flatly.

"Petite Mort," she echoed, her cheeks going instantly pink. "Really?"

"Really." He held up the ticket stubs for inspection.

She stared at them. "Okay, then. That's certainly… interesting."

He lifted a brow.

"Petite mort means 'little death' in French," Ophelia said, with the seriousness of a reference librarian. She'd decided to tackle the awkwardness of the situation head-on, apparently. Much to Artem's chagrin, he found this attitude immensely sexy. "It's a euphemism for…"

"Orgasm." Artem was uncomfortably hard. In the champagne line at the ballet. Marvelous. "I'm aware."

What had he done to deserve this? Fate must be seriously pissed to have dealt him this kind of torturous hand. Of all the ballets…

Petite Mort.

He'd never seen this performance. In fact, he knew nothing about it. Perhaps it wasn't as provocative as it sounded.

It didn't matter. Not really. His thoughts had already barreled right where they didn't belong. Now there was no stopping them. Not when he could feel the tender warmth of Ophelia's body beneath the palm of his hand. Not when she was right there, close enough to touch. To kiss.

He looked at her, and his gaze lingered on the diamonds decorating the base of her throat. That's where he wanted to kiss her. Right there, where he could feel the beat of her pulse under his tongue. There. And elsewhere.

Everywhere.

His jaw clenched again. Harder this time. *Petite Mort.* How was he supposed to sit in the dark beside Ophelia all night and not think about touching her? Stroking her. Entering her. How could he help but envision what she looked like when she came? Or imagine the sounds she made. Cries in the dark.

How could he not dream of the myriad ways in which he might bring about *her* little death? Her *petite mort.*

"Sir?" Somewhere in the periphery of Artem's consciousness he was aware of a voice, followed by the clearing of a throat. "Mr. Drake?"

He blinked against the image in his head—Ophelia, beneath him, bare breasted in the moonlight, coming apart in his arms—and forced himself to focus on the bartender. They'd somehow already made it to the front of the line.

He forced a smile. "My apologies. My mind was elsewhere."

"Can I get you anything, sir?" The bartender slid a pair of cocktail napkins across the counter, which was strewn with items for sale. Ballet shoes, posters, programs.

Artem glanced at the *Petite Mort* program and the photograph on its cover, featuring a pair of dancers in flesh-colored bodysuits, their eyes closed and limbs entwined. His brows rose, and he glanced at Ophelia to gauge her reaction, but her gaze was focused elsewhere. She wore a dreamlike expression, as if she'd gone someplace faraway.

Artem could only wonder where.

Ophelia had to be seeing things.

The pointe shoes on display alongside the *Petite Mort* programs and collectible posters couldn't possibly be hers. Being back in the theater was messing with her head. She was suffering from some sort of nostalgia-induced delusion.

She forced herself to look away from them and focus instead on the bartender.

"I hope you enjoy the ballet this evening." He smiled at her.

He looked vaguely familiar. What if he recognized her?

She smiled in return and held her breath, hoping against hope he didn't know who she was.

"Mr. Drake?" The bartender didn't give her a second glance as he directed his attention toward Artem.

Good. He hadn't recognized her. She didn't want her past colliding with her present. It was better to make a clean break. Besides, if anyone from Drake Diamonds learned who she was, they'd also find out exactly why she'd stopped dancing. She couldn't take walking into the Fifth Avenue store and having everyone there look at her with pity.

*Every*one or a certain someone?

She pushed that unwelcome question right out of her head. She shouldn't be thinking that way about Artem. She shouldn't be caressing his face in the back of limousines, and she shouldn't be standing beside him at the ballet with his hand on the small of her back, wanting nothing more than to feel the warmth of that hand on her bare skin.

And the repertoire. *Petite Mort.*

My God.

She sneaked another glance at the pointe shoes, mainly to avoid meeting her date's penetrating gaze. And because they were there. Demanding her attention. One shoe tucked into the other like a neat satin package, wound with pink ribbon.

They could have been anyone's pointe shoes, and

most probably were. The company always sold shoes that had been worn by the ballerinas. Pointe shoes that had belonged to the principal dancers sometimes went for as much as two-fifty or three hundred dollars, which provided a nice fund-raising boost for the company.

She told herself they weren't hers. Why would her shoes be offered for sale when she was no longer performing, anyway?

Still. There was something so familiar about them. And she couldn't help noticing they were the only pair that didn't have an autograph scrawled across the toe.

Beside her, Artem placed their order. "Two glasses of Veuve Clicquot Rosé, please."

He removed his hand from her back to reach for his wallet, and she knew it had to be her imagination, but Ophelia felt strangely unmoored by the sudden loss of his touch.

He looked at her, and as always it felt as though he could see straight inside her. Could he tell how fractured she felt? How being here almost made it seem like she was becoming the old Ophelia? Ophelia Baronova. "Anything else, darling?"

Darling.

He shouldn't be calling her darling. It was almost as bad as princess, and she hated it. She hated it so much that she sort of loved it.

"The pointe shoes." With a shaky hand, she gestured toward the pastel ballet shoes. "Can I see them please?"

"Of course, miss." The bartender passed them to her while Artem watched.

If he found it odd that she wanted to hold them, he

didn't let it show. His expression was cool, impassive. As always, she had no idea what he was thinking.

And for once, Ophelia didn't care. Because the moment she touched those shoes, she knew. She *knew*. If flesh had a memory, remembrance lived in the brush of her fingertips against the soft pink satin, the familiar heaviness of the shoe's box—its stiff square toe—in the palm of her hand and the white powder that stull clung to the soles from the backstage rosin box.

Ophelia had worn these shoes.

The ones she now held were custom-made by a shoemaker at Freed of London, as all her shoes had been. A maker who knew Ophelia's feet more intimately than she knew them herself. She remembered peeling back the tissue paper from the box the shoes had come in. She'd sewn the ribbons on them with her own hands. She'd pirouetted, done arabesques in them. She'd danced in them. She'd dreamed in them. They were hers.

She glanced at Artem, who was now busy paying for the champagne, and then fixed her gaze once again on the shoes clutched to her chest. She wanted to see. She needed to be sure.

Maybe she was imagining things. Or maybe she just wanted so badly to believe, she was spinning stories out of satin. Heart pounding, she unspooled the ribbons from around the shoes. Her hands shook as she gently parted the pink material and peered inside. Penned in black ink on the insole, as secret as a diary entry, were the words she most wanted to see:

Giselle, June 1. Ophelia Baronova's final performance.

The pointe shoes in her hands were the last pair of ballet slippers she'd ever worn.

"What have you got there?" Artem leaned closer, and Ophelia was so full of joy at her fortuitous discovery that she forgot to move away.

"Something wonderful." Not until she beamed up at him did she notice the intimacy of the space between them. But even then she didn't take a backward step. She was too happy to worry about self-preservation.

For once, she wanted to live in the moment. Like she used to live.

"I'd ask you to elaborate, but I'm already convinced. Anything that puts such a dazzling smile on your face is priceless as far as I'm concerned." Without breaking eye contact, Artem slid two one-hundred-dollar bills out of his slim leather wallet and handed them to the man behind the counter. "We'll take the shoes, too."

Unlike the kitten incident, Ophelia didn't utter a word of protest. "Thank you, Artem. Thank you very much."

He pocketed his wallet, lifted a brow and glanced curiously at the pointe shoes, still pressed lovingly to Ophelia's heart. "No arguments about how you can't accept them? My, my. I'm intrigued."

"Would you like me to argue with you, Mr. Drake?"

"Never," he said. "And somehow, always."

She shrugged, feigning nonchalance, while her heart beat wildly in her chest. Part of her, the same part that still yearned to kiss him with utter abandon, wanted to tell him the truth. But how could she possibly explain that the satin clutched to her chest was every bit as priceless as the Drake Diamond itself? Maybe even more so.

The pointe shoes her grandmother had worn for her final performance lived in a glass case at the Hermitage in Saint Petersburg, alongside the shoes of other ballet greats like Anna Pavlova and Tamara Karsavina. Ballerinas went through hundreds of pointe shoes during the course of their career. Usually more than a hundred pairs in a single dance season. But none was ever as special as the last pair. The pair that marked the end.

Until this moment, Ophelia hadn't even known what had become of them. She remembered weeping as a nurse at the hospital removed them from her feet the night she'd fallen onstage. Then there'd been the MRIs, the blood tests, the spinal tap. And then the most devastating blow of all. The diagnosis. In all the heartbreak, her pointe shoes had been lost.

Like so much else.

Jeremy must have taken them. And now by some twist of fate, she'd found them again. Artem had bought them for her, and somehow it felt as though he'd given her back a missing part of her heart. Holding the shoes, she felt dangerously whole again.

The massive chandeliers hanging from the lobby ceiling flickered three times, indicating the start of the performance was imminent.

"Shall we?" Artem gestured toward the auditorium with one of the champagne flutes.

Ophelia took a deep breath, suddenly feeling as light and airy as one of the tiny bubbles floating to the top of the glass in his hand. "Lead the way."

They were seated on the first ring in private box seats, which shouldn't have come as a surprise, but somehow did. Ophelia had never come anywhere near such prestigious seating in the theater. When she'd been with the ballet, she always watched performances from the audience on her nights off. But like the other dancers, she'd sat in the fourth ring, at the very tip-top of the balcony. The nosebleed section. Those seats sold for twenty dollars each. She couldn't even fathom what the Drake Diamond seats must have cost. No doubt it was more money than all the dancers combined got paid in a year.

What exactly did tens of thousands of dollars get you on the first ring of the theater? For one, it got you privacy.

The box was closed in all sides, save for the glorious view of the stage. Ophelia sank into her chair with the ballet shoes still pressed to her heart, and her stomach fluttered as she looked around at the gold crown molding and thick crimson carpet. This was intimacy swathed in rich red velvet.

The lights went black as Artem handed her one of the glasses of champagne. His fingertips brushed hers, and she swallowed. Hard.

But as soon as the strains of Mozart's Piano Concerto no. 21 filled the air, Ophelia was swept away.

The music seemed filled with a delicate ache, and the dancers were exquisite. Gorgeous and bare, in their nude bodysuits. There was no hiding in a ballet like *Petite Mort*. There were no fluffy tutus or elaborate costumes. Just the beauty and grace of the human body.

Ophelia had never danced *Petite Mort*. She'd never thought she had what it took to dance such a provocative ballet. It was raw. Powerful. All-consuming. In the way perfect sex should be.

Not that Ophelia knew anything about perfect sex. Or ever would.

No wonder she'd never danced this ballet. How could she dance something called *Petite Mort* when she'd never had an orgasm? Things with Jeremy hadn't been like that. He'd been more interested in the height of her arabesque than the height of passion. She'd never been in touch with her own sensuality. She'd done too much dancing and not enough living. And now it was too late.

She watched the couple performing the pas de deux onstage turn in one another's embrace, legs and arms intertwined, and she'd never envied anyone more in her entire life. Somehow, some way…if she had the chance, she'd dance the hell out of that ballet now.

If only she could.

She felt different about her body than she had before. More appreciative. Maybe it was knowing that she'd never dance, never make love, that made her realize what gifts those things were. Or maybe it was the way the man sitting beside her made her feel…

Like a dancer.

Like a woman.

Like a lover.

Artem shifted in his chair, and his thigh pressed against hers. Just the simple brush of his tuxedo pants against her leg made her go liquid inside. She slid her gaze toward him in the dark and found him watching her rather than the dancers onstage. Had he been looking at her like that the entire time?

Her breath caught in her throat, and the ache between her legs grew almost too torturous to bear. What was happening to her? The feeling that she'd had in the limo was coming back—the desire, the need. Only this time, she didn't think she had the power to resist it. It was the shoes. They'd unearthed a boldness in her. Ophelia Baronova was struggling to break through, like cream rising to the top of a decadent dessert.

The shoes in her hands felt like a sign. A sign that she could have everything she wanted.

Just this once.

One last time.

Another dance. Another chance.

Intermission came too soon. Ophelia's head was still filled with Mozart and dark decadence when the lights went up. She turned to face Artem and found him watching her again.

"What do you think?" he whispered, and the atypical hoarseness in his voice scraped her insides with shameless longing.

Just this once.

"I think when this is over—" she leaned closer, like a ballerina bending toward her partner "—I want to dance for you."

Chapter Seven

A better man would have stopped her.

A better man would have asked the limo driver to take her back to her apartment instead of sitting beside her in silent, provocative consent as the car sped through the snowy Manhattan streets toward the Plaza. A better man wouldn't have selected Mozart's Piano Concerto no. 21 once they'd reached the penthouse and she'd asked him to turn on some music.

But Artem wasn't a better man. And he couldn't have done things differently even if his overindulgent life had depended on it.

Instead he sat in the darkened suite watching as she slipped on the ballet shoes she'd chosen at Lincoln Center, and wound the long pink ribbons around her slender ankles. He could feel the music pulsing dead center in his chest. Or maybe that rhythmic ache was simply a physical embodiment of the anticipation that had taken hold of him since she'd leaned into him at intermission, eyes ablaze, face flushed with barely contained passion.

I want to dance for you.

Artem would hear those words in his darkest fantasies until the day he died.

"Are you ready, Mr. Drake?" Ophelia asked, settling in the center of the room with her heels together, toes pointing outward and willowy arms softly rounded.

So damned ready.

He nodded. "Proceed, Miss Rose."

The lights of Fifth Avenue drifted through the floor-to-ceiling windows, casting colorful shadows between them. When Ophelia began to move, gliding with slow, sweeping footsteps, she looked almost like she was waltzing through the rainbow facets of a brilliant cut gemstone. Outside the windows, snow swirled against the glass in a hushed assault. But a slow-burning simmer had settled in Artem's veins that the fiercest blizzard couldn't have cooled. His penthouse in the sky had never seemed so far removed from the real world. Here, now, it was only the two of them. He and Ophelia. Nothing else.

No other people. No ghosts. No rules.

I want to dance for you.

The moment Ophelia rose up on tiptoe, Artem knew that whatever was transpiring before him wasn't about ballet. This was more than dance. So much more. It was passion and heat and life. It was sex. Maybe even more than that.

The only thing Artem knew with absolute certainty was that sitting in the dark watching the adagio grace of Ophelia dancing for him was the single most erotic moment he'd ever experienced.

It was almost too much. The sultry swish of her ballerina dress, the exquisite bend of her back, the dizzying pink motion of her pointed feet—all of it. Artem had to fight against every impulse he possessed in order to stay put, to let her finish, when all he wanted was to rise out of his chair, crush his lips to hers and make love to her to the timeless strains of Mozart.

To keep himself from doing just that, he maintained a vise grip on the arms of the leather chair. Ophelia fluttered past him on tiptoe with her eyes closed and her lips softly parted, so close that the hem of her skirt brushed against his knee. Artem's erection swelled to the point of pain. Had he been standing, his arousal would have crippled him. Dragged him to his knees. For a moment, he even thought he saw stars. Then he realized the flash of light came from the diamonds around Ophelia's neck.

It didn't occur to Artem to wonder about the shoes or how she'd known they would fit. Nor did he ask himself how she could move this way. Questioning anything about this moment would have been like questioning a miracle. A gift.

Because that's what she'd given him.

Every turn of her wrist, every fluid arm movement, every step of her pink satin feet was a priceless gift. Then she stopped directly in front of him and began a dizzying sequence of elaborate turns, and he swore he could feel the force of each jackknife kick of her leg dead center in his heart. He could no longer breathe.

Artem wasn't sure how long Ophelia danced for him. Somehow it felt like both the longest moment of his life and, at the same time, the most fleeting. He only knew that when the music came to an end, she stood before him breathless and beautiful, with her breasts heaving and her porcelain skin glistening with exertion. And he knew that he'd never witnessed such beauty in his life. He doubted he ever would again.

Without breaking her gaze from his, Ophelia lowered herself into a deep curtsy. At last—at *long* last— Artem rose and closed the distance between them. As gently as he could manage while every cell in his body throbbed with desire, he took her hand in his and lifted her to her feet.

She rose up on the very tips of her toes, so that they were nearly eye level. When she smiled, it occurred to Artem that he'd never seen her so happy, so full of joy. Even her eyes danced.

He glanced down at her feet and the satiny pink ribbons that crisscrossed her ankles in a neat X.

"I used to be a dancer," she whispered, by way of explanation.

Used to be? *Used to be* was ridiculous. Artem didn't know what had happened in her past, but something clearly had. Something devastating. It didn't matter what that something was. He wasn't about to let it steal anything from her. Or make her believe she was anything else less than what she was.

"No." He took her chin in his hand. "Ophelia, you *are* a dancer."

Her eyes filled, and a single tear slipped down her lovely cheek. Artem wiped it away with the pad of this thumb.

He wished he had a bouquet of roses to place in her arms. Petals to scatter at her feet. She deserved that much. That much and more. But all he had to offer was the ovation rising in his soul. So he did what little he could. He brought her hand to his lips and pressed a tender kiss there.

"Artem." With a waver in her voice, she took a backward step, out of his reach.

For a single, agonizing moment, he thought she was going to run away again. To glide right out of the penthouse on her pink-slippered feet. He wouldn't let her. Not this time.

She didn't run, though. Nor did she say a word.

She simply reached her lithe arms behind her and unfastened the bodice of her strapless gown. Artem felt like he lived and died a thousand *petite morts* in the time it took her dress to fall away. It landed on his floor in a whispery puff of tulle, right where it belonged, as far as he was concerned.

She was gloriously naked, save for the diamonds around her neck, just as he'd imagined. Only no fantasy could have prepared him for the exquisite sight of her delicate curves, her rose-tipped breasts and all that marble-white flesh set off to perfection by the glittering jewels and the pink satin ribbons wrapped round her legs.

"Ophelia, my God." He swallowed. "You're beautiful."

* * *

Who is this woman I've become?

By putting on the shoes and dancing again, Ophelia had thought she could be her old self just for a moment. Just for a night. But this bold woman standing in front of Artem Drake and offering herself in every possible way wasn't Ophelia Baronova any more than she was Ophelia Rose. This was someone she didn't recognize. Someone she'd never had the courage to be.

Someone who actually believed Artem when he called her beautiful.

She *felt* beautiful, adorned in nothing but diamonds and pink satin shoes. Beautiful. And alive.

And aching.

She needed him to touch her. Really touch her. She needed it so much that she was on the verge of taking his hand and placing it exactly where she wanted it.

She stepped out of the pile of tulle on the floor and went to him, feeling his gaze hot on her exposed skin. Then she wrapped her arms around his neck, rose up en pointe and touched her lips ever so gently to his.

Artem let out a long, agonized groan, and to Ophelia, the sound was sweeter than Mozart. She'd never had such an effect on a man before. She'd never considered herself capable of it. And now that she knew she could—on this man, in particular—it was like a drug. She wanted to see him lose control, for once. She wanted him as raw and needy as she felt.

She got her wish.

His tongue parted her lips and he kissed her violently. Hard enough to bruise her mouth. He pulled her against him, and it seemed wholly impossible that this could be their first kiss. Their lips were made for this. For worshipping one another.

God, was it supposed to feel this way? So deliciously dirty?

She slid against him, reveling in the sensation of his wool tuxedo against her bare skin. Her eyes fluttered open as his mouth moved lower, biting and licking its way down her neck until he found her nipples. She cried out when he took her breast in his mouth, and a hot ribbon of need seemed to unspool from her nipple to between her legs. In the glossy surface of the snow-battered window, she caught a glimpse of their reflection and was stunned by what she saw—her bare body writhing against Artem, who had yet to shed a single article of clothing.

Before she could bring herself to feel an ounce of shame, he gathered her in his arms and carried her to his massive bed, that blanketed wonderland that had so intimidated her the first time she'd been here. Had it been only fourteen days ago that they'd sworn to one another they had no desire to sleep together?

She'd been lying then. Lying through her teeth. Ophelia had wanted this since the moment she'd set eyes on Artem Drake. No, not *this*. Not exactly. Because she hadn't known anything like *this* existed.

She struggled to catch her breath as Artem set her down on the impossibly soft sheets. Then he leaned over her and kissed her again, with long, slow thrusts of his tongue now, as if his body was telling her they had all the time in the world and he intended to make good use of every wanton second. As his hands found her hair and unwound her ballerina bun, she couldn't stop touching his face—his perfect cheekbones, his chiseled jaw and that secret place where his dimple flashed in those rare, unguarded moments when he smiled. The most beautiful man she'd ever seen, looking down at her as if he'd been waiting for this moment as long as she had. It hardly seemed possible.

He wound a finger in the diamonds around her neck and grinned as wickedly as the devil himself. "My grace."

Ophelia balled the sheets in her fists, for fear she might float away. Everything seemed to be happening so fast, yet somehow not quickly enough. She wasn't sure how long she could survive the heavenly warmth flowing through her. It was beginning to bear down on her. Hot and insistent. Then Artem moved his hand lower, and lower still, drawing a tremulous, invisible line down her body, until with a gentle touch he parted her and slipped his fingers inside her.

"Oh," she purred, in a voice she'd never heard come out of her mouth.

"Ophelia, open your eyes. Look at me."

She obeyed and found him watching her, his gaze filled with dark intention. His hand began moving faster. Harder, until she had to bite her lip to keep from crying out.

Before she knew what was happening, he'd begun kissing his way down her body. And were those really her breasts, arching obscenely toward his mouth?

And were those her thighs, pressed together, holding his hand in place?

Yes, yes they were. Artem's touch had made her a slave to sensation. She'd lost all ability to control her body, this body she'd once moved with such perfect precision.

Then his mouth was poised over her center, and she found she couldn't breathe for wanting.

"Please," she whimpered. *Oh, please.*

She wasn't even sure what she was begging for. Just some kind of relief from this exquisite torture.

"Shh," Artem murmured, and his breath fluttered over her, causing a fresh wave of heat to pool between her legs. It was excruciating. "I'm here, kitten."

Kitten.

Oh, God.

He pressed a tender kiss to the inside of one thigh, then the other, and the graze of his five o'clock shadow against her sensitive, secret places nearly sent her over the edge.

Then his mouth was on her, kissing, licking, tasting, and it was too much. She suddenly felt too exposed, too vulnerable. She was drowning in pleasure, and she knew that if she let it pull her under, there would be no turning back. No forgetting.

How could she return to normal life after this? How could she live the rest of her life alone, knowing what she was missing?

"Relax, kitten," Artem said in a hoarse whisper. He sounded every bit as wild and desperate as she felt. "I want to see you come. Let go."

He slipped a finger inside her again and she closed her eyes, tangled her fingers in his hair and held on for dear life. She didn't want to lose this moment to worry and fear. She wanted to stay. Here.

In this bed.

With this man.

So she did it. She let go. And the instant she stopped fighting it and let the blissful tide sweep her away, she shattered.

Stars exploded behind her eyes and she went completely and utterly liquid. She felt like she was blossoming from the very center of her being, and for the first time, the concept of *petite mort* made sense. *Little death.* Because it was like she'd died and gone someplace else. Somewhere dreamlike and enchanted. She could feel herself throbbing against Artem's hand, and it seemed as though he held her entire life force, every heartbeat she'd ever had, in the tips of his fingers.

And still he lapped and stroked, prolonging her pleasure, until it began to build again. Which seemed wholly unbelievable. She wouldn't survive it again. So soon? Was that even possible?

"Artem," she protested, even as she arched beneath him, seeking it again, that place of impossible light. Wanting him to take her there.

"Yes, kitten?" He pressed a butterfly-soft kiss to her belly and stood.

Ophelia had come completely apart, and there he was. Still fully dressed in a tuxedo, with his bow tie crooked just a fraction of an inch. He looked like he could have just walked out of a black-tie board of directors meeting…aside from the impressive erection straining the confines of his fly.

Ophelia swallowed. Hard. She needed to see him, to feel him.

Now.

She rose up on her knees and ran her hands over the expanse of his muscular chest. He cupped her breasts and pressed a kiss to her hair as she slid her palms under his lapels and pushed his jacket down his arms. It landed on the floor with a soft thud.

"Are you undressing me, Miss Rose?" he growled, and bent to take a nipple in his mouth. That crimson ribbon of need unwound inside her again, and she arched into him.

"I am." She sighed, dispensing with his shirt as quickly as she could manage. One of his cuff links flew off and bounced across the floor. Neither of them batted an eye.

She had no idea what she was doing. She'd never undressed a man in her life, but she was no longer nervous, hesitant or the slightest bit bashful. He'd unlocked something in her. Something no man had ever come close to discovering. Something wild and free.

She unzipped his fly and slid her hand inside, freeing him. He was hard—harder than she'd imagined he could possibly be—and big. Intimidatingly big. But the weight of his erection in her hands sent a thrill skittering up her spine.

She linked her gaze with Artem's and stroked him. He moaned, and his eyes went dark. Dreamy. *Bedroom eyes*, she thought. Watching him watch her as she pleasured him made her head spin. As if she'd done too many pirouettes. Ophelia's pulse pounded in the hollow of her throat, right where Princess Grace's diamonds nestled.

When she bent to take him in her mouth, Artem's hands found her hair. He wound her curls around his fingers and she could feel a shudder pass through him as surely as if it had passed through her own body. After this, after tonight, they would be tied to one another. Forever. Years from now, when her condition grew worse and she could no longer dance or even walk, she would remember this night. She would remember that she had once been cherished and adored. And when she closed her eyes and came back to this bed in her dreams, the face she would see in those stolen moments would be Artem's.

He might forget her someday. He probably would. There would be other women in his life, other mistresses. She wasn't foolish enough to believe that making love to her would change anything for him.

But it would change everything for her. It already had. *He* already had.

"Oh, kitten…" He hissed, and his fists tightened their grip on her hair.

She looked at up him. She wanted to etch this moment in memory. To somehow make it permanent.

He pulled her back up to her knees on the bed and rested his forehead against hers. "I need to be inside you," he whispered.

A knot lodged in her throat. Unable to speak, barely able to breathe, she nodded. *Yes, yes please.*

Then he was on top of her, covering her with the heat of his perfectly hard, perfectly male body. He stroked her face and kissed her closed eyelids as his arousal nudged at her center.

Ophelia had expected passion. She'd expected frenzy. And Artem had given her those things in spades. But this unexpected tenderness was more than she could bear. Then he groaned as he pushed inside, and she realized exactly how unprepared she'd been for the dangers of making love to Artem Drake.

Her pulse roared in her ears.

Remember.

Remember.

Remember.

Then with a mighty thrust, he pushed the rest of the way inside and Ophelia knew there would be no forgetting.

How could she ever forget the way the muscular planes of his beautiful body felt beneath her fingertips, or the glimmer of pleasured pain in his dark eyes, or the catch in her throat when at last he entered her? And the fullness, the exquisite fullness. She felt complete. Whole. Healed.

She knew it didn't make sense, and yet somehow it did. With Artem moving inside her, everything made sense. Because in that moment of sweet euphoria, nothing else mattered. Not her past, not her future, not even her disease. Nothing and no one else existed. Just she and Artem.

Which was the sort of thing someone in love would think.

But she wasn't in love with him. She couldn't be in love. With *anyone*. Least of all Artem Drake.

This was lust. This was desire. It wasn't love. It couldn't be. Could it?

No. Please no. No, no, no.

"Yes," Artem groaned, gazing down at her with an intensity that made her heart feel like it was ripping in half. Two pieces. Before and after.

"Yes," she whispered in return, and she felt herself nodding as she undulated beneath him, even as she told herself it wasn't true.

You don't love him. You can't.

She could feel Artem's heartbeat crashing against hers. She was free-falling again, lost in sensation and liquid pleasure. Her breath grew quicker and quicker still. She looked into his eyes, yearning, searching, and found they held the answers to all the questions she'd ever had. Somewhere behind him, snow whirled in dreamlike motion as he reached between their joined bodies to stroke her.

"Die with me, Ophelia," he whispered.

La petite mort.

Die with me.

With those final words, she perished once again and fell alongside Artem Drake into beautiful oblivion.

Chapter Eight

Artem slept like the dead.

Hours later, he woke to find Ophelia's shapely legs entwined with his and the pink ballet shoes still on her feet. Moonlight streamed through the windows, casting her porcelain skin in a luminescent glow. He felt as though he had a South Sea pearl resting in his arms.

What in the world had happened? He'd done the one thing he'd vowed he wouldn't do.

He wound a lock of Ophelia's hair around his fingers and watched the snow cast dancing shadows over her bare body. God, she was beautiful. Artem had seen a lot of beauty in his life—dazzling diamonds, precious gemstones from every corner of the earth. But nothing he'd ever experienced compared to holding Ophelia in his arms. She was infinitely more beautiful than the diamonds that still decorated her swan-like neck. Thinking about it made his chest ache in a way that would have probably worried him if he allowed himself to think about it too much.

There would be time for thinking later. Later, when he had to sit across a desk from her at Drake Diamonds and not reach for her. Later, when all eyes were on the two of them and he'd have to pretend he hadn't been inside her. Later, when he walked into his office and saw the portrait of his father.

He wasn't Geoffrey Drake. Artem may have crossed a line, but that didn't make him his father. He refused to let himself believe such a thing. Especially not now, with Ophelia's golden mane spilled over his pillow and her heart beating softly against his.

He let his gaze travel the length of her body, taking its fill. Arousal pulsed through him. Fast and hard. What had gotten into him? She'd reduced him to a randy teenager. Insatiable.

He should let her rest awhile. And should remove the pointe shoes from her feet so she could walk come morning.

He slipped out of bed, trying not to wake her, and gingerly took one of her feet in his hands. He untied the ribbon from around her ankle, and the pink satin slipped like water through his fingers. As gently as he could, he slid the shoe off her foot. She let out a soft sigh, but within seconds her beautiful breasts once again rose and fell with the gentle rhythm of sleep.

Artem cradled the pointe shoe in his hands for a moment, marveling at how something so lovely and delicate in appearance could support a woman standing on the tips of her toes. He closed his eyes and remembered Ophelia moving and turning across his living room. Poetry in motion.

He opened his eyes, set her shoe down on the bedside table and went to work removing the other one. It slipped off as quietly and easily as the first.

As he turned to place it beside its mate he caught a glimpse of something inside. Script that looked oddly like handwriting. He took a closer look, folding back the edges of pink satin to expose the shoe's inner arch.

Sure enough, someone had written something there.

Giselle, June 1. Ophelia Baronova's final performance.

Artem grew very still.

Ophelia Baronova?

Ophelia.

It couldn't be a coincidence. That he knew with the utmost certainty. It wasn't exactly a commonplace name. Besides, it explained why the shoes had fit. How she'd known she could dance in them. On some level, he'd known all along. Tonight hadn't been some strange balletic Cinderella episode. These were Ophelia's shoes. They always had been.

It explained so much, and at the same time, it raised more questions.

He studied the sublimely beautiful woman in his bed. Who was she? Who was she really?

He fixed his gaze once again on the words carefully inscribed in the shoe.

Baronova.

Why did that name ring a bell?

"I can explain." Artem looked up and found Ophelia holding the sheet over her breasts, watching him with a guarded expression. Her gaze dropped to the shoe that held her secrets. "It was my stage name. It's a family name, but my actual name is Ophelia Rose. I didn't falsify my employment application, if that's what you're thinking."

Her *employment application*? Did she think he was worried about what she'd written on a piece of paper at Drake Diamonds, while she was naked in his bed?

"I don't give a damn about your employment application, Ophelia." He hated how terrified she looked all of a sudden. Like he might fire her on the spot, which was absurd. He wasn't Dalton, for crying out loud.

"It's just—" she swallowed "—complicated."

Artem looked at her for a long moment, then positioned the shoe beside the other one on the nightstand and sat next to her on the bed. He could deal with complicated. He and complicated were lifelong friends.

He cradled her face in his hands and kissed her, slowly, reverently, until the sheets slipped away and she was bared to him.

This was how he wanted her. Exposed. Open.

He didn't need for her to tell him everything. It was enough to have this—this stolen moment, her radiant body, her passionate spirit. He didn't give a damn about her name. Of all people, Artem knew precisely how little a name really meant.

"Please," she whispered against his lips. "Don't tell anyone. Please."

"I won't," he breathed, cupping her breasts and lowering his head to take one of her nipples in a gentle, openmouthed kiss. She was so impossibly soft.

Tender and vulnerable.

As her breathing grew quicker, she wrapped her willowy legs around his waist and reached for him. "Please, Artem. I need you to..."

"I promise." He slid his hands over her back and pulled her close. Her thighs spread wider, and she began to stroke him. Slow and easy. Achingly so.

She felt delicate in his embrace. As small and fragile as a music-box dancer. But it was the desperation in her voice that was an arrow to his heart.

It nearly killed him.

Which was the only explanation for what came slipping out next. "I'm not really a Drake, Ophelia."

No sooner had the words left his mouth than he realized the gravity of what he'd done. He'd never confessed that truth to another living soul.

He should take it back. Now, before it was too late.

He didn't. Instead, he braced for her reaction, not quite realizing he was holding his breath, waiting for her to stop touching him, exploring him...until she didn't stop. She kept caressing him as her eyes implored him. "I don't understand."

"I'm a bastard," he said. "In the truest sense of the word."

"Don't." She kissed him, and there was acceptance in her kiss, in the intimate way she touched him. Acceptance that Artem hadn't even realized he needed. "Don't call yourself that."

His father had used that word often enough. Once he'd found out about Artem's existence, that is. "My real mother worked at Drake Diamonds. She was a cleaning woman. She died when I was five years old. Then I went to live in the Drake mansion."

Dalton had been eight years old, and his sister Diana had been six. Overnight, Artem had found himself in a family of strangers.

Wouldn't the tabloids have a field day with that information? It was the big, whopping family secret And after keeping it hidden for his entire life, he'd just willingly disclosed it to a woman he'd known for a fortnight.

"Oh, Artem." Her lips brushed the corner of his mouth and her hands kept moving, kept stroking.

And there was comfort in the pleasure she offered. Comfort and release.

Artem didn't know her story. He didn't have to. Ophelia was no stranger to loss. Her pain lived in the sapphire depths of her eyes. He could see it. She understood. Maybe that was even part of what drew him toward her. Perhaps the imposter in her had recognized the imposter in him.

But he couldn't help being curious. Why the secrecy? *Slow down. Talk things through.*

But he didn't want to slow down. Couldn't.

"Kitten," he murmured, his breath growing ragged as he moved his hands up the supple arch of her spine.

She was so soft. So feminine. Like rose petals. And she felt so perfect in his arms that he didn't want to revisit the past anymore. It no longer felt real.

Ophelia was the present, and she was real. Nothing was as authentic as the way she danced. Reality was the swell of her breasts against his chest. It was her tender voice as she whispered in his ear. It was her warm, wet center.

Then there were no more words, no more confessions. She was guiding him into her, taking him fully inside. All of him. His body, his need, his truths.

His past. His present.

Everything he was and everything he'd ever been.

He didn't know what time it was when he finally heard the buzzing of his cell phone from inside the pocket of his tuxedo jacket, still in a heap on the floor. Pink opalescent light streamed through the windows, and he could hear police sirens and the rumble of taxicabs down below. The music of a Manhattan morning.

Artem wanted nothing more than to kiss his way down Ophelia's body and wake her in the manner she so deserved, but before he could move a muscle the phone buzzed again. Then again.

And yet again.

Artem sighed mightily, slid out of bed and reached for his tuxedo jacket. He fished his phone from the pocket and frowned when he caught his first glimpse of the screen. Twenty-nine missed calls.

Every last one of them was from his brother.

Bile rose to the back of his throat as he remembered the last time Dalton had blown up his phone like this. That had been two months ago, the night of their father's heart attack. By the time Artem had returned Dalton's calls, Geoffrey Drake had been dead for more than four hours.

He dialed his brother's number and strode naked across the suite, shutting himself in his small home office so he wouldn't wake Ophelia.

Dalton answered on the first ring. "Artem. Finally."

"What's wrong?" he asked, wondering why Dalton sounded as cheerful as he did. Artem wasn't sure he'd ever heard his brother this relaxed. Relaxing wasn't exactly the elder Drake's strong suit.

"Nothing is wrong. Nothing at all. In fact, everything is right." He paused. Long enough for alarm bells to start sounding in the back of Artem's consciousness. Something seemed off. "You, my brother, are a genius."

Now he was really suspicious. Dalton wasn't prone to flattery where Artem was concerned. Although he had to admit *genius* had a better ring to it than *bastard*. "What's going on, Dalton? Go ahead and tell me in plain English. I'm rather busy at the moment."

"Busy? At this hour? I doubt that." Artem could practically hear Dalton's eyes rolling. At least something was normal about this conversation. "I'm talking about the girl."

Artem's throat closed. He raked a hand through his hair and involuntarily glanced in the direction of the bed. "To whom are you referring?"

The girl.

Dalton was talking about Ophelia. Artem somehow just knew. He didn't know why, or how, but hearing Dalton refer to her so casually rubbed him the wrong way.

"Ophelia, of course. Your big discovery." Dalton let out a laugh. "She's not who we think she is, brother."

So the cat was out of the bag. How in the world had Dalton discovered her real name?

"I know." But even as he said it, he had the sickening feeling he didn't know anything. Anything at all.

"You know?" Dalton sounded only mildly surprised. "Oh. Well, that's good, I suppose. Although you could have told me about her connection to the Drake Diamond before I had to hear about it from a reporter at *Page Six*."

Artem froze.

The Drake Diamond? *Page Six?* What the hell was he talking about?

"I can't believe we've had Natalia Baronova's granddaughter working for us this entire time," Dalton said. "You did a good thing when you recommended her designs. A really good thing. Like I said, genius."

Baronova. No wonder the name had rung a bell. "You mean the ballerina who wore the Drake Diamond back in the forties? *That* Natalia Baronova?"

"Of course. Is there another famous ballerina named Natalia Baronova?" Dalton laughed again. He was starting to sound almost manic.

"Ophelia is Natalia Baronova's granddaughter," Artem said flatly, once he'd put the pieces together.

He remembered how passionately she'd spoken about the stone, the dreamy expression in her eyes when he'd spied her looking at it, and how ardently she'd tried to prevent him from selling it.

Why hadn't she told him?

I can explain.

But she hadn't explained, had she? She'd just said that Baronova had been a stage name. She'd said things were complicated. Worse, he'd let her get away with it. He'd actually thought her name didn't matter. Of course, that was before he'd known her family history was intertwined with *his* family business.

Artem had never hated Drake Diamonds so much in his life. He'd never much cared for it before and had certainly never wanted to be in charge of it. He could remember as if he'd heard them yesterday his father's words of welcome when he'd come to live in the Drake mansion.

I will take care of you. You're my responsibility and you will never want for anything, least of all money, but Drake Diamonds will never be yours. Just so we're clear, you're not really a Drake.

Artem had been five years old. He hadn't even known what the new man he called Father had even meant when he said, "Drake Diamonds." Oh, but he'd learned soon enough.

He should have tendered his resignation as CEO just like he'd planned. It had been a mistake. All of it. He'd stayed because of her. Because of Ophelia. He hadn't wanted to admit it then, but he could now. Now that he'd tasted her. Now that they'd made love.

It was bad enough that she had any connection to Drake Diamonds at all. But now to hear that she had a connection to the diamond... Worse yet, he had to hear it from his brother.

He should have pushed. He should have known

something was very wrong when she'd mentioned her employment application. He should have demanded to know exactly whom he'd taken to bed.

Instead he'd told her things she had no business knowing. Of course, she had no business in his bed, either. She was an employee. Just as his mother had been all those years ago.

Pain bloomed in Artem's temples. He'd been at the helm of Drake Diamonds for less than three months and already history had repeated itself. *Because* you *repeated it.*

"Natalia Baronova's granddaughter. I know. That's what I just said." Dalton cleared his throat. "I've set up a meeting for first thing Monday morning. You. Me. Ophelia. We've got a lot to discuss, starting with the plans for the Drake Diamond."

A meeting with Dalton and Ophelia? First thing Monday morning? Spectacular. "There's nothing to talk about. We're selling it. My mind is made up."

"Since when?" Dalton sounded decidedly less thrilled than he had five minutes ago.

"Since now." It was time to start thinking with his head. Past time. The company needed that money. It was a rock. Nothing more.

"Come on, Artem. Think things through. We could turn this story into a gold mine. We've got a collection designed by Natalia Baronova's granddaughter, the tragic ballerina who was forced to retire early. Those ballerina rings are going to fly out of our display cases."

Tragic ballerina? He glanced at the closed door that

led to the suite's open area, picturing Ophelia, naked and tangled in his sheets. Perfect and beautiful.

Then he thought about the sad stories behind her eyes and grew quiet.

"I'll crunch the numbers. It might not be necessary to sell the diamond," Dalton said. "Sleep on it."

Artem didn't need to sleep on it. What he needed was to get off the phone and back into the bedroom so he could get to the bottom of things.

Tragic ballerina…

He couldn't quite seem to shake those words from his consciousness. They overshadowed any regret he felt. "You mentioned *Page Six*. Tell me they're not doing a piece on this."

Not yet.

He needed time. Time to figure out what the hell was going on. Time to get behind the story and dictate the way it would be presented. Time to protect himself.

And yes, time to protect Ophelia, too. From what, he wasn't even sure. But given the heartache he'd seen in her eyes when she'd asked him to keep her stage name a secret, she wasn't prepared for that information to become public. Not now. Perhaps not ever.

Tragic ballerina…

He'd made her a promise. And even if her truth was infinitely more complicated than he'd imagined, he would keep that promise.

"Why on earth would you want me to tell you such a thing? The whole point of your appearance at the ballet last night was to create buzz around the new collection."

"Yes, I know. But…" Artem's voice trailed off.

But not like this.

"The story is set to run this morning. It's their featured piece. They called me last night and asked for a comment, which I gave them, since you were unreachable."

Because he'd been making love to Ophelia.

"You can thank me later. We couldn't buy this kind of publicity if we tried. It's a pity about her illness, though. Truly. I would never have guessed she was sick."

Artem's throat closed like a fist. He didn't hear another word that came out of his brother's mouth. Dalton might have said more. He probably did. Artem didn't know. And he didn't care. He'd heard the only thing that mattered.

Ophelia was sick.

Ophelia woke in a dreamy, luxurious haze, her body arching into a feline stretch on Artem's massive bed. Without thinking, she pointed her toes and slid her arms into a port de bras over the smooth surface of the bedsheets, as if she still did so every morning.

It had been months since she'd allowed her body to move like this. In the wake of her diagnosis, she'd known that she still could have attended ballet classes. Just because she could no longer dance professionally didn't mean she had to give it up entirely. She could still have taken a class every so often. Perhaps even taught children.

She'd known all this in her head. Her head, though,

wasn't the problem. The true obstacle was her battered and world-weary heart.

How could she have slid her feet into ballet shoes knowing she'd never perform again? Ballet had been her love. Her *whole* life. Not something that could be relegated to an hour or so here and there. She'd missed it, though. God, how she'd missed it. Like a severed limb. And now, only now—tangled in bedsheets and bittersweet afterglow—did she realize just how large the hole in her life had become in these past few months. But as much as she'd needed ballet, she'd need this more. *This*. *Him*.

She'd needed to be touched. To be loved. She'd needed Artem.

And now...

Now it had to be over.

She squeezed her eyes closed, searching for sleep, wishing she could fall back into the velvet comfort of night. She wasn't ready. She wasn't ready for the harsh light of morning or the loss that would come with the rising sun. She wasn't ready for goodbye.

This couldn't happen again. It absolutely could not. No amount of wishing or hoping or imagining could have prepared her for the reality of Artem making love to her. Now she knew. And that knowledge was every bit as crippling as her physical ailments.

I'm not really a Drake, Ophelia.

Last night had been more than physical. So much more. She'd danced for him. She'd shown him a part of herself that was now hers and hers alone. A tender, aching secret. And in return, he'd revealed himself to her. The real Artem Drake. How many people knew that man?

Ophelia swallowed around the lump in her throat. Not very many, if anyone, really. She was certain. She'd seen the truth in the sadness of his gaze, felt it in the honesty of his touch. She hadn't expected such brutal honesty. She hadn't been prepared for it. She hadn't thought she would fall. But that's exactly what had happened, and the descent had been exquisite.

How could she bring herself to walk away when she'd already lost so much?

She blinked back the sting of tears and took a deep breath, noting the way her body felt. Sore, but in a good way. Like she'd exercised parts of herself she hadn't used in centuries. Her legs, her feet. Her heart.

It beat wildly, with the kind of breathless abandon she'd experienced only when she danced. And every cell in her body, every lost dream she carried inside, cried out, *Encore, encore!* She closed her eyes and could have sworn she felt rose petals falling against her bare shoulders.

One more day. One more night.

Just one.

With him.

She would allow herself that encore. Then when the weekend was over, everything would go back to normal. Because it had to.

She sat up, searching the suite for signs of Artem. His clothes were still pooled on the floor, as were hers. Somewhere in the distance, she heard the soothing cadence of his voice. Like music.

A melody of longing coursed through her, followed by a soft knock on the door.

"Artem," Ophelia called out, wrapping herself in the chinchilla blanket at the foot of the bed.

No answer.

"Mr. Drake," a voice called through the door. "Your breakfast, sir."

Breakfast. He must have gotten up to order room service. She slid out of bed and padded to the door, catching a glimpse of her reflection in a sleek, silver-framed mirror hanging in the entryway. She looked exactly as she felt—as though she'd been good and thoroughly ravished.

Her cheeks flared with heat as she opened the door to face the waiter, dressed impeccably in a white coat, black trousers and bow tie. If Ophelia hadn't already been conscious of the fact she was dressed in only a blanket—albeit a fur one—the sight of that bow tie would have done the trick. She'd never felt so undressed.

"Good morning." She bit her lip.

"Miss." Unfazed, the waiter greeted her with a polite nod and wheeled a cart ladened with silver-domed trays into the foyer of the suite. Clearly, he'd seen this sort of thing before.

Possibly even in this very room, although Ophelia couldn't bring herself to dwell on that. Just the idea of another woman in Artem's bed sent a hot spike of jealousy straight to her heart.

He doesn't belong to you.

He doesn't belong to you, and you don't belong to him. One more night. That's all.

She took a deep breath and pulled the chinchilla tighter around her frame as the waiter arranged everything in a perfect tableau on the dining room table. From the looks of things, Artem had ordered copious amounts of food, coffee and even mimosas. A vase of fragrant pink peonies stood in the center of the table and the morning newspapers were fanned neatly in front of them.

"Mr. Drake's standard breakfast." The young man waved at the dining area with a flourish. "May I get you anything else, miss?"

This was Artem's standard breakfast? What must it be like to live as a Drake?

Ophelia couldn't even begin to imagine. Nor did she want to. She would never survive that kind of pressure, not to mention the ongoing, continual scrutiny by the press...having your life on constant display for the entire world to see. Last night had been frightening enough, and she hadn't even been the center of attention. Not really. The press, the people...they'd been interested in the jewelry. And Artem, of course. She'd just been the woman on Artem Drake's arm. There'd been one reporter who had looked vaguely familiar, but she hadn't directed a single question at her. Ophelia had been unduly paranoid, just as she had with the bartender.

"Miss?" the waiter said. "Perhaps some hot tea?"

"No, thank you. This all looks..." Her gaze swept over the table and snagged on the cover of *Page Six*.

Was that a photo of *her*, splashed above the fold? She stared at it in confusion, trying to figure out why in the world they would crop Artem's image out of the picture. Only his arm was visible, reaching behind her waist to settle his hand on the small of her back. A wave of dread crashed over her as she searched the headline. And then everything became heart-sickeningly clear.

"Miss?" the waiter prompted again. "You were saying?"

Ophelia blinked. She was too upset to cry. Too upset to even think. "Um, oh, yes. Thank you. Everything looks wonderful."

She couldn't keep her voice from catching. She couldn't seem to think straight. She could barely even breathe.

The waiter excused himself, and Ophelia sank into one of the dining room chairs. A teardrop landed in a wet splat on her photograph. She hadn't even realized she'd begun to cry.

Everything looks wonderful.

She'd barely been able to get those words out. Nothing was wonderful. Nothing at all.

She closed her eyes and still she saw it. That awful headline. She probably always would. In an instant, the bold black typeface had been seared into her memory.

Fallen Ballet Star Ophelia Baronova Once Again Steps into the Spotlight…

Fallen ballet star. They made it sound like she'd died.

You did. You're no longer Ophelia Baronova. You're Ophelia Rose now, remember?

And now everyone would know. *Everyone.* Including Artem. Maybe he already did.

He'd promised to keep her identity a secret. Surely he

wasn't behind this. Bile rose up the back of her throat. She swallowed it down, along with the last vestiges of the careful, anonymous life she'd managed to build for herself after her diagnosis.

She felt faint. She needed to lie down. But most importantly, she needed to get out of here.

One more night.

Her chest tightened, as if the pretty pink ribbons on her ballet shoes had bound themselves around her heart. There wouldn't be another night.

Not now.

Not ever.

Chapter Nine

Beneath the conference table, Artem's hands clenched in his lap as he sat and watched Ophelia walk into the room on Monday morning. He felt like hitting something. The wall, maybe. How good would it feel to send his fist flying through a bit of Drake Diamonds drywall?

Damn good.

He couldn't remember the last time he'd been as angry as he had when he'd finally ended the call with Dalton and strode back to the bedroom, only to find his bed empty. No Ophelia. No more ballet shoes on his night table. Just a lonely, glittering strand of diamonds left behind on the pillow.

He'd been gone a matter of minutes, and she'd left. Without a word.

At first, he simply couldn't believe it. There wasn't another woman in all of Manhattan who would dare do such a thing. No other woman had even had the chance. Artem had firm rules about sleepovers. He didn't partake in them.

Until the other night.

Nothing about his involvement with Ophelia was ordinary, though, was it? Since the moment he'd first spotted her in the kitchen at Drake Diamonds, he'd found himself doing things he'd never before contemplated. Staying on as CEO. Adopting kittens. Exposing dark secrets. He scarcely recognized himself.

He sure hadn't recognized the man who'd stormed through the penthouse suite, angrily searching for something. A sign, perhaps? Some leftover trinket, a bit of pink ribbon that would ensure that he hadn't imagined the events of the night before. A reminder that it had all been real. That spellbinding dance. The intensity of their lovemaking...

Then he'd seen the newspaper lying on the dining table, and he'd known.

She'd been the cover story on *Page Six*, and the article had been less than discreet. Worse, Ophelia had clearly seen it before he'd had a chance to warn her. The newsprint had been wet with what he assumed were tears, the paper still damp as it trembled in his hands. He must have missed her getaway by a matter of seconds.

"Mr. Drake." Without quite meeting his gaze, Ophelia nodded as she entered the room.

So they were back to formalities, were they? It took

every ounce of his self-control not to remind her that
the last time they'd seen one another, they'd both been
naked. And gloriously sated.

Just imagining it made him go instantly hard, which
did nothing to soothe his irritation.

"Miss Rose," he said, sounding colder than he'd intended. "Or should I call you Miss *Baronova*?"

She went instantly pale. "I prefer Miss Rose."

"Just checking." Artem did his best impression of a
careless shrug.

He did care, actually. That was the problem. He cared
far too much.

Multiple sclerosis.

My God, how had he not known she was sick? How
had he looked into those haunted eyes as he'd buried
himself inside her and not realized it?

Artem was ashamed to admit that although he'd
donated money to the National MS Society and even
attended a few of their galas, his knowledge of the condition was less than thorough. He'd spent a good por-
tion of the weekend online familiarizing himself with
its symptoms and prognosis.

The article in *Page Six* had offered little hope and
predicted that Ophelia would eventually end up in a
wheelchair. Artem found this conclusion wholly beyond his comprehension. The idea that she would never
dance again was impossible for him to accept. And it
made the gift she'd given him all the more precious.

The story alleged she hadn't danced at all since her
diagnosis. Artem hadn't needed to read those words to
know it was true. There'd been something undeniably

sacred about the ballet she'd performed for him. He could still see her spinning and twirling on pink satin tiptoes. As he slept, as he dreamed...even while he was awake. It was all he saw. Day and night.

Dalton had stood as she entered the room. "Good morning, Ophelia," he said now.

"Good morning." She aimed a smile at his brother. A smile that on the surface seemed perfectly genuine, but Artem could see the slight tremble in her lips.

He knew those lips. He knew how they tasted, knew what it felt like to bite into their pillowy softness.

Ophelia's smile faded as she glanced at him, then quickly looked away. Being around him again clearly made her uncomfortable. Good. He'd felt distinctly uncomfortable every time he'd tried to call her since her disappearing act. He'd felt even more uncomfortable when his knocks on her apartment door had gone unanswered. He'd felt so *uncomfortable* he'd been tempted to tear the door off its hinges and demand she speak to him.

He could help her. Didn't she know that? He could hire the best doctors money could buy. He could fix her...if only she'd let him.

Dalton cleared his throat. "We have a few things to discuss this morning."

The understatement of the century perhaps. Although what could Artem actually say to Ophelia with Dalton present? Nothing. Not a damn thing.

Ophelia nodded wordlessly. As angry as he was, it killed him to see her this way. Quiet. Afraid. His arms itched to hold her, his body cried out for her, even if logically he knew it would never happen. She'd made that abundantly clear.

Artem should have been fine with that. He should have been relieved. He didn't want a *relationship*. Never had. He didn't want marriage or, God forbid, children. His own childhood had been messed up enough to turn him off the idea for life. Even if he did want a relationship, she was still his employee. And Artem was *not* his father, recent behavior notwithstanding.

But sitting an arm's length away from Ophelia right now felt like torture. He felt anything but fine.

"I'd like to propose a new marketing campaign for the ballerina collection now that certain, ah, facts have come to light." Dalton nodded.

So he was going right in for the kill, was he? Artem's fists clenched even tighter.

"A new marketing campaign?" Ophelia's eyes went wide, and the panic Artem saw in their sapphire depths took the edge off his anger and softened it a bit. Changed it to something that felt more like sorrow. Deep, soul-shaking sorrow.

"Yes. I'm thinking a print campaign. Artful black-and-white shots, perhaps even a few television commercials, featuring you, of course."

"Me?" She swallowed, and Artem traced the movement up and down the slender column of her throat.

For a moment, he was transfixed. Caught in a memory of his mouth moving down Ophelia's neck. In his mind, he heard the soft shudder of a moan. He felt the tremulous beat of her pulse beneath his tongue. He saw a sparkling flash of diamonds against porcelain skin.

Then he blinked, and he was back in the conference room, with Ophelia appraising him coolly from the opposite side of the table.

If only Dalton weren't present. Artem would tell her exactly how enraged he felt about being ghosted. Or maybe he'd simply lay her down on the smooth oak surface of the table and use his mouth on her until she shattered.

Perhaps he'd do both those things.

But Dalton was most definitely there, and he was talking again. Going on about advertisements in the *Sunday Times* and a special catalog for the holidays. "You'll wear ballet shoes, of course. And a tutu."

Finally, *finally*, Ophelia looked at Artem. Really looked at him. If he'd thought he'd caught a glimpse of brokenness in her gaze before he'd known about her MS, it would have been unmistakable now. Somewhere in the sapphire depths of her gaze, he saw a plea. Someone needed to put a stop to what was happening.

The things Dalton was proposing were out of the question. How could his brother fail to understand that dressing the part of what she could no longer be would kill Ophelia? Artem could almost hear the sound of her heart breaking.

He cleared his throat. "Dalton…"

But his brother wasn't about to be dissuaded so easily. Clearly, he'd been mulling over new marketing strategies all weekend. "You'll wear the Drake Diamond, of course. I'd like to get it reset in your tiara design as soon as possible. You'll be the face of Drake Diamonds. Your image will be on every bus and in every subway station in New York. Possibly even a billboard in Times Square. Now I know you haven't performed in a while, but if you could dance for just a bit, just long enough to tape a commercial segment, we'd be golden."

Artem couldn't believe his ears. Now Dalton was asking Ophelia to dance? No. Just no. Ballet was special to her. Far too special to be exploited, even if it meant saving Drake Diamonds. Maybe Dalton wasn't capable of understanding just what it meant to her, since he'd never seen her dance. But Artem had.

He knew. He knew what it felt like to go breathless at the sight of her arabesque. He knew how just the sight of her arched foot could cause a man to ache with longing. Artem would carry that knowledge to his grave.

And Dalton expected her to dance for him? In a television commercial, of all things?

Ophelia would never agree to it. Never. Even if she did, Artem wouldn't let her.

Over his dead fucking body.

Ophelia did her best to look at Dalton and focus on what he was saying, as ludicrous and terrifying as it was, but he was beginning to look a bit blurry around the edges.

Not now. Please not now.

She hadn't even managed to get back to her own apartment on Saturday morning before her MS symptoms began to make themselves felt. She'd taken a cab rather than the subway, afraid of being spotted in public in her ball gown from the night before. The same ball gown she was wearing on the front page of the morning newspaper. As she'd sat in the backseat of the taxi, biting her lip and staring at the snow swirling out the window while she'd tried not to cry, she'd felt a strange numbness creeping over her.

It had started with her fingertips. Just a slight tingling sensation, barely noticeable at first. She'd stared down at her hands, clutching the pointe shoes she'd almost left behind, and realized she was shaking. That's when she'd known.

She'd been unable to stop the tears when she realized she'd become symptomatic. Fate hadn't exactly been kind to her lately, but this seemed impossibly cruel. Too cruel to believe. Her lips had still been swollen from Artem's kisses, her body still warm from his bed. Why did it have to happen then? Why?

Logically, she knew the answer. Stress.

The doctors had been clear in the beginning—stress could make her condition worse. Even a perfectly healthy body responded to stress, and as Ophelia was only too aware, her body was neither perfect nor healthy. Her medical team had counseled her to build a life for herself that was as stress-free as possible, which was why she'd begun volunteering at the animal shelter. And one of the multitude of reasons why she'd never considered dating. Or even contemplated the luxury of falling in love.

She'd slipped. Once. Only once.

For a single night, she'd forgotten she was sick. She'd allowed herself to live. Really live. And now her life, her secrets, everything she held dear, was front-page news. Something to read about over morning coffee.

All of that would have been stressful enough without the added heartbreak of knowing that Artem would see those words and that he'd never look at her the same way again. Never see her with eyes brimming with desire rather than pity.

It was no wonder her fingertips had gone numb. No wonder she'd fallen down when she'd exited the cab. No wonder the tingling sensation had only gotten worse when Artem had shown up at her apartment and practically beaten down the door, while she'd curled in the fetal position on the sofa with Jewel's tiny, furry form pressed to her chest.

She'd wished then that the numbness would overtake her completely. That it would spread from her fingers and toes, up her arms and legs, until it reached her heart. She wished she could stop feeling what she felt for him.

She missed him.

She missed him with an intensity that frightened her.

So the blurry vision really should have come as no surprise as she sat across from Artem in the Drake Diamonds conference room and listened to his brother's horrifying idea for promoting her jewelry collection.

Dalton wanted her to dance. On television.

"No," Artem said. Calmly. Quietly. But the underlying lethality in his tone was impossible to ignore.

"I beg your pardon?" Dalton said, resting his hands on the conference table.

"You heard me."

Dalton cast a tense smile in Ophelia's direction. "I think the choice is Ophelia's, Artem."

Ophelia cleared her throat. She suddenly felt invisible, which should have been a relief. But there was something strangely disconcerting about the way Artem studiously avoided her gaze, even as he came to her rescue.

Why was he doing this, even after she'd refused to take his calls or see him? She didn't know, and thinking about it made her heart hurt.

"That's where you're wrong, brother. The choice isn't hers to make because there *is* no choice. We're not doing the campaign. We're not resetting the Drake Diamond. It's going up for auction three weeks from today."

Wait. *What?*

Dalton let out a ragged sigh. "Tell me the contract hasn't been signed. Tell me it's not too late to undo this."

Artem shrugged as if they were discussing something as banal as what to order for lunch rather than a priceless gem that glittered with family history. Both his and hers. "The papers are on my desk awaiting my signature, but I'm not changing my mind. Ophelia will not wear your tiara, and neither will she dance in your ad campaign."

Silence fell over the room, so thick that Ophelia could hardly breathe.

She shook her head and managed to utter a single syllable. "Don't."

"Don't?" Artem turned stormy eyes on her. "Are you telling me you actually *want* to go along with this marketing strategy?"

"That's not what I'm saying at all." She slid her gaze to Dalton. "Dalton, I'm sorry. I can't. Won't, actually."

She'd needed to say it herself. The truth of the matter was she didn't need Artem to fight her battles. She could—and *should*—be fighting them herself.

She might be on the brink of a relapse, but she could still speak for herself and make her own decisions. Besides, Artem wouldn't always be there to take her side, would he? In fact, she couldn't figure out why in the world he was trying to protect her now. Other than the obvious—he felt sorry for her. Pity was the absolute last thing she wanted from him.

Exactly what do you want from him?

So many things, she realized, as a lump formed in her throat. Maybe even love.

Stop.

She couldn't allow herself to think that way. Despite his wealth and power, the man had obviously had a tumultuous emotional life. Could she really expect him to take on a wife who would certainly end up a burden?

Wife? *Wife?* Since when had she allowed herself to even fantasize about marriage? She needed to have her head examined.

"I don't understand." Dalton frowned.

"There's nothing to understand. You heard Miss Rose. She isn't dancing, and the diamond is going up for auction. Case closed." Artem stood and buttoned his suit jacket, signaling the meeting was over.

How was everything happening so fast?

"Wait," Ophelia said.

She'd lost her family. And her health. And ballet.

And she'd never have Artem, the only man she'd ever wanted.

But she would *not* lose the Drake Diamond. She

knew Artem would never understand. How could he? But that diamond—that *rock*, as he so frequently called it—was her only remaining connection to her family.

She would never marry. Never have children. Once she was gone, the Baronova name would be nothing more than a memory. She could live with that. She could. But that knowledge would be so much easier to swallow if only something solid, something real, remained. A memory captured in the glittering facets of a priceless jewel. A jewel that generations of people would come to see. People would come and look at that diamond, and they would remember her family.

The Baronovas had lived. They'd lived, and they'd mattered.

"Please, Artem." Her voice broke as she said his name. She was vaguely aware of Dalton watching her with a curious expression, but she didn't care. "Don't sell the diamond. Please."

Her eyes never left Artem's, despite the fact that being this close to him and pretending the memory of their night together didn't haunt her with every breath she took was next to impossible. She'd had no idea how difficult it would be to see him in this context. To sit a chaste distance apart when she longed for his touch. To see the indifference in his gaze when she could all but still feel him moving inside her. It was probably the hardest thing she'd ever done in her life apart from hearing her diagnosis. Maybe even worse.

Because if she'd only taken his calls or answered the door when he'd pounded on it, he wouldn't be looking at her like that, would he? He wouldn't be so angry he couldn't look her in the eye.

"I'm sorry, Miss Rose." But he didn't sound sorry at all.

Then he focused on the floor, as if she was the last person in the world he wanted to see. In that heartbreaking moment, Ophelia understood that pity wasn't the worst thing she could have found in his gaze, after all.

"My mind is made up. This meeting is adjourned."

Chapter Ten

Ophelia was certain Artem would change his mind at some point in the weeks leading up to the auction. He couldn't be serious about selling the diamond. Worse, she couldn't understand why he'd made such a choice. And why didn't Dalton put up more of a fight to keep it in the family?

Granted, the decision was Artem's to make. He was the CEO. The Drake family business was under *his* leadership. Not that he took to the mantle of authority with enthusiasm. After all, he'd been set to resign on the day they'd met.

And now she thought she knew why.

I'm not really a Drake, Ophelia.

She got a lump in her throat every time she thought about the look in his eyes when he'd said those words.

Storm-swept eyes. Eyes that had known loss and longing. Eyes like the ones she saw every time she looked in the mirror.

She and Artem had more in common than she would ever have thought possible.

But if what was being printed in the newspapers was any indication, he had every intention of going through with the sale of the diamond. And why wouldn't he, since he clearly felt no sentimental attachment to it?

She did, though. And now Artem knew exactly how much that diamond meant to her. The fact that he apparently didn't care shouldn't have stung. But it did.

She hated herself for wishing things could be different. She'd slept with Artem. She'd thrown herself at him, naked in both body and soul, knowing it was for only one night. What had she thought would happen?

Not this.

Not the persistent ache deep in the center of her chest. Not the light-headed feeling she got every time she thought about him. Not the constant reminders everywhere she turned.

Artem's face was everywhere. On the television. On magazines. In the papers. Details of the auction were front-page news. Appraisers speculated about the purchase price. Most of them agreed the diamond would go for at least forty-five million. Probably more.

If there was a silver lining to the sale of the diamond, it was that in the excitement over the auction, *Page Six* had all but forgotten about Ophelia. Up until the press release, her photo had been in the paper every day. The paparazzi gathered outside her building and followed her to work in the morning. They followed her to the subway station. They even followed her to her volunteer shifts at the animal shelter. It was beyond unnerving. Ophelia lived in fear of losing her balance and being photographed facedown on the pavement. She knew that was what the photographers were waiting for. A disastrous stumble. A breakdown. An image that showed how far she'd fallen since her glory days as a promising ballerina. Something that would make the readers cry for her. With her.

She was determined not to give it to them. She'd lost Artem. And now she was losing the diamond. She refused to lose her dignity. It was all she had left.

But once news of the auction broke, the mob outside her door vanished. Overnight, she became yesterday's news.

She knew she should be grateful. Or at the very least, relieved. But it was difficult to feel anything but regret as days passed without so much as a word from Artem. Or even a glimpse of him.

He hadn't set foot inside Drake Diamonds since that awful Monday morning in the conference room. Three weeks of silence. Twenty-one days of absence that weighed on her heavier than a fur blanket.

Even on the lonely Friday morning when the armed guards from Sotheby's showed up to remove the Drake Diamond from its display case on the sales floor, Artem had been conspicuously absent. Ophelia couldn't bring herself to watch.

Not until the day of the auction did she finally come to accept that not only was Artem actually going through with the sale of the diamond, but he might never return to Drake Diamonds. She might never see him again. Which was for the best, really. Absolutely it was. She wasn't sure why the prospect made her feel so empty inside.

Because you're in love with him.

No.

No, she wasn't. She was in love with the way he'd made her feel. That was different, wasn't it? It had to be. Because she couldn't be in love. With anyone. Least of all, Artem Drake.

The auction was set to begin at noon sharp, and the store had set up an enormous television screen in the ground level showroom. Champagne was being served, along with platters of Drake-blue petits fours and rock candy in the shape of emerald cut diamonds. It was a goodbye party of sorts, and half of Manhattan had shown up.

Ophelia shut herself in her tiny office and tried to pretend it was a regular workday. Her desk was covered in piles of half-drawn sketches for the new collection she was designing to mirror the art deco motif of the Plaza. But losing herself in her work didn't even help, because Artem's absence was there, too. The memory of their night together lived in the glittering swirl of the pavé brooch she'd finally finished. The unbroken pattern of the diamonds mirrored the whirl of a midnight snowfall, and the inlaid amethysts were as pale pink as her ballet shoes.

Would it always be this way? Was she destined to live in the past? In the grainy black-and-white photos of her grandmother's tiara and in the jewels that told the story of the night she'd made what had probably been the biggest mistake of her life?

Her fingertips tingled and the pencil slipped out of her hand. She tore the sheet of paper from her sketchpad and crumpled it in a ball, but she couldn't even manage to do that properly. It fell to the floor.

Ophelia sat staring at it, and reality hit her. Hard and fast. This was her present. Right here. This moment. Dropping things. Feeling frustrated. Missing someone.

It would also be her future. Her future wouldn't be one of diamonds and dancing or making love while a snowstorm raged against the windows of Artem's penthouse in the sky. It wouldn't be ballet or music or the velvet hope of a darkened theater. Her future would be moments just like this one.

She should never have slept with him.

She'd done what she'd set out to do. She was a jewelry designer at the most prestigious diamond company in North America, if not the world. She'd reinvented herself.

And still, somehow, it wasn't enough.

Artem slipped out of Sotheby's once the bids exceeded twenty million dollars, the sum total of the Drake Diamonds deficit, thanks to dear old dad and his worthless Australian mine.

Ophelia's ballerina diamonds had brought in close to five million in under a month, which was remarkable. Sometimes Artem wondered if it would have been enough. If they'd only had more time.

If...

Artem had never been one to indulge in what-ifs. Since his night with Ophelia, he'd been plagued with them. What if he'd been able to warn her about the article on *Page Six* before she found it herself? What if he wasn't her boss? What if she wasn't sick?

What if he'd never agreed to sell the diamond?

But none of that mattered, did it? Because all those obstacles existed. Now he just wanted to forget. He wanted to forget Drake Diamonds. He even wanted to forget Ophelia. He would have done anything to erase the memory of the way he'd felt when he'd seen her dance. Spellbound. Captivated. And now that night haunted him.

He just wanted out. *Needed* out.

So the moment the bidding escalated and he knew that Drake Diamonds would live to see another day, he left. Walked right out the door, and no one even seemed to notice. Even the reporters gathered at the back of the room were focused so intently on the auctioneer, they didn't see him as he strode past. For the first time in weeks, he slid into the backseat of his town car without being photographed.

"Home, sir?" the driver asked, eyeing him in the rearview mirror.

Artem shook his head. "The store."

"Yes, sir."

It was time to put an end to things. For good.

As expected, the showroom was a circus. The auction was still in progress, apparently, so once again his presence went wholly undetected. Good. He'd go upstairs, leave his letter of resignation on Dalton's desk and set things right. He'd do what he should have done weeks ago, before he'd gotten so hopelessly distracted by Ophelia Baronova.

The tenth floor was a ghost town. For once, there wasn't a single pair of doe-eyed lovers in Engagements trying on rings over champagne and petits fours. Artem wasn't sure whether he found the heavy silence a relief or profoundly sad. Perhaps a little bit of both.

He wasn't sure why he glanced inside the kitchen as he walked past. Probably because that's where he'd first seen Ophelia, where everything had changed. With one look. One word. One tiny bite of cake.

His gaze flitted toward the room, and for a moment, he thought he was seeing things. There she was, in all her willowy perfection, surrounded by champagne flutes and petits fours just as she'd been all those weeks ago. As if somehow his desire had conjured her into being.

He blinked and waited for her image to shimmer and fade, as it always did. Since the night she'd spent in his bed, he'd been haunted. Tormented. She moved through the shadows of his penthouse in balletic apparitions. A ghost of a memory.

He'd intentionally stayed away from the store so he wouldn't be forced to look at her. But still he'd seen her everywhere. So he was almost surprised when she spoke to him, confirming that she was, in fact, real and not just another one of his fantasies.

She said one word. His name. "Artem."

Her voice faltered a little.

He glanced at the petit four in her hand. It trembled slightly, either from nerves or a by-product of her MS. An ache formed in the center of his chest.

He'd once enjoyed toying with Ophelia, rattling her, getting under her skin. That was before he'd seen her so boldly confident when she'd stood before him and let her dress fall to the floor. He wanted that Ophelia back. He didn't want to frighten her. He wanted her fearless and bold. He wanted her breathless. He wanted her bared.

He wanted her.

Still. He always would.

How could she possibly be sick? Time and again, he'd tried to wrap his mind around it. He'd read all the articles about her in the papers. He'd even Googled the coverage of her incident onstage—the sudden fall that had led to her diagnosis. No matter how many times he saw the words in print, he still couldn't bring himself to believe it. It just didn't seem possible that a woman who could dance the way Ophelia had danced for him could have a chronic medical condition. She'd moved with such breathless abandon. How could it be true?

That dance was all he could think about. Even now. *Especially* now, as he stood looking at her in the Drake Diamonds kitchen. Again.

This was where they'd begun. He supposed it was only fitting they should end here, as well.

He just needed to get in and get out, to at *long last* tender his resignation and never set foot in the building again. He'd done what he needed to do. He'd sold the diamond. He'd saved the company.

He wasn't needed at Drake Diamonds anymore. Dalton could take it from here. It's what his brother had always wanted, anyway, and Artem was only too happy to let him.

"We must stop meeting like this, Ophelia," he said, trying—and failing—not to look at her mouth.

"You're back." She sounded less than thrilled. Good. *Get mad, Ophelia. Feel something. Anything.*

He shook his head. "Not really."

She rolled her eyes. "Don't tell me you're quitting again."

"As a matter of fact, that's exactly why I'm here."

She lowered the petit four to the plate in her hand and set it down on the counter. "I was joking."

He shrugged. "I'm afraid I'm not."

How ridiculous that the last conversation they would ever have would be about business. It was absurd.

"You're quitting?" Her voice softened to almost a whisper, but somehow it still seemed to carry the weight of all the words they'd left unsaid. "Is this because…"

Every muscle in Artem's body tensed. "Don't say it, Ophelia." He did *not* want to discuss his illegitimacy. Not here. Not now. "I'm warning you. Don't go there."

"You're the one who should be running this company, Artem. It's your birthright, just as much as it is Dalton's." She rested her hand on his forearm. Her touch was as light as a butterfly, but it was nearly his undoing. If he stayed another minute, he would kiss her. Another five, and he'd be tempted to lay her across the kitchen table.

He shrugged her off. "We're not having this discussion."

"Fine. But you should at least talk to your brother about it before you do something ridiculous like resign."

"You're the last person who should be lecturing me about quitting," he said, knowing even as he did that he was taking things too far. He couldn't seem to make himself stop, though.

"What are you talking about? I'm not the one quitting my job." She jammed her pointer finger into his chest. "You are."

"You're right about that. I'm quitting my job." He crossed his arms. "But you, my darling, have quit everything else. You've quit life."

Her eyes glittered with indignation. "You don't understand."

"Make me, Ophelia. Make me understand." He reached for her hand, but she pulled away.

Then she threw his words right back at him. "We're not having this discussion."

"As you wish." He nodded.

This was better. Anger was better than ache. She didn't want to discuss her illness any more than he wanted to discuss his family history. They had nothing left to say to one another.

Other than goodbye.

He took a deep breath. *Just say it. Say the words. Goodbye, Ophelia.*

"Goodbye, Artem." She brushed past him with an indifference he would have envied if he'd bought it for even a second.

He turned to stop her just in time to see her stumble.

The world seemed to move in slow motion as she lost her footing and fell against the kitchen counter. Artem rushed to her side, but she gripped the counter instead of his arm. She righted herself, then refused to meet his gaze.

"Are you all right?" He regretted the words the moment they left his mouth.

Of course she wasn't all right. She was sick. Nothing about that was right.

"I'm fine," she snapped.

But she didn't look fine. Far from it. Her skin had gone ghostly pale. He had the strangest feeling that she wasn't altogether there. As if in the midst of a conversation, she might fade and disappear.

"Don't." She shook her head. "Do not ask me if I'm all right. And please don't look at me like that."

"Like what?" he prompted. He was looking at her the only way he knew how. Like he missed her.

Because by God, he did. He knew he shouldn't. But he did.

"Like you feel sorry for me. Like I'm this fragile, broken creature that needs to be fixed." She lifted her chin and finally looked him in the eye. "That's not how I want you to see me."

"Your illness is the last thing I see when I look at you, Ophelia. Surely you know that."

She blinked, but her eyes didn't seem to fully take him in.

Artem needed her to hear him. He needed her to understand that he didn't see her as a tragic waif, but as a balletic beauty. Desire personified. Nothing would ever change that. Not even the goodbye that was on the tip of his tongue.

"Artem," she whispered. "I think I…"

Her voice was the first thing to fade away, then her lovely sapphire eyes drifted shut and she fell unconscious into his arms.

Chapter Eleven

She had to be dreaming.

The heat of Artem's body, the rustle of his smooth wool suit jacket against her cheek, the sheer comfort of once again being in his arms…none of it could be real.

She had to be dreaming.

Ophelia fought the instinct to open her eyes. Railed against it. She wanted to linger here in the misty place between sleep and wakefulness, the place where she could dream and dance. The place where things hadn't gone so horribly wrong.

No matter how hard she tried, though, she couldn't seem to stop the sounds of the real world from pressing in—the ding of a bell, a familiar grinding noise and the soothing cadence of Artem's voice.

"Ophelia, wake up. Please wake up."

Her eyes fluttered open, and though things looked hazy, as if she were seeing them through a veil, the familiarity of Artem's chiseled features was unmistakable. Her heart gave a little lurch as she took in the angle of his cheekbones and the sureness of his square jaw.

He was so close she could have reached out and traced the handsome planes of his face with her fingertips, if only she could move. But her arms seemed impossibly heavy. And she couldn't feel her legs beneath her at all. She *wasn't* dreaming, but what on earth was happening?

"Ah, Sleeping Beauty. You've returned." Artem smiled down at her.

He was here. He was smiling. And, oh, God, he was *carrying* her in his strapping arms.

She managed to lift one hand and push ineffectively against his chest. His solid, swoon-worthy chest. "Put me down."

His smile faded, which did nothing to lessen the effect of his devastating good looks. If anything, he was more handsome when he was angry, which was wrong on so many levels.

"No," he growled.

"Artem, I'm serious." Why did her voice sound so slurred?

"As am I. You fainted, and now I'm taking you to the hospital."

Fainted? *Hospital?*

She heard another ringing sound and managed to tear her gaze away from Artem. She recognized the close quarters now—the neat row of numbered buttons, the dark wood paneling, the crystal chandelier overhead. They were standing in the posh elevator of Drake Diamonds. Correction—*Artem* was standing. She most definitely was not.

"Put me down. I'm not letting you carry me through the showroom and out the front door of the store." There were hundreds of people downstairs, including the media.

He glared down at her. "And have you faint on me again? No, thank you."

The fog in her head began to clear, and things started coming back into focus. She remembered sneaking off to the kitchen. It had been the first time she'd set foot in there since the day she'd met Artem. When would she learn her lesson? And just what did the universe have against her indulging in a tiny bit of cake every now and then?

But had it really been a coincidence? Or somewhere deep inside had she been hoping he would come?

"Artem, please." She fought the sob that was making its way up her throat. "The photographers."

His blue eyes softened a bit, and he lowered her gently to her feet. He kept a firm grip on her waist, though, and all but anchored her to his side. "Hold on to me while we walk to the car. My driver is meeting us at the curb."

She nodded weakly. She felt impossibly tired as the reality of what just happened came crashing down on her.

She'd fainted. At work.

She'd fainted only one other time in her life, and that

had been the day her dancing career had ended. Why was this happening again? She was relapsing. It was the only explanation. For weeks now, she'd been experiencing minor symptoms. She'd been so ready to chalk them up to stress. But this was serious. She'd passed out.

In front of Artem, of all people.

The elevator chimed as they reached the ground floor, and he pulled her closer against him. In the final moments before the elevator doors swished open, he took her hand and placed her arm around his waist, all but ensuring they looked like lovers rather than what they were.

What were they, anyway? Ophelia didn't even know.

The doors opened. She blinked against the dazzling lights of the showroom and stiffened, resisting the instinct to burrow into Artem's side.

He whispered into her hair, "Do not let go of me, Ophelia. If you try to walk out of here on your own, I'll turn you over my shoulder and carry you out caveman-style while every photographer in Manhattan snaps your photo. Understood?"

Her cheeks flared with heat. "Fine."

The man was impossible.

And no, she didn't understand. Why was he doing this? Why didn't he just call an ambulance and let the paramedics carry her away on a stretcher? Surely he wasn't planning on actually accompanying her all the way to the hospital? When she'd fainted midperformance at the ballet, not one person had ridden with her to the ER. Not even Jeremy.

She kept her gaze glued to the floor as Artem escorted her across the showroom, through the rotating doors and onto the snowy sidewalk. Beside her, he spoke politely—charmingly even—to the photographers as the shutters on their cameras whirred and clicked. At first she didn't understand why. Then she realized he was putting on a show, distracting them from what was really going on. Everyone would think they were a couple now, but at least she wouldn't look sick and vulnerable in front of the entire world.

The press peppered him with questions. At first, they didn't make sense. Then, as she looked around, she realized what had happened. While she and Artem had been arguing in the kitchen, the auction had ended.

"Mr. Drake, do you have anything to say about the auction? Are you happy with the purchase price of fifty-six million?"

"How do you feel about the Drake Diamond moving to Mexico City?"

Mexico City? The diamond wouldn't even be in the country anymore.

Ophelia's knees began to grow weak as they approached the car. Artem's driver held the door open and she slid across the bench seat of the limousine. Artem followed right behind and eyed her with concern as she exhaled a deep breath and sank into the buttery leather.

Snowflakes swirled against the car windows and her heart suddenly felt like it could beat right out of her chest. This—Artem, the snow, the unexpected intimacy of the moment—stirred up every memory she'd been fighting so hard to repress, and brought them once again into sharp focus. She couldn't be here. Not with him. Not again.

"Artem." She would tell him to leave. To just go back inside and let the driver drop her off at the hospital. She'd be fine. She'd done this before all by herself. Why should this time be any different?

"Ophelia." He reached and cupped her cheek, and despite her best intentions, she let her head fall into the warmth of his touch.

She went liquid, as liquid as the sea, powerless to fight his pull. Because Artem was as beautiful as the moon, and whatever this was between them felt an awful lot like gravity.

"Thank you," she whispered.

Artem paced back and forth in Ophelia's hospital room, unable to sit still. At least he'd managed to get her immediately moved to a private room rather than the closet-sized space where they'd originally placed her. He'd walked in, taken a look around and marched right back out.

If she suspected his influence was behind her relocation to more acceptable surroundings, she didn't mention it. Then again, she wasn't exactly in fighting form at the moment. Case in point—she hadn't tried to kick him out of her room yet, which was for the best. Artem would rather avoid a nasty scene, and he had no intention of leaving her here. Alone.

She looked as beautiful as ever, asleep on the examination table with her waves of blond hair spilled on the pillow like spun gold. She looked like Sleeping Beauty, awaiting the kiss that would bring her back to life. The comparison brought an ache to Artem's gut.

She'd scared the hell out of him when she'd fainted. His heart had all but stopped the moment she slumped into his arms. He needed to know she was okay before he even thought about walking out the door.

Or out of her life.

But she wasn't okay. MS didn't simply go away. Artem could throw all the money he had at the situation, and it wouldn't do a bit of good. He'd never felt so helpless, so out of control, in his life. It didn't sit well. He'd thought he could fix this, if only she'd let him. Now he realized how very wrong he'd been.

The door opened, and a nurse in blue scrubs walked in. "Miss Rose?"

"She's sleeping," Artem said.

"I just have a few questions." The nurse smiled.

Artem did not.

They'd already listened to her heart, taken her pulse and filled up three vials with her blood. He was ready for answers or, at the very least, a conversation with an actual doctor.

He forced himself to quit pacing and stand still. "Is that really necessary?"

"I'm afraid so, Mr, ah…" She flipped through the folder in her hand until her gaze landed on a name. "…Davis."

Artem lifted a brow. "I beg your pardon. Who?"

"Miss Rose's emergency contact. Mr. Jeremy Davis. I'm sorry. I assumed that was you." She frowned down at the papers in her hand. Clearly, the staffers in the emergency room hadn't filled her in on Artem's identity, which probably would have irritated him if he hadn't been momentarily distracted by being called by another man's name. "Shall I give Mr. Davis a call?"

"No." Ophelia, awake now, sat bolt upright on the exam table. "Absolutely not. In fact, take his name off my paperwork."

Artem crossed his arms and regarded her as she studiously avoided his gaze.

The nurse made a few notes and then looked back up as her pen hovered over the page. "Whose name would you like to write down in place of Mr. Davis?"

"Um…" Ophelia cleared her throat. "Can we just leave that space blank for now? Please?"

The nurse shook her head. "I'm afraid we must have an emergency contact. It's hospital policy."

"Oh." Ophelia stared down at her lap. "In that case, um…"

"Allow me." Artem reached for the nurse's clipboard and pen.

"Artem, don't." Ophelia struggled to her feet.

"Sit. Down." His command came out more sternly than he'd intended, but he'd already had enough of a fright without watching her faint again and hitting her head on the hospital's tile floor.

Ophelia sat and fumed in silence while Artem finished scribbling his name and number, then thrust the clipboard back at the nurse. "Done. Now when can we talk to the doctor?"

He didn't want to think about why he thought it only proper that he should be Ophelia's emergency contact.

Nor did he want to contemplate the identity of Jeremy Davis. He just wanted to make Ophelia better.

What in the world was he doing? He'd never taken care of anyone in his life. He'd certainly never been anyone's emergency contact. Not even for his siblings. The truth of the matter was he'd carefully arranged his life in a way to avoid this kind of obligation. He'd had enough of those. He'd been an obligation his entire life—the child the Drakes had accepted because they'd had to. It was easier to remain entirely self-contained.

Except Ophelia didn't feel like a chore. She felt more like a need he couldn't quite understand.

This wasn't him.

"The doctor will be by any minute. We're just waiting on some test results from the lab." The nurse turned her attention back to Ophelia. "Can you tell me more about your symptoms? Have you been experiencing any dizziness before this morning?"

Ophelia nodded. "A little."

This was the moment he should leave. Or at the very least, step into the hallway. He'd delivered Ophelia to the hospital. He'd seen to it that she would have the best care money could buy. But in reality, her health was none of his business.

He glanced at her, fully expecting to be given his marching orders. She'd certainly never minced words with him before, which made it all the more poignant when she said nothing, but instead looked back at him with eyes as big as saucers.

She was afraid.

She was afraid, and if he left her now, she'd be sitting

in this sterile room in her flimsy paper gown, waiting for bad news all alone.

Artem felt an odd stirring in his chest. He sat beside her on the examination table and took her hand in his.

The nurse pressed on with more questions. "Any other problems associated with your MS? Tingling? Numbness?"

"Yes." Beside him, Ophelia swallowed. "And yes. In my hands mostly."

Artem stared down at their interlocked fingers He'd had no idea she'd become symptomatic. Then again, since their night together he'd seen her only once—at that awkward meeting in the conference room.

"And how long has this been going on?" the nurse asked.

"Three weeks ago last Saturday," she said, with an unmistakable note of certainty in her tone.

Three weeks ago last Saturday. The morning after. That dark winter morning when everything had spun so wildly out of control.

Shit.

Artem felt like pummeling somebody. Possibly himself. The nurse gathered more information, but he could barely concentrate on what was being said. When she'd finally filled what seemed like a ream of paper with notes, she flipped her folder closed and left the room.

Before the door even clicked shut behind her, Ophelia cleared her throat. Artem knew what was coming before she said the words.

"You don't have to stay. I mean, thank you for everything you've done. But I understand. You don't want to be here, and that's fine. I don't blame you." She let out a laugh. "I don't want to be here myself."

"Stop," he said.

"What?"

He reached for her chin, held it in place and forced her to look at him. "Stop telling me how I feel. I'll leave when I'm good and ready. Not a minute before. Understood?"

She narrowed her gaze and prepared to argue, which he'd fully expected. Things that had perplexed and frustrated him before were beginning to make more sense—her reluctance to adopt the kitten, her abrupt announcement on the first day she'd set foot in his penthouse that she didn't have relationships. Or sex. Something...or some*one*...had convinced Ophelia that having a medical condition meant she had to close herself off from the rest of the world. He could see it now, as clear and sharp as a diamond.

Of course, that made it no less frustrating.

"I—" she started.

He cut her off, ready to get to the crux of the matter. "Who is Jeremy Davis?"

She lifted an irritated brow. He'd struck a nerve. Good. An angry Ophelia was far preferable to a frightened Ophelia.

"He's the director of the ballet company," she said primly.

"*And* your emergency contact?" he prompted, noting—to his complete and utter horror—how very much he sounded like a jealous boyfriend.

"Yes." She waited a beat, then added, "And my former fiancé."

"Fiancé?" Now he didn't just sound like a jealous boyfriend. He felt like one, too. Except he didn't have any claim on Ophelia. He had no right at all to these unwelcome feelings that had taken hold of him.

He wasn't sure why people called it the green-eyed monster. While indeed monstrous, there was nothing green about it. His mood was as black as ebony. "What happened? Why didn't you marry him?"

"Isn't it obvious?" She gestured toward their sterile surroundings. "It was for the best, really. I didn't love him. I thought I did, but it wasn't love. I know that now."

If the idiot named Jeremy Davis had been standing beside them, Artem would have given the man a good reason to make use of the hospital's facilities. He didn't need to know what Ophelia's former fiancé had said or what, exactly, he'd done. He didn't need to know anything else at all, frankly. The truth was written all over Ophelia's face. It showed in the way she locked herself away from the world.

He'd hurt her.

Maybe Ophelia's biggest problem wasn't her MS. Maybe it was her past.

Yet another thing they had in common.

"I'm sorry," he whispered, and gave her hand a tender squeeze.

"For what?" The quaver in her voice nearly slayed him.

"For everything."

He meant it. Every damn thing. He was sorry for not

trying harder to reach her after the news of her medical condition became a front-page story. He was sorry he hadn't forced her to see him. He was sorry for selling the diamond, when he knew how much it meant to her. He should have found a way to keep it, to let her hold on to just one thing.

But most of all he was sorry for every bad thing that had ever happened to her. He was sorry for the past, both hers and his, and the way it seemed to overshadow everything. Never had he wanted so badly to let it all go.

The door swung open. A woman in a white coat entered and extended her hand toward Ophelia. "Miss Rose, I'm Dr. April Larson."

"Hello." She shook the doctor's hand and gestured toward Artem. "This is Artem Drake, my, ah…"

"Emergency contact," he said, and smiled.

"Wonderful. It's great to meet you both." Dr. Larson sat on the stool facing them and spread a folder open on her lap. "So, Ophelia. You had a fainting spell this morning? How are you feeling now?"

Beside him, Ophelia took a deep breath. "A little tired, actually."

Dr. Larson nodded. "That's completely normal, given your condition."

"My condition. Right." She smiled, but it didn't reach her eyes.

The doctor nodded again. "I'm afraid so. You need to get some rest, Ophelia. And I would suggest that you avoid stress as much as possible. There's not much else we can do for you."

"I see. So it's that bad, is it? The symptoms I've been

experiencing and the fainting…" She blinked back tears. "I'm no longer in remission. I'm relapsing. This is only the beginning. It's going to get worse, much worse. Just like last time. I'm on the verge of a full-blown MS attack. Is that what's happening?"

"What?" The doctor leaned forward and placed a comforting hand on her knee. "No, not at all."

Ophelia shook her head. "I don't understand."

But Artem did.

The godforsaken past was repeating itself. And this time, it was all his doing. He had no one to blame but himself. It wasn't enough to sit at his father's desk and run his father's company. How had he let this happen? How had he actually allowed himself to become the man he most despised?

The doctor smiled. *Don't say it. Do* not. "You're not relapsing, Ophelia. You're pregnant."

Chapter Twelve

*P*regnant?

Ophelia couldn't believe what she was hearing. There had been a mistake. Of course there had. She couldn't possibly be pregnant.

With *Artem's* child.

She couldn't even bring herself to look at him. He'd gone deadly silent beside her. She could feel the tension rolling off him in waves. She wished he were somewhere else. *Anyplace* else, so she could have had an opportunity to figure out how and when to tell him. Or *if* she would have told him.

But she would have. Of course she would. Having someone's child was too important to keep secret.

A child.

She couldn't have a child! "But I'm on birth control

pills. I've been on them since my diagnosis. My primary physician said there was evidence that the hormones in oral contraceptives helped delay the onset of certain MS symptoms."

She'd never imagined she'd use them for actual birth control. But still. They were called *birth control pills* for a reason, weren't they?

Dr. Larson eyed Ophelia over the top of her glasses. "Did your primary doctor also tell you that your MS medications could decrease the effectiveness of oral contraceptives?"

"No." Of course not. She would have remembered an important detail like that. Or would she? She'd decided never to have sex again. And if she'd stuck to that decision—as she so clearly should have—that detail wouldn't have been so important. It wouldn't have mattered at all.

She dropped her head in her hands. "I don't know. It's possible. I hadn't planned on—" Goodness, this was mortifying. How could she have this discussion with Artem right here, seething quietly beside her? "—meeting anyone."

"Well, the heart has its own ideas, doesn't it? Congratulations." Dr. Larson smiled and shot a wink in Artem's direction. "To you both."

Obviously, the doctor had seen past Artem's introduction as her emergency contact and detected there was something more between them. Even though there wasn't. Other than the fact that he was apparently the *father of her unborn child.*

Ophelia felt faint again, but this time she knew it was

just psychological. She'd been so sure she was relapsing. She almost wished she were. How could she possibly raise a child? And what about the physical demands of pregnancy? Could she even do this?

According to what the doctor was saying, yes. Of course she could. She was even talking about how pregnancy frequently eased MS symptoms. Women with MS had children every day. Dr. Larson was going on about how having children was a leap of faith for anyone, and there was no reason why she shouldn't have a healthy, loving family.

Except there was. Two months ago, Ophelia couldn't bring herself to adopt a kitten. And now she was supposed to have a family? She was supposed to be someone's *mother* when she was terrified that one day she wouldn't even be able to take care of herself?

She didn't hear another word the doctor said. It was too much to wrap her mind around. She felt sick to her stomach. What was she going to do? Could she raise a baby? All on her own?

A baby changed everything. How could she have been so incredibly foolish? She'd wanted one night with Artem.

Just one.

But that wasn't altogether true, was it? She wasn't sure when it had happened—maybe when he'd kissed her hand after she'd danced for him, when he'd whispered the words she so desperately needed to hear. *Ophelia, you* are *a dancer.* The exact moment no longer mattered, but sometime on that snowy night she'd begun to want more. More life. More everything. But most of all, more of *him*.

"Ophelia."

She blinked. Artem was standing now, holding all her paperwork in one hand and cupping her elbow with his other.

"Let's go, kitten." He smiled. But it was a sad smile, one that nearly tore her heart in two.

What had she done?

"I didn't do this on purpose," she said, once they were settled in the backseat of his town car. "I promise."

"I know." His tone was calm. Too calm. Too controlled, given the fact that the set of his jaw looked hard enough to cut diamonds. "I know it all too well."

She nodded. "Good."

Artem's driver glanced over his shoulder as the car pulled away from the curb. "To the Plaza, sir?"

"No." Artem shook his head. Thank goodness. Ophelia had no intention of accompanying him back to his penthouse. Or anywhere. She needed a little time and space to come to grips with her pregnancy and figure out what she was going to do. "City hall, please."

City hall?

She slid her gaze toward Artem. "Have you got a parking fine you need to take care of or something?"

"No, I do not," he said. Again, in that eerily placid tone he'd adopted since they'd left the hospital. "You're an intelligent woman. You know very well why we're stopping at city hall."

Ophelia stared at him in disbelief. Surely he didn't expect her to marry him. Here. Now. Without even so much as a discussion about it. Or a proposal, for that matter. "I'm afraid I don't."

"We're to be married, of course." He couldn't be serious. But he certainly looked it as he stared back at her, his gaze steely with determination. "Straight away."

The driver—usually the epitome of professional restraint—let out a little cough. Artem didn't seem to notice. Apparently, he was so laser focused on the idea of a wedding that other opinions didn't matter. Hers included.

A hot flush rose to her cheeks. "I'm not marrying you, Artem."

Marrying him was out of the question. He knew that. She'd told him in the beginning that she didn't have relationships. Of course, she'd also told him she didn't have sex.

But still.

Artem Drake could marry anyone he chose. He couldn't possibly want to marry her. This was about the pregnancy. *Not* her. And even if the prospect of having a baby terrified her more than she would ever admit, she wouldn't marry a man who didn't love her.

Even if that man was Artem. And even if the thought of being his wife made her heart pound hard in her chest, just like it did when she danced.

"Yes, you are," he said, as if their marriage was a foregone conclusion.

Our marriage. Something stirred inside Ophelia. Something that felt too much like love.

Stop. You cannot *consider this.*

"If you want a more formal affair, or even a church

wedding, we can do that later. Whatever and wherever you wish. Vegas, Paris, Saint Patrick's Cathedral. Your choice. We can plan it for next week, next month or even after our baby is born, if that's what you prefer." *Our baby.* Ophelia's throat grew tight. She couldn't seem to swallow. Or breathe. "But we are getting legally married at city hall. Today. Right now."

It would have been so easy to say yes, despite the fact that he'd ordered her to marry him rather than actually asking. And despite the fact that she still couldn't forget the things Jeremy had once said to her. *Burden. Too much to deal with...*

Marrying Artem would mean she would have help with the baby. She wouldn't have to face her questionable future all alone. None of that mattered, though. The only thing that did was that marrying him would mean she could pledge her heart, her soul, her life to the man she loved.

She loved him. There was no more denying it. She'd loved him since the moment he'd seen past the wall she'd constructed around her heart and forced a kitten on her. Maybe even before then.

She loved him, and that's exactly why she couldn't marry him.

"Artem, please don't." She fixed her gaze out the window on the snowy blur of the city streets. She couldn't bring herself to look at him. Why was this so hard? Why did she have to fall in love? "I can't."

"Ophelia, I will not father a child out of wedlock. That is unacceptable to me. Please understand." He reached for her hand and squeezed it. Hard. Until she finally tore her gaze from the frosted glass and looked him in the eyes, the tortured windows to his soul. "Please."

His voice had dropped to a ragged whisper. A crack in his carefully measured composure. At last... That look, coupled with that whisper, nearly broke her.

Please understand.

She did. She understood all too well. She understood that Artem didn't want his baby to grow up without a father. His desire to get married had more to do with his past than it did with her. He was offering her the world. Paris. London. He was offering her everything she wanted, with one notable exception.

Love.

He hadn't said a single word about loving her. Maybe he did. But how could she possibly know that if he didn't tell her? And this ache she felt—the longing for him that seemed to come from deep in the marrow of her bones—was so intense it was dangerous. Desperate. Could something so wholly overwhelming possibly be reciprocated?

Because if it wasn't, if this was unrequited love, and Artem wanted to marry her out of obligation to their child, or as a way of mending his past, what would happen when her MS became worse? What would happen if she was one of the unlucky ones, one of the patients who ended up severely disabled? What then? If he loved her, they could get through it. Maybe. But if he didn't...

If he didn't, she would be a burden. Just as Jeremy had predicted. Artem would grow to resent her, and the thought of that frightened her even more than trying to raise a child by herself.

It would never work.

"I'm sorry." She shook her head and tried her best to maintain eye contact, but she just couldn't. She focused on the perfect knot in his tie instead. It grew blurry as she blinked back tears. *Say it. Just say it before you break down.* "I can't marry you, Artem. I can't, and I won't."

Chapter Thirteen

Artem sat seething across the desk from Dalton, unable to force thoughts of Ophelia and their unborn child from his mind. Fourteen hours and half a bottle of Scotch hadn't helped matters. If anything, he was more agitated about the unexpected turn of events than he'd been the night before.

She'd said no.

He'd asked Ophelia to marry him, and she'd said no. Rather emphatically, if memory served.

I can't marry you, Artem. I can't, and I won't.

"What's this?" Dalton asked, staring down at the envelope Artem slid toward him.

My long overdue letter of resignation. His personal life might be in a shambles at the moment, but he was determined to end the farce of his reign as CEO of

Drake Diamonds. At least that's why he told himself he'd come into the office today. If it had been to ask Ophelia to marry him—*again*—he would have been out of luck, anyway. Her office door had remained firmly closed for the duration of the morning.

Artem nodded at the letter. "Just read it."

Why should he disclose the contents when Dalton would know what the letter said as soon as he opened it?

If he opened it.

"Whatever it is can wait," he said calmly. *No. No, it can't.* "There's a matter we need to discuss."

Dalton tossed the sealed envelope on his desk, opened the top drawer and pulled out a neatly folded newspaper. Artem sighed and closed his eyes for a moment. He knew what was coming before he even opened them and found Dalton leaning back in his chair, waiting for some sort of explanation. As if there could possibly be a plausible excuse for the photographs of him and Ophelia entwined with one another as they climbed into the car the day before.

"Well?" Dalton tapped with his pointer finger the copy of *Page Six* spread open on the desk.

Artem gave the paper a cursory glance. He didn't like looking at the picture. Seeing it reminded him of how he'd felt watching Ophelia fall, lifeless, into his arms. Powerless. Stricken.

Artem sighed. "What is your question, exactly?"

He had no desire to beat around the bush. The past twenty-four hours had been a godforsaken mess, and he was fresh out of patience.

I can't marry you, Artem. I can't, and I won't.

Why couldn't he get those words out of his head?

Dalton cleared his throat. "For starters, is the caption correct? Was this photo taking *during* the auction, when you were supposed to be at Sotheby's?"

At that moment, if Artem hadn't been the CEO, he might have begged to be fired. But alas, he couldn't be terminated. Much to his chagrin, he was untouchable.

"Yes." There wasn't a hint of apology in his voice. If anything, that simple syllable contained a thinly veiled challenge.

His mood was black enough to be ripe for a fight. At least if Dalton was his opponent, he'd have a decent chance of winning. Because Ophelia had shown no sign of surrender. After refusing to marry him, she'd asked the driver to drop her off at her apartment, and had all but ran inside in order to get away from Artem.

She wasn't going to get away with ghosting him again. Not when she was pregnant with his child. She would talk to him before the day's end. He'd seen to that already.

"I suppose it doesn't matter. The auction was successful." Dalton stared at the picture again, then lifted a brow at Artem. "But you're sleeping with Ophelia. That much is obvious. While you were away on your latest disappearing act, she started designing another collection. It's good. Brilliant, actually. The auction pulled us out of the red, but we need her."

Artem shifted in his chair. *We need her. I need her.* "It's not what you think, brother."

"Not what I think?" Dalton let out a laugh. "So you're not sleeping with her?"

"I didn't say that."

Another sigh. "Have you thought about what will happen when you get bored and still have to work with her every day?"

Bored? Not likely. Not when she had a certain knack for driving him to the brink of madness. In his bed, as well as out of it. "She's pregnant."

Why hide it? If he got his way, she'd be living under his roof within hours. Months from now, she'd be giving birth to his son or daughter. He'd never wanted to be a father, never even imagined it. But that no longer mattered. Artem had every intention of being a doting dad.

Marriage or no marriage.

The set of his jaw hardened, as it always did when he thought back on her trembling refusal. *I can't. I won't.*

"Pregnant?" Dalton paused. "With *your* child?"

Artem's mood grew exponentially blacker. "Of course the child is mine."

"Sorry, give me a minute. I'm still trying to wrap my head around this. Given our family past..." Dalton cleared his throat. Artem had to give him credit for choosing his words delicately, rather than just coming out and saying what they were both thinking. *Given the fact that you're my bastard brother...* "I'm surprised you weren't more careful."

So was Artem, to be honest. He'd never bedded a woman without wearing a condom. Never. Until Ophelia. But nothing about that night had been ordinary. The music, the ballet, the snow. The way he'd forgotten how to breathe when he'd seen her bare body for the first time.

It had been a miracle he'd remembered his own name, never mind a condom. "This was different. *She's* different."

Dalton eyed him with blatant curiosity. "How, exactly?"

Because I love her.

By God, he did. He loved her. That's why he'd insisted on signing that emergency contact form before he'd even known she was pregnant. It's why he hadn't been able to work, sleep or even think since the morning she'd disappeared from his bed. It's why he wanted so very badly to take care of her. To make love to her again. And again.

To marry her.

It wasn't just the baby. It was *her.*

Artem cleared his throat and tried to swallow the realization that he was in love. With the mother of his child. With the woman who'd made it clear she had no intention of marrying him.

"My God, you're in love with her, aren't you?" Dalton said, as if he'd somehow peered right inside Artem's head.

"I didn't say that." But it was a weak protest. Even Artem realized as much the moment the words left his mouth.

"You don't have to. It's obvious." Dalton shrugged one shoulder. "To me, anyway."

Artem narrowed his gaze. It hadn't been obvious to himself until just now. Or maybe it had, and he hadn't wanted to believe it. "How so?"

"If you didn't love her, you would have never allowed this to happen. It's simple, really."

Artem wished things were simple. He'd never wished for anything as much. "You give me far too much credit, brother. Why don't you go ahead and say what we're both thinking?"

Dalton's gaze grew sharp. Pointed. "What is it I'm thinking?"

"The truth. I've become our father." No matter how many times he'd thought it, believed it, Artem felt sick saying it aloud. Like reality was a vile, dark malady crushing his lungs, stealing his breath.

Dalton looked at him for a long, silent moment before he finally replied. "That couldn't be further from the truth, brother. In fact, it might be the biggest load of bullshit I've ever heard."

If Dalton had ever been the type to humor him, Artem would have taken his reaction with a grain of salt. But Dalton hadn't been that sort of brother. Ever. If anything, Dalton had been hard on him, with his sarcastic comments about Artem's lavish lifestyle and what Dalton considered to be his less-than-stellar work ethic. As if any normal person's work ethic could compare to his workaholic brother's.

No, Dalton didn't make a practice of mincing words, but what he was saying made no sense. "Think about it. I've done exactly what Dad did. I had a fling with an employee, and now she's pregnant."

It was a crude way of putting it, and in truth, it didn't feel at all like what had happened. But it was, wasn't it?

No. It was more. It had to be.

Dalton shook his head. "You're forgetting something. Dad was married with two kids, and you are most assuredly not."

He had a point.

Still...

"I just can't believe this has all happened right after I stepped into his place here at the office. It's like he knew something I didn't." Artem dropped his head in his hands. "It should have been you, Dalton."

Dalton wanted to run the company. Artem didn't. He never had. He hated that he'd been the one chosen. Worse, he hated thinking their father had done it on purpose. That he'd known how alike they really were.

Like father, like son.

"No," Dalton said quietly. "It should have been you. It *had* to be you. Don't you get it?"

Artem lifted his head and met his brother's gaze. "*What?* No."

"*Yes.* Dad knew he was sick, Artem. He also knew about the mine."

This was news to Artem. "You mean he knew it was worthless before he died?"

Dalton nodded. "The accountant confirmed it last week. If you'd bothered to show up at the office before now, I would have told you."

"I was trying to keep my distance from Ophelia." He'd thought he could get her out of his system. What a waste of time that had been. "He knew about the mine. What does that have to do with me?"

"*Everything.* It has everything to do with you. Dad knew the only way to save the company was to sell the diamond, and he knew I'd never do it. Hell, he couldn't even do it himself, otherwise he would have arranged for its sale as soon as he knew the mine was worthless."

Artem let this news sink in for a moment. Dalton was right. Their father never would have auctioned off the diamond. To him, it would have been like selling his family heritage. Worse, it would have been an admission that he'd failed. He'd failed the company and the long line of Drakes that had come before him.

Artem didn't give a damn about the long line of Drakes. Or the diamond. He didn't give a damn about being CEO. Ophelia was the only reason he'd stuck around as long as he had.

"You were the only one who would do it," Dalton said. "That's why he chose you, Artem. He didn't appoint you because he thought you were like him. He appointed you as CEO because you weren't like him at all."

Artem concentrated on breathing in and out while he processed what his brother was saying. He wanted to believe Dalton's theory. He wanted to believe it with everything in his soul.

"Listen to me, brother. What you did saved the company," Dalton said.

"It also helped push Ophelia away. That diamond meant something to her." He could still hear the desperation in her voice that day in the conference room. *Please, Artem. Don't sell the diamond. Please.* He hadn't listened.

He'd told himself he was doing the right thing. He'd been trying to put a stop to Dalton's ridiculous ad campaign. He'd been trying to protect her.

Maybe he had. But he'd also hurt her in the process. And now there was no going back.

"The fact remains that you saved the family business, and that makes you more of a Drake than anybody. More than me. More than Dad."

Artem wished he could take comfort in those words. There was a time when hearing Dalton say such a thing would have been a balm. Those words may have been all the healing he'd needed. Before.

Before Ophelia. Without her, they meant nothing. *He* meant nothing.

"About this." Dalton picked up the envelope containing Artem's letter of resignation. "Is this what I think it is?"

"It's my notice that I intend to step down as CEO," Artem said.

Dalton tore it neatly in half without bothering to open it. "Unaccepted."

For crying out loud. Could one thing go as planned? Just one? "Dalton…"

"Think on it for a while. Think about the things I've said. You may change your mind. The position pays awfully well."

As if Artem needed more cash. "I don't care about the money. I have plenty."

"You sure about that? After all, soon you'll have another mouth to feed." Dalton smiled, as if jumping at the chance to become a doting uncle.

A child. He and Ophelia were having a *child*. He'd been so stunned at the news, so abhorred by the idea that he'd become his father, that he hadn't realized how happy he was.

Ophelia was having his baby. That's all that mattered now. That, and convincing her to speak to him again. But he already had that covered.

"Think on it," Dalton said again. "I like having you around. It's about time we Drakes stuck together."

Ophelia blinked against the swirling snow and pulled her scarf more tightly around her neck as she stalked past the doorman of the Plaza, who was dressed, as usual, in a top hat and dark coat with shiny gold buttons. After hiding out in her office all day specifically to avoid facing Artem, she couldn't believe she was willingly setting foot in the hotel where he lived.

But he'd given her no choice, had he? He infuriated her sometimes. He had since the very beginning. But now…now he'd gone too far.

"Welcome to the Plaza." The concierge smiled at her, then before she even told him who she was, handed her a familiar-looking black key card, plus another, slimmer card. *Odd.* "The black card will give you access to the penthouse elevators and the other is the key to Mr. Drake's suite. He's expecting you."

I'll bet he is.

"Thank you." She did her best to smile politely. After all, the concierge had nothing to do with this ridiculous situation.

Or maybe he did. Who knew? Even Artem couldn't have pulled off a stunt like this without help.

And what was with the key to his suite? That had to

be a mistake. No way was she going to walk into his penthouse without knocking first. Although she supposed she was entitled, after what he'd done.

The elevator ride felt excruciatingly slow. Since arriving home from work and realizing what had happened, she hadn't stopped to think. She'd simply reacted. Which was no doubt what Artem had been counting on.

Now that she was moments away from seeing him again, she was nervous. Which was silly, really. She was having the man's baby. She should at least be able to carry on a simple conversation with him.

That was the trouble, though, wasn't it? Her feelings for Artem were anything but simple.

Yes, they are. You love him. Plain and simple.

She swallowed. That might be true, but it didn't mean she had to act on it. Or, God forbid, say it. But what *would* she say to him after refusing to marry him? And how could she see him again, so soon? She'd kept her office door closed all day for a reason. She didn't think she could take being in the same room with him without being able to touch him, to kiss him, to tell him how hard it had been to refuse him yesterday.

To pretend she didn't love him.

She'd told herself she'd done the right thing. Just because they were having a baby didn't mean they should get married. No matter how badly one of them wanted to.

She'd started to wonder, though, which one of them really wanted marriage. In her most honest moments, she realized it was her.

She didn't know what to do with these feelings. Everything had been so much easier when she'd kept to herself, when she'd gone straight home after work every day. No kitten. No nights at the ballet. No Artem.

Was it better then? Was it really?

At last the elevator reached the eighteenth floor, and Ophelia stepped into the opulent hallway. When she reached the door to penthouse number nine, she pounded on it before she had time to chicken out.

Artem opened it straightaway and greeted her with a devastating smile that told her she'd played right into his hand, just as she'd suspected. "Ophelia. Hello, kitten."

Her heart leaped straight to her throat, and to her complete and utter mortification, a ribbon of desire unfurled inside her. In an instant, her center went hot and wet.

She willed herself not to purr. "Kitten? Interesting choice of words, given the circumstances."

"Enlighten me. What would those circumstances be, exactly?" He crossed his arms and leaned casually against the door frame. Apparently, he was intent on making her go through the motions of this ludicrous charade.

"Artem, stop. You and I both know that you kidnapped my cat." She brushed past him into his suite, scanning the surroundings for a glimpse of Jewel.

Ophelia had been panicked when she'd come home from work and the little white fluffball hadn't greeted her at the door, winding around her ankles as she did every night. Then she'd seen the bouquet of white roses on the coffee table and Artem's business card propped against the lead crystal vase. No note. Just the card. *Artem Drake. Chief Executive Officer. Drake Diamonds.*

Chief Executive Ass was more like it.

Artem had broken into her apartment. He'd barged right in, and he'd stolen her cat.

"I beg your pardon. *Your* kitten?" He raised a sardonic brow. "As I recall, I'm the one who adopted her from the animal shelter when you refused to do so. That would make her *my* cat, would it not?"

No. Just…

No.

She looked over his shoulder and saw Jewel curled into a ball in the middle of his massive bed, right on top of the chinchilla blanket. The same blanket she'd wrapped around her naked self the last time she'd stood in this room. It was surreal. And possibly the most manipulative thing Artem Drake—or any other self-entitled male—had ever done.

"You can't be serious," she sputtered.

"Surely you remember how adamant you were about not adopting. I thought it best to relieve you of your cat-sitting responsibilities." He glanced at the kitten on the bed. "She rather likes it here. It's not such a bad place to be, Ophelia."

She heaved out a sigh and looked at Jewel. Memories of being in that same bed hit her, hard and fast. She envisioned herself waking up with her legs wrapped around Artem, her head nestled in the crook of his neck…

But wait, she wasn't actually considering letting him get away with this, was she? No. Of course she wasn't.

"Artem, you can't do this. I'm not marrying you, and if you think repossessing your kitten is going to change my mind, you're sorely mistaken."

"Who said anything about marriage? You don't want to marry me? Fine. I'm a big boy. I can take it." His tone went soft, sincere. The switch caught her off guard, and she felt oddly vulnerable all of a sudden. "But if you think I'm going to stand by and let you do this by yourself, you're the one who's mistaken. Let me be there for you, kitten. Let me take care of you. At least stay here."

"Stay here? With you?" She rolled her eyes.

"With me. Yes." There wasn't a hint of irritation in his tone. He'd dropped the overbearing act and was looking at her with such tenderness that her heart hurt.

Let me take care of you.

It was so close to *I love you* that it almost made her want to forgive him for breaking into her home. Seriously, who did that?

The man she was in love with. That's who.

"I shouldn't have come here." She shook her head and headed for the door.

She couldn't do this. If she stayed here for even one night, she'd end up back in his bed. And she'd never be able to leave him. Not again.

"Ophelia, stop. Please." Artem chased after her.

She shook her head. "I don't… I can't…"

He slid between her and the door, raised her chin with a gentle touch of his fingertips and forced her to look him in the eyes. "He was wrong, Ophelia. I don't know what Jeremy Davis said to you to make you believe that your MS made you unlovable, undesirable, but he was wrong. Dead wrong."

She took a few backward steps and wrapped her arms around herself in an effort to hold herself together. Because it felt like the entire world was falling to pieces around her. Not just her heart. "Artem..."

"I'm not going to force you to stay here. And I'm sure as hell not going to force myself on you. I'm leaving town for a few days, and I'd love nothing more than to find you here when I come back." He walked past her and grabbed a messenger bag from the table in the center of the room.

Ophelia couldn't believe what she was hearing. He'd taken her cat and lured her here, and now he was leaving? "You're *leaving*? Where are you going?"

"I'd rather not say. I've been called away for work, and I'll be back as soon as I can. The hotel staff has orders to provide whatever you need. You'll find them rather accommodating. Make yourself at home while I'm gone." His gaze flitted around the penthouse and paused, just for a moment, on the closed door to his home office. The room where he'd shut himself off on the morning she'd slipped away. "Take a look around."

Then he turned and walked right out the door.

Ophelia stared after him, dumbstruck. *This is insane.*

She walked to the bed and scooped Jewel into her arms, fully intending to give Artem a five-minute head start before going back downstairs and hailing a cab home.

She couldn't believe he actually expected her to stay here while he was gone. As if she could sleep in his bed, rest her head on his pillow, wake up every morning in his home and not wonder what it would be like to share it with him. Impossible. She couldn't do it.

"Come on, Jewel." She held the kitten closer to her heart. "Let's go home."

Home.

She blinked back tears. Damn Artem Drake. Damn him and his promises. *Let me take care of you.*

He was tender when she least expected it, and it messed with her head. As ridiculous as it seemed, she preferred it when he did things like break into her apartment and steal her cat.

She needed to get out of here. Now. She couldn't keep standing in his posh penthouse while the things he said kept spinning round and round in her head. She marched toward the door, but as she passed his office, her steps slowed.

Take a look around. What had that meant, anyway?

Nothing, probably.

She lingered outside the room, wanting to reach for the doorknob, even though she knew she shouldn't. She rolled her eyes. What could possibly be in there that would change her mind about anything?

Nothing. That's what.

He'd probably bought a crib. Or a bassinet. No doubt he thought she'd see it and go all mushy inside. Well, he was wrong. If he'd bought a crib—now, when she was only weeks pregnant—she'd know that the only reason he wanted to marry her was because of the baby. Giving the baby a proper, nuclear family was all he could think about. Just to prove it, if only to herself, she turned the knob and stepped inside his mysterious, secret room.

What she saw nearly made her faint again.

There was no crib. This wasn't a baby's room, and it most definitely wasn't an office. Ophelia's reflection stared back at her from all four of the mirrored walls. Beneath her feet was a smooth wood floor that smelled like freshly cut pine. A ballet barre stretched from one end of the room to the other.

Artem had built her a ballet studio, right here in his penthouse.

A lump formed in her throat. She couldn't swallow. She could barely even breathe.

Ophelia, you are *a dancer.*

He'd whispered those words before he knew about her illness, before he knew she was Natalia Baronova's granddaughter. She hadn't believed him then. Even as she'd danced across the moonlit floor of his living room, she'd doubted. She'd been performing a role, playing a part. That part had been the ballerina she'd been. The woman who could have done anything, been anything. A dancer. A mother. A wife. Once upon a time.

Ophelia, you are *a dancer.*

He'd really meant it. And now, standing in this room, she almost believed it, too.

Almost.

Chapter Fourteen

Artem was away longer than he'd planned. Three days, three nights. He'd hoped to take no more than an over-night trip, but things hadn't gone as smoothly as he'd anticipated. He hated being away and not knowing what was going on with Ophelia, but he'd been prepared to be gone as long as it took to set matters straight.

He returned to New York on the red-eye, hoping against hope he wasn't coming home to an empty pent-house. According to Dalton, Ophelia had been at work in the store on Fifth Avenue every day and seemed to be in perfectly good health. No fainting spells. No indi-cation whatsoever that she was sick, or even pregnant. She hadn't missed a beat at work. But Artem had drawn the line at checking in with the staff at the Plaza to see whether or not she'd been staying in his suite. In truth, he hadn't been sure he wanted to know. Probably because he was almost certain she'd gone straight back to her own apartment after he'd left.

Sure enough, when he slipped inside the penthouse at 2:00 a.m.—quietly so as not to wake her, because a shred of optimism survived somewhere deep in his gut—the penthouse was empty. As was his bed.

Shit.

He let his messenger bag slide from his shoulder and land with a thud on the floor, its precious cargo forgotten. The air left his lungs in a weary rush. Until that moment, he hadn't realized he'd been all but holding his breath in anticipation as he'd flown clear across the continent.

He needed to see her. Touch her. Hold her. Three days was a damn long time.

He loosened his tie, crossed the room and collapsed on the bed. Eyes shut, surrounded by darkness, he could have sworn he caught Ophelia's sweet orchid scent on his pillow. The sheets felt sultry and warm. He must have been even more tired than he'd realized, because his empty bed didn't feel empty at all. He had to remind himself he was only being swallowed in sheets of memories.

But he could have sworn he heard the faint strains of music. Mozart's Piano Concerto no. 21. *La Petite Mort.* What was wrong with him? Clearly, he'd lost not only his Ophelia, but his mind, too.

You haven't lost her. Not yet.

There was still a ray of hope. A whisper of possibility. It was small, but he could feel it. He could see it in his mind's eye. It glittered like a gemstone.

Thud.

Out of nowhere, something landed on his chest, surprising him. He coughed and reached to push whatever it was off, and his hand made contact with something soft. And furry. And unmistakably feline.

He sat up and clicked on the light on the bedside table. Ophelia's tiny, white fluffball of a cat blinked up at him with wide, innocent eyes.

"Jewel. What are you doing here?" He gave the kitty a scratch on the side of her cheek and she leaned into it, purring furiously.

Artem had never been so happy to see an animal in his entire life. "Where's your mama, huh? Where's my Ophelia?"

My Ophelia.

There was no way she would have left the cat at his penthouse all alone. No possible way. She had to be here somewhere, but where?

He stood while Jewel settled onto his pillow, kneading her paws and purring like a freight train. At least someone was happy to see him.

The cat was in his apartment, though. That had to be a good sign.

"Ophelia?" His gaze swept the penthouse twice before he noticed a pale shaft of light coming from beneath his office door. Or what had *been* his office.

The ballet studio. Of course. He'd been so weary from the stress of the past few days that he'd almost forgotten he'd arranged a place for her to dance. Because she needed such a place, a room where she could let her body dream. If his trip had been a failure, if he could have given her only one thing, it would be the knowledge that she was perfect just as she was. Just as she'd always be. Ophelia would forever be a dancer. No illness, and certainly no man, could ever take that away from her.

He smiled to himself. The music hadn't been a product of wishful thinking, after all. Nor had it simply been a tender, aching memory. It was real, and it swelled as he approached the closed door, until the subtle strains of the violin exploded into a chorus of strings and piano notes that seemed to beat in time with the pounding of his heart.

He paused with his hand on the knob, remembering the last time he'd seen her dance to this music. He knew every moment, every movement by heart. He still dreamed about that dance every night, the whisper of her ballet shoes in the moonlight and the balletic bend of her spine when she'd arched against him as he'd entered her. Even his body remembered, perhaps more so than his mind. Because hearing that wrenching music and knowing Ophelia was right on the other side of the door, pointing her exquisite feet and arching her supple back, sent every drop of blood rushing straight to his groin. He was harder than he'd ever been in his life, hard as a diamond, and he'd yet to even set eyes on her.

With exaggerated slowness, he turned the knob and pushed the door open. The room was dark, the music loud. So loud she didn't notice his presence. She hadn't bothered to turn on the lights, and moonlight streamed through the skylights casting a luminescent glow on the smooth wood floors he'd had installed less than a week ago.

Ophelia stood at the barre with her back to him, wearing nothing more than her pink-ribboned pointe shoes and a sheer, diaphanous nightgown that ended just above her knees. In the soft light of the moon, Artem could see no more than a hint of her graceful spine and the curve of her ballerina bottom through the thin, delicate fabric. She rose up on tiptoe, reached her arm toward the center of the room, then bent toward the barre in an achingly glorious curve.

Seeing her like this, lost in her art, was like being inside a lucid dream. A lovely, forbidden fantasy. Part of him would have been happy to remain there in the doorway, a worshipful voyeur in the shadows. A sudden, fierce urge to inspect her body, with the thrill of knowing she was expecting his child, seized him. He took in the new softness of her frame, hips lush with femininity and a delicate voluptuousness that pierced his soul. But the other part of him—the demanding, lustful part that refused to be ignored—wanted to rip her gossamer gown away and bury himself inside her velvet soft warmth.

He prowled closer, footsteps swallowed by Mozart's tremulous melody. Artem didn't stop until he was close enough to feel the heat coming from her body, to see the dampness in the hair at the base of her swan-like neck. His fists clenched at his sides as he suppressed the overwhelming urge to touch her. Everywhere.

She turned on her tiptoes, and suddenly they were

face-to-face. Mouths, hearts, souls only inches apart. Artem would have given every cent he had for a sign— *any* sign—that she was happy to see him, that while he'd been gone she'd lain awake in his bed craving his hands on her body, dreaming of him bringing her to shattering climax with his mouth, his fingers, his cock.

"Artem." Her eyes were wide, her voice nothing but a breathy whisper, and for an agonizing moment, he thought she was on the verge of dancing away from him. As she'd done so many times.

But she didn't. She stayed put, breathing hard from exertion, breasts heaving with new fullness, her rose-petal nipples hardening beneath her whisper-thin gown. Pregnancy had changed her body in the most beautiful of ways, and knowing he'd been the one responsible for that divine transformation sent a surge of proprietary pride through him. The baby growing inside her was his. *She* was his, and he had every intention of showing her how profoundly that knowledge thrilled him.

She looked at him with eyes like flaming sapphires. And when the heat of her gaze dropped to his mouth with deliberate intent, it was all the invitation he needed.

"Kitten," he groaned, and pulled her to him, molding her graceful body to his.

His lips found hers in an instant, and the desperation that had been building in him in the weeks since he'd last tasted her reached its crescendo. He poured every bit of it into that kiss—all the fitful, restless nights, all the moments of the day when he'd thought of nothing but making love to her again. And again. And again.

They'd had one night together. He'd known it hadn't

been enough, but now he realized he'd never get his fill of her. If he lived a thousand years and spent every night buried in the sanctity of her precious body, he'd still want more.

Her hands found his hair and he deepened the kiss, trying to get closer to her. And closer still, until she let out a little squeak and he realized he'd pushed her up against the ballet barre.

Somehow he tore his mouth from hers long enough to gather her wisp of a nightie in his hands and lift it over her head. Then his lips found her again, this time at the base of her neck, where the erratic beat of her pulse told him how badly she'd wanted this, too. Needed it. Missed it. Missed *him*.

He cupped her breasts, lowered his head and kissed one nipple, then the other, drawing a deep moan of satisfaction from Ophelia's lips. She was so soft, so beautiful. Even more perfect than he remembered.

Time and again, he'd told himself that if he ever got to make love to her again, he'd go slow. He'd draw out each kiss, each caress, each lingering stroke as long as possible. He'd savor every heartbeat that led to their joining. But his blood boiled with need. He couldn't have slowed down if his life depended on it. And Ophelia matched his breathless hunger, sigh for sigh. She pulled at his hair, then clutched at his tie and wrapped it around her hand, holding him tightly to her as he drew her breast into his mouth, suckling. Savoring.

"Please, Artem," she begged. "Please."

"I'm here, kitten," he whispered against the soft

swell of her belly, where life—the life they'd created together—was growing inside.

He was here. And this time there would be no leaving. On either of their parts.

He unclenched her hands from his tie and placed each one on the ballet barre, curled them in place.

"I suggest you hold on," he murmured against her mouth, dipping his tongue inside and sliding it against hers for a final, searing kiss before dropping to his knees.

He slid his hands up and down the length of her gorgeous legs, parting her thighs. She had the legs of a dancer, legs that were made for moving to music and balancing on tiptoe. And for wrapping around his waist when he pushed himself inside her. But first, this. First the most intimate of kisses.

He devoured her like a starving man. And still he couldn't seem to get enough, even when she spread her ballerina thighs wider to give him fuller access. Somehow he grew only hungrier as she ground against him and her breathy little sighs grew louder and more urgent, rising with the music. He had to have her like this, wild and free and unafraid, forever.

Forever and always.

"Artem, I…" Her hands tightened in his hair with so much force that it bordered on pain, and he hummed against her parted flesh.

He wouldn't have stopped, even if she begged, even if she slid right down the wall into a puddle on the floor. Not until she found her release. Blood roared in his ears. If he hadn't been on his knees, his legs would have buckled beneath him. He was on the verge of coming himself and he'd yet to shed a single article of clothing.

Not yet.

He wanted her spent and trembling when he finally drove into her. He'd lived with the torture of wanting her for weeks, since he'd last touched her. They'd wasted so much time. Days. Weeks. Time when he'd fought his feelings for her and told himself what he'd done was wrong, when it couldn't have been more right.

Did she have any idea the kind of restraint it had taken not to act on his desire? To see her and pretend every cell in his body wasn't screaming to love her?

He needed her to know. He needed her to feel it with explosive force.

He moved his hands up the back of her quaking thighs, and the moment he dug his fingertips into the lush flesh of her bottom, she convulsed against him in rapturous release. And when she finally let herself go, the words on her lips were the ones Artem had waited a lifetime to hear.

"I love you."

Oh, my God.

Ophelia tightened her grip on the ballet barre as Artem rose to his feet and began to undress, his fiery gaze decisively linked with hers.

She was grateful for the barre, for the way it felt solid and familiar in her hands. She needed something real, something substantial to hold on to because this couldn't possibly be reality. This was too heavenly, too much like a beautifully choreographed dance—the kind that left you with a lump in your throat and tears running down your face at the end—to possibly be real.

She was naked and shivering and ravished, and she'd never felt more alive, more whole in her entire life. What had just happened? What had she just *said*?

I love you.

The words had slipped out before she could stop them, and now she'd never be able to take them back. Artem had certainly heard them—the Artem who stood in front of her, naked and hard now, more aroused than she would have thought humanly possible, plus the roomful of Artems reflected in the mirrored walls. He was everywhere. Here. Now. Surrounding her with his audacious, seductive masculinity.

She couldn't think, couldn't breathe, couldn't even figure out where to look. Her gaze flitted from the hard, chiseled planes of his abdomen to the mirror where she could see the sculpted sinews of his back and his firmly muscled backside. He was beautiful, like a god—the Apollo of Balanchine's *Orpheus*, an embodiment of poetry, music, dance and song, all the things she held most near and dear to her heart.

"Oh, kitten," he whispered, sliding a hand through her hair and resting his forehead against hers.

His erection pressed hot and wanting against her stomach, and in that perfect, precious moment he felt so big and capable that anything seemed possible. He was bigger than her fears. Bigger than her past. Bigger than her illness.

"I love you, too," he breathed, as he pushed inside her, pressing her into the barre. "I've loved you all along."

It was such ecstasy to have him filling her again, she could have wept. She'd been waiting for this since the morning she'd fled his penthouse. She just hadn't wanted to admit it. How could she have been so foolish to think she could live without this, without *him*, when the notion was impossible in every way? She rested her hands on his chest, wanting to imprint her touch there somehow, to mark him as hers, this magnificent man who refused to let her push him away.

At the moment of their joining, he groaned and she slid her hands down and around, reaching for his hips so she could anchor him in place. She wanted to hold on to this moment, this moment of coming together, while her entire body sighed in relief.

She could feel him throbbing and pulsing deep in her center, and it was almost too much. Too much pleasure. Too much sensation. She was going to come again. Soon. And he hadn't even moved.

"Do you have any idea how I've missed you?" he whispered into her hair, as he started to slide in and out. Slow at first, with languid, tender strokes as the pressure gathered and built, bearing down on her with frightening intensity.

"Yes," she whimpered. "I do… I do."

I do.

Wedding vows.

"My bride," he murmured, with aching sincerity in his voice as he thrust faster. Harder.

And she didn't fight it this time. Couldn't, even if she'd wanted to. Because since the moment she'd walked into this room, this mirrored place of hope, all

her fractured pieces had somehow come together. She'd
stayed at Artem's penthouse while he'd been gone. Because of this room. Every night, she found herself slipping on her ballet shoes and dancing again. Because
of this room. She was healing. Because of this room.

She didn't feel like Ophelia Rose anymore—that sad,
sick girl who'd given up on life. On dance. On love. Nor
did she feel like Ophelia Baronova, because that Ophelia
had known nothing but ballet. She'd never known how
it felt to come apart in the arms of a man who loved her.
She'd never lived with secret knowledge that life was
growing inside her. A future. A real one.

A family.

No, she felt different now. Hopeful. Whole. The woman
she felt like now was a dancer, a lover, a mother. And her
name was Ophelia Drake.

"Tell me," Artem commanded, his eyes going sober,
his strokes longer, deeper. She didn't think it was possible to love him more, but the deeper he pulsed inside
her, the deeper she fell. "Look at me, kitten. I need to
hear it. I love you with everything I have, everything I
am. Tell me you'll be my wife."

"Yes," she whispered, unable to stop the tears from
filling her eyes. "I will."

He kissed her with a tenderness so different from
the violent climax building inside her that it felt like a
dream. A beautiful, impossible dream.

"Don't be scared, baby," he murmured against her
lips.

"I'm not." She clenched her inner muscles around

him, drawing a moan of pure male satisfaction from his soul. "Not anymore."

Then he was slamming into her with such delicious desperation that she could no longer keep her orgasm at bay. It tore through her and she cried out just as Artem pushed into her with a final mighty thrust. He shuddered and groaned his release as her back pressed harder against the ballet barre, and somehow she had the wherewithal to open her eyes so she could watch him climax. She wanted to see the perfection of his pleasure mirrored back at her, silvery reflections as plentiful and exquisite as the facets of a diamond.

They stayed that way, against the wall with their hearts crashing into each other, until their breathing slowed and the music went silent. Then, and only then, did Artem pull back to look at her. He brushed the hair from her eyes and covered her face with tender kisses.

I love you.

I love you.

I love you.

She wasn't sure if the words were hers or his. If they were merely thoughts or if one of them said them aloud. It had become like a heartbeat. Natural. Unstoppable.

Artem lowered his lips to her ear and whispered, "I think this occasion calls for a diamond. Don't you?"

Laugher bubbled up her throat. "Don't tell me you still have Princess Grace's necklace lying about?"

"No." He shook his head. His sensual lips were curved in a knowing grin, but the look in his eyes was pure seriousness. "Better."

She swallowed. Hard. "Better?"

Had he bought her an engagement ring? Was he about to reach into his suit pocket on the floor and retrieve one those infamous Drake-blue boxes with a white satin bow?

"Wait here," he ordered, his gaze flitting ever so briefly to her discarded nightgown pooled at her feet. "And don't even think about getting dressed."

She grinned as her heart pounded against her rib cage. "As you wish."

He blew her a kiss and strode naked out of the room, while she stared openly at his beautiful body. She could hardly believe this breathtaking man was going to be her husband. The father of her baby.

She slid her hands over her belly and marveled at the subtle, firm swell and the new heaviness in her breasts that meant Artem's child was growing inside her. It felt like a miracle. The doctor at the hospital had been right. Her breakout MS symptoms had all but gone away over the past few days. She felt healthier now, more her-self, than she had since before her diagnosis. Some new mothers with MS experienced a relapse shortly after giving birth, but she wasn't worrying about that yet. She had the best doctors money could buy, and what-ever happened, she could deal with it. Just like other new mothers did.

"You're beautiful, you know. More beautiful than I've ever seen you," Artem said, as he walked back into the studio holding a large black velvet box. Far too large for a simple engagement ring. "I have a mind to keep you barefoot and pregnant."

Ophelia laughed. "Are you forgetting I have a job

that I love? Besides, I'm not barefoot. There are ballet shoes on my feet."

She pointed a toe at him, and he grinned. "Even better, kitten. Be still my heart."

"What have you got there?" she asked, eyeing the velvet box. "Elizabeth Taylor's bracelet? Queen Elizabeth's tiara?"

"No," he said quietly. "Your grandmother's."

He lifted the lid of the box to reveal a glittering diamond tiara resting on a dark satin pillow. Eight delicate scrolls of tiny, inlaid diamonds curled up from the base, surrounding a stunning central stone. A yellow diamond. Just like…

"No." She started to tremble from head to toe. "This isn't…"

She couldn't even form the words. *The Drake Diamond*. It was too much to hope for. Too much to even dream.

"Yes, kitten." It is. He lifted the tiara from the box and placed it gingerly on her head. "The Drake Diamond has found its way home."

She caught a glimpse of her reflection in the mirror and nearly fainted again. The Drake Diamond was back. In New York. Reset in its original design. And she wasn't looking at it in a fancy glass case, but sitting on her very own head.

She bit her lip to keep from crying. "But I don't understand. How is this possible? I thought a buyer in Mexico City bought it at the auction."

Realization dawned slowly. Mexico City… Artem's urgent business trip. *Oh, my God.*

Artem shrugged. "I bought it back."

"Drake Diamonds bought it back? Just days after it was auctioned off?" She started to shake her head, but was afraid to move when a priceless stone was sitting atop her head.

"No." Artem's voice softened, almost as if he were imparting a secret. "*I* bought it back. Not Drake Diamonds."

"You? *Personally?*" It was too much to wrap her bejeweled head around. Did Artem have that kind of money? Did anyone?

"Yes, me. So not to worry. There won't be any more talk about resigning as CEO. It looks like I'll be working at Drake Diamonds for the rest of my life now." He let out a laugh. "With Dalton, actually. We've decided to share the role."

"I think that's perfect," she said through her tears. "But why? You didn't have to do this for me. It's too much."

She was crying in earnest now, unable to stop the flow of tears. She'd never expected this. She'd come to terms with the loss of the diamond. It had been hard, but she'd accepted it. She was pretty much an expert on loss now.

Not anymore, a tiny voice whispered inside. *Not anymore.*

Artem gathered her in his arms and pulled her against his solid chest. "Shh. Don't cry. Please don't cry. I wanted you to have it. I want you to wear that diamond tiara when you walk down the aisle to me on the day I make you my wife. You were right. It's not just a stone. It's a part of family history. Mine. Yours."

He raised her chin with a touch of his finger so her gaze met his. It seemed as if all the love in the world was shining back at her from the depths of his eyes. "And now ours."

Then he kissed away each and every one of her diamond tears.

* * * * *

If you liked this story about finding love in the glittering world of jewels and New York City, don't miss the next two books in the DRAKE DIAMONDS trilogy, available April 2017 & July 2017 wherever Mills & Boon Cherish books and ebooks are sold.

www.millsandboon.co.uk

MILLS & BOON®

Cherish™

EXPERIENCE THE ULTIMATE RUSH OF FALLING IN LOVE

MILLS & BOON®

EXCLUSIVE EXTRACT

Sheikh Ibrahim al-Ansari must find a bride,
and quickly... Thankfully he has the perfect
convenient princess in mind—his new assistant,
Ruby Dance!

Read on for a sneak preview of
THE SHEIKH'S CONVENIENT PRINCESS
by Liz Fielding

'Can I ask if you are in any kind of relationship?' he
persisted.

'Relationship?'

'You are on your own—you have no ties?'

He was beginning to spook her and must have realised
it because he said, 'I have a proposition for you, Ruby,
but if you have personal commitments...' He shook his
head as if he wasn't sure what he was doing.

'If you're going to offer me a package too good to
refuse after a couple of hours I should warn you that it
took Jude Radcliffe the best part of a year to get to that
point and I still turned him down.'

'I don't have the luxury of time,' he said, 'and the
position I'm offering is made for a temp.'

'I'm listening.'

'Since you have done your research, you know that
I was disinherited five years ago.'

She nodded. She thought it rather harsh for a one-off

incident but the media loved the fall of a hero and had gone into a bit of a feeding frenzy.

'This morning I received a summons from my father to present myself at his birthday majlis.'

'You can go home?'

'If only it were that simple. A situation exists which means that I can only return to Umm al Basr if I'm accompanied by a wife.'

She ignored the slight sinking feeling in her stomach. Obviously a multimillionaire who looked like the statue of a Greek god—albeit one who'd suffered a bit of wear and tear—would have someone ready and willing to step up to the plate.

'That's rather short notice. Obviously, I'll do whatever I can to arrange things, but I don't know a lot about the law in—'

'The marriage can take place tomorrow. My question is, under the terms of your open-ended brief encompassing "whatever is necessary", are you prepared to take on the role?'

Don't miss
THE SHEIKH'S CONVENIENT PRINCESS
By Liz Fielding

Available February 2017
www.millsandboon.co.uk

MILLS & BOON®

Why shop at millsandboon.co.uk?

Each year, thousands of romance readers find their perfect read at millsandboon.co.uk. That's because we're passionate about bringing you the very best romantic fiction. Here are some of the advantages of shopping at www.millsandboon.co.uk:

* **Get new books first**—you'll be able to buy your favourite books one month before they hit the shops

* **Get exclusive discounts**—you'll also be able to buy our specially created monthly collections, with up to 50% off the RRP

* **Find your favourite authors**—latest news, interviews and new releases for all your favourite authors and series on our website, plus ideas for what to try next

* **Join in**—once you've bought your favourite books, don't forget to register with us to rate, review and join in the discussions

Visit **www.millsandboon.co.uk**
for all this and more today!